CONSTELLATION DRACO

J. R. Bacon

First published by On the Write Path Publishing
5023 W. 120th Ave. #228
Broomfield, CO 80020
martinmcleanlit@aol.com

ISBN-13: 978-1-64990-601-4

ISBN -10: 1-64990-601-3

This book is printed on acid-free paper.

Printed in the United States of America

For Patt, my best friend.
You're always there for me.

Acknowledgments

I want to take this opportunity to express my appreciation to several people for helping me achieve this goal, the publication of this science fiction novel.

First, I want to thank two people who have given me a lot of good feedback and constructive criticism, my wife, Patt, and my older son, John. Both of them have been invaluable.

Second, I want to thank my agent, Lisa Martin, for her good advice and her continuing faith in me.

Finally, I do want to thank Dave Petty for the excellent photo on the back cover of this novel.

Cast of Characters

Mayan:

Aten Imhotep (46)   Aten Imhotep (95)
Isis - wife (45)
Khons - son (21)   Amun Imhotep - son (71)
                                     Naomi Nefera - wife (71)
                                     Intef - daughter (44)

Commander Ramses Tutan (70)   Tia Hapmen (77)
          Naqada - wife (67)   Capt. ERC Moses Hapmen (49)
          Intef – Daughter (44)   Ninsu - wife (46)

Dr. Sethos Pithom (62) - environmental specialist
Dr. Ahmose Buhen (56) - astrophysicist
Dr. Avaris Taharqa (63) - rocket propulsion engineer

Chancellor –   Apis Dahshur (62)
Councilman –   Tanis Narmer (52)
                Peret - wife (47)

Alternate Starship Commander - Seth Menes (59)
Starship Pilot - Captain Amarna Mastaba (43)

Colonel Djoser Ra (58) - military commander
Sergeant Abydos Smendes (42) - military noncom
Corporal Badari Gerzean (29)
Private Sile Kamose (32)
Lieutenant Saite Manetho (38) - ERC + Security Police
Captain Avaris Khufu (28)

Hyksos:

Zeus (34)
Aphrodite - wife (33)
Achilles - son (13)

Diomedes (36)
Athena - daughter (17)
Alexander - son (15)

Cronos - fishing boat captain (36)

CHAPTER ONE
"Loved Ones"

Starship Hope
Compartment 82
Level 5
Pod 2
4M, Day 28, 95 A.D.
4:43 p.m.

"Look, Mom, we're just concerned about you here alone. This flyby Planet 6 is gonna be big. That's what the experts are sayin'. We're just tryin' to make sure you're gonna be all right."

"I'll be fine. I've been taking care of myself all these years. I'm sure I can take care of myself during this flyby. What you don't remember was the Jupiter flyby when you were just a baby." Tia Hapmen pointed at the first of four living room chairs on aluminum pedestals. "I sat right there and held you in my arms. You weren't but a few weeks old."

Moses grinned. "Mom, you've only told me about that a hundred times since I was a little kid."

"Well, it happened. I brought you here to live in your daddy's compartment. He was a fine man. He saved the whole starship. Gave his life to save everybody else."

Moses leaned close to his wife's ear. "I've also heard this one a million times," he whispered.

Ninsu's pretty mouth made a sweet smile. "She's just rememberin', Honey," she whispered.

Tia Hapmen spun around. "Are you two talking about me?"

Moses grinned and moved closer to his mother. "We sure are, Mom. So, Ninsu will come here to this compartment tomorrow mornin', probably pretty early." He turned to his wife. "Eight o'clock, maybe?"

Ninsu nodded. "Yes, eight to eight-thirty."

"You don't have to come, Ninsu."

"But Mrs. Hapmen. . ."

"I keep telling you, Ninsu, it's Miss Hapmen. I never did marry Moses' father. We were planning it before those things happened. Hell, just call me Tia."

"I don't feel comfortable doing that."

"Then call me Miss H."

Ninsu made an uncomfortable smile. "If you like."

"You don't have to come here tomorrow, My Dear."

"Mom, the flyby is gonna be very dangerous. This planet is much bigger than Jupiter. I think they said it was about one-third bigger. So things are gonna get broken and knocked around. I want Ninsu with you to make sure you're all right."

Tia raised her hands in a gesture of helplessness. "Okay, okay. It'll be nice having the company anyway. It's supposed to last three or four hours."

Moses smiled. He was greatly relieved. His mother could be very stubborn, but he had been warned that this flyby of Planet 6, as they called it, was going to be extreme.

The starship was traveling at approximately 172,000 miles per second, just short of the speed of light. As their starship entered this solar system, they had to really slow down if they were going to be able to establish an orbit around Planet 3, the one they called Hyksos.

That third planet was their target planet. They had been collecting more and more information about its surface over the almost fifty years of their journey across the Galaxy. Hyksos did seem habitable and that's where they hoped to finally start a new life.

Moses had never known anything but this starship. He had seen the old videos of life back on their home planet, Mars. It looked really kind of cool. This new planet would be different. At least that's what he had been told. This Hyksos planet was supposed to have more water than Mars and more vegetation.

Of course, all this was guessing. They wouldn't really know the details until they went into orbit above the planet and sent unmanned drones down into the atmosphere to have a look around.

He had heard rumors that some of the people aboard the starship might not be able to go down to the surface of this new planet. The engineers were calculating how much fuel would be needed for the shuttle to make all those trips.

But maybe that was just a rumor. Maybe it was just somebody's idea of being funny. He hoped so. Actually, it wasn't all that funny.

But he did wonder if the older people like his mother would be able to survive a trip down to Hyksos. That kind of glide down into the turbulence of the atmosphere might be extreme and his mother was seventy-seven years old. Not exactly young.

Moses put his hands on his mother's shoulders. "Give me a hug, Mom. I have to go on duty tonight. We're gettin' everythin' ready for this flyby."

Tia Hapmen put her arms around her son and kissed his cheek. "You keep them in line. I've heard you're doing a good job running the ERC, taking care of all those emergency repairs. Years ago, that's what I did. Of course the starship was a lot newer then. Not too many problems, unless you had a meteor strike – like the one that killed your father."

Ninsu stood by the door, waiting.

Moses was happy that his wife was willing to stay with his mother, just in case there was a problem. He bet that everything would go off just fine, but you never knew about these things.

He moved over next to Ninsu and slapped his hand on the blue lighted rectangle to the right of the pocket door.

It rattled open.

Moses turned to his mother. "Ninsu will come in the mornin', Mom."

"I'll be here."

"Bye, Miss H."

"Good-bye, Ninsu."

The young woman smiled at her mother-in-law and then stepped over the curved threshold out into the narrow corridor. Moses followed her.

The pocket door sucked shut.

Ninsu moved down the corridor toward the elevators at the far end. "She didn't want me to come."

Moses was walking right behind her. "Mom's just stubborn, Honey. She really wants somebody there with her. Otherwise she would be scared to death, but she would never admit it."

They stopped in front of the first elevator door. Ninsu pressed the UP button.

Number 2 elevator light glowed and the door rumbled open.

They stepped inside.

There was a young man at the back right corner of the small box-like space. To Moses, he looked like a college student – probably harmless.

The door rattled shut.

Moses pressed the 3 button.

The elevator jerked upward.

He glanced back over his shoulder at the male student. Then he turned to his wife. "We've been talkin' about who to send from the ERC down to the surface once we get to Hyksos."

"How many ERC people are you sendin' down, Honey?"

"Just one. That's all we're allowed right now."

"How come?"

"There's gonna be limited space on the shuttles and, besides, we need a big crew up here in the starship."

"Can we go down?"

Moses shook his head. "Not at first. They need me up here." He hesitated. "I know the technician I want to send down."

"Who's that?"

There was a subtle "ding" and the elevator jolted to a stop.

"Here we are." Moses glanced over his shoulder.

The young male was staring at the screen of the control on the inside of his left wrist.

Moses figured that probably it was an incoming text. He stepped out into Level 3 corridor.

Ninsu followed.

He turned to face her and let her go by him so she could walk in front.

The elevator door rattled shut.

Ninsu began walking down the corridor. "You haven't told me who you want to choose."

"I didn't want to talk about it where I could be overheard."

His wife stopped in front of the door labeled "Compartment 43" and slipped her card into the slot to the right of it.

The pocket door sucked open.

She pulled her card out of the slot and stepped over the curved threshold into the interior.

Moses followed.

The door sucked shut behind him.

"Aren't you gonna to tell me?"

Moses shrugged. "Sure. It's Saite Manetho."

"Which one is he?"

"He's the one I told you about. His great uncle was a Secret Police captain back on Mars. He talks about it all the time, as if it's some kind of badge of honor or somethin'. From what I've heard, the Secret Police weren't all that popular."

"You're actin' as if you don't like this guy very much."

Moses thought about this for a minute. "Yeah, I guess I do sound that way." He sat down on the first barstool next to the kitchen counter and looked up at Ninsu. "He's just different. I guess that's why I'm plannin' on sendin' him down to the surface of the planet."

"Bein' different isn't bad, Moses."

"Oh, I know that. I mean – this guy is really good at his job. He has great mechanical skills and he's always calm, even in the worst situations, and that's real important for this kind of work. And he's real smart."

"Then why?"

Moses shrugged. "I don't know. I mean – everyone else stops at the beer counter in the cafeteria after work to sit around and bullshit. But not Saite."

"Is he unfriendly or somethin'?"

"Not exactly. He's just kind of weird."

"I still don't get it."

"Well, for instance, when you look into his eyes, there's nothin' there. It's like he's not friendly, but he's not angry either. It's like he's not any-thin'. It's real weird."

"How does he feel about goin' down to the planet?"

"I haven't told him yet."

"You may want to tell him right away."

"Why's that?"

"So he can get used to the idea."

"I kind of thought I'd tell him today."

"I think you're doin' the right thing, Sweetie."

"I guess." Moses stood up. "Well, I should be goin'. I'm on at five-thirty. I'll be gettin' back at about three in the mornin'." He hesitated. "Do you want me to wake you up?"

"Why would I want you to do that?"

Moses could feel his face getting warm. "You know."

Ninsu grinned. "Oh, really? So I'm supposed to be hot to trot at three in the mornin'?"

Moses shrugged. "I just thought. . ."

Ninsu stepped over to him and gave him a quick kiss on the lips. "Sure, wake me up, there, Cutie. And bring the mouthwash in from the bathroom."

Moses thought of something. "I wish we could still put in for havin' children."

Ninsu's brown eyes became sad. "I know. I feel the same way. But, hey, maybe when we get to this Hyksos planet, they'll take away those rules, so we can have kids whenever we want." She touched Moses' cheek. "I've never been pregnant. I'd like to know what that feels like just once in my life."

Moses wondered if they would change the rules. He had bought lottery tickets every year from the time he was twenty-two until he was twenty-nine and he had not gotten one single winning ticket. Ninsu had done the same thing and, again, no winning ticket.

Maybe now they could have a kid. When he thought this way, Moses wondered about his father, the mysterious man he had never known. Moses Shipharah was the man who had saved the starship by sacrificing his own life.

Well, that was his mother's version of things. It could have been a lot different than that. Maybe he'd ask around, just out of curiosity. Somebody had to remember his father.

CHAPTER TWO
"Tough Decision"

Starship Hope
The Bridge
4M, Day 28, 95 A.D.
7:46 p.m.

Ramses Tutan stared at the spray of starry light filling the wraparound windshield of the spaceship. The spray swept upward in a giant blue-white swirl across the blackness of space. It was the Constellation Draco.

Ramses could remember the start of this long journey. It seemed so long ago and so far away and, really, it was both of those things. They had traveled some 47 light years distance across the Milky Way Galaxy to find their new home. Now they were here.

He glanced at the time on the face of his wrist control strapped underneath his left wrist. He had to go to that meeting in Conference Room 2. They held all their important meetings in that conference room because it was soundproof and there was only one entrance – easy to secure the access and egress of people.

He wasn't looking forward to this particular meeting. Maybe that's why he was procrastinating about leaving the bridge. The meeting started at eight o'clock. Perhaps he should get going. He might have to wait for the elevator and that would slow him down.

Of course, at this time of the evening most Mayans aboard this starship were in their compartments with their families or out working on the second shift. The bad times to move around were any time near 6:00 p.m. or 12:00 noon or 12:00 midnight or 6:00 a.m. That's typically when shifts changed and there was a lot of traffic in the corridors and elevators.

"Gentlemen, I have to leave for that meeting."

The two men at the control consoles turned. The one on the left smiled. "Aye, Aye, Commander. Don't drink too much."

"It's not that kind of meeting, Captain Mastaba."

"Whatever you say, Sir."

Ramses smiled and then moved toward the pocket door on his right. He stopped and turned. "You can, of course, reach me on my wrist. Use the priority channel."

"Yes, Sir," said Mastaba.

The other officer waved. "Have a good time, Sir."

"I'll bring drinks back for you two."

Mastaba grinned. "Why, thank you, Sir."

"Think nothing of it, Captain." Ramses placed his thumb on the blue pad to the right of the pocket door.

It sucked open to the left.

He stepped over the curved threshold out into the short corridor.

The door sucked shut behind him.

Straight ahead was the door to supply room number 3. To his right at the end of the short corridor was the elevator.

He moved down the corridor, stopped in front of the elevator door and pressed the DOWN arrow, the only one on this panel. The bridge was the top level on the starship.

Above the door the number 3 was lit. It flickered out and then number 2 lit.

Ramses pressed the DOWN button again.

Number 1 lit, and then went out.

The bridge was above level 1. It had no level designation.

The elevator door jolted open. The elevator was empty.

Ramses stepped inside and turned to face the doorway.

The door rattled shut.

He pressed number 1.

The elevator jerked downward and after several seconds there was a "ding" and the elevator came to a stop.

The door rattled open.

Ramses stepped out into an empty corridor.

This meeting tonight involved a matter of making a decision. Ramses knew there would be objections, but there were some fundamental realities that had to be faced. That was all there was to it. He had specifically set the meeting before the day of the flyby because everyone who was not in the meeting would assume that it had to do with that issue.

He stopped in front of the door marked with bold black figures, "CONFERENCE ROOM 2." He pressed the small black button on the wall to the right of the pocket door.

There was a loud "buzz!"

He could not actually see it, but he knew there was a guard peering through the peephole in the upper middle of the shiny aluminum door.

The door sucked open.

A large guard with a pistol in a shoulder holster under his left arm reached out his hand. "Your I.D., Sir."

Ramses held out his left arm with his wrist control facing the tiny screen toward the guard.

The large man aimed an electronic reader at it.

There was a "beep."

The guard raised the reader in front of his face. He lowered his arm. "Very good, Sir. Of course I knew who you were, Commander. It's just procedures, Sir."

Ramses made a brief smile. "I understand, Sergeant."

The guard stepped aside. "Come-in, Sir."

Ramses stepped into the room.

The door sucked shut behind him. The room was filled with the low murmur of conversation.

As Ramses expected, everyone was already here. All of them were probably wondering why he had called this meeting.

Apis Dahshur, the chancellor, was at the far end of the rectangular table. He would have expected the chancellor to do that. Even though Dashshur wasn't calling this meeting or doing a presentation, he would choose a position of command because he did those things.

Ramses moved over to the last remaining seat at the side of the table near the corner, right next to the engineer, Doctor Avaris Taharqa, who was sitting at this end of the table. Probably Taharqa had saved the seat for Ramses next to him because it might be the two of them against the rest of the men in the room. Actually, Ramses liked Taharqa. The man had good instincts and he was pleasant to be around. That was not true of everyone here, unfortunately.

When Ramses slipped into the end swivel seat on the left side of the table, Chancellor Dahshur made eye contact. Then his eyes moved over to the engineer in the seat next to Ramses at the end of the table. Probably the chancellor had figured out the alliances in the room already. The man had extraordinary political instincts.

Ramses leaned over close to the engineer. "Doctor Taharqa," he whispered, "could we, perhaps, change seats?"

The other man stared at Ramses through the lenses of his thick glasses. "I don't understand, Commander."

Ramses leaned close. "It's a political strategy, Avaris. It'll help our cause," he whispered.

The other man stared at him again. Then he smiled and nodded. "Sure." He rose from the end chair and picked up his folder.

Ramses stood up and stepped around behind the bulky man.

Now Doctor Taharqa sat in the first seat at the left side of the table.

Ramses remained standing. "Gentlemen. . ."

The room quieted.

"I'd like to welcome Chancellor Dahshur, as well as our renowned astronomer, Doctor Ahmose Buhen." He nodded and smiled at the astronomer. "Our environmental expert, Doctor Sethos Pithom." He nodded toward the man on the right side of the table. Then he turned to Avaris Taharqa on his near left. "And finally, Doctor Avaris Taharqa, our rocket propulsion engineer."

Ramses made eye contact with Chancellor Dahshur at the other end of the table. "I have called you here this evening for several announcements. First off, you know we're heading into the solar system of CM Draconis in the Constellation Draco. Tomorrow afternoon we will begin a flyby of Planet 6 in this solar system.

"This flyby will create tremendous turbulence and strain on the structure of this starship. However, it is absolutely necessary for our successful deceleration as we enter the Draconis solar system. We will also, by the way, do a flyby of Planet 5 in a matter of two to three months. That time frame will be determined by the amount of deceleration we achieve by doing this flyby of Planet 6.

"We have several contingency plans, of course. The first contingency is Planet 5 of this solar system. It is about half the size of Planet 6 but we may do a flyby there as well. That depends upon how much deceleration we achieve with the other two larger planets' gravitational fields. We will also do a flyby of planet 4, if necessary. That planet is approximately the same size as planet 5.

"Now, in the worst case scenario, we will use Planet 3, our target planet – also called Hkysos – as a fourth flyby, then circle around and begin the deceleration process all over again from Planet 6.

"We are currently traveling at approximately 172,000 miles per second. We have never traveled in any spaceship at that speed before so we are not sure just how many flybys this deceleration process will take. We can only determine what works as we go through the process itself.

"I will begin discussing the next issue by saying that when you are the commander of a starship, you sometimes have to make decisions that result in some people being very unhappy. I called this meeting on this particular day so that most people on the starship who hear about it will think this meeting has to do with the flyby exclusively.

"Actually, that's not the case. The more important issue is the one I'm about to discuss with you.

"So far, there have been very few life and death decisions aboard this vessel. There was that one incident where I ordered the ERC, the Emergency Repair Crew, to leave a compartment sealed after a meteor had ripped a hole across the outside of the compartment. I then ordered an exterior maintenance crew to do an extravehicular repair to that compartment.

"While it is true people died in that situation, more people would have died if I had opened that compartment to the starship."

"Are you trying to make a point, Commander?"

Ramses made eye contact with the handsome, grey-haired man at the far end of the table. He had never liked Chancellor Dahshur, mostly because of the man's smugness.

Ramses had always felt that Dahshur had this strange idea that Ramses was his competitor. That was ridiculous, especially when one considered that they were adult males who were supposed to be working together.

"Chancellor Dahshur, I was laying the groundwork for a decision I will announce presently." Ramses turned to the engineer, next to him. "But perhaps I should let Doctor Taharqa take things from here."

The engineer pointed at the chest of his white lab coat and made eye contact with Ramses.

"Yes, Avaris, why don't you get up and explain the situation."

Doctor Taharqa rose from his swivel chair.

Ramses looked over at the engineer. "You all know Doctor Avaris Taharqa. Doctor Taharqa is our rocket propulsion engineer. He has some pertinent information to share with us."

Ramses sat down in his swivel chair. "Go ahead, Avaris."

The bulky-bodied engineer with flattened black hair looked around the table. "This is not going to be good news." He glanced down at his folder on the table. Then his gaze came up. "We have studied the situation with regard to our rocket fuel. I'm referring to the rocket fuel for our shuttle."

He glanced around the table. "As all of you know, that is the way we will be able to descend to the surface of Planet 3. We of course have to establish that it's habitable first." He gestured toward Doctor Sethos Pithom, the environmentalist. "As Doctor Pithom will tell you, so far the indications are very good."

The bulky man looked down at his folder again. He removed a sheet of paper and held it up above his head under the recessed ceiling lights. "This is a sheet of the calculations we have made regarding the shuttle fuel. My staff and I have gone over these figures hundreds of times and we keep coming up with the same conclusion."

He stared through the thick lenses of his glasses at the men around the table. "According to our calculations, there will not be enough shuttle fuel to transport the entire complement of passengers in this starship down to the surface of Planet 3."

The thick glasses with the oversized, distorted eyes behind them scanned the faces around the table. "I cannot decide who goes down there and who stays. I can only report to you the facts about our fuel situation with regard to the shuttle."

The engineer's head turned and he made eye contact with Ramses.

"Thank you, Avaris." Ramses rose from his seat.

"You're welcome." The engineer plopped his large body down into his swivel chair.

Doctor Ahmose Buhen, the astronomer, raised his hand.

Ramses nodded toward him. "Yes, Doctor Buhen?"

"Commander, we are not completely sure what the gravitational situation will be for Planet 3."

Ramses turned to the engineer. "What about that, Avaris?"

The engineer leaned forward and put his forearms on the table. "Doctor Buhen, we have run all kinds of scenarios, even with a gravitational field less than our home planet, Mars, and the results are the same. We might be able to make one more trip down to Planet 3 with a very low level of gravity, but only one more and that still wouldn't take everyone down to the surface."

The environmentalist raised his hand.

Ramses nodded toward him. "Yes, Doctor Pithom?"

"Commander, can our engineer friend inform us as to what percentage of the people will not be able to go down to the planet's surface?"

"Certainly." Avaris studied the sheet of paper in front of him. Then he looked up and lowered the paper to the tabletop. "We have estimated that somewhere between seventeen and twenty-eight percent of the people aboard this starship will not be able to go down to the surface of Planet 3.

"This, of course, is contingent upon the gravitational field of that planet and atmospheric conditions – even the ease with which we can find that first area in which to land. The first shuttle flight down might have to be airborne for some period of time before a suitable landing area can be found."

"I thought we were planning on sending down an unmanned drone to study the surface of this planet."

The engineer's enlarged eyes behind the lenses focused on Doctor Pithom, the environmentalist. "Yes, we are. However, there are always unforeseen problems with landing in an unprepared, unfamiliar area.

"The shuttle will land vertically the first time. This uses a greater amount of fuel. Once we have prepared a landing strip, all subsequent shuttle landings will be horizontal, using its landing gear and a drogue parachute."

"This will be a bombshell aboard this starship when the people find out."

Ramses looked down the table at Chancellor Dahshur. "That's true, Chancellor. However, I think if we announce one particular bit of information, it may alleviate some of that problem."

"What information is that, Commander?"

"I have made the decision, as commander of this starship, that anyone of sixty years or older cannot go down to the surface of the planet."

Ramses turned to Doctor Pithom. "I have had numerous conversations with Sethos, here, and I have gathered from what he has said that unless the gravitational field on this planet is exceptionally weak, there are some serious challenges for our older passengers to even make it down to the surface alive. In addition, conditions down there might be extremely primitive. If they are, it will be no place for older citizens."

"That would include you and your wife, Commander."

Ramses made eye contact with the handsome, grey-haired man at the far end of the rectangular table. "That's true, Chancellor Dahshur. And I'm assuming you and your wife will remain up here as well."

The chancellor nodded. "Yes."

Ramses glanced around the table. "In fact, I think that might be true of most of the people around this table. . . except, perhaps, for Doctor Buhen."

The astronomer sitting several seats down the left side of the table smiled. "I'm going to stay in the starship. I'd rather be up here anyway. It's where I belong. I can spend the rest of my life studying the stars in this new area of the galaxy. Actually, I'm really looking forward to that."

"I'm sure that's true, Doctor Buhen." Ramses glanced around. "I will also inform my crew that they have to stay. We need to be able to make this starship function as a home for the people left here for many years. So that means approximately fifty some crew people staying behind."

Ramses turned to the engineer. "Avaris, did you happen to get any statistics about how many people there are aboard the starship who will be sixty or over when we arrive?"

The engineer shook his head. "No, I didn't."

Sethos Pithom cleared his throat. "Commander, I believe the number is somewhere around three to four hundred people."

Ramses nodded. "We figured it would be about that number. Would you be able to get that information for us, Doctor Pithom?"

"Of course, Commander."

Ramses glanced around the group. "Now, let me make something very clear. Because we don't know the exact number of people sixty or older, we won't know for sure that this will be the absolute cutoff number. It might be fifty-five, or we might have to figure into the equation the issue of a person's health.

"Consequently, this discussion we've had this evening should not be revealed to the public. It should stay in this room." He glanced around the group. Then he made eye contact with the chancellor, Apis Dahshur. "Is everyone in agreement with that?"

All the men around the table nodded. Someone muttered, "Of course."

Ramses noticed that the politician, Chancellor Dahshur, did not nod or say anything. "Are you in agreement with this, Chancellor?"

The handsome man sat forward and leaned with his elbows on the table. "It seems to me, Commander, that you've taken an awful lot of responsibility – and power – on your own shoulders. This is a decision that must be made by the public."

"I totally disagree."

Doctor Buhen, the astronomer, turned to Chancellor Dahshur. "You want the people to decide this? You want the turmoil, arguments in the corridors, fights and all kinds of other unspeakable things to happen? You're mad, Dahshur, absolutely mad."

"Perhaps we should put this to a vote right here, Gentlemen." Ramses looked around the group. "Is that agreeable with everyone?"

Several of the men nodded.

"All right, those who agree that we should absolutely not put this issue up to a public vote, raise your right hand."

The engineer raised his hand, then the astronomer, Doctor Buhen.

Doctor Pithom rubbed his face with his hands. Finally he said, "I abstain."

Ramses raised his hand and looked around the group.

Chancellor Dahshur sat with his arms folded across his chest.

Ramses glanced around again. "What I see is three in favor, one against and one abstention. The issue passes. We will not put this up to a public vote. And, again, I would strongly advise that you not reveal the subject of this meeting to the people on this starship. Don't even tell your wives. I'm not going to. That way we can be sure it stays right here."

"You're going to have to tell the people at some point, Commander."

Ramses focused on the handsome face at the far end of the table. "I realize that, Chancellor, but we'll have to carefully plan the time to do that and the way we'll do it."

Right after he had said this, Ramses wondered if the good chancellor would actually keep his mouth shut. He doubted it, especially if this information gained Dahshur some political advantage, or even just some perceived political advantage.

At this moment, Ramses really wished Chancellor Apis Dahshur was not aboard this starship.

CHAPTER THREE
"Forever Among the Stars"

Starship Hope
Compartment 28
Level 5
Pod 1
4M, Day 29, 95 A.D.
7:02 a.m.

"You should have somethin' to eat. You've been workin' all night."

"I'm not hungry, Mother. Just leave me alone."

"What's makin' you all cranky this mornin'?"

Saite shrugged. "Nothing special."

"Somethin' goin' on. Got your lower jaw draggin' on the floor like somebody gut-punched you or somethin'."

"They're sending me down to the surface of the planet."

"You mean that Hyksize place?"

"Hyksos, Mother."

"Whatever." Inti Manetho swallowed some coffee and turned toward the pot to pour more. She picked up the pot. "What's this? Did you take all the fuckin' coffee?"

"Don't go at me, Mother. I've had a bad night. I was on duty with a really dumb dipshit and nothing happened all night, except he talked about all the girls he's laid, which was a whole lot of lies."

Inti stood by the counter, holding the nearly empty coffee pot. "You've had a bad night? What the fuck do you think it's like with your kid livin' with you when he's almost forty years old?"

"Mother, for God's sakes, don't go on about this – not this morning. I'll make you a new pot of coffee."

"I don't have time to wait for a new pot of coffee. So there, You Little Shit!"

"I wish you were older, Dear Mother, much older!"

Inti turned to face her son. "What did you just say?"

"I said I wished you were older – like sixty or sixty-five."

"What the fuck does that have to do with anythin'?"

"Then they'd leave you up here on the starship and you'd just stay here until your fat old ass rotted away. Considering the huge size of your fat old ass, that would be a hundred years!"

Saite saw his mother's arm swinging around above the kitchen counter before he saw the actual coffee pot.

He dropped off the stool at the breakfast bar and lurched to the right.

The coffee pot with the small amount of black coffee sloshing inside its glass globe came toward him.

He ducked down behind the counter.

The pot glanced off the exit door to the compartment and smashed against the corner of the small side table next to one of the living room chairs.

Saite clambered to his feet. "What the hell are you doing?"

His mother was standing in the kitchen with both hands on her hips. Her face was bright pink and her brown eyes were full of anger. "You always were a stupid little shit!"

"You're the stupid one, Mother. I'm just sorry you're not older, then you would stay up here forever among the stars and I'd never have to see you again. They're sending me down to the surface, but once both of us are down there, you're on your own, you old bitch!"

His mother grabbed the sugar bowl from the counter.

"Throw that, Bitch, and I'll slap your ugly fat face!"

His mother stood rigid with the sugar bowl poised above her right shoulder.

"That sugar bowl's not supposed to be left loose, or didn't your little brain remember that, Mother?"

Inti Manetho's right hand did not move. It was as if she were frozen in position. Finally, she lowered the sugar bowl to the counter. "I don't need this. I don't need some ungrateful asshole of a son tellin' me that I should be older." Her eyes filled with tears. "Don't you pity your old mother, workin' every day like I do? I don't have a man to provide for me – never did. Raised you all by myself."

"No man would have you, Mother."

"Shut your mouth, you ungrateful little shit!"

Saite found that amusing for some reason and began to chuckle. "You're pathetic, Mother, you really are."

"I'll tell you who's pathetic – it's you!"

Saite chuckled again. He couldn't help but be amused. He had just experienced one of those very long nights.

It all started when that Moses Hapmen had told him that he was the one chosen to go down alone to the planet as the repair person. Hapmen had told him that Commander Tutan had said that only one ERC person would be allowed to go down with the crew, and Hapmen chose him.

It wouldn't have mattered so much but Saite knew already that he was the outsider in the Emergency Repair Crew. The other guys were polite most of the time, but not friendly. They talked about him. Sometimes he would walk in on a conversation and the voices would stop. That was a sure sign.

Saite supposed he should have become used to that by this time. He had been the outsider as long as he could remember, and that would be since the second grade. He was always the kid that the teacher had to match up with somebody else or put in some group. He was the one not chosen, or if he was chosen, he was always the last one.

You felt those things deeply. He tried to deny their importance to him, but the pain was still there. One girl in third grade had told him that being different meant you were better. She was kind of an outsider too, but she had seemed to make peace with it. Saite never had.

He had heard from his Aunt Bes years ago that he was a lot like his great uncle, Tanis Manetho, a captain in the Secret Police. For some reason he could not understand, Saite had always felt a bond with this great uncle he had never met.

It was ridiculous, when you tried to make some sense out of it, but that didn't matter. A person had to have something to hold onto. A person had to possess some sort of validation.

"You can clean up the mess. I clean up other people's messes all day long." His mother was standing at the door with her bag containing her cleaning overalls.

"I'll think about it."

His mother rolled her eyes. "Ungrateful children – what the hell are you gonna do with them?"

"Tell me, Mother, what should I be grateful for? Living with you? Oh my! Living with you has been such a treat – my crabby old mother always belittling me about everything. Well, frankly, I don't give a good fuck if there's coffee all over the floor. You made the mess. You clean it."

His mother spun around. "I want you out of here! Move out!"

Saite smiled. "Gladly, Bitch!"

His mother stabbed her index finger at him. "Today!"

"I'll be gone from your life by the time you come home, Mother. And I hope you rot in hell!"

His mother turned around and slapped her hand against the blue pad to the right of the door.

The pocket door sucked open.

She stepped out and the door shut.

Saite stood by the breakfast bar, waiting. He wondered if she was trying to look through the peephole. If she was, she wouldn't see much. Those things only worked for peering at a person who was outside, not the other way around.

He moved over toward the table where the coffee pot had broken. Maybe he should clean this up and then put the glass in his mother's bed. That would be hilarious.

At the thought of his mother screaming when she climbed into bed, Saite chuckled. Then he laughed some more. That image of his enraged mother jumping out of bed just amused him so, so much.

Well, maybe he could have a few hours of peace away from that old bitch. He wouldn't move out just yet. It wasn't so much that he enjoyed living with her. He hated that. But he did enjoy aggravating her. There was just something so amusing about antagonizing that old bitch.

Maybe he ought to sleep in one of the bunk beds at the Emergency Repair Crew quarters up in Level 3.

Well, maybe not. He would much rather stay around and irritate his mother. If he was still here, he could do a crazy prank to really scare her during the flyby. That would be lots of fun.

Something occurred to him, something that would scare his mother so much she would definitely scream.

Saite hurried back through the living room to a small closet in the hallway next to the bathroom. He unhooked the door latch and slid the door back into the wall pocket to his right.

He crouched down and then reached into the closet and dragged out a soft cloth bag filled with tools. He unzipped the bag and dug around inside.

His fingers fumbled among the hard, cold metal objects until they touched a crescent wrench. He wiggled the wrench out from the tangle of tools, stood up and walked back into the living room.

During the last flyby, his mother had sat in the living room chair nearest the kitchen counter. She had told him that this would enable her to grab the counter and pull herself into the kitchen if either one of them wanted something to eat.

Saite crossed the living room to that particular chair. He knelt down next to the aluminum post under the chair and slid the open end of the wrench around two of the flat sides of the head of the bolt holding the right side of the safety belt.

He pulled the wrench away and with his thumb rolled the adjustment. The wrench opening narrowed.

Saite slid the wrench around the flat sides of the bolt head a second time.

The wrench was still a little large.

Without moving it, he rolled the adjustment.

Now it was tight.

Saite leaned forward, pressing the wrench handle in a counterclockwise direction.

The bolt held for a split second - then released.

Saite turned the wrench counterclockwise again, one full turn - then again, and again.

Now the bolt was loose.

He placed the wrench on the floor. Then with the index finger and thumb of his right hand he clasped onto the bolt head and turned counterclockwise. He continued to turn the bolt until it came loose.

Then he turned the bolt back into the threaded hole in a clockwise direction one turn. Now he tested it by turning it counterclockwise until it came loose again.

Saite turned the bolt back into the threaded hole just enough so that it held.

He leaned back until the cheeks of his buttocks were against the heels of his tennis shoes, and he chuckled. "Shit, that will be so funny," he whispered. "Mother will just scream her fucking head off."

He grabbed the crescent wrench and rose to his feet. He stared down at the loose bolt sticking out from the side of the chair post. "She'll never notice. Too bad I can't be here to see it. I'll be on duty."

He put the fingers of his free left hand up to his mouth and giggled. "My God, that will be so fucking funny."

Saite moved across the living room toward the closet. "Right now, I have to get some sleep." When he reached the open door, he crouched down and slid the wrench back into the cloth pouch.

He zipped it, slid the closet door shut, and then rose to his feet. "Nighty night, Mommy." He chuckled. "That will be so fucking funny."

CHAPTER FOUR
"Love and Respect"

Starship Hope
Bridge
4M, Day 29, 95 A.D.
3:07 p.m.

Amun wondered how his father felt about being up here on the bridge for this flyby. The man had seen a lot of life. He'd actually been born the year the last of the domes were built back on their home planet, Mars. That was ninety-five years ago.

Sure, it was a long time, but what made it seem even longer was how much had happened since. His father used to tell him about what it had been like those first years in the domes, living inside clear plastic bubbles on the surface of a planet that was dying.

Those first years the Mayans had been so confident they could solve the problem of the disappearing atmosphere. After all, they had two hundred years to deal with this. Then the government scientists discovered a frightening truth. They were losing atmosphere at a very high rate and they had less than fifteen years to do something about it.

That's when construction began on this starship. By that time, the Mayans knew they would have to leave the planet.

"Are you comfortable, Dad?"

Aten Imhotep's full head of white hair turned on the padded surface of the headrest. "I'm fine. It's beautiful up here on the bridge." He swept out his right hand. "You can see all this. In the rest of this starship you're not aware of where you are, really. Can't see what's outside."

Amun stared out at the spray of stars swept in an upward swirl in front of the giant windshield that curved around above the instrument filled control panel. This Constellation Draco was certainly beautiful.

For some reason, however, today Amun was feeling kind of melancholy. Maybe it was because he had always felt somewhat apologetic around his father.

Aten Imhotep, his father, was a person of great achievements. He had a Ph.D. in engineering. He had designed the living quarters aboard this starship.

Amun, himself, had planned to go into engineering, but once he began his studies, he realized that it wasn't really his thing and that he had probably chosen the field out of respect for his father, rather than for his own interest. There was also some sort of misplaced expectation, on Amun's part, that his father wanted him to be an engineer.

So often Amun had felt like he had to explain or apologize for becoming a mathematics teacher. He had always loved his work. The thing about teaching that he loved was working with teenagers. He enjoyed their energy, their enthusiasm and their successes and he liked helping them deal with their difficulties. "Dad. . ."

His father's head turned.

"I never told you why I went into teaching."

"You don't have to tell me anything about that, Amun."

"I'm just not the engineer, Dad. I love working with young people."

"There's no need to explain, Son."

Amun shrugged. "I don't know why but I've always felt I had to explain."

"Amun, you're seventy-one years old and semi-retired. You've had a very successful career as a teacher. Your mother . . ." Aten hesitated. "Your mother and I were always proud of you, even when you were jailed for being in that protest. We were fearful about what would happen to you, but we were still proud of you for standing up for your principles.

"Son, you've always been a person who has stood for his principles. You wanted to become a math teacher and so you did. You don't have to apologize for a successful teaching career."

Amun nodded. "I know. It's just that you were so well known for your work on this starship."

"I made a contribution, but there were thousands of people who did important work on this starship."

Commander Ramses Tutan rose to his feet. His seat was ahead of Aten and Amun, but behind the starship pilots. He turned to Amun. "I would suggest that you sit down, Amun, and put on your safety harness. We're accelerating now because of the gravitational field of Planet 6. We should be feeling some turbulence at any time."

Ramses walked back around his seat and stood in front of the old man. "Mister Imhotep, how are you doing, Sir?"

"Hey, I'm doing fine, Ramses. . . I mean, Commander Tutan."

Ramses grinned. "This flyby will be getting kind of rough, Mister Imhotep. I was going to offer to have you taken back to your own compartment, but I guess it isn't any safer there. Would you feel more comfortable in your own compartment?"

"Absolutely not. I wouldn't miss this for anything. I want to be up here where the action is."

Ramses patted the old man on his shoulder. "Okay, Sir." He made a visual check of Aten's safety harness. "It looks like you're all buckled up."

The starship shuddered.

Ramses grabbed the back of Aten's seat. He glanced toward Amun who was sitting to the right of his father. "You okay?"

Amun nodded. "I'm fine."

The starship shuddered again.

"It's beginning." Ramses waited for the shaking to stop. Then he walked back to his seat behind the two pilots. He dropped onto the vinyl surface, pulled up the belts from both sides and snapped them together at his waist. He pulled the strap to tighten it.

The starship shook violently.

This time Amun was shaken so hard that he was sure his eyeballs had slammed up into his forehead.

When the shaking stopped, his stomach was sore from the safety harness straps.

The starship began shaking in a regular rhythm.

Amun pulled the safety harness tighter. He turned to his father on his left. "Are you straps tight, Dad?"

The white hair turned and his father smiled. "I'm fine, Son."

The starship shook. The shaking was so violent that Amun's body felt like it was permanently suspended in the air.

Just as suddenly, his body slammed back into the padding of his seat. The cushions compressed flat and Amun could feel the chair's shape pressed hard against the back of his body.

He wanted to turn to see how his father was doing, but he couldn't move his head. For some reason, however, he felt he had to do this.

Amun focused. Then he pushed against the extreme pressure on his face. He was able to turn far enough so in the periphery of his vision he could see his father. The man's head was tipped to the side so that it was pressed against the outside edge of the headrest. He was facing Amun.

"Dad!" His mouth wouldn't open all the way and the word came out sounding like some kind of weird noise.

Something was wrong with his father, but Amun couldn't do anything about it. He was helpless, trapped in his seat.

For some reason, which Amun couldn't begin to understand, he suddenly felt a warm sweep of emotion about his father. He so much wanted to tell the man that he loved and respected him. That would have to wait, however.

CHAPTER FIVE
"Sweet Dreams"

Starship Hope
Compartment 28
Level 5
Pod 1
4M, Day 30, 95 A.D.
7:06 p.m.

Saite Manetho slipped his plastic key card into the slot to the right of the door a second time. As before, there was a whirring sound, but the door didn't move.

The starship had been shaken-up pretty badly in that flyby yesterday. It lasted through the afternoon and most of the night. He supposed that the whole structure of this giant spaceship had been compromised in little ways.

They had experienced no leaks during the flyby and there had been no meteorite strikes. That was fortunate because for most of the flyby time, the whole Emergency Repair Crew was strapped into their seats at the Repair Center storage area. They couldn't move because the gravitation and the shaking were so extreme.

He had heard about that Jupiter flyby fifty years ago. This flyby of Planet 6 had to be much worse than Jupiter. The whole ERC group had spent the last few weeks studying the information about Jupiter left by that crew. As it turned out, very little of it applied to this situation. The reason? This planet was almost a third larger than Jupiter.

Saite stared at the door to Compartment 28. Finally, he had this great idea. Suppose he did the card thing and banged the door with his fist? Would that work? Hell, he wouldn't know until he tried.

He had to get inside. His mother was still in there, as far as he knew. Well, maybe that bolt had held after all, but if it hadn't, she might be injured. Then, what would he do? Actually, he wasn't sure.

Saite stabbed the plastic card into the slot.

The light flickered green and there was a "whir."

He banged his fist on the door.

It slid left into the pocket in the wall.

Inside the compartment the living room wall was spattered with blood. His mother was lying in a heap in a corner to the right, up against the wall. Directly above her was a splotch of smeared blood.

Saite glanced around to see if anybody was nearby. Then he stepped into the compartment.

There was a subtle "whir" but the door didn't move back.

He banged his fist on the wall.

The door rattled shut.

Saite turned around and cautiously moved by the kitchen counter with its four bar stools. He stepped into the living room. As he did, he looked toward the front seat next to the kitchen counter.

The right safety strap lay on the floor still latched together to the other half of the harness. The bolt had broken loose.

He glanced around the room. The bolt wasn't visible. Perhaps he should find it before he left and screw things back together.

At this juncture, Saite might have entertained some feelings of regret for what he had done, but he told himself that he really didn't have time for any of that, especially with regard to his mother. She had been such a bitch to live with.

Now to check on her.

He crossed toward the far corner of the living room where the woman's body was lying, pressed up against the wall.

When he reached the body, Saite crouched down. "So, Mother, what kind of day are you having?" He giggled. He couldn't help himself. This was just so damned funny.

It was quite different from anything he had ever seen before and, besides that, it was rather interesting. His mother's nose was bloody and was bent far over toward her left cheek. Her lips were a bloody pulp, and as Saite scrutinized the area, he spied the end one of her top front teeth protruding through the bloody flesh.

Then he noticed something else. Her chest was moving up and down in a regular rhythm and there was a subtle wheezing sound near the mangled mouth. "Oh, Dear Mother, you're still alive," he whispered. "How special."

He knelt on the blood-smeared floor next to her body and leaned closed to the bloody pulp at the bottom of her face. "Poor, poor mother.

Don't fret. I promise that I will take away all of the pain, and very shortly too."

The left eye was black and swollen shut, but the right one jerked open. It stared at Saite.

"Don't fret, Mother Dear." He just couldn't help himself. He giggled. "Some makeup might help." Saite chuckled again. "On second thought, maybe reconstructive surgery would be a better idea." He raised his right hand to his mouth and laughed.

When he felt like he had gotten control of himself again, he pointed with his right index finger upward toward the ceiling. "But do not fret, Mother. I will alleviate your pain. In fact, I will end it."

Saite rose to his feet and crossed to the living room chair nearest the kitchen counter. He unsnapped the cushion.

Suddenly he felt thirsty.

He dropped the cushion on the chair and walked into the kitchen. He unhooked the safety latch from the refrigerator door and opened it. He checked the beverage holder on the inside of the door.

There were two bottles of Cairo Blue.

He grabbed one of the brown bottles with blue labels, then closed the refrigerator and reconnected the safety latch. He had to return things to the way they were before the flyby. If the authorities checked, they would find his fingerprints all over the compartment, but this was where he lived. So what?

Saite twisted off the beer cap. Then he opened a recycling bin near the sink and dropped the cap inside and closed it. He took a swig of beer and sauntered over to the chair.

He picked up the cushion and moved back toward his mother. When he reached her crumpled body, he stood above her, looking down. He held the cushion against his chest with his left arm. "I'll bet you think I'm going to put this cushion under your head. I'm so sorry, Mother, that's not my plan. Instead, My Dear, I'm going to put it over your terribly messy face." He giggled and sipped from the bottle of beer.

He motioned with his head toward the four seats in the living room. "I'm going back here to sit awhile and drink this beer, Mother. I've had a very long day." He smirked. "I'll bet you have too." He giggled again.

Still clutching the chair cushion, he moved back into the small living room and sat down in the last seat on the right. He placed the bottle of beer on the small table between the two seats. He then reached underneath, tripped off the release and swiveled the chair around so that he could see his mother.

He picked up the bottle of beer and guzzled several swallows.

He supposed it was rather cruel, sitting here like this, but he was waiting for his mother's chest to stop moving. Of course, he might have to wait several hours and, besides, it would be much more merciful to just end it right away. In a way, though, this was quite enjoyable.

Saite took a deep drink of beer, tilting the bottle up high. He swallowed, and then belched. He placed the bottle on the small side table again and rout from the chair.

Still clutching the cushion, he moved slowly across the compartment to the crumpled body.

He then knelt on the floor next to his mother and stared down at the mangled lips. "You certainly do need a facelift." He giggled.

He slapped the pillow over the pulpy mouth and pressed. "Sweet dreams, Mommy Dear."

CHAPTER SIX
"Blessings"

Starship Hope
Compartment 775
Level 3
Pod 2
2M, Day 18, 96 A.D.
(10 months later)
6:23 p.m.

Amun Imhotep loved his family with all his heart. He had invited them here to his compartment for dinner because he had something to tell them. This was going to be difficult, but Naomi, his wife, had agreed that this was the way to do it.

Of all these people he loved, she was the one he loved the most. Of course, she was the one he had known the longest.

He turned to his right and watched her as she ate.

Her head came up and her eyes narrowed. "What?"

"Just looking at the pretty lady."

Naomi's brown eyes focused on his for a split second, and then she looked away toward their son across the breakfast bar. "What are you painting now, Aten?"

Their son looked up from his food plate, as if surprised.
"Oh, just something I photographed in front of an elevator. Nothing special. But the expression on the face of this old grandfather is priceless. I can't wait to get down to this planet. There will be so many things to paint."

"We're just two days away from establishing an orbit."

His son put down his glass of water and swallowed. "Will they have to go around again, like they said?"

Amun shook his head. "No, not from what Ramses says." Right on the edge of Amun's tongue was the issue he had brought the family here for tonight. It was something that was not easy to talk about.

Naomi had been willing to do this duty. She was such a wonderful partner – strong and able. Actually, it was probably her abusive childhood that made her so strong.

However, Amun had told her that this should really be his to tell. After all, he was the father and it was his duty to do this.

There was this sort of given in most Mayan households that the father was the reporter of bad news, no matter what it was. The mother was there to soothe and heal. Of course, that was rather silly, considering the fact that some mothers weren't exactly good healers and some fathers weren't very strong. But that's the way it was in Mayan society and it had probably been that way for many centuries.

Amun looked around the compartment. This was originally his father's place. Now his father was gone. It was just as well in many ways. His dad had missed his mother so much. She had died eleven years before he did.

His father had suffered a heart attack during the Planet 6 flyby. But that was the way to go – quickly.

Amun smiled. It was like most things his father did. They were always accomplished the right way. Nothing was ever haphazard.

"What're you smiling about, Dad?"

Amun looked across the counter. "I was thinking how your grandfather always seemed to get everything just right. He even died just right. He got to see the Constellation Draco from the bridge and experience the flyby – well at least part of the flyby. Then he died quickly."

"Can we talk about something else, Dear?"

Amun turned to Naomi. "Sorry." She did look very pretty tonight. Naomi loved being with her family. It seemed to empower her. "Yes, I should change the subject."

Amun faced his son again. He placed his fork on his plate. "I should get down to the reason I asked you guys to come here tonight."

His grandson, Khons, looked up from the food he had been devouring.

Amun smiled at him. Then he turned to his daughter-in-law, Isis. As far as he was concerned, Aten had chosen a winner there. "This concerns all of us. You, no doubt, have heard that the Council has been in an extended session and is even sleeping in Conference Room 2."

"Yeah, Dad, what's that all about?"

Amun made eye contact with his son. "It's about a problem we have. Ramses tipped me off. He said he wouldn't have done this except that the Council has been stupid about this issue - one member in particular,

Tanis Narmer. Apparently this guy has been filibustering and stopping them from taking a final vote.

"The issue has to do with a problem we have." Amun glanced at Naomi. "The shuttle doesn't have enough reserve fuel to move everyone down to the surface of the planet, Hyksos.

"Ramses made it clear that, because he has the final word as commander of this ship, senior citizens, meaning people of sixty years and older, will not be able to go down.

"He said he made that decision based upon the likelihood that many such people might not survive the trip down and even if they did, the rigors of living in primitive conditions on the planet would kill most of them anyway. In fact, because they might already be suffering from all kinds of ailments and diseases, it would make things even more difficult to deal with for everyone."

Amun looked around at his family. "There, I've said it."

"Who made this decision, Dad?"

"Ramses."

"It doesn't seem fair."

Amun's eyes rested on his grandson. "I know it doesn't seem fair, Khons. But, think about it. There would be a lot of old people down on that planet living in, perhaps, tents in a very primitive place, maybe even living without running water or electricity for a period of time. That would be really difficult. It'll actually be difficult for even the younger people."

Aten looked at his father with sad eyes. "I never thought anything like this would happen, Dad."

Amun nodded. "Me either." He turned to Naomi. Her eyes were filled with tears. He put his hand on her shoulder. "How are you doing, Sweetie?"

She shrugged. "I'm all right." She glanced at him. "No I'm not."

He leaned and kissed her cheek. "Me either."

"We ought to refuse to go down."

Amun turned to his grandson and smiled. "Khons, you're a protester, just like your grandfather."

"I remember you said you were a protester, Grandpa. You protested because your friend Khons was imprisoned. That's how I got my name."

"Yes, he was a really good guy - about your age, in fact. After he was imprisoned, I was also imprisoned because I protested his imprisonment." Amun could feel his smile vanish.

"Pretty bad, huh?"

"Yes, it was." Amun looked around the group. "Frankly, I wouldn't protest, if I were you. There will be others besides the senior citizens who will not be able to go down to the surface of the planet. There just isn't enough fuel. You don't want to be among those people who can't go. If you protest, that could happen."

"Can't they use fuel from the starship?"

Amun shook his head. "No, Aten. I asked that same question. The starship uses a hydrogen fuel. The shuttle uses a solid, granular fuel. Totally different combustion systems." He glanced around the breakfast bar.

The room was silent.

"I couldn't let my family find out any other way but by telling you guys myself." He glanced at Naomi. "While you're working hard down on the new planet, your mother and I will be up here working on her favorite project, storing all the historical information about our culture, personal and otherwise, for future generations. We'll put it on DVDs.

"Your mother says that's very important because this starship journey and the end of life on Mars are critical turning points in our culture's history and, frankly, I think she's right. So, we're going to be really busy up here working with the Mayan Historical Society to preserve these things."

"We'll be able to come up to see you won't we, Grandpa?"

Amun turned. "No, Khons, I'm afraid not. There won't be enough fuel for that."

The room was silent again.

"I've been wrestling with this, guys, ever since Ramses told me. I guess the only way I can accept it is to believe that all of you are going to have a wonderful life down there on this new planet. Besides, you're going to be doing something important, creating a new beginning for the Mayan people."

Naomi was staring at him now. She made a sweet smile. "I love you," she whispered.

Amun could feel tears rising into his eyes. He placed his hand atop hers, resting on the counter.

Then he turned to his son and daughter-in-law. "We're strong people. We can handle this. I'm sure we'll be talking by phone every day. That way we'll be keeping in touch. It'll be like you're living in another city far away. It's not the optimum situation, but I'm sure all of us can handle it."

Aten looked at him. "You're right, Dad. It's just that it's going to be difficult."

"I know, Son. I feel the same way, but I have to look at it from the most selfless perspective I can. It's the right thing to do, under the circumstances.

"Ramses says that the rest of the population, aside from the people critical to security and such, will be taking part in a lottery. That's how they'll determine who goes down."

Amun looked around at his family. "And because of my father's position as the designer of these compartments and his prominence in the Mayan Space Agency, we are evidently a shoe-in. You, Isis and Khons are going down to the planet for sure."

"That isn't fair."

Amun looked at his grandson. "No, it isn't, but I wouldn't fight it if I were you, Khons. Let me tell you something – if my father, your great grandfather, had not been so prominent in the Mayan Space Agency, we would have had to enter the lottery back on Mars and take our chances about getting onboard this starship.

"In fact, it's entirely possible that if he hadn't been a person of prominence, I would have stayed in that Secret Police prison. And maybe I would have eventually disappeared like my friend, Khons."

He smiled at his grandson. "So, Kiddo, you should count your blessings."

CHAPTER SEVEN
"The Threat"

Starship Hope
Compartment 28
Level 5
Pod 1
2M, Day 21, 96 A.D.
7:42

"Tell me, Sergeant, what have you observed about this Saite Manetho."

Abydos shrugged. "Not a hell of a lot, Colonel, Sir. He's kind of a loner but he seems harmless enough. From what I've been seein' at the Emergency Repair Center, the rest of the crew doesn't like him all that much."

"What makes you say that?"

Abydos shrugged again. "Well, Sir, one of them said he was weird."

"Which one was that, Sergeant?"

"This guy named Khufu."

"Did his remark seem credible?"

"I guess. He said Manetho doesn't spend any time with the rest of them after work. They all hang out together when they're not workin', all except this Manetho."

"What does Captain Hapmen, the ERC leader, say?"

"He says Manetho's a good worker, has good skills and does a good job. Sir, can I ask you somethin'?"

"If it pertains to this case, Sergeant, of course."

"It does, Sir. Why have we been doin' all this checkin' on this guy when his mother got killed durin' the flyby? It was an accident – right?"

"It seems that way, Sergeant, except for one thing. We found some evidence that was kind of strange."

"We did?" To Abydos, it seemed like the colonel wasn't going to tell him. As far as he was concerned this whole thing was a waste of time. He didn't like Manetho much himself, but that didn't mean this guy did anything to his mother.

Colonel Ra cleared his throat. "There was blood on the cushion of one of the chairs, Sergeant, and our forensic people can't seem to explain that."

"From what I saw of the pictures, Sir, there was blood all over the compartment."

"That's true, Sergeant, but the forensic people say that this blood doesn't fit the pattern."

The control on the colonel's wrist rang. He raised his hand. "Just a minute, Sergeant." With the index finger on his right hand, he tapped the surface of the control on the inside of his left wrist and held it up to the side of his face. "Colonel Ra."

Abydos watched the other man's face.

"Keep him inside the conference room, Corporal. I'll send a couple of men down right away." Colonel Ra turned away from Abydos. "And don't let him talk you into letting him out of there." Colonel Ra tapped the surface his wrist control with his right index finger.

He turned to Abydos. "You have to go up to Level 1, Conference Room 2. Take Private Gerzean with you. There's been a problem with a councilman, one in particular, Tanis Narmer."

"I know who he is, Sir."

"Yes, Sergeant, I'm sure you do. His reputation precedes him."

"Isn't he the one who voted against the lottery?"

"He's the one."

Sergeant Abydos Smendes could not stand the sight of that Narmer guy. As far as he was concerned, Narmer was an asshole - pure and simple.

"Look, Sergeant, I know that most of us don't care for the man. However, it is our duty to maintain a secure environment aboard this starship. There have been threats against his life."

"Sir, if I may say so, Sir. . ."

"No you may not, Sergeant." The colonel rose from his chair. "I expect you to take Private Gerzean with you and I expect you to go up to Level 1, Conference Room 2, and I expect you to escort Councilman Tanis Narmer to his living quarters. Do you understand that order, Sergeant?"

Abydos jumped up from his chair and snapped to attention. "Yes, Sir."

"I also expect you to leave Private Gerzean at the door of Narmer's living quarters as his guard. Tell Gerzean that he will be relieved from that duty in six hours and tell him that Narmer must not leave his quarters until notified that he may do so. Is that understood, Sergeant Smendes?"

"Yes, Sir."

"In the meantime, Sergeant, I will form a detail to investigate the source of these threats against him. When you go to my outer office, Sergeant, tell my assistant, Private Coptos to come in here."

"Yes, Sir."

"You are dismissed, Sergeant."

Abydos saluted. "Yes, Sir." He did an about-face and strode to the door.

"Sergeant, Smendes."

Abydos stopped and turned. "Yes, Sir?"

"Gerzean is in the weapons storage room cleaning pistols."

Abydos saluted. "Thank you, Sir."

The colonel returned the salute. "Get to it, Sergeant."

"Yes, Sir." Abydos slapped his palm against the blue panel to the right of the door.

It rattled open.

He stepped into the outer office.

The door sucked shut behind him.

The young assistant looked up from his desk.

"The colonel wants to see you, Coptos."

"Right now?"

"Not tomorrow, Coptos."

"Yes, Sergeant." The young private jumped up from his chair and hurried around the edge of the desk and across the small office.

Abydos moved across the office to a side door. He put his hand on the blue panel.

The door sucked open.

Two young men in uniform and sitting on the floor looked up from pistols they held in their hands.

"Gerzean. . ."

A skinny, white-skinned young soldier jerked to a standing position.

"Come with me, Gerzean. Oh, by the way, you'll need a pistol and ammo."

The young private stopped. "A pistol?"

"Is there a fuckin' echo in here?"

The private didn't answer.

"Also bring your bulletproof vest."

"Put it on?"

"No, shove it up your ass, Gerzean."

The other man chuckled.

"Hey, this is not fuckin' funny! Get a pistol and bulletproof vest, Gerzean – now!"

"Yes, Sergeant." The young private grabbed a pistol off the tabletop and a cartridge belt. Then he moved over to a shelf and snatched a bulletproof vest.

"Grab a couple of helmets, Gerzean."

The private turned to another shelf and removed two helmets. He then crossed the room to Abydos. "Here you are, Sir."

"Thanks a lot, Gerzean. By the way, we're gonna be guarding Tanis Narmer."

The young private stared at him.

"And no I'm not kidding, Gerzean." Sergeant Smendes crossed the small space and picked up a bulletproof vest. It occurred to him that both of them might be the first targets for a would-be assassin.

He crossed to the door and pressed his hand against the blue pad next to it.

The door sucked open and Smendes stepped through. He could feel the young soldier behind him.

"This guy is a real asshole, Sergeant."

Smendes stepped into the outer office. Coptos was still gone. "I didn't say that, Gerzean."

"No, Sir. I did, Sir."

Abydos grinned. "You're right this time, Gerzean. I think that's the first time you've ever been right in your whole miserable life. But let me make somethin' very clear. It doesn't make any fuckin' difference. We have to guard him all the way to his compartment. Then you're gonna be standin' outside his compartment for the next six hours guardin' his life. Got that?"

"But, Sir. . ."

Abydos pointed at the private's face. "Gerzean, don't give me any of your shit. You signed up for the military and now you have to follow orders. And if you fuck this up, I'm gonna kick your ass so hard you won't find it till the day you die. Got that?"

"Yes, Sir."

"Good. Now swipe your pistol, these vests and helmets in front of that sensor on Coptos' desk." The sergeant pointed at the sensor.

Sergeant Smendes pulled out his pistol and snapped the slide back. Then he lowered the hammer carefully to the rest position and turned on the safety.

When he looked up, Gerzean was staring at him. "What are you lookin' at?"

"You just put a round in the chamber."

"No shit, Gerzean?"

"I saw you, Sergeant."

"Of course you did. Narmer's life's been threatened. I expect you to get your pistol ready to fire as well. Run those items by the scanner so we can get the hell out of here. Come on. Get your ass in gear."

"Yes, Sir."

CHAPTER EIGHT
"Close Call"

Starship Hope
Conference Room 2
Level 1
Pod 2
2M, Day 21, 96 A.D.
8:03 a.m.

"Commander, I really don't see why I have to stay in here. This is tantamount to imprisonment."

Ramses Tutan smiled at the councilman. "You don't have to make a big fuss about it, Tanis. There are no TV cameras or microphones here recording this. Our purpose is to prevent you from getting hurt - or even killed."

"Do you actually think those ruffians would attempt to do something?"

"We don't know, Tanis. We're just trying to protect you. That eleven hour filibuster of yours really upset some people."

"I'm rather disappointed in this whole process, if you must know, Commander. The people aboard this ship expect a democratic process and that's what I was trying to give them. Just because some weirdo threatens my life, I'm not going to run and hide."

"We don't expect you to hide, Tanis. However, you did filibuster the vote for the lottery. People see this as obstruction."

"I wasn't trying to obstruct anything. I was objecting to the way this process was going to be conducted. I still think we can get more people onboard those shuttle flights. This lottery presumes that we can't move more than one hundred eight people down in one flight. My figures show that we could move as many as one hundred twenty-one."

"I don't know where you got your figures, Tanis, but they're wrong. One hundred eight is all we can safely transport down at once. If that changes at some point, then we'll make adjustments to accommodate more passengers."

Tanis Narmer shook his head. "I still think we can do more than we are." At this juncture Tanis wasn't going to pursue this any longer. Obviously he wasn't getting anywhere, just like he couldn't with the High Council.

However, Tanis would keep his options open. He was absolutely sure they could transport more people down to the planet Hyksos in each of these flights.

The first ship down was going to carry aluminum strips to make a runway for the next landing. As a consequence, the first flight would be engineers and construction people. There would also be a small contingent of military to secure the area.

Now, what was all this falderal about these threats on his life? He supposed people misunderstood his motives. Perhaps they thought he was trying to delay the shuttle flights. Not at all.

Of course, until the council had approved the lottery concept, the lottery couldn't begin, so it might appear to someone who was ill-informed that he was delaying the process.

The starship was in orbit around Hyksos. There was no big hurry. The military had to send down a drone to scout out the surface of the planet anyway.

Councilman Tanis Narmer wasn't trying to delay. He just wanted to get things right. He realized that the masses of people aboard this starship were not well informed about the political process. He had actually expected a more enlightened attitude. Making threats? How childish.

Tanis thought that the selection process for this starship back on Mars when they started this journey had skimmed some pretty good people off the top of society. He supposed the kind of people aboard this starship would be of superior intelligence. Perhaps not. Maybe some real cretins had made it through the selection process.

"The important thing, Tanis, is that people misinterpreted what you were doing. All they saw was delay. They're already upset because not all of them will be able to go down to the surface of this new planet."

Tanis nodded. "I realize that, Commander."

There was a loud "buzz" at the door.

Commander Tutan turned. "Get that, Private."

"Yes, Sir." The young soldier dressed in camouflage khakis standing next to the door, did an about-face. He peered through the peephole, and then turned back to Commander Tutan. "It's the military escort for Councilman Narmer, Sir."

"Let them in, Private. But do check their identifications." Ramses pulled his pistol out of his holster and snapped the slide back. He held the black pistol at his side and faced the doorway.

The young soldier put his thumb against a blue panel to the right of the door.

It sucked open.

In front of him were two soldiers in helmets and bulletproof vests. They were wearing pistols.

The private held out his hand. "Identification, please."

The sergeant tilted his head. "Kamose, you know who I am."

"Yes, Sergeant, but the Commander told me to check all identifications."

Sergeant Smendes dug inside the collar of his tee shirt behind his bulletproof vest and pulled out a metal tag on a chain.

The guard clasped the metal tag in his fingers and studied the surface. "Sergeant Abydos Smendes." He stood aside. "You may come in, Sergeant."

Abydos stepped around him and entered Conference Room 2. He moved over next to Councilman Narmer and stood facing the doorway.

Private Kamose checked the other soldier's military identification tag. "Private Badari Gerzean." Kamose stepped aside and the other soldier moved into the conference room.

The door sucked shut.

Sergeant Smendes turned to Councilman Narmer. "It's my responsibility to see that you get back to your compartment safe. While we're movin' back to your compartment I will be in charge. Do you understand that, Doctor Narmer?"

"This is preposterous! A lowly sergeant giving me orders."

"It's for your safety, Sir."

Narmer raised his hand and waved it. "I refuse to do this! It's ridiculous!"

"Sir, it's either you cooperate or I'll put you in handcuffs and haul you to your compartment."

"You wouldn't dare!"

Ramses stepped over next to Councilman Narmer. "Tanis, I will order him to put you in handcuffs if you don't cooperate."

"I'll have you court-martialed!"

Ramses grinned. "Take your best shot, Tanis." He turned to Smendes. "Put him in cuffs, Sergeant."

The soldier reached around to the small of his back.

"I refuse!"

"You won't refuse if these two men wrestle you to the floor, Tanis."

A hand suddenly clamped onto Tanis's right shoulder and squeezed.

His right arm went numb and his left arm was yanked around behind his back. He heard a distinct "click" and felt cold metal against his wrists. "You can't do this!"

"We just did, Tanis. Now you're under the direct orders of Sergeant Smendes."

The sergeant stepped around in front of him. "This is the way it's gonna be, Councilman." He motioned with his head toward the other soldier. "Private Gerzean will walk in front of you and I will walk behind you. If we tell you to drop to the floor, you do it."

"You can't treat me like this."

"Look, Narmer, I really don't give a good fuck if somebody shoots your ass and throws you down a garbage chute so that you float out there in space above Hyksos for the rest of eternity, but I have orders to deliver you to your compartment alive and I'm gonna do that, even if I have to knock you on the head and carry you there. Got that?"

Tanis Narmer stared at the muscular face with the lumpy nose. This peasant was going to tell him what to do. Well, maybe he really had no choice, after all. Probably it was just better to go along. "Sometime, Sergeant, I'll discuss my political and social views with you. Of course, I'm not sure you'd understand something that complicated."

"Tanis. . ."

The councilman turned to Commander Tutan.

"Tanis, these men are going to be protecting your life. If I were you, I would treat them with at least the minimum of respect."

Councilman Narmer stared into Ramses' blue eyes. Then he looked at Sergeant Smendes.

Perhaps it would be wiser to treat this cretin better. Tanis doubted these threats were real, but of course, one never knew for sure. "You can take off the cuffs."

Ramses stared into Tanis's eyes. "You realize, Tanis, that he's just trying to keep you safe."

"The cuffs are very uncomfortable."

Ramses turned to the noncom. "Take them off, Sergeant."

Smendes stared at Ramses. "With all due respect, Sir. I don't have to. My assignment is to deliver him safe. I will carry that out, no matter what anybody says."

"I understand, Sergeant. But I think Tanis is going to behave himself now. If he doesn't, just snap those cuffs back on." Ramses looked at the councilman. "I would."

"Yes, Sir." The sergeant pulled a key out of his pocket and unlocked the cuffs. He reached around to the small of his back and re-inserted them into his belt. "You stay close to us, Councilman. There are a whole bunch of people out there who are pissed-off at you."

Smendes turned to the young private. "Gerzean, you go first. Walk with your hand on the butt of your pistol. Is your safety off?"

"Yes, Sir."

Smendes nodded toward the door. "Go ahead."

Gerzean stepped over to the door.

The guard pressed his thumb against the blue panel.

The door sucked open.

Private Gerzean stepped out into the corridor and moved to his left. He placed his right hand on the butt of his pistol.

"Go ahead, Councilman."

Narmer turned to the sergeant. "I don't like being treated like a child."

"Do it!" Sergeant Smendes eyes were angry.

The councilman stepped out into the corridor and turned left.

Sergeant Smendes followed.

The door to the conference room sucked shut.

Smendes leaned around the councilman. "Go ahead, Gerzean. When you get to the elevator door, go beyond it. I want to look inside."

Several feet down the corridor Gerzean stopped.

Sergeant Smendes turned to the elevator panel and punched the DOWN button.

The number 2 lit above the elevator door, then 1. "Ding."

The elevator door rumbled open.

Sergeant Smendes grabbed the edge of it. He scrutinized the two people inside. One was a brown-haired girl wearing a backpack. Smendes studied the small, pudgy man in the back corner to the right.

"Step inside, Councilman, over against the wall on the left."

Tanis Narmer didn't like being given orders.

"Do it, Councilman. . . now!"

Tanis stepped into the elevator. He stood near the left wall.

Sergeant Smendes stepped in next to him on the right. He glanced at the man in the corner, then turned around and stood to Narmer's left, facing the open doorway.

The door began to move.

Private Gerzean grabbed it, then stepped inside to the left and turned around in front of the panel.

"Level 3, Gerzean," said Smendes.

The young private punched the 3 button.

The door rumbled shut and the elevator jerked downward.

Tanis Narmer had no idea what was happening until he heard the man behind him "gasp."

He turned.

Sergeant Smendes was holding the handle of a knife up against the man's stomach.

There was blood on Smendes' hand.

The girl behind Narmer screamed.

Sergeant Smendes held the knife hard into the man's stomach and pushed against him. His face was intense.

The man slid down the back wall to the carpeted floor.

The elevator bell rang.

When the door rumbled opened, Smendes looked up at the girl from where he was crouched over the man's body. "Do you know this guy?"

"No!"

"Gerzean, get her name and compartment number."

The private pulled a pencil and pad out of his shirt pocket. He handed it to the girl.

She scribbled on the pad, all the while staring at the body in the corner.

Sergeant Smendes held his left wrist up near his mouth. He tapped the surface of his wrist control with his bloody right index finger. "This is Sergeant Abydos Smendes. Private Gerzean and I are in Elevator 5 at Level 3, Pod 2. We need backup right now. And send up a medic."

"Got it, Sergeant," said a male voice. "Sending up two men and a medic."

Tanis Narmer started to move.

Smendes grabbed his left arm. "Stay right here. This man tried to stab you. There may be somebody workin' with him. Don't go anywhere." He motioned with his head toward the girl. "Get off and find another elevator."

She handed the pad and pen to Gerzean. Then she stared down at the man with empty eyes crumpled in the corner.

Dark blood was pooling on the carpeted floor of the elevator.

"Go!"

The girl pushed by Councilman Narmer out into the corridor. She glanced back, and then ran.

"He just saved your life, Councilman."

Tanis Narmer looked at the young private.

Gerzean nodded toward Smendes. "He saved your ass. That guy down in the corner was tryin' to stab you."

Tanis Narmer turned to Smendes who was crouched next to the body. "Thank you, Sergeant." He held out his hand.

Smendes looked at the proffered hand, then up at Councilman Narmer. "It's my job." He turned back to the body and pressed his bloody right index finger against the left side of the man's neck. "Pulse is weak."

It suddenly dawned on Tanis Narmer that even though he didn't particularly like this crude Sergeant Smendes, the man had, indeed, saved his life. Maybe he could do something for him as a thank you. Of course, this guy wasn't all that bright, so perhaps a gesture of this kind would be way over his head.

Tanis figured he should try to do something, nevertheless. The important thing was that these gestures were always good for a politician's image, even if they weren't appreciated by the recipient.

CHAPTER NINE
"More Surprises"

Starship Hope
The Bridge
2M, Day 21, 96 A.D.
9:58 a.m.

Ramses stood at the left side of the three men, sitting in front of the video monitor.

Outside the curved windshield of the starship floated a blue and green planet with puffy white clouds. A great portion of the planet was the blue of large bodies of water. Green continents sprawled throughout the blue.

The scientific experts had decided to focus the first part of their probe into the atmosphere of Hyksos with the drone in areas where there should be moderate temperatures. Doctor Buhen, the astronomer, had determined that the planet did tilt on its axis throughout a period of some length of time, perhaps three hundred or more days, but it was only a slight tilt, less than three degrees.

As a consequence, there would be only a slight change of seasons in the lower and upper hemispheres. Therefore, he decided that it would not be wise to go too far upward or downward away from the more temperate climates near the middle area of the planet.

Ramses turned to the small group of men. "Gentlemen, Lieutenant Harkhuf will turn on the camera shortly. The drone is currently flying its way down into the atmosphere of Hyksos to observation level. I wanted you all here to help us make decisions about whether we can land our shuttle and if we can, where it's possible to land.

"You are obviously the most knowledgeable people with regard to these issues – Doctor Pithom, our environmental expert, whose task is obvious. Then we have Doctor Buhen, our astronomer, who will tell us the general characteristics of this planet, and, of course, our engineer, Doctor Taharqa, who will help us with the logistics of where to land."

Ramses moved over next to the monitor so that he was facing the three men. "This is the moment we have planned for since we left Mars forty-nine years ago."

He scanned the three faces. "I'm not sure what we'll find, Gentlemen. However, I would suggest that we keep what we see to ourselves until a proper public announcement can be made over the video system aboard this starship, perhaps with some of these pictures we're recording today."

Ramses focused on Doctor Sethos Pithom. "We're recording sound as well, Doctor Pithom, so any comments you want to make will be appreciated. I would think when it comes to environment that any little detail would be important."

"Sir. . . sorry to interrupt."

Ramses' head jerked around to the young military officer manning the control module in front of a small video screen off to the left side of the pilot's console.

"Commander, the drone's moving below the layer of clouds now, Sir. I'll turn on the video monitor."

"Thank you, Lieutenant." Ramses stepped away from the video monitor and stood at the end of the row of three men who were seated.

The large screen blinked on and a color picture of a vast forest appeared.

There was a list of white numbers next to the left exterior edge of the video monitor screen.

"Doctor Pithom, what are your first reactions?"

The pudgy man leaned forward and studied the screen. "I'd say this is a sub-tropical forest with thick undergrowth. We can hope for some occasional open grassy areas or, perhaps, high plateaus with treeless plains." He pointed at the numbers in the left margin of the screen. "We're reading twenty-two percent oxygen, seventy-seven percent nitrogen. The last one percent contains argon, carbon dioxide and some other minor gases." He turned to Ramses. "Commander, this planet will definitely sustain animal life."

Pithom stared at the screen. "This is fascinating."

Ramses smiled. "I'm sure it is, Doctor."

The pudgy man raised his head above the monitor and addressed the military officer at the controls. "What is the ambient temperature your drone is recording at this altitude, Lieutenant?"

"Seventy-two degrees, Sir."

"Commander, I think we've chosen the right planet."

Ramses nodded. "That's great to hear."

Ahmose Buhen, the astronomer, pointed. "A river."

The river disappeared.

Ramses moved around to the side of the monitor. "Lieutenant, can we go back to that river and slow down some?"

The young officer glanced back. "Certainly, Sir."

The picture pivoted around in a sweeping circle of blurry greenery.

As Ramses stared at the screen, he felt a slight sense of vertigo. He moved away from the monitor and gripped onto the back of Doctor Pithom's chair.

The man looked up at him. "Kind of makes your head spin."

The river appeared again.

Pithom looked up at Ramses again. "Commander, may I direct the lieutenant?"

"Certainly, Doctor Pithom."

The environmental expert peered over the top of the video monitor. "Lieutenant, slow the drone and follow that riverbed. In fact, if you can drop the altitude a bit, that would be very helpful."

The scenery flowing by slowed ever so slightly, then the angle of the picture changed. It changed again and the river valley came closer and closer. The drone leveled out.

Lieutenant Harkhuf glanced back over his left shoulder. "That's three hundred feet altitude, Sir. I don't dare go any lower. Some of those trees are pretty tall."

Pithom waved his hand. "That's fine, Lieutenant." His eyes were riveted on the river.

He glanced up at Ramses. "That's fresh water and it's very clear. There certainly doesn't seem to be any pollution of any kind, which would make me guess that this is far away from any civilization – no towns or cities."

He rose slightly from his seat and looked over the monitor toward the young lieutenant. "Can you make your drone hover over the river, Lieutenant Harkhuf?"

"No, Sir, but I can make it circle."

The scenery shifted dizzily to the left.

"Making a hard right turn, Sir."

Ramses watched as the forest of green trees swept by. For just a split second, there was a break in the foliage and he saw charging animals. "Lieutenant, stop the turn."

"Yes, Sir."

The sweep stopped and the probe moved over the trees in a straight line. Suddenly the ground came close.

"Wow!" The lieutenant pulled back on the small joystick.

The drone climbed skyward, and then it leveled out.

On the video screen was a flat plain with tall yellow grass. Suddenly a black animal body appeared.

"Bison!"

Ramses pointed. "More bison. They're running."

"It's a huge herd." Doctor Pithom turned to Ramses. "Bison mean food, Commander."

"Look!" Ahmose Buhen, the astronomer pointed toward the screen.

In the upper left corner of the screen appeared a white-skinned humanoid on horseback. His hair was a mass of thick, orange curls. He was wearing a loose-fitting animal skin shirt and short animal skin pants and animal skin moccasins.

"My God, it's a human!"

The figure had a long spear raised high above his right shoulder.

Then the figure disappeared and the screen was full of black bison.

Ramses moved forward. "Lieutenant, can you turn so we can see that humanoid again."

"Yes, Sir."

The drone swept to the right, making the yellow grass and the black muscular backs of the bison sweep to the left.

When it completed its turn, a humanoid on horseback slipped under it.

"Take it up a hundred feet, Lieutenant," said Doctor Pithom.

"Yes, Sir."

The angle of the drone tipped up.

What they saw next almost stopped Ramses' breath.

Out in front of the drone camera was a giant herd of bison and along the right side of the herd rode seven humanoids on horseback with spears raised above their right shoulders.

One threw a spear and a bison stumbled and another bison tripped over that one and was speared by another humanoid.

The group of humanoids stopped, forming a barrier with their horses around the two downed bison.

The stampeding bison swerved away like a sea of undulating blackness.

The drone flew over the humanoids.

"Circle back," said Doctor Pithom.

The drone swept to the right. This time it approached the humanoids from the side.

"Can you slow it down, Lieutenant?"

The young officer glanced back at Doctor Pithom. "Not much, Sir. I don't want it to stall."

When the drone approached the humanoids, the bison herd was gone.

One of the humanoids pointed at the drone. Then he slipped a crossbow up onto his saddle, cocked it, raised it and fired.

"He's shooting at the drone."

"Moving higher, Sir."

The view from the drone was blue sky with puffy clouds.

"I'm taking it up a couple hundred feet, and then I'll circle. I can extend the camera focus."

The drone leveled out and swept to the right. The camera angle tilted downward and the lens zoomed outward. The small plane circled around the large open area filled with yellow grass.

Below in the center of its circle were eight orange-haired humanoids. A smaller one was holding the horses while the others were kneeling next to the downed bison.

Ramses pointed. "One of the horses is hitched to a travois."

Doctor Pithom turned to him. "That's the way they'll take the meat back to the village. Therefore, the village would have to be fairly close."

The drone lazily circled far above the tiny figures.

Doctor Pithom pointed toward the screen. "They all have orange hair."

Ramses moved slightly closer to the video screen. "And very white skin."

"Yes." Doctor Pithom stood up. "Lieutenant, can you fly around in a pattern, perhaps at a higher altitude, please. There has to be a village nearby. They won't haul that meat on a travois more than a few miles, I wouldn't think."

"Doctor Pithom, do you think this place is habitable for us?"

The pudgy man swung around. "Yes, absolutely. Our only problem is that we may be competing with these people for food. Of course, they could be quite friendly."

Ramses stared at the screen as the drone rose to a higher altitude and swept back and forth, first to the right, then to the left. "Doctor Pithom, suppose they're not friendly?"

The environmental expert shrugged. "Well, we have the technological advantage. I would estimate that they're living in a late stone age or an early bronze age. That's what it looks like to me. If we could see one of those spears up close,
I'm sure we could figure it out pretty quickly."

Ramses wondered what was in store for the Mayans once they landed on this alien planet.

Doctor Pithom walked around the counter with the large monitor above it. He moved over next to the man near the controls. "Lieutenant, go back to the river. That's where we'll find the village."

The young man looked up at him. "Certainly, Sir."

The drone swept to the left.

Then the angle of the camera moved upward, revealing a panoramic view of the plateau and the steep slope with short, thinly foliated scrub trees dropping abruptly down into a thickly forested green valley.

Beyond it was the river, now a silver ribbon meandering through the thick clusters of green treetops.

As the drone approached the river, Pithom tapped the lieutenant's monitor. "Look, it's a village! My God, it's right there!"

Now Ramses could see it on the big monitor.

Away from the river, along a flat area below the sheer walls of rock on the side of the plateau was a cluster of circular huts.

Ramses held out his right hand with the index finger pointing. He began counting. ". . . five, six, seven, eight."
He stared at the cluster of huts. "There have to be fifteen to twenty huts in that village."

Doctor Sethos Pithom looked over his left shoulder at Ramses. "Can you believe it? This is marvelous!" He turned back to the young officer's monitor. "Lieutenant, when you get near the village, drop down in altitude."

"Yes, Sir." The lieutenant pushed the small joystick on the control panel.

Pithom turned around. "This is quite a little town, Commander."

Ramses thought it was fascinating too. However, he just hoped these humans with orange hair were friendly.

CHAPTER TEN
"First Encounter"

Hyksos (Planet 3)
2M, Day 28, 96 A.D.
8:26 a.m.

Sergeant Abydos Smendes held onto the armrests of his seat as the shuttle descended backward to the surface of the planet. The skin on his face was stretched back from the g-force and the shaking made his body vibrate inside the safety harness he thought he had strapped tight. Right now it didn't feel all that tight.

That environmentalist guy, Pithom, had told them that the gravitation on this planet would be greater than Mars, their home planet. He said they would feel heavy and clumsy at first because they had lived on the starship with sixty percent gravity. They would also have to be careful about muscle pulls.

Abydos had been working out every morning for the last seven months aboard the starship to prepare for this. He had always worked out, but lately he had increased the length of time and the levels of resistance. He figured he wanted to be ready for anything.

When the shuttle finally touched down on the low plateau above the riverbed, there was a sudden silence.

"All passengers and crew members, please stay in your seats until we have stabilized the landing gear," said a male voice over the public address system.

There was the "whirr" of hydraulics and the shuttle shifted. Then another "whirr."

Finally electric motors whined.

The front of the compartment slowly descended downward in an arc. When it reached approximate level there was another "whirr" of hydraulics.

The cabin rotated toward the left until it was level, then the "whirr" ceased.

"All passengers may remove their safety harnesses. The temperature outside the hull of the shuttle is eighty-one degrees. Oxygen readings hover at around twenty-two percent. The air is breathable, gentlemen."

Abydos unbuckled his safety harness and stood up.

Colonel Ra walked up to him. "Sergeant, we will be the first off. Make sure the men have their firearms ready to use with all safeties off. The assault rifles are in the locker to your right and left as you go through this compartment exit." He pointed to the doorway behind him.

"We will form a perimeter around the area designated in our discussions yesterday. That will be where the landing strip is constructed. Assign sentinels immediately. We must have people whose jobs are dedicated to security from the get-go. Got that, Sergeant?"

"Yes, Sir, Colonel."

"Carry on, Sergeant."

"Yes, Sir." Abydos turned to the soldiers standing in the aisle next to their seats. They were wearing camouflage uniforms and brown boots. "Okay, listen up!"

The shuttle went silent.

"Private Gerzean and Private Kamose - I want you guys to form sentinel packs of seven men each! We will form a sentinel perimeter around the landin' strip! Make sure your wrist controls are workin' and make sure your assault rifles are loaded and ready to fire!

"To all you men - you will find assault rifles in the lockers to the right and left as you leave this compartment! Got that?" He looked around the group of men. "Any questions?"

One man in the back raised his hand. "Sir, if we see hostiles, what should we do?"

"Fire a warnin' shot above their heads, crouch down and call me on your wrist control. I'll take it from there. And by the way, if they happen to be standin' between you and the shuttle or the construction crew, fire your warnin' shot somewhere else!"

There was a low chuckle.

"Okay, men, let's get to it! Form a line, facin' the door!" Sergeant Abydos Smendes moved down the narrow aisle, pushing his way around the men as he went.

At the exit to the compartment, he turned to the locker door and slid it aside.

Lined up in racks inside were assault rifles and at the bottom of the locker was a box of ammunition clips.

Abydos grabbed one of the assault rifles and yanked it out of the plastic stand. He held it up above his head. "Take your assault rifle and two clips of ammo!"

He bent down, opened the green plastic case at the bottom of the locker and removed two clips. He stuffed them into the two box-like cloth containers on the wide cartridge belt around his waist and pressed the Velcro strips at the tops of the containers. Next, he reached down for a third clip and snapped it into the rectangular opening on the bottom of the assault rifle in front of the trigger.

He then moved to the doorway.

What surprised him were the fragrances that wafted into his face. These were sweet smells he had never known before. The sun felt warm. For just a split second he was mesmerized.

At least this would be interesting. That lottery today on the starship should be interesting too. The military had to keep a presence on the starship at the lottery sites, just so there wouldn't be any trouble. People were really uptight about this lottery thing.

Abydos slipped the assault rifle strap over his right shoulder and turned around. Facing backwards, he stepped outside to the egress ladder.

Gripping the handles on the side of the door casing he descended the ladder the first few steps. Then gripping onto a ladder rung above his head, he descended step-by-step.

He jumped off the ladder two rungs from the bottom and his boots landed in the tall, spongy grass. Sergeant Smendes snapped back the bolt on his assault rifle and moved a few feet from the base of the ladder. "All clear!"

Abydos Smendes realized something. He would be the first man down that ladder. He'd be the first man on this planet.

Hey, he was all right with that. It was because he was Colonel Ra's noncom. Colonel Ra was an okay commander, but if Abydos was commanding this unit himself, he would have been the first one down the ladder. He wouldn't have sent a sergeant. But that was Colonel Ra. He was kind of a sissy.

Sergeant Smendes didn't exactly dislike the guy. Ra was all right, but the sergeant had often wondered when the chips were down if his colonel would stand and fight, or maybe he would run like a little girl.

Smendes scanned the field around him. Then he turned so he was looking beyond the body of the shuttle toward a wooded area. For just a second, he thought he saw something move.

Still staring toward the wooded area, he felt along his cartridge belt with his left hand. His fingers found his binocular case. He ripped open the Velcro strip at the top and slid out the binoculars.

Still holding his assault rifle ready with his right hand, he lifted the binoculars to his eyes with his left.

The image was blurry.

"See something, Sir?"

Abydos adjusted the wheel until the image cleared. "I thought I saw some motion over there, Gerzean."

"What do you think it is?"

Orange hair and white skin appeared in front of the binocular lens. "People."

"No shit?"

"No, shit, Gerzean." He lowered the binoculars and turned to the private. "Make sure the men you pick aren't some trigger-happy twerps, Private. We don't want anybody hurt. All the same, everybody should have a clip in his weapon and his weapon should be ready to fire. Got it?"

"Yes, Sir."

A string of soldiers wearing green and brown camouflage was descending the ladder.

Abydos pointed. "Take some men over there, Gerzean and set up a perimeter.

"Yes, Sir, Sergeant."

"Get to it."

"Yes, Sir."

Gerzean moved in among the men, calling out names.

Sergeant Smendes watched for another second. Then he forced himself to move away from the shuttle to a position between the shuttle and the trees where he had seen the humans.

Smendes held up his binoculars again to check. He saw nothing.

Then he took off his hat and slipped the binocular strap over his head. He pulled the soft hat back down on his close-shaven head and tugged the brim down to shade his eyes from the bright sun.

At that moment he thought he heard voices. What startled him, how-ever, was that the voices were not coming from behind him, but in front of him - from somewhere in the woods.

He studied the edge of the woods. Suddenly his eyes caught a motion in a tree. He stared at the tree. In the shadows behind foliated branches he could see a silhouette.

The fingers of his left hand found his binoculars, resting against his chest. His hand raised them up in front of his eyes.

His left index finger rubbed against the ribbed wheel.

The shadowy silhouette cleared.

Abydos Smendes could see a small man crouched in the interior of the large tree. The man seemed to be wearing clothes of some kind. He had red bushy hair and his skin was very white. "Ugly little sucker," he whispered.

Then he saw what looked like a crossbow.

Abydos dropped the binoculars, crouched down to one knee and raised his assault rifle to his shoulder. He aimed into the top of the tree above the man with the crossbow and pulled the trigger.

The stutter of automatic fire shattered the silence and the sound echoed into the trees and the surrounding hills.

In the bottom of his vision, Abydos saw the human figure drop out of the tree.

He caught a glimpse of white skin.

Then he heard multiple voices and a scurrying sound in the brush around the tree.

"What is it, Sergeant?"

Abydos remained on one knee with his eyes riveted on the trees. "Some little guy with a crossbow."

"A crossbow?"

"That's what I said, Sir."

The colonel knelt next to him with his own assault rifle poised against his right hip. "Do you think he was going to shoot at you?"

"I don't know, Sir."

Colonel Ra scanned the line of trees. "We'll have to remain on high alert, Sergeant."

"Yes, Sir."

The colonel rose to his feet.

Abydos glanced in his direction and remained on one knee. "When you move back, Sir, I'd turn and check behind yourself every so often. I think I scared them away, but there may be somebody still in the trees with a crossbow." Abydos thought for second. "Just a suggestion, Sir."

"Actually, Sergeant, it's a good idea."

Abydos Smendes remained on one knee, scanning the line of trees with his eyes. He was sure the colonel would now spend the whole day near the shuttle where he felt safe. Abydos knew that was going to happen for sure.

This made Sergeant Smendes almost chuckle. His colonel was such a wimp. Why the hell would you sign up for the military when you were a wimp?

The sergeant rose to his feet. He checked the line of trees again, and then turned to check on his men.

There were clusters of soldiers moving outward toward the line of woods on the far side of the field.

Abydos raised his left arm up near his face. He tapped the screen of his wrist control with the index finger of his right hand. "Gerzean, are you all set up?"

There was a brief pause. "Yes, Sir. We're getting men placed around the perimeter of the field. Kamose is off to my right." There was a pause. "I guess you'd call that east."

"I'm seein' Kamose movin' some men out toward the woods."

"What was the shooting about, Sir?"

"I saw a man in a tree with a crossbow."

"Did you say, 'Crossbow', Sir?"

"Yes, Gerzean. Keep your eyes open. One of these little guys might take a shot at you."

"I'll tell the men, Sir."

"Do that, Gerzean."

Sergeant Smendes heard the whinny of a horse behind him.

He swung around.

A small herd of horses bolted out of a thin area in the woods and charged toward him through the tall grass.

Smendes was surprised. Why would horses charge at you?

Then he caught a glimpse of something hanging down on the far side of the body of the horse.

He held his left wrist up near his face and tapped the surface of his control. "Gerzean, I think we're being attacked! Get your men ready!"

The sergeant dropped to his right knee and brought his assault weapon down so it was aimed at the lead horse.

Arrows filled the air.

Smendes dropped to his stomach. He heard the "whizz" of an arrow near his head.

He fired his assault weapon into the ground in front of the lead horse.

The stutter of automatic weapon fire echoed in the hills.

The horse reared and fell.

The remaining horses turned and their riders swung up onto their backs and rode away.

Abydos jumped to his feet and charged toward the downed horse.

When he was near it, the horse clambered to its feet and ran.

"Halt!"

A small red-haired man started to run.

Abydos fired in front of him. Dust and dirt splattered the man's legs.

The stuttering of the automatic weapon echoed in the woods. The man stopped.

"Hands up!"

The figure turned and faced him.

Smendes gestured with his left hand above his head.

The figure raised both hands.

When Sergeant Smendes stopped a few feet away, he was looking at a very white man with bushy orange hair and blue eyes. The man was wearing black animal skin short pants and an animal skin shirt. He stood about five feet, seven inches tall.

CHAPTER ELEVEN
"Realistic"

Starship Hope
Cafeteria
Level 3
Pod 2
2M, Day 28, 96 A.D.
2:26 p.m.

When Khons walked into the cafeteria, there was a meeting going on toward the back. A small group of young men was sitting around in a loose cluster and a slightly older man was talking to them.

From the backpacks and the faces, he figured most of them were college students. Khons just hoped there wasn't going to be any trouble. That lottery today had stirred up a lot of noise on the starship. There had even been some arrests. One soldier was hit by a hammer. Luckily he wasn't hurt badly.

Khons knew why people were upset. He was upset too. In his case, it wasn't because he didn't get a ticket to go down to the planet. He did. However, his girlfriend, Opet, didn't.

She was waiting for him in the back of the cafeteria by the dispensing machines in the corner across from the meeting of those guys. He wondered what that was about – probably the lottery.

Khons really dreaded this. He had begged his father to do something for Opet. His father had told him that it just wasn't possible. He had said that if Khons' great grandfather were still alive, then maybe he could have done something, just because of his prominence in the Mayan Space Agency. Otherwise, there was no chance.

This really bummed him out. Khons was seriously attached to Opet. She was a good person and they had been dating for two years now. They had known each other since elementary school.

But what would he do about the fact that she wasn't going? A solution had crossed his mind. He could stay up here on the starship. But he was so awfully curious about that planet below them. What would it be like to live down there? He had entertained all kinds of fantasies about it, some of them pretty ridiculous.

He knew the construction crew and a military contingent were down on the surface right now. Man, that would be so exciting! A whole new planet! And he had heard that there were people on this planet. It had been one of those rumors moving around the starship since they had established their orbit.

He stopped in front of Opet. "Hi."

She looked up at him with sad eyes.

Khons sat down next to her on the aluminum bench. "What's the matter?"

"I can tell by the way you're acting that it didn't work."

Khons looked down at the fingers of his right hand, playing with the strap of his wrist control. He had been doing things like that lately, nervous things.

Opet turned to face him. "Look – I know you tried, okay? But I think this is a lot of shit. We travel all these millions and millions of miles across the galaxy and now they tell us we have to stay up here in this starship. We can't go down to the planet and the plan all along was to go down to this planet. It's stupid."

"That's true."

"I knew it wasn't going to work. You're this crazy idealist that believes if it's right, then it'll work out. Things don't always work out, Khons. Sometimes they screw up."

"I don't know what to say."

"You don't have to say anything."

Khons looked away. He watched the speaker in front of the small group at the other side of the cafeteria. He wondered what those people expected to do – stop this lottery thing from working? No, maybe they felt just like he felt – desperate.

He turned to Opet. "I asked Dad what would happen if we got married."

The young woman's head turned. "What did he say?"

"He said he didn't know, but then. . ." Khons couldn't finish the sentence.

"Don't keep me waiting." Opet stared at him. "That didn't work either, did it?"

Khons shook his head. "No. He checked with the Department of Health. They said that you and I would become another family and that we'd have to buy a lottery ticket and take our chances."

"That's stupid. They say the shuttle trips are already full. Why would anybody buy a ticket now?"

Khons shrugged. "That's what the Department of Health person told my father."

"I thought you said your family had some pull with these government people."

"Dad says that, because my great grandpa is dead now, our pull just doesn't work anymore."

"Except that your whole family gets to go down to the planet."

Khons stared at the metal tabletop. His head came up. "I'm sorry, Opet, I really am."

She stood up. "I should be going."

"Want to meet for coffee tomorrow?"

Opet folded her arms across her chest. "Why?"

"I just thought. . ."

"You're a nice guy, Khons, but you're a dreamer, an idealist. You have this weird belief that people are good and everything's really all right. It's part of what attracted me to you. But, Khons, you need to be realistic to survive. When you get down to that planet, life's going to be tough. Not everyone is good. Not everything is all right."

Khons stared at the pretty face. "I really wish you could go down with us, Opet. I tried so hard."

Tears rose into her brown eyes. She sniffed. "I believe you. But it's not going to happen, so that's that."

Opet hurried away down the aisle lined with dispensing machines on the wall to the left and tables to the right. At the doorway in the middle of the wall, she stepped through and disappeared.

CHAPTER TWELVE
"Bridging the Gap"

Hyksos
The Encampment
2M, Day 28, 96 A.D.
8:31 p.m.

In the flickering light from the fire at the center of the group of soldiers, Colonel Ra studied the little man across from him. This humanoid had bushy orange hair, very white skin and blue eyes. His ankles and his hands were tethered so he was obviously harmless.

Colonel Ra wondered if maybe it was time to try to find out some things.

He put his MRE container of stew on the ground and pushed himself to his feet. He turned to a tall man eating a few feet away. "Private Nefera. . ."

The man scrambled to his feet. "Yes, Sir?"

"Do you have some of those translator ear pieces?"

"Yes, Sir." The younger man placed his MRE on the ground and swung his backpack around. He unzipped a side compartment and pulled out a C-shaped earpiece.

"Do you have another one of those, Nefera?"

"Yes, Sir." He dug out another earpiece.

Colonel Ra took both ear pieces and stuffed them into the pocket of his bulletproof vest. "Thank you, Nefera. You may continue your meal." The colonel glanced around the encampment. There were five guards at various points in a perimeter beyond the loose circle of soldiers eating food.

The construction crew was in the shuttle doing the same thing, eating. It had been a long, hard day.

The colonel moved over to a case of water bottles, bent down and pulled one out. He turned to the case of MREs and then leaned and extracted one. He checked the label. This one was hotdogs and beans. Oh, well, who knows what this alien person might eat.

He moved across the center of the circle, skirting around the fire. Then he dropped down in front of the small man with bushy orange hair.

"I wouldn't do that, Sir."

Colonel Ra looked upward over his right shoulder. Sergeant Smendes was standing with an MRE in his hands.

"I'll be careful, Sergeant. I just think it's important to try to find out about these people. We may not get another chance like this."

"I don't trust him, Sir."

Colonel Ra looked into the blue eyes in the white face under the low brow of bushy orange hair. "I think I'll be all right, Sergeant." The colonel turned to Smendes. "If you think there's any danger, Sergeant, then you can stay close."

"I'd be careful, Sir."

"I just want to see what he has to say."

The colonel was going to clip the translator onto the alien's ear but he wondered if this guy trusted him.

He twisted the cap off the water bottle. He held it out toward the strange-looking man.

The man didn't move.

Then Colonel Ra thought about this attempt at reaching the man. If this guy didn't trust him, maybe he should show him that this water bottle was harmless.

The colonel raised the bottle to his own mouth tilted it upward and drank. Then he lowered the bottle and held it out toward the man.

He didn't move.

The colonel leaned forward and pressed the bottle to the man's lips.

The man's tongue shot out and touched the water. Then he tilted his head.

Colonel Ra tipped up the bottle.

The man drank and drank and finally jerked back from the bottle.

"You were thirsty. I'm sorry I didn't give you some water earlier." The colonel recapped the bottle and laid it on the grass. Then he reached into his vest pocket and pulled out the translators.

The man's eyes focused on the translators.

Colonel Ra slipped a translator onto his right ear.

The man watched him.

Now Colonel Ra leaned toward the orange-haired man with the other translator held out in front of him.

The man's upper body pulled back and his tethered hands rose up in defense.

"It's okay. I won't hurt you."

The blue eyes focused on Ra. Then the hands dropped.

The colonel leaned forward and clipped the translator onto the small ear. Then he moved back and placed his left hand over his mouth. The trainers had told them to do this because in the first moments of conversation the other person would look at your lips moving the wrong way and become confused.

"How do you do. I am Colonel Djoser Ra."

The colonel focused on the man's eyes so he wouldn't be confused by the strange lip movements of this man speaking his own language.

The little man's lips moved. "I am Zeus, the greatest hunter of the Upriver Hyksos."

"It is good to meet you, Zeus." Colonel Ra could hear the feet of several soldiers moving up behind him in the grass. "Zeus, you are wearing a translator so that we can speak, even though we know two different languages. I speak Mayan and you speak the language of the Hyksos people."

"It is good to speak. We want to know why you come out of the sky in this big fire-stick." Zeus nodded toward the shuttle some twenty yards away.

"We have come here, Zeus, to start a new life. We have come. . . from a place far up in the sky to live here and we would like to live in peace with the Hyksos people."

"Not all Hyksos are peaceful. Some make war all the time. But we are peaceful people."

Colonel Ra's eyes fell on the MRE just beyond his left knee. "Would you like something to eat?"

"Do you have any bison or fish?"

"No. We have a Meal Ready to Eat." The colonel picked up the packet. "Here, we can open this and pull the strip to heat it." He ripped open the top of the package, then pulled a grey strip along the right side.

There was a small puff of smoke.

Zeus lurched back.

The colonel placed the MRE on the grass to let it heat. Then he rose up on his knees. "Zeus, I'm going to cut the zip strip from your wrists. I expect you'll behave yourself."

The man stared at him out from under his orange eyebrows.

Colonel Ra pulled out his bayonet.

Zeus stared at him. The blue eyes were intense.

The colonel held out the point of the bayonet toward Zeus. "Put out your wrists and I'll cut off the strip."

"I wouldn't do that, Colonel," said Sergeant Smendes' voice behind him.

"He won't do anything, Sergeant. We're all here around him."

Zeus held out his bound wrists.

Colonel Ra slowly reached out to the zip strip and touched the surface.

It jerked apart.

Zeus rubbed his wrists.

Colonel Ra opened the MRE and took out a plastic spoon. He handed it to Zeus with the MRE.

The small man stared at it.

The colonel made a motion of sweeping something up to his mouth.

Zeus continued to stare at him.

Captain Ra dipped the spoon into the pork and beans and put some of the moist bean compound into his own mouth. Then he chewed.

Zeus watched him.

"Hand me a clean spoon."

"He won't care, Colonel."

Colonel Ra turned to Smendes. "I don't want to give him any bacteria, Sergeant."

A clean spoon appeared next to the colonel's face.

He grabbed it. "Thanks." Then he handed it to Zeus and pushed the MRE toward him.

Zeus stared down at the food, and then he dug his spoon in and tasted the beans. Then his spoon went down again and he scooped out more beans. He ate those. Then his spoon found a hotdog piece. He held it up toward Colonel Ra.

"Hotdog."

Zeus put it into his mouth and chewed. Then he nodded and smiled. "Good."

"Yes. This is called hotdogs and beans."

"Very good." Zeus ate ravenously. He spooned into the syrupy bean mixture and shoved one spoonful after another into his mouth and chewed with gusto.

Colonel Ra pushed the water bottle toward him.

Zeus glanced at him.

Colonel Ra gestured toward the bottle. "Drink. It's water."

Zeus nodded his understanding. He tried to yank the cap off.

"Let me help you." Colonel Ra held the bottle in front of Zeus and twisted the cap off, then handed him the bottle.

Zeus twisted the cap on, then off, as if he was fascinated by the threaded cap and bottle top.

"Threads." Colonel Ra pointed to the neck of the bottle.

Zeus held out the cap. "Threads."

Colonel Ra nodded. "Yes, a threaded bottle cap." He pointed at the bottle. "Bottle." Then at the cap. "Bottle cap."

"Threads?"

Colonel Ra touched the threads. "Threads."

Zeus pointed his spoon toward the black star-filled sky. "Where you come from?"

At that moment the colonel wondered if this primitive man could begin to understand. Then he turned to the soldiers behind him. "Does anyone have a star map?"

Private Sile Kamose walked up to Colonel Ra. "I have one, Sir."

"Can I see it, Kamose?"

"Let me get it out of my backpack." He swung his backpack to the ground. "Sir. . ."

"Yes, Kamose?"

"I'd like it back, Sir."

"Fascinated by the stars, Kamose?"

"Yes, Sir."

"I'll make sure you get it back."

"Thank you, Sir."

Colonel Ra took the folded sheet of paper inside the plastic bag and moved over so that he was sitting next to Zeus.

Zeus moved away from him.

"I'm not going to hurt you, Zeus." Colonel Ra pulled the paper map out of the plastic pouch and unfolded it. He searched for the top of the map and finally, could tell by the print along the edge which side was up.

He stared at the large piece of paper in the fire light. Then he reached inside his left shirt pocket and pulled out a small flashlight and flicked it on.

Zeus jerked back and stared at the white beam of light on the paper. He pointed. "Fire?"

Colonel Ra turned to him. "No. . . light."

Zeus stared at the flashlight.

Colonel Ra studied the sheet of paper.

Private Kamose pointed. "This is where we are, Sir." He pointed to the far right on the sheet of paper. "And this is where we came from."

Colonel Ra motioned toward Zeus. "Come here, Zeus, and see this map."

The little man stared at Colonel Ra.

"I gave you food and water. I won't hurt you. I want to show you where we came from."

Zeus seemed to understand. He moved closer.

Colonel Ra pointed at the large sheet of paper. "We came from here." He pointed at an area to the left of the first area. "This is where we are now."

Zeus shook his head. He stabbed the ground. "We are here."

"Yes." Colonel Ra pointed at the sheet of paper. Then he asked himself something. Did these people actually know how to read and write?

"Colonel. . ."

He turned to Kamose.

The private pointed toward the western part of the night sky. "Sir, that's where we came from."

Zeus looked up.

Colonel Ra folded the star map closed. "Zeus."

The little man turned to face him.

"Zeus, we came from up there." Colonel Ra pointed toward the south western sky.

Zeus pointed toward the same area. "There?"

"Yes, that's where we came from."

Zeus studied that area of the night sky. Then he turned to Colonel Ra. "It must have been a journey of many, many days."

CHAPTER THIRTEEN
"Separation"

Starship Hope
Conference Room 2
Level 1
Pod 2
2M, Day 29, 96 A.D.
7:58 a.m.

Naomi Imhotep was enthusiastic about her project. Of course the difficulty might be convincing these people. Sometimes people with power and big egos didn't like to be pushed in new directions. They had their own agendas and didn't want those jeopardized.

She was sitting at the conference table, waiting. Ramses was at her left at the end of the table, peering at some data sheet in a folder in front of him.

The two scientists, Doctor Ahmose Buhen and Doctor Sethos Pithom, were standing closer to the door of the compartment, huddled in earnest conversation.

Naomi leaned over close to Ramses. "What are we waiting for?" she whispered.

Ramses looked up. "Dashur," he whispered. "He's always late."

Naomi was sure she was going to have a difficult time selling this idea. It had all come to her as kind of a hunch. She just knew this was going to be one of the most important things they could do for the Mayan people.

The door sucked open and a tall handsome man with wavy grey hair entered the conference room.

Naomi watched as the guard checked the man's identification. She averted her eyes when the chancellor looked toward her. She had heard that he was a flirt and a womanizer. He was terribly handsome but she had no time for immature men.

Naomi supposed that she always found it difficult to step forward and initiate new things because of her fundamental lack of confidence. That probably came from her childhood of abuse.

This idea she was going to present this morning made her nervous. She just wished that Chancellor Dahshur would sit down so she could get started.

When she thought back to how she had gotten aboard this starship forty-nine years ago, she was amused. How daring. A kid without even a bachelor's degree posing as a college teacher – that was truly crazy.

The amazing thing was that it had worked. Of course she had been found out. Then, to her great surprise, the dean of University Five had let her continue teaching because she had been very effective. She had worked on her master's degree in Mayan History and eventually she had even finished her Ph.D.

She was still doing some teaching, just a few hours each semester. She liked working with the younger college students.

Ramses rose out of his seat. "Gentlemen, could we all sit down, please."

Both Doctor Pithom and Doctor Buhen walked over to the table and dropped into seats across from each other. Avaris Taharqa, the rocket engineer, was already sitting at the far end of the table, facing Ramses.

The chancellor moved away from the door. He crossed the room with a confidence that suggested that this place was his. He finally sat down to Taharqa's right near the end of the table.

Ramses glanced around the table. "Gentlemen, I have brought you here today to discuss an issue that Doctor Imhotep has brought to my attention." Ramses held his hand out toward Naomi. "For those of you who haven't met her, this is Doctor Naomi Imhotep, history professor at University Five."

Doctor Pithom smiled and nodded.

Ramses pointed around the table. "Doctor Imhotep, this is Doctor Ahmose Buhen, our resident astronomer." He pointed across the table. "And this is Doctor Sethos Pithom, our environmentalist and, finally, down at the end of the table is our rocket engineer, Doctor Avaris Taharqa. You of course know Apis Dahshur, our chancellor aboard the starship."

Naomi smiled politely and made eye contact with the chancellor.

"Doctor Imhotep has brought to my attention a very important aspect of our situation that needs attention." He turned toward Naomi. "But I'll let her tell you." He dropped down into his chair. "Go ahead, Doctor."

Naomi rose to her feet. She was somewhat nervous, but she also knew that once she began to talk, everything would fall into place. "A society, Gentlemen, is shaped by four things - the needs of the moment, its leadership, its people and its history.

"I became cognizant of an important missing ingredient involved with our arrival here at Hyksos. Once the announcement was made that there would be a limited number of flights down to the surface of the planet and that no more than a third of the people on this starship would be able to travel down to Hyksos, I realized that we had to do something very important.

"You see - what will inevitably happen, Gentlemen, is that two separate cultures will evolve because of this separation of our people. In the future, we Mayans up here in this starship will live in one environment and those who are down on the planet will live in another entirely different environment. According to what Commander Tutan says, the reports coming up from the planet are promising, but there will also be huge challenges for our people who go down to the surface.

"It seems important, in my estimation, that our people bind themselves together as one culture as much as possible. We didn't travel some forty-seven light years across this galaxy to save the Mayan people and culture, only to lose it to neglect or careless oversight.

"I have started a project with one of my Mayan History classes. It's a section of undergraduate fourth year students who are quite talented. What I have asked them to do is two things. First, collect information about their families and the history of their families. Second, store that information as data and as visuals on DVDs.

"There are two things I'd like to have you consider. First, suppose, for some reason, communication with our people down on the planet breaks off. All of our communication devices run by batteries. Eventually those batteries down on the planet will die out."

"They can be recharged, Doctor Imhotep."

Naomi's eyes focused on the chancellor down at the end of the table. "Will their recharging devices last forever? We can't resupply them with new devices."

Doctor Pithom raised his hand. "They're constructing a charging station made out of a windmill near the landing strip."

"What happens when that needs replacement parts?"

Doctor Pithom shrugged and looked across the table at Doctor Buhen. Then he turned toward the engineer at the far end of the table. "What about that, Avaris?"

The engineer put his fist to his mouth and cleared his throat. "Excuse me. Doctor Imhotep has a point, Gentlemen. Once we run out of shuttle fuel, we won't be able to supply the people on the surface with anything. We're sending down as many supplies as we can initially, but we have to weigh the quantity of supplies against the number of people we send down to the surface. And people are the priority."

Naomi glanced around the group of men. "What I see happening, Gentlemen, is a breach of communication at some point. Even the simplest radio will eventually need parts. On the surface of that planet there will be life in its most basic form. I'm sure Doctor Pithom, our environmentalist can attest to that.

"If you think about it, Gentlemen, in the foreseeable future, there won't be a connection between the people down on Hyksos and us up here in this starship. If you know anything about living in primitive conditions, you also know that close to ninety percent of the effort of people in those circumstances is devoted to survival.

"Once they run out of MREs and other food supplies, they will have to find other sources of food. They will start by living in tents but they will eventually have to build more substantial shelters.

"Our life up here will be much easier. Therefore, we will have the time and the energy to work on preserving one of our most valuable assets – our history. Up here, we have the means and the time to record this history for future generations.

"My students are already doing this for a class project. I'm trying to make them aware of how important this will be in future years. If you think about it, Gentlemen, when we lose contact with the people down on the planet, this lost contact could go on for many generations, perhaps a century or two. They will contact us again when they have the means to manufacture communication devices or have fuel to fly up here again."

Doctor Pithom raised his hand.

"Yes, Doctor Pithom?"

"I just wanted to reinforce what Doctor Imhotep is saying, Gentlemen. I can't emphasize enough the struggle our people will be going through on the surface of that planet to find enough food and create enough shelter to survive. They will also have to cope with new diseases and such things as that." He nodded toward Naomi. "Go on, Doctor Imhotep."

Naomi smiled and nodded toward the environmentalist. "Thank you, Doctor Pithom." She glanced around the group. "Our environmental struggle on Mars years ago and our great journey across this Milky Way Galaxy have both been monumental events in our history.

"If you think I'm trying to sell this idea as strictly a sentimental gesture, Gentlemen, you're terribly wrong. We learn from our mistakes. Our history not only records our great achievements, but our big mistakes as well.

"Perhaps our people at some time in the future will be faced with decisions which may have an impact on their environment. Don't you think they should know about the mistakes we made on Mars that led to the deterioration of our atmosphere?

"Besides that information, don't you think our future generations should know about this epic journey we have made across the galaxy? Don't you think they should know where we came from?

"Perhaps, Gentlemen, someday they will want to return to our home solar system. I understand, Doctor Pithom, that at some time in the distant future, the planet Earth might be habitable."

The environmentalist nodded. "Yes, that is a distinct possibility."

"Our people, Gentlemen, should know that fact and should know the way back to our mother solar system. All of this we must record for future generations."

Naomi looked around the group of men. She was sure that most of them were onboard with this idea. The only holdout might be Chancellor Dahshur. He had, of course, not said anything to that effect, but there was something Naomi intuited from seeing him here in this room.

"What do you propose we do, Doctor Imhotep?"

Naomi turned to Doctor Pithom. "What I suggest is that we have all families aboard the starship record data and pictures about their family history on a single DVD. If this is given to me via the regular couriers aboard the starship, I will have my classes sort through this information and compress it for storage on our mainframe computer and on DVDs.

"Obviously I have come here to get your approval because then we can make that request through the starship's political system." Naomi looked down the table at Apis Dahshur. "Chancellor, will you help us with this important project?"

"We have years to do this, Doctor Imhotep. What's the hurry?"

"A large number of our people will be going down to the surface of Hyksos during this next month, Chancellor. We want their family information before they leave."

The handsome man nodded several times. "I see." Then he shrugged. "I don't see why this isn't doable."

Naomi smiled. "Thank you for your support, Chancellor."

"Let me say, however, Doctor Imhotep. I wouldn't think it would be wise to tell these people all that you've said to us. We don't want to frighten them unnecessarily."

Naomi smiled and nodded. "I agree, Chancellor." She looked around the group. "Are there any other questions, Gentlemen?"

The engineer at the far end of the table raised his hand.

"Yes, Doctor Taharqa?"

"Would you like all of us to contribute to this record?"

"Yes, of course. We want to create the most complete picture possible for future generations of the Mayan people."

CHAPTER FOURTEEN
"Invasion"

Hyksos
The Encampment
2M, Day 30, 96 A.D.
2:56 a.m.

Private Sile Kamose lay on his back with the telescope up to his right eye. Zeus was lying next to him.

Kamose just loved staring at all those stars up in the night sky. He often imagined that people were living up there somewhere. Hell, there were people here on Hyksos. There always had been. Why wouldn't there be people other places?

Sure - he knew he was supposed to be guarding this guy, but Zeus was such a little runt and, besides, he was zip-stripped around his hands and ankles. How was he going to get away? And he was asleep anyway.

More important, Sergeant Smendes was asleep. The tough-ass sergeant was over there a few feet away sleeping like a little boy, snoring up a storm. At least that's the way the asshole looked about an hour ago when Kamose came on duty.

He glanced over at the prisoner.

Zeus was sound asleep.

Kamose put the rubber eyepiece up in front of his left eye and scanned to the right, toward the area where they had come from. Somewhere forty-seven light years away was the planet Mars. They say it had died from a combination of pollution and an asteroid strike.

He would just love to go there someday. Hell that would be impossible. Well, he could, but he would be an old man by the time he got there. Let's see. . . he was thirty-two and if you add forty-nine to twenty-seven you get. . .

Something bumped Kamose's arm.

He jumped and pulled the telescope away. "What?"

Zeus was staring at him. He tapped his left ear with both hands. It was the ear where the translator had been.

Kamose dug into his shirt pocket behind his bulletproof vest. He pulled out the translators. He then reached toward Zeus and clipped one onto his ear.

Kamose clipped the second translator onto his right ear.

Zeus pointed up at the stars. "Where is your home?"

Kamose held his index finger to his lips. "Shhh. Don't talk so loud," he whispered. He pointed up toward the western sky. "Up there."

Zeus nodded toward the telescope. "Can you see home with that?"

"No. Too far away."

Zeus reached out with both hands. "Let me look."

Kamose hesitated. He really did prize this telescope, but this guy couldn't hurt it. He handed the little telescope to Zeus.

The small, orange-haired man grabbed it with his tethered hands and peered through the lens.

Kamose noticed that he was aiming in the wrong direction.

"Home." Zeus lowered the telescope and pointed with it toward the night sky.

Kamose held out his right hand. "Let me see," he whispered.

Zeus handed the telescope over to him.

Kamose put it up to his right eye and moved it. He saw nothing but distant stars. Then he moved it slightly to the left.

A small, blue-green planet popped into view. "Planet Four." He lowered the telescope.

"What is Planet Four?"

Kamose thought a minute. Then he put the telescope back into the cloth case attached to the strap hanging around his neck.

He glanced around the ground until he spied a stick. He picked it up and drew a small circle in the dirt a few feet from the fire. He pointed at the circle. "Sun."

Zeus pointed at Kamose. "Son?"

Kamose shook his head. "No – sun." He pointed up toward the sky. "The daytime sun."

Zeus nodded. "Yes, sun."

Kamose drew another much bigger circle, then another and another. He pointed to the first circle. "This is where Planet One is located." He pointed at the next circle. "Planet Two."

Zeus pointed with his bound hands at the third circle. "Planet Three?"

Kamose nodded. "Yes, Planet Three." He pounded his hand against the ground. "This is Planet Three."

Zeus stared at him.

"You live on Planet Three."

Zeus pointed at himself. "Planet Three?"

Kamose patted the ground. "No. This is Planet Three."

Zeus stared at him again. Then he pounded the ground with his bound hands. "Planet Three?"

"Yes."

Zeus pointed his two hands upward. "Home?"

"No. Planet Four."

Zeus stared at Private Kamose. "Planet Four is home?"

"No. My home is much farther away."

"Longer trail, many days."

"Many years."

"What is 'years'?"

"Three hundred, sixty-five days is one year."

"I don't understand years. We have twelve Love Moons then the seasons come around again."

Kamose thought a minute. "The Love Moon is a month?"

"Don't understand this month."

"Twelve Love Moons must be one year, Zeus."

"One year?"

"Yes. One year."

"You said many years to journey here."

"Forty-nine."

Zeus stared at him in the dim light from the fire. "I am four hundred and eight Love Moons or thirty-four years old. You left your home before I was born."

"Yes. And long before I was born. I'm thirty-two years old."

Zeus looked up at the star-filled sky.

A light appeared in the eastern sky.

Kamose's head snapped around. "What's that?"

"The Man Moon. Every night is a Man Moon. Twelve nights a Woman Moon. When the Man Moon catches the Woman Moon, this is the Love Moon night. It happens one night only."

Kamose nodded. "That's like some kind of poetry."

"No, that is the way it is here on Hyksos."

Kamose pulled out the telescope again. "Do you want to look at Planet Four again?"

Zeus shrugged. "I will look once."

Kamose held out the telescope toward Zeus.

He didn't take it. "I have something to ask."

Kamose shrugged. "Sure."

"Will the ugly one kill me tomorrow?" He nodded toward a man in the sleeping bag ten feet away.

Kamose looked in the direction Zeus had moved his head. "Oh, you mean Sergeant Smendes."

"The one who captured me."

"Yes, Smendes."

"Kill me?"

Kamose shook his head. "No. The colonel won't let him do that."

Zeus smiled. "Ah, good. I still have to teach my son, Achilles to hunt better. He is so young that he is a crazy hunter. He has no patience. I have to teach him patience. I wasn't very patient when I was young. I remember that. It took me a long time to learn to hunt from my father, Archimedes. He was a great hunter. All of the old ones many love moons ago were great hunters."

Private Kamose thought about this. These people were living in an age far back in history. He held out his telescope toward Zeus. "Do you want to look at Planet Four again?"

In the distance, there was a soft "thump."

Kamose glanced around. Everything seemed fine.

"I am tired. I will sleep. You look through the magic tube at Planet Four." Zeus turned and lay down on his right side, facing away from Kamose. The translator was still on his left ear.

Kamose was going to remove it, but then he thought it would be all right just to leave it there.

He dropped down to his back and put the telescope to his right eye. Planet Four was a milky turquoise color, but now with the Man Moon it was harder to see clearly.

Something sharp touched his neck.

"Don't move, Private Kamose," whispered a voice.

The telescope was pulled out of his hand. Zeus hovered over him. "This is my son, Achilles."

Kamose's eyes rolled upward.

Behind him was another Hyksos with red bushy hair. In the flickering yellow light from the fire, Kamose could tell that this one was younger.

"You should not move, Private Kamose. Achilles has a knife at your neck and he will use it if he has to."

"Sure." Kamose turned his eyes toward Zeus.

"It has been interesting staying with you people who fell out of the sky. You have many magic things, but you are not good at keeping the Hyksos warriors out of your camp."

"Zeus, you won't kill me, will you?"

The small man with bushy orange hair grinned. "No, we will just stab you with a dart. It will give you a very peaceful sleep." Zeus slipped the telescope into the pouch on Kamose's chest. "I gave back your magic tube. Now sleep."

Something sharp pricked Sile Kamose's neck. In seconds, everything became blurry. . . then black.

CHAPTER FIFTEEN
"Casualties"

Hyksos
The Colony
3M, Day 27, 96 A.D.
(one month later)
8:32 a.m.

In the dim light of the large tent, Aten held up a book sealed in a clear plastic case. He held it out in front of Khons. "See this? It's a written record of our history. Your grandmother prepared it for me."

Khons knelt down next to his father. "Why did Grandma Naomi send it down here with you?"

"Because she's convinced that the starship and this colony will become more and more separated over time. She told me that we needed a record of our history with us to preserve for our descendents. The shuttle's gone up to the starship for the last time and won't come back again – not enough fuel. Maybe she's right after all.

"Your grandmother had it sealed in this plastic case so that it wouldn't be damaged, even over a long period of time."

Khons stared down at the thick brown book molded inside the clear plastic case. A HISTORY OF THE MAYAN PEOPLE was printed in gold letters on the brown cover. "That's actually pretty cool, Dad."

"I wanted you to know about it because someday it will be yours and then you can give it to your son and so forth."

Khons smiled. "Sure. It's like we'll all be connected together by this book."

Aten patted his son on the back. "That's the idea."

"I have to get outside, Dad. They need help with the fortifications and Councilman Narmer wants to plant some crops out in that field that we cleared."

Aten chuckled. "Narmer is a real pain sometimes, but he does have good ideas. His father brought some crop seeds from Mars aboard the starship. I guess his grandfather was a farmer in the hydroponic gardens back on Mars."

"We won't have hydroponics here for a long time." Khons rose to a standing position. His head bumped the top of the tent. "I can't get used to these tents."

"We won't be in them forever, Son. I expect that once we get the fortifications done, we can build some houses."

"Man, I'm all for that."

"I'll keep this book in my clothes bag, Khons. If anything ever happens to me, you should grab it and take it with you."

"Come on, Dad, nothing's going to happen to you."

"I'm just saying."

"Hey - understood." Khons pulled the tent flap back.

"Tell them I'll be right out, Son."

When Khons stepped outside, he was greeted with the buzzing of chain saws and the sound of men's voices. Across the small field with rows of tents he could see a gathering of men. He recognized the tall, slightly bent figure of Councilman Narmer and there was a soldier standing directly in front of Narmer. The soldier was gesticulating with his hands.

That would probably be where he could find out how he could help.

At the west end of the open area was a windmill standing high above the edge of the forest. The blade was turning very slowly.

Khons had been told that it was built a hundred feet high so it would clear the height of the trees. It was supposed to generate enough electricity for the colony and also provide a means for everyone to recharge their batteries. There were some solar batteries, like on the translators, but even those had to be recharged at some point.

Khons hurried across the field. He was wearing some boots he had taken out of the community clothing lockers yesterday. He figured they would come in handy. The tennis shoes they had worn on the starship were not the right footwear down here.

As he neared the cluster of men, Khons realized there was an argument going on between the soldier and Narmer. Of course, this was not all that unusual with Councilman Tanis Narmer. He was an opinionated man who seemed to have no trouble getting into confrontations with almost anybody.

The soldier was leaning on one hip with his right hand resting on the butt of the pistol in the holster attached to the wide belt around his waist. He turned to look at Khons as he came near.

Narmer was talking. ". . . so, as you can see, Sergeant Smendes, both of these functions are necessary for the betterment of the community."

"Look, Narmer, there are these little runt-like humans with orange hair livin' out there in that forest and they're not all that friendly."

"Sir. . ."

The military man turned to Khons. "What is it?"

"Sir, I came to offer to work on whatever needs to be done."

"Do you know how to use a chainsaw?"

"No."

"A shovel?"

"Sure."

Sergeant Smendes pointed toward a group of men digging a trench bordering the woods some forty feet away, along the east side of the colony. "Go over there and grab a shovel. Private Kamose will tell you what to do."

"Now, just a minute, Sergeant." Councilman Narmer put his hand on Khons' shoulder. "This young man can help us in the fields, digging and planting seeds."

The sergeant stared at Narmer. "You are the dumbest fuck I have ever met, Narmer. Your goddamn seeds won't mean a fuckin' thing if everybody's killed by these ugly little Hyksos assholes."

"Please don't spew your foul mouth at me, Sergeant. Show a little respect for your superiors."

"Superiors? You dumb sack of shit!"

Khons decided he'd better go before this got ugly. "Councilman Narmer, I'm going over here to work on the trench. When you're ready to go out to the fields, come by and maybe I'll go out to help you - okay?

"And, by the way, there's something I have to say here. I don't get why you guys are spending all this time arguing when we have so much work to do."

Khons turned away and began walking across the open area toward the east. Ahead of him was a crew of bare-chested men digging a deep trench. Their backs, visible above the edge of the trench, gleamed with perspiration. Occasionally a head of dark hair would pop up - someone who was taking a momentary break.

When he reached the trench, Khons stopped next to some shovels lying on the ground. "Is Private Kamose here?"

A muscular slender man at the end of the trench turned. "I'm Kamose."

"I'm supposed to ask you what I can do to help. Sergeant Smendes sent me."

Kamose nodded toward the row of tools to Khons' right. "Grab a shovel and start digging."

Khons bent over and picked up a shovel. Then he jumped down into the trench next to a blond man and stabbed his shovel into the dirt.

This was different. He had never dug anything before in his whole life. When you're brought up in a starship, you have no contact with any natural environment, unless you perhaps worked in the hydroponic gardens and then all you came in contact with was just that ugly mulch-like stuff.

Khons had worked there for a period of time between semesters at University Five, and he had hated it. In the hydroponics it was always humid and warm and it smelled of human excrement and other pungent odors.

The neat thing down here on the planet was that the general smell was kind of sweet like flowers and there were these pine trees that had a sort of fruity fragrance. One of the things that he missed was hearing the constant hiss of the ventilation system on the starship. You kind of get used to hearing that subtle noise all the time. It was with you every minute of every day and every night.

On Hyksos, it was insect sounds or the wind in the trees, which he actually kind of liked. Down here at night it was real quiet. You could sometimes hear howling. His father had told him that those were wolves. Then there were the little dogs he had seen around. They were called coyotes. They yipped at night sometimes. In a way, though, it was kind of cool with all these sounds and smells.

Khons turned to the blond man next to him. "I don't know about you, but I've never done this before."

The other man looked at him with cold grey eyes. "I think about things I enjoy and the time goes by very fast."

"What do you think about?"

"My mother."

"How does she like it down here?"

"She's not down here. She had an accident."

"On the way down?"

"During the flyby of Planet Six."

Khons reached out his right hand. "I'm Khons Imhotep."

The blond man with the strange grey eyes stared at the hand as if he didn't know what to do. Then he reached out and shook it once. "Saite Manetho."

Khons didn't like the handshake. It was weak and almost slimy, but – hey – at least the guy was reasonably friendly.

As he continued to dig, something wedged itself in the back of Khons' mind. That name, Manetho, sounded kind of familiar. But where had he heard it before? Maybe it was at University Five.

He threw a shovelful of dirt up on the side of the trench. "Is your father a professor at University Five?"

The other man's grey eyes scrutinized Khons. "Why would you ask that?"

"Your name's familiar."

"I don't know what my father did. My mother used to say he didn't do much, and that's about all she ever said about him."

"I'm sure I've heard the name before."

"My great uncle was a captain in the Secret Police back on Mars, but you wouldn't remember that because I don't and you're younger than I am."

Khons turned away immediately and stabbed his shovel into the sandy dirt. He pushed the shovel down with the boot on his right foot. He lifted the shovel and flung the dirt up onto the flat ground beside the trench.

Now, he finally remembered where he had heard that name before. It was a Captain Manetho who had imprisoned his grandfather back on Mars when his grandfather had protested against putting his friend in jail.

Khons didn't know much about this guy, this Saite Manetho, but, now, just the prospect of knowing the grandnephew of the man who had jailed his grandfather didn't have all that much appeal. In fact, it made him feel kind of creepy. Maybe if he just kept digging and stayed quiet it would be a good idea.

The next thing Khons never saw coming. He had been digging away at the trench, trying to follow the pattern of the other diggers, and he had avoided talking to this Manetho guy. In fact, he was kind of in his own little zone.

Then he heard this voice. "Young man. . ."

Khons turned.

Tanis Narmer was standing above him near the edge of the trench. "Young Man, I could use some help out in the fields. I seem to have enlisted a pretty good-sized group of females, but no males. We're going to need strong, young backs out there. Would you like to come?"

Khons glanced over at the grandnephew of the Secret Police captain, this Saite Manetho, and decided that he might, in fact, like it better out in the fields. "Sure."

He clambered up the side of the trench and was about to return the shovel to the loose grouping of digging tools, when Narmer touched his arm. "Bring the shovel with you. We're going to need to do some digging out there as well. We'll have to turn over the soil."

Khons raised the shovel handle to his right shoulder and walked next to the tall councilman.

Narmer looked over at him. "I don't think I got your name, young man."

"Khons Imhotep."

"Was your grandfather, by chance, Aten Imhotep?"

"My great grandfather, yes."

"Now there, by God, was a real genius. You know - he actually designed the interior of that starship."

"Yes, he told me about that."

"I understand he died during that first flyby."

"Yes, he did, Sir."

"I was sorry to hear about that. We need smart men like your great grandfather now that we're down here."

They reached the small group of young women.

Narmer stood in front of them. "This is Khons Imhotep, people. He's going to be helping us out in the fields today."

Khons smiled. "Hello." He recognized an older cousin of his, Intef Tutan. She was the starship commander's daughter. "Cousin Intef, hi."

"Hi, Khons."

Actually Khons felt a little out of place because there were no other men, aside from Narmer of course. However, it was good to get away from that Saite Manetho. He was a little strange.

Councilman Narmer picked up a canvass bag of sticks he had apparently left with the group of girls and began walking south out of the colony.

Khons fell in next to him.

"You know, young man, we don't have any plows, so we're going to have to be inventive when it comes to cutting furrows. I've asked my friend, Moses Hapmen, to see if he could fashion one out of whatever materials he can find. He thought he might be able to use some of those aluminum strips from the landing field."

Narmer turned to Khons. "He's the head of the ERC, Emergency Repair Crew. Evidently he was going to stay up on the starship and run his crew up there but then it became obvious that we'd need handy people down here, and that man is truly handy. Let's just hope he can come up with a plow.

"These Hyksos people have horses. If we could talk one of them into giving us a horse we'd have the means to move a plow across a field. I'm sure Hapmen could make a harness for a horse."

Minutes later, they reached the planting field. It was a low, moist grassland.

With a length of string, Councilman Narmer measured a rectangular plot and marked it off with wooden stakes shoved down into the soft ground.

Khons watched.

Narmer walked back to him. "We can't do this all in one day, since we have only one man to dig. Some of these females will dig too, but it's going to be slow." He pointed toward the southeast corner of the field. "Why don't you start down there?"

"Sure."

"Just dig it up and turn it over. Then chop up what you dig."

"Sounds easy enough."

Narmer smiled. "It's hard work, but you're young. I'm going to do some digging too, and spell off some of these girls." He patted Khons on the side of the shoulder. "Thank you for helping."

"We all have to chip in, Councilman. That's what my father says."

"Maybe he'll help us too."

Khons shrugged. "Could be, but I think he's back in the village helping out there."

"Well, we'd better get at it. Every journey starts with a single step."

"If you say so, Sir." Khons walked away with the shovel handle resting across his shoulder.

Ever since he had been down here on the planet, Khons' muscles had been sore. He had done the recommended resistance exercises on the starship before they reached Hyksos, but in these circumstances all that exercise didn't seem to make much difference.

He stopped at the southeast corner where there was a stake. There he jammed the tip of his shovel into the moist, grassy surface. Then he put his right foot on the right top, flattened edge of the shovel and rose up so that his whole weight pushed down onto the top edge of the shovel.

It slid downward into the moist soil.

Khons dug up the chunk of dirt and turned it over. He then glanced toward his left. He seemed to be about even with the stake over at the southwest corner.

He moved slightly west and jammed the point of the shovel into the soft soil. Then he put his right foot on it and rose up and pushed down with his whole body.

To the north he could see the village of tents clustered in the middle of a field. On either side were the huge brown gashes of the trenches being dug as a protective barrier against animals and maybe even human intruders.

Toward the far end of the trenches, he could see the men with chainsaws cutting logs. They were putting up a bulwark of these pointed logs along the inside of the trench.

Any animal or human trying to get into the village would have to cross through the trench which was about four feet deep and six feet wide, then climb up over a cluster of pointed logs jammed into the ground. Colonel Ra had even talked about putting water in the trench.

Khons wondered how Opet was doing up in the starship. It was too bad she couldn't be here. She would love the beauty of this planet, all the trees and the birds and the way the river meandered down the valley. She wouldn't like the bugs and the dirt and the sweating. She had always been very particular about the way she looked.

Khons dug up another tuft of grass and turned it over. He checked down the row.

He was wearing only a tee shirt and some old jeans but he would probably take off the tee shirt at any time. He was getting pretty hot. Khons was sure glad he found these boots at the supply tent.

What he was trying to avoid, when he thought about Opet, was this sense of loss or maybe loneliness. He wasn't sure exactly which one it was – not that it mattered. He just felt kind of empty. He had known her since fifth grade and she had always really been his girl.

Khons had never been one to hang around with the guys and he wasn't into sports all that much. Things just kind of clicked with Opet. He would sure miss her, but there wasn't anything he could do about it, especially now that the shuttle flights had stopped.

By the time Narmer came over to see how he was doing, Khons had dug up a large square of dirt. It was far from perfect but it was turned over.

"We're going to have to invent some kind of cultivator, Khons, to chew up this ground and make it so we can plant some seeds."

"Maybe that guy you mentioned before could do something."

"Moses Hapmen? Yes, he could. He's really quite clever. I understand his father was some kind of hero – fell against a meteor hole in the star-ship to stop the leak - died saving the ship. That's the way the story goes. His name was Moses just like this guy."

Narmer checked the time on his wrist control. "We'll take a mid-morning break in a little while, Khons. Do you need some water?"

"No, I'm fine for now, Sir."

"You don't want to go too long without water in this heat."

There was a loud "POP!"

The stutter of automatic weapon fire echoed off the trees.

"Get down!" Councilman Narmer dropped face first to the tilled ground.

Khons dropped his shovel and crouched down to his knees. He waved at the cluster of girls digging at the northeast corner of the field. "Get down!"

One of the girls lurched and fell backward. The others dropped down, some lying prone on the ground. His cousin, Intef, crawled to the girl who had fallen. She turned toward Councilman Narmer. "She's been shot!"

Khons rose up to his knees. "Do we have a first-aid kit?"

"Back in the village," said Narmer.

"They need help." Khons charged forward down the side of the field close to the trees, staying low and trying to stay behind the occasional large stump from a cut tree.

In the distance he could hear the "pop, pop" of gunfire and the nearly constant stutter of automatic weapons.

When he reached the wounded girl, he dropped to his knee next to her. He stared down at the frightened brown eyes in the dirty face.

"Where is it?"

Intef pointed to the wounded girl's left arm. "Here! She's bleeding!"

Khons pulled his damp tee shirt up over his head and wrapped it around the area just above the wound. He tied it in a lose knot, and then pulled it tighter. "Tell me when it feels too tight."

The wounded girl stared at him with her mouth open.

"Is that okay?"

The girl didn't answer.

Khons pulled the tee shirt knot tighter. "Now?"

"Too tight!"

He loosened the knot.

The bleeding had slowed.

Khons heard heavy breathing. He turned.

Councilman Narmer was on his knees behind him. "How's she doing?"

"Better. We have to get her to a doctor."

"I don't have my instruments or bandages. They're in the clinic." Narmer nodded toward the village. Besides, they're still at it up there."

Khons could see clearly the group of orange-haired horsemen riding through the village wielding spears and crossbows.

One turned and spotted them. He kneed the sides of his horse, which then charged toward them.

Khons looked around for something – anything. He spotted shovels. He scrambled off to his right and grabbed two shovels.

The rider pulled his horse to a halt and raised his crossbow.

Khons held up the two shovels.

The arrow "clanked" on the shovel and deflected off to the left.

Khons swung back the shovel in his right hand and flung it.

The shovel spun wobbly through the air and whacked the rider's chest.

The rider fell from the horse.

Khons charged forward clutching the other shovel.

The horse shied away.

When Khons saw the orange hair, he swung with all his might.

The shovel landed with a loud "clunk!"

The Hyksos warrior dropped to the ground.

Khons raised the shovel above his head.

"Don't!"

Councilman Narmer was standing next to him. "You knocked him out. Don't kill him. We want to talk to him - get intelligence. I've got some rope. We can tie him up."

Khons looked off toward the village. The engagement was over. Then he noticed something. The windmill was lying on the ground, some of its blades bent, others broken off.

He pointed. "They got the windmill."

Narmer turned to look. "I hope Hapmen can repair that. He's the best. Where's the generator?"

"I don't know, Sir. Looks like they took it."

There was a low groan.

Khons swung around to face the downed Hyksos warrior. "Better get that rope, Sir."

"Yes." Narmer hurried away. "Good, girl. We have a horse."

Khons turned. One of the girls was holding the reins of the Hyksos warrior's horse and she was petting its nose.

Khons heard another groan. He swung around and raised his shovel above his right shoulder. "Don't move!"

The warrior held up his right hand above his head, as if in defense. He started to stand up.

Khons pointed at the ground. "Stay down!"

The warrior dropped to the newly turned dirt and sat, waiting.

Minutes later, Narmer returned with rope and a jackknife. When he neared the warrior he stopped and opened the jackknife.

The Hyksos warrior scrambled backward on the dirt.

Narmer held up the rope. "I'm going to tie your hands." He cut a short length out of the rope. Then he folded the jackknife and handed it to Khons. "Take this. I don't want him getting his hands on it."

Khons took the jackknife with his left hand and stuffed it into the pocket of his jeans.

Narmer walked around behind the warrior, grabbed his hands and pulled them back. He tied a slipknot on the right wrist, and then tied it to the left. Next he tied the end of the rope to the man's leather waist tie and pulled it tight and tied it again.

Narmer beckoned. "Come here, Intef, and guard this guy." He picked up the crossbow, took one of the arrows out of the quiver hanging from the side of the horse and cocked the bow back.

Narmer handed her the bow. "Here, Intef. Aim it at this fellow." He pointed at a wooden stub below the center slot. "This is the trigger. If you touch this, you'll shoot him."

Intef stood with her feet planted wide apart and the arrow aimed at the Hyksos on the ground.

"Give me a hand, Khons." Narmer led him back to the wounded girl.

Khons and Narmer helped her to her feet.

"Can you walk?" asked Narmer.

"Yes."

"You help her, Khons. Besides, I think she likes you."

The girl appeared to be twelve or thirteen years old. Khons smiled at her. "Okay, I'll help you walk, but I'm not carrying you."

"Come on, ladies, let's get back to the village. They may need our help. . . and bring that horse. We may be able to use him."

Khons moved with the girl along the uncultivated ground next to the tree stumps. Twenty or so feet off toward the right was the beginning of the forest. None of the trees had been cut back that far.

This girl was cute and all, but Khons was twenty-one and she looked more like somebody's younger sister than a girl he'd be interested in dating or anything. Of course, down here there wasn't much time for any of that anyway.

When the group reached the south end of the village, Khons heard a noise. He raised his hand. "Stop."

Intef was at the front of the group with the crossbow pointed at the back of the Hyksos warrior. She turned around.

Narmer moved up next to Khons, holding the handles of three shovels lying across his right shoulder. "What is it?"

"I heard something."

There was the noise of shuffling brush and a groan.

Khons looked around. They would need the crossbow to guard this Hyksos. Then he spotted something sticking up from the waistband of the warrior, an animal bone or antler of some kind.

He moved up to the warrior's right side and yanked upward on the handle.

The warrior's head jerked around.

Khons now held a dagger with a yellowish metal blade.

The warrior stared at Khons.

He turned around to face Councilman Narmer. "I'm going over there to see what that is."

Khons moved across the open area, passing three large tree stumps. When he reached the edge of the forest, he crouched down. What occurred to him was that he was entering this dark area with bright sunlight behind him. If somebody was in there, that person would be able to see him for sure.

He pushed aside the tall yellow grass along the edge of the dense stand of trees and moved into the darkness. Then he dropped to one knee.

What Khons noticed immediately was that the temperature had dropped dramatically. It was cool in here.

There was another moan.

Crouched low, he inched his way forward.

There was a "snort."

He dropped to his knee and scanned the area, looking for the source of the sound.

When his eyes fully adjusted to the dark, he saw a horse standing with its head hanging down.

Khons moved forward. What was foremost in his mind was why this horse would be standing like this in the woods. There had to be a human around somewhere.

Then he heard a groan.

He stopped and crouched lower.

The horse looked up and shook its head.

Khons moved forward again.

He stepped into a small clearing next to the horse.

A Hyksos warrior was lying face down with an arrow protruding from his back.

Khons reached for the arrow, as if to pull it out, but then he stopped.

He reached out slowly and touched the horse's nose.

The horse made a guttural noise.

Khons clamped his hand onto the reigns and turned his head. "Narmer, come here! I need help!"

CHAPTER SIXTEEN

"Issues"

Hyksos
The Colony
3M, Day 27, 96 A.D.
1:42 p.m.

"**S**it down, Gentlemen." Colonel Ra motioned toward the two canvass chairs next to his desk inside the Command Center tent.

Sergeant Smendes sat down in the chair directly in front of the colonel's desk.

Councilman Narmer moved the other chair as if he were choosing a better location on the grass. Then he worked the chair as if to settle it down into the soft ground.

Colonel Ra knew what Narmer was doing. He had dealt with politicians before, and Narmer in particular. The man was staking out his territory, making his presence known and was saying, in essence, that this was not Colonel Ra's meeting. It was, in fact, his and he was in control.

Colonel Djoser Ra had learned to tolerate these ploys and let them slide right off. He ignored them to death, and usually that worked. In this situation, he was not about to let Narmer control the meeting and – no – he was not going to be manipulated into doing anything that he didn't think was to the advantage of this colony. It just wasn't going to happen.

The colonel leaned back in his canvas chair. "Gentlemen, I've brought you here today to let you know where we are now and what our options are going to be in the future."

He made eye contact with Smendes, then Narmer. "This colony is essentially a military operation at this point. However, I don't run military operations without consulting the other leaders involved." He nodded toward Smendes. "You, Sergeant, are my expediter, the man I depend upon to get things done."

He faced Narmer. "And Councilman Narmer - you are our civilian liaison."

Narmer was leaning back in his chair, trying to look regal and in control.

The colonel made sure his face was passive as his eyes moved off the man, back to Smendes. "I'm also bringing Commander Ramses Tutan and his people into this conversation today, mostly because we have some pressing problems. I'm putting him on speaker phone."

The colonel turned to his right and pressed a button on the surface of a rectangular module sitting on a stand atop his desk. "Good afternoon, Commander."

"Good afternoon to you, Colonel Ra," said the voice on the small speaker.

"Commander, do you have your contingent of experts with you today?"

"Yes, I do. Doctor Pithom, our environmentalist, Doctor Buhen, our astrophysicist, and Doctor Taharqa, our rocket propulsion engineer."

"Very good. Commander, let me begin by saying that we were attacked by Hyksos warriors earlier today. We have seven dead, twelve people wounded, most of them not too serious, and we killed twenty-three of their numbers. We also have two prisoners, one who is being interrogated, without much success I might add, and one who is wounded and is currently in surgery."

"I'm sorry to hear about the attack, Colonel. I thought these Hyksos people were rather friendly."

"They're not, Sir."

The colonel scowled at Sergeant Smendes. "That's enough, Sergeant."

"Is there a problem, Colonel?"

"No, Sir, we're fine. Well, actually there are some problems, two of them in fact. First, we're going to need more ammunition. We brought some down, but didn't expect we'd be in a conflict with these people. Is there any way we can move more ammunition down to the surface of Hyksos?"

"Just a minute, Colonel. Let me ask."

On the radio there was the murmur of distant voices.

Colonel Ra knew that with the many shuttle flights down here, there was always an issue of weight. Passengers were the first priority. He had chosen to bring down a certain number of cases of ammunition. He had assumed that his specifications would be honored. They weren't.

His ammunition allotment had been cut twenty percent weight-wise, and he had to make some choices. Luckily he had chosen in favor of light weapons but even there, he wasn't given much priority. He had tried to sneak just anything aboard each flight down, yet all too often, his numbers were cut.

Now they had a problem. They were running low and they were, apparently, surrounded by hostiles.

"Colonel. . ."

Djoser Ra faced the phone module. "Yes, Commander?"

"Doctor Taharqa, our rocket propulsion engineer, says that based upon his calculations, the shuttle would not have enough fuel to make another trip down to the surface of Hyksos, even if we didn't try to bring it back. He said the real danger would be that the shuttle might run out of fuel near the end of the flight and crash near the base, injuring people."

Colonel Ra stared up at the cloth ceiling of the tent. It was a beige cloth and sunlight seeped through, lighting the inside. That was a great help for lighting the place. However, in the later afternoon, it was so hot in there that he often made a point of doing something out of doors, where temperatures were at least tolerable.

"I'm sorry, Colonel, but I don't think sending down ammunition is possible."

Colonel Ra sat forward, leaning his forearms on his desk. He shrugged. "Well, I guess we'll just have to make do, Commander."

"We're really sorry, Colonel, but there doesn't seem to be any answer that would work. You had a second problem?"

The colonel nodded his head. "Yes, Sir. The Hyksos warriors who attacked this morning lassoed and pulled over the windmill. It sustained serious damage. Not only that, but they took the generator motor with them. Consequently, we have no electrical power. We're on batteries totally.

"And that brings up the greater problem. In a matter of days our batteries are going to run down. Therefore, we're only going to contact you in emergencies. I'm going to give orders to confiscate all phones and other battery devices so that our military contingent has a large supply of batteries.

"I haven't wanted to do this because I know that some people contact relatives and friends up on the starship, but our security is the most important issue, and if our military people don't have the means to communicate, it compromises our ability to function and, therefore, our security."

The desk phone was silent.

Councilman Narmer leaned forward. "You can't do this, Colonel. The people won't stand for it."

"I have no choice."

"Gentlemen. . ."

Colonel Ra turned toward the rectangular phone module. "Yes, Commander?"

"Obviously, we don't approve of your plan to confiscate phones. However, your survival is the most important thing. Do what you have to do, Colonel. It's your call."

"Thank you, Sir."

"We have some issues up here ourselves, Colonel. At least, we have one issue. Doctor Buhen, our resident astronomer, has spotted a meteor storm out beyond Planet Four. He says it's possible that it may be headed our way.

"As a consequence, we're going to be busy up here getting ready for this event. Buhen says that it's possible this meteor storm will miss us completely, but as you well know, Colonel, one must always prepare for the worst-case scenario."

"I wish, Commander, that we could be of some help."

"Thank you, Colonel. I think we'll be fine. I wish we could do something for you as well, but our hands are tied."

Colonel Ra nodded. "I understand, Sir."

"May the Gods be with you, Colonel."

"Same to you, Commander." Colonel Ra punched a button on the surface of the rectangular phone module and turned to Councilman Narmer. "Tanis, if I could do anything else in this situation, I would. You have to know that."

"I know no such thing, Colonel."

Colonel Ra leaned back in his chair and folded his arms. "Don't make this harder than it has to be, Tanis."

"Do you think sucking up to me and using my first name is going to dissuade me from fighting this?"

Colonel Ra wanted to punch this fool in the face right then, but with Tanis Narmer the more you blustered, the better he liked it. Staying calm worked the best.

The colonel unfolded his arms. "I would suggest, Tanis, that you look beyond your own ego and realize that what I'm about to do is for the security of this encampment. If you try to stop me, I will lock you up. You will not stop me from performing this necessary action. This meeting is over."

Colonel Ra rose from his canvas chair, picked up his camouflage hat and pulled it on. Then he walked toward the open flap at the front of the tent.

He had to check on the interrogation of the prisoner. There was the important matter of prisoner treatment. He didn't trust Sergeant Smendes to do the right thing in every situation.

Colonel Ra knew that Smendes didn't like him. The sergeant thought he was soft. Of course, Colonel Ra could always promote the guy to lieutenant. That would increase his pay, which down here didn't mean anything. However, there was the issue of pride, and Smendes had a lot of that.

Maybe a promotion would make him happier and if Smendes was happier, he might be easier to handle. The promotion was an interesting idea. Of course, when it came right down to it, Colonel Ra didn't totally trust Smendes.

There was something inside the guy that was angry. The colonel had no idea what it was, but he had seen it. In any case, he'd have to take his time when considering this promotion idea. He didn't want to make a mistake.

Colonel Ra began walking toward the prisoner retention tent at the back of the compound. At that moment, he was reminded that being a base commander was largely a matter of handling people – all kinds of people.

When he reached the retention tent, the colonel looked back over his right shoulder.

Councilman Narmer was standing in front of the command center with his arms folded across his chest.

The colonel wondered if that old asshole was planning something. On the other hand, maybe he really didn't want to know.

CHAPTER SEVENTEEN
"The Arrow"

Hyksos
The Colony
Hospital Tent
3M, Day 27, 96 A.D.
7:02 p.m.

Khons had been bothered by the circumstances of this event the whole afternoon. It had been an impossible day and he was exhausted. He had helped to carry the litters with the wounded after the attack. Then he had spent the rest of the day digging in the trench.

Sergeant Smendes had been very forceful about digging the trenches and he was carrying this assault rifle with him the whole afternoon, as were all the rest of the army guys.

All afternoon Khons had worked next to a Private Kamose. When Smendes wasn't around, Kamose would tell the men to take a break. Most of them needed it. The temperature had been pretty high during the afternoon, probably in the nineties and it always seemed to be humid.

What bothered Khons was that this Hyksos he had found in the woods had an arrow stuck in his back. He hadn't been shot with a bullet. What that said to Khons was this guy had been wounded by one of his own people. Or maybe there were other tribes of Hyksos.

When Khons stepped into the hospital tent, he was confronted with the smell of antiseptic and there was one man in the back who was moaning. He was probably going to do more digging today, but first he had to talk to that Hyksos who was shot in the back with an arrow.

"Young Imhotep, why didn't you go back out into the field and dig in the garden again?"

Khons turned around. "Oh, hi, Councilman Narmer."

The councilman moved toward him. He was wearing a blue smock with blood stains on the front. "Intef said you didn't go back out into the field."

"Sergeant Smendes drafted me into trench digging, Sir."

"Yes, he's pretty focused on that ditch." Narmer looked down at the front of his smock. His head came up. "By the way, excuse my appearance. I've been assisting the surgeon, Doctor Osiris, all afternoon. We had quite a few casualties - most of them not too serious. There was one man, however, who had a spear lodged in his thigh. That was pretty difficult, and messy."

"Sir, where is that Hyksos I found in the woods?"

The councilman nodded toward the back of the tent. "He's over there." Narmer began walking in that direction.

Khons dodged around a tent pole. "How is he doing, Sir?"

"Pretty well, actually. There's a young private back here talking to him – a fellow named Sile Kamose."

"Sir, I have a question."

"Ask away, Young Man."

"Where is the arrow that was in his back?"

"It's on the table next to his bed. This Kamose asked about it. Why is that so important, Imhotep?"

"Sir, you can call me Khons."

"Khons – good Mayan name. But tell me, why is that arrow so important?"

"Well, Sir, if you think about it, the whole thing is rather strange. He wasn't wounded by our soldiers. He was shot by his own people. Why would they do that?"

Narmer's eyes squinted and he nodded thoughtfully. "Yes, that is a very good question. Perhaps we should ask him."

Khons followed the doctor down the narrow grass aisle between the rows of cots with wounded men.

Narmer stopped three cots from the end and turned inward. "How are we doing here, Private?"

Kamose rose from a canvas stool next to the bed. He was wearing a translator earpiece. "Fine, Sir."

Narmer nodded toward the Hyksos. "How is our patient doing?"

Kamose shrugged. "Achilles seems fine."

"His name is Achilles?"

"Yes, Sir. I've met him before. We captured his father that day we landed and built the airstrip for the shuttle. This one came at night to save his father – held me at knife point. Then he pricked me with some kind of dart with a drug on it and it knocked me out."

"Oh, yes, I heard about that. All the sentries were shot with darts covered with some kind of drug – put them out too."

"We've been talking. He wants to get back to his village and that may be a good idea."

Narmer turned to Khons. "This is the fellow who found Achilles out in the woods - young Khons Imhotep. He's quite curious about that arrow that was in Achilles' back."

Private Kamose swung around to the table. "It's right here." Kamose picked it up from the surface of the table and handed it to Councilman Narmer.

"Can I ask Achilles some questions, Private Kamose?"

The young soldier looked at Khons then shrugged. "Sure."

Khons reached out for the translator piece on Kamose's ear. The young private pulled it off and held it out. Khons slipped the piece onto his own ear. "Hello, Achilles."

The Hyksos stared at him. "Who are you?"

"I found you in the woods and brought you to the hospital with Doctor Narmer, here."

The blue eyes studied Khons' face. "I owe you a debt. You have saved my life."

"Well, then maybe you can tell me something." Khons reached for the arrow.

Councilman Narmer handed it to him.

Khons held it out toward the young Hyksos. "What I don't understand, Achilles, is why you were shot by your own people."

"Not my people. That arrow is from the downriver tribe. They attack us all the time." He reached out, then winced and pulled his arm back. "Give it to me and I will show you."

Khons leaned forward and handed him the arrow.

The young Hyksos studied the arrow in the dim light. Then he tapped the surface of the arrow back by the feathers tied to the shaft. "Here is their sign." Achilles handed the arrow back.

Khons held it up close to his face and studied the area near the feathers. He turned toward the lantern hanging from the ceiling a few feet away.

What he saw was a wedge shape, resembling an incomplete triangle, carved into the wood. "Yes, I see it now." He lowered the arrow and looked at Achilles. "Then you weren't attacking us."

"No. I was watching the pretty girls. Many of them are ugly but some are pretty too. The day before I watched you digging your trench, then I reported back to my tribe."

Khons smiled. "Were you going to report about the girls?"

Achilles white face broke into a smile. "No. I was doing that for me only."

"Smendes wants to interrogate him."

Khons looked at Private Kamose. "Why? He didn't attack us."

Kamose glanced around the tent. "Smendes is sometimes kind of over the top about things," he said in a low voice.

"Report him."

The private looked up at Councilman Narmer. "And be given the shittiest jobs for a month? No thanks. Besides - Colonel Ra likes his sergeant. He probably wouldn't do anything to Smendes anyway."

Khons had an idea. "Achilles, what tribe do you belong to?"

"Upriver." He pointed toward the north.

"Do you think your people would kill us if we took you back to your tribe?"

"They will thank you."

Councilman Narmer folded his arms across his chest. "Actually, Khons, that's a very sound idea. If we can establish a working relationship with this upriver tribe, then we have an ally."

"You'd better get him out of here before Smendes gets a hold of him."

Khons held out the translator. "You sound serious."

Private Kamose slipped it onto his ear. "That other guy we captured Smendes beat up pretty bad until the colonel stopped him. I think Smendes enjoys that kind of thing – gets off beating the shit out of other people."

The private waved his hand next to his face. "I'm not saying another word. I just think we should get Achilles out of here. He doesn't know anything anyway. He's just a kid."

Achilles said something to Kamose.

The young soldier turned. "You're father doesn't think you're some great hunter. He says you have a lot to learn and he's still teaching you."

"How old is he?"

Kamose stood up. "He's twelve years old. His father explained how they count their months and years. In their culture that's one hundred forty-four Love Moons."

"If what you say about Smendes is true, Private, we have to get Achilles out of here as soon as we can."

Private Kamose nodded. "I'll go with you."

Khons turned to Narmer. "You're a doctor, Councilman."

"Yes, and I'll be glad to help. In fact, I'd like to meet the leaders of this tribe. Maybe we can work on some kind of an alliance with them."

"When do you want to do this?"

Narmer thought a minute. "Actually he could be moved right now, Khons, but I'd rather wait until tomorrow. Let him heal a little more."

"How about early in the morning? Why don't we meet here at six." Khons looked at Private Kamose. "Will that work for you?"

"Smendes is going to be mad." He turned to Achilles. "But we've got to get him out of here. He's only a young kid." The young private faced Khons again. "Yeah, I'll do it. Six sharp."

Khons looked up at the councilman. "How about it, Doctor Narmer?"

"I hate early morning."

"You don't want Smendes messing with him, Sir."

The councilman turned to the young private. "Yes, I'm sure you're right. I'll be here. We can put him on his horse to transport him. I don't think it would be a good idea for him to walk. He might pull out his stitches."

CHAPTER EIGHTEEN
"Moment of Love"

Hyksos
The Colony
3M, Day 28, 69 A.D.
3:26 a.m.

Sergeant Abydos Smendes liked the nights best.

He leaned back in his canvas chair in front of the campfire and stared up at the star-filled sky. At night you were alone with the darkness. At night he was usually off duty and he could drink. When he drank, he felt relaxed and mellow. It took off the edge.

A lot of the day for the sergeant involved emotional pain. Actually his life had been that way since he was a kid. He had pretty much been uncomfortable most of his life.

Tonight he had downed a whole shitload of beer. Most of the day was a pain in the ass, and most of this pain in his ass had to do with that fuckup, Tanis Narmer, the councilman. Narmer was a stupid shit for sure, but the thing about him was that Narmer didn't realize he was stupid.

In a way, Abydos thought that was funny, especially now that he'd drunk so many beers. It was funny because this mouthy, arrogant piece of shit, this Councilman Narmer, thought he was brilliant, but he wasn't.

"A penny for your thoughts, Sergeant."

The sergeant looked up from the campfire. In front of him was that guy who had helped dig the trench today, the one with the weird eyes and the blond hair. Abydos had never met anyone with grey eyes before. This guy had them. "What do you want?"

The tall, slender man sat down on a large log near the fire. He threw up his hands in a gesture of not caring. "Oh, nothing in particular. However, I do know that you want something and I know what that is."

"What the fuck are you talkin' about?"

"Councilman Narmer. You absolutely abhor that man."

"Who sent you?"

"No one."

"Narmer sent you."

"I wouldn't give that fucking twit the time of day."

Abydos stared at the man with the grey eyes. "Why should I believe you?"

The man shrugged. "I have no idea. I'm just trying to tell you like it is. You know. . . if you had any guts at all inside that camouflage uniform, you'd do something about Narmer."

"Hey, Buster, you talk so fuckin' big - why don't you get out there and do somethin' yourself?"

"Do you want me to? I'd be delighted to shove a knife into his ribs."

Sergeant Smendes stared into the grey eyes. This guy had said that thing about the knife like he might have told you he was going to tie his shoes. Man, this asshole didn't show any emotion at all. Abydos had never seen anything like that before. "You'd really do it, wouldn't you?"

Saite Manetho shrugged. "Sure, why not?"

Abydos Smendes drank from his can of beer. He had drunk so much of it that he could hardly taste it anymore. But he liked the mellow feeling.

He glanced at his wrist control. Fuck - it was late. He hated the idea that he had to get up in the morning and work. He knew he was going to feel like shit in the morning. He had to get his ass out of bed at seven. He would get some fucking MRE fake egg breakfast and drink gallons of coffee, and then he would have to bring all those assholes out to work again in the ditch.

"Want to see my pet mouse?"

"You have a pet mouse?"

"Yes, indeed. I found him in the field today and I fed him some potato chips. Then I stapled him to a little board. I did that so he wouldn't run away."

"Isn't that kind of mean?"

"He's just a mouse."

"But he can't defend himself."

Saite held out the board.

Sergeant Abydos Smendes stared at the tiny figure with its legs stapled to the small board. He wasn't one of those animal rights people or a tree hugger or anything, but this just wasn't right.

The mouse's legs were spread open and there was a staple at each paw holding it tightly onto the board. The mouse's head moved back and forth as if it was in some kind of strange trance. "Kill the damn thing. For God's sakes, just kill it."

"No, no. Ralphie's all right."

"What do you mean, he's 'all right'?"

"He is, believe me."

"I don't believe you. And let me tell you somethin' else, Asshole, if you don't kill him, I will."

"Why don't you kill Narmer?"

"Because I take orders from Colonel Ra."

"That pansy guy who is trying to save the world?"

"He's not a pansy."

"Sure he is and you know it too."

"This conversation's over." Sergeant Smendes rose to his feet.

"You're the one who knows how to keep this encampment safe. Narmer has no idea how to do that. He's just interested in doing what he wants to do. If things keep going this way, we won't last more than a few months."

"You've been listenin', haven't you?"

"Listening to what?"

"To what I've been sayin' about Narmer."

"Everybody knows about it."

"That's not true. I don't tell anybody anythin'."

"Maybe not, but I know what you're thinking."

"Are you some kind of fuckin' mind reader or somethin'?"

The grey-eyed man rose to his feet and slipped the mouse board into his right jacket pocket. "No, but I can feel things about people."

Sergeant Smendes held the blue can of beer up to his lips, tilted back his head and drank down the last of the tingly liquid.

Up in the sky were two white moons, the larger of the two above the other and slightly behind it. They called this the Love Moon night, the one when the two moons seemed to almost come together in the sky. The smaller one below was the Man Moon and the upper, larger one was the Woman Moon.

The sergeant thought that this old tale must have been made up by a woman. It was kind of cool actually. He had been told that Mars, the planet they had come from, also had two moons. He was born on the starship so he never saw any of that stuff.

Being on a planet was kind of cool in many ways, but he didn't like the mosquitoes and other bugs. The heat could get bad too, especially when it was real humid, and it was humid most of the time.

Sergeant Smendes turned to the grey-eyed man. "Tell you what – if you kill the mouse, maybe I'll do the other thing."

The grey eyes studied him. "What other thing, Sergeant? Be more specific."

Sergeant Smendes crushed the beer can with his right hand. How could he trust this guy to keep his yap shut? This creep was weird. He had a screw-up mind or something.

Smendes tossed the can into the fire.

Sparks burst upward into the smoke.

"How would you like to work for me?"

Saite Manetho's grey eyes stared at him. "Me?"

"Yeah, you."

"Doing what?"

Smendes shrugged. "Oh, I don't know. . ." He looked at Saite. "You ever kill anybody?"

The grey eyes stared at him. Then there was a giggle.

Abydos Smendes felt a chill sweep up his back. Seconds ago he had been sweating, so what the hell was this?

Saite put the fingers of his right hand up to his mouth and laughed. "I'm not going to tell you." He seemed to pull himself together. "I refuse to answer that question on the grounds that it might incriminate me." He giggled again.

Sergeant Smendes felt another chill. He was sure this guy had done something real bad. He didn't know what or where, but it was definitely bad.

Smendes had heard about people like this guy who tortured animals and later tortured people and even killed them. If you had a guy like this working for you, then you could scare the shit out of anybody, anytime you wanted.

"Will you work for me?"

"How much would you pay me?"

"Do I look like I could pay anybody?"

"Then, why should I work for you?"

"Because. . . I could let you do things you like to do."

"Like what?"

Sergeant Smendes nodded toward Saite's jacket pocket. "Like stapling that mouse to a board."

"You can't staple people."

"You can do other things."

The air around them hung silent.

Behind him, the sergeant could hear the fire crackling. A puff of light breeze swept across the back of his neck.

The grey-eyed man stared up at the Love Moons in the eastern sky.

Smendes noticed that the lower Man Moon had moved away from the Woman Moon above. The moment of love had passed. "I have one requirement."

Saite Manetho turned around. "You have a requirement? I haven't said I'd work for you yet."

"You will."

"You sound terribly confident, Sergeant."

"I'm givin' you a chance to do the things you love to do."

A twitch quivered around the edges of Saite Manetho's small, sensitive mouth. Finally he smiled and nodded. "You've found me out." He giggled. "What's your requirement?"

"Kill the mouse."

"Then I won't have a pet anymore."

"You can always find another one, and by the way, if you want to keep a mouse, find a little cage. You don't have to staple him to a board to prevent him from runnin' away."

"That's not why I did it."

"Then why?"

Saite Manetho shrugged. "I don't know. It just seemed like fun."

CHAPTER NINETEEN
"The Stew"

Hyksos
The Forest
3M, Day 28, 96 A.D.
5:58 a.m.

Khons was munching on a granola bar. He checked in his shirt pocket for the two translators he had put in there right after he had gotten up. He would need them today. The tips of his fingers touched the two small C-shaped devices at the bottom of his pocket.

Maybe he should put one on now while he was thinking about it. With the fingers of his left hand, he slipped a translator out and clipped it onto his left ear.

He had been here for only about ten minutes in front of the hospital tent, but it seemed like hours. Last night, he had dreamed about Sergeant Smendes, something about him ordering people around and being angry. It didn't make much sense.

Then he had awakened just a little after four-thirty. Last night he had set the alarm on his wrist control at five forty-five, figuring that would give him just enough time to eat something and brush his teeth. But he woke earlier. It was that nightmare about Smendes.

Private Sile Kamose appeared out of the dark with Councilman Narmer. Narmer was leading a horse by the reigns.

Kamose glanced at his wrist control. "Let's get him out of here quick. We don't have much time."

Khons followed them into the dim tent.

Private Kamose flicked on a small flashlight.

Achilles was sitting on the side of his bed. He had pulled on his animal skin bottoms.

Khons picked up the top. "Do you want this?" he whispered.

Achilles slipped on the translator. "What did you say?"

"Do you want your jacket?"

"Yes."

Khons held it for him while he slipped his arms through the side holes.

Achilles tied the leather strands on the front.

Kamose helped Achilles stand up.

They guided him toward the opening of the tent.

Suddenly a light popped on. "Who is it?"

Councilman Narmer walked over to the wounded soldier. "We're moving somebody. Go back to sleep."

"Strange time to be movin' somebody."

"Orders," said Narmer.

"Yeah, fuckin' orders. See where they got me."

Narmer patted the man on the shoulder. "Go to sleep." He flicked off the man's bed light and walked to where Khons and Private Kamose had led Achilles.

Outside the tent, when the horse saw Achilles, it shook its head and made a guttural noise.

Achilles rubbed the horse's nose and whispered something in its ear.

The horse snorted.

Kamose laced the fingers of both hands together, making a cradle. "Here, step up onto my hands."

Achilles' left moccasin slipped into Kamose's hands.

Kamose grunted under the weight as he lifted Achilles.

The small Hyksos rose up and swung his leg over the horse's back. When he sat down on the horse, it shook its head and made a low guttural sound.

Kamose stared down at the ground for several minutes. Then, finally, he looked at Narmer. "I don't dare cross Smendes. You guys are going to have to go it alone. Sorry."

He ripped off the Velcro from the cover of his holster and pulled out a black pistol. "Here." He held it out. "Take this for protection."

Khons stared at the black pistol. "I don't know anything about guns. I don't want it."

"You need protection."

Khons shook his head. "I don't want it. Guns scare me."

"Private, I'm carrying a pistol."

Kamose turned to Narmer.

The councilman held out a small silver pistol.

Kamose grinned. "That's just a peashooter. You need a real gun. Take this." He held out the larger pistol.

Narmer shook his head. "No. We shouldn't need guns."

"Sorry about not going. I just think Smendes will court- martial me or something."

"We'll be fine, Private." Narmer grabbed the reigns of the horse.

Khons fell in next to him.

They walked down the muddy lane between the rows of tents toward the garden area south of the colony.

Off to the east the sky was becoming light. Up high it was a delicate blue. Then it blended eastward into a subtle yellow and finally orange.

Right now Khons was glad he had these boots from the supply tent. The ground was rough and they would be walking in the woods. Boots protected your ankles and lower legs.

At the end of the trench on the south side of the colony they turned left and crossed the narrow grass area and moved into the woods. There seemed to be a natural path leading deep into the forest.

That was good because it was hard to see.

Khons wondered how Opet would like this. Actually she wouldn't. She tended to be one who preferred the modern conveniences, and down here those conveniences were not always available. He wondered how she would have dealt with the heat and the bugs. Probably not very well.

At least Khons liked to think that was the case. Then he would be off the hook for not getting her a passage on the shuttle. Now the shuttle was up there permanently with the starship so it didn't make any difference anyway.

There had been talk of bringing the shuttle down with more supplies and leaving it down here on the surface of the planet. He had heard, however, that there actually might not even be enough fuel to make a flight down one last time.

Khons hated getting up this morning. The minute he flipped back the covers and moved his legs, he felt the soreness in his body. He was still adjusting to the heavier feeling of his body here in the greater gravity and he was working hard outside every day. This was not something he'd ever experienced before.

This morning when he got up, his parents had been sound asleep at the far end of the tent. His dad had worked cutting logs yesterday. He had learned how to use a chainsaw.

Khons figured he ought to learn that too. It might come in handy at some point. Of course when they ran out of fuel for the chainsaws, what would they do?

Based upon what Private Kamose had said about his sergeant last night, Khons had wanted to get out of the colony as soon as possible this morning. Kamose said that Sergeant Smendes got up at seven promptly every morning no matter what time he went to bed. Khons didn't want to start the day arguing with some nasty army sergeant.

Once they were in the dark woods, Narmer flicked on his flashlight. They were moving slowly, but that was all right because they didn't want to jar Achilles and pop open the wound.

When they had been traveling for what Khons guessed had to be about ten minutes, he heard a sound behind them, a sound like breaking twigs. "Hold it," he whispered to Narmer.

The councilman brought the horse to a stop.

Achilles' head was turned. "It is a man," he whispered.

A flashlight beam swept across them.

"It's me – Sile Kamose."

There was heavy breathing and Private Kamose moved by the horse to Narmer. He was carrying an assault rifle. "I got to worrying about you guys out here all alone." He nodded toward Narmer. "And you with that little peashooter."

"What about Smendes?"

The army private turned to Khons and shrugged. "I'll take my chances. Maybe Councilman Narmer can talk him out of doing anything too bad."

"I'll be glad to vouch for you, Young Man."

Kamose grinned. "I figured you would." He looked around. "Tell you what – why don't I lead since I've got the assault rifle. You can bring up the rear, Khons. Do you want my pistol?"

"No, I don't think so."

"Probably not a good idea if you don't know how to use one. I don't want to get shot in the back. Just keep your eyes open for anything, any motion on the ground or up in the trees. These Hyksos people know how to climb trees like goddamn monkeys." He looked up at Achilles. "Am I right?"

"Hyksos warriors know how to do many things."

Random beams of sunlight filtered down through the treetops into the woods.

Private Kamose checked the control module on his wrist. "It's close to six forty-five. Let's get going. I don't want Smendes coming out here looking for us. I want to be far gone before he knows we left the colony."

Khons moved around the side of the horse's belly to the rear.

Private Kamose leaned around the horse. "Just keep your eyes open. Whistle, or whatever, if you see or hear anything."

The private moved forward down the path, holding his assault rifle slung over his right shoulder.

It seemed to Khons that since he had been down here on this planet, he had lived through the number of events in just four days that many people had not experienced in a lifetime.

There was no going to the cafeteria to drink coffee with your girlfriend, and forget the whole idea of going to the gym to work out. There was no gym down here and, besides, there was so much physical labor every day that workouts were definitely not necessary.

A lot of the things he had accepted as part of life were completely gone now. He had wondered about a career teaching history, much like his grandmother. History had always fascinated him.

When they had arrived at Hyksos, Planet Three, he had been at a point in his life where he was just finished with his bachelor's degree from University Five. He was considering what he would do for a living, sort of in-between things. He was still living in his parents' compartment and he was dating Opet. Life for him was in a holding pattern.

Now, looking back at all those things, most of it seemed rather silly. It's not that a career teaching history would be a bad thing. In fact, it was great, but right now the issue was survival.

A group of teachers had set up a daycare and an elementary school in the colony. This was to assure the education of the children, but it was also a necessary babysitting service because down here everybody worked, men and women alike.

They had very little time for their children during the day. Just surviving from day to day was a monumental task and everyone had to take part in making it happen.

Now in the forest, the sun was above the treetops and morning bird sounds echoed among the giant trees. The rays of sunlight splayed down through the mist rising off the wet ground, and there was a kind of ambient fog lingering in the open spaces.

In front of the short line, Sile Kamose raised his hand. "Hold it!" he whispered.

The army private lowered his assault rifle off his shoulder and snapped back the latch.

The rattle of metal echoed in the thick, silent woods.

Khons knelt down to the right of the horse.

Private Kamose crouched and moved forward through the trees until Khons could no longer see him.

Achilles leaned down slightly. He winced. "It's a deer," he whispered.

Private Kamose appeared in front of Councilman Narmer. "Didn't see anything."

"Achilles said it was a deer."

Sile looked at Khons. "How can he tell?"

"I know these things," said Achilles. "I am a great hunter."

Khons grinned. "Well, you got your answer."

Private Kamose didn't smile.

Khons had the distinct impression that this army guy was nervous about the way his sergeant was going to deal with him. It was strange, really. Kamose was willing to do this, even though he might be considered disobeying orders.

What he had told Khons last night was that since Sergeant Smendes had not given the order yet, he couldn't be accused of disobeying the order.

He hadn't given the order not to leave the colony. At least that's what Private Kamose had told him. However, Khons wasn't sure Smendes would see it that way. Also, he was convinced that Private Kamose, in spite of his statements to the contrary, wasn't sure either.

Khons wouldn't have gone along with this whole idea in the first place if he hadn't been worried about what the military guys would do to Achilles. But maybe a greater reason for going with Achilles was that Khons was curious about this Hyksos village.

The young private motioned for them to move forward.

Khons followed behind Achilles' horse as they trudged through the short grass and broken twigs on the forest floor.

He hadn't told his father what he was doing exactly. Khons had just said that he had to go out early in the morning with Private Kamose.

Off to the right, brighter light gleamed through the trees.

Kamose turned toward the light. "It's hard to move in this forest. Let's get out into the open."

"Stay close to the trees."

Kamose stopped. He turned around and looked up at Achilles. "Why?"

"It's harder for your enemies to see you."

The army private nodded. "You're probably right."

Achilles smiled. "I know I'm right. I am a great hunter. Also, if you stay next to the forest, you have a place to hide."

Narmer looked up at Achilles. "We don't have to hide from your people, do we?"

"No. But the downriver Hyksos are always around. They like to fight."

"Those are the ones who shot you."

"Yes. I will find out who did it and I will wait for him outside his village and I will kill him."

Narmer took off his wide-brimmed hat and swept a handkerchief across his forehead. "I thought your people didn't like killing."

"We only kill those who try to kill us."

Narmer placed his hat back onto his head and stuffed his handkerchief into his back pocket. "I guess I can understand that."

"Let's keep moving." The army private waved his hand as if to urge them forward.

When they came into the clearing, Hyksos warriors appeared out of the woods, like silent phantoms.

Kamose dropped to one knee and aimed his assault rifle toward a Hyksos at the front who was carrying an animal skin shield.

"Those are my people."

"How do you know?" asked Kamose from in front of them.

"I recognize Diomedes and Alexander."

"Which one is Diomedes?"

"The one with the shield." Achilles leaned forward. "Give me the reigns."

Narmer held up the reigns.

The young Hyksos laced them in between his thumbs and index fingers and kicked the sides of the horse.

It ambled through the tall yellow grass across the small field.

Diomedes smiled and held up his spear.

Achilles stopped the horse next to the other Hyksos.

Khons watched as they talked.

Diomedes seemed quite excited about something.

After several minutes of conversation, Achilles motioned for Kamose to come forward.

The army private rose to his feet, but still held his assault rifle pointed ahead of him.

Narmer pointed at the rifle. "Private, I would put that away if I were you. You don't want to threaten these people. They might not like it."

"He's right, Private."

Sile looked over his shoulder at Khons. "They make me nervous."

"Hey, we brought back one of their guys alive. We saved him. They should be happy about that."

Kamose twisted the safety and hung his rifle strap over his right shoulder. He waved his hand. "Come on." He moved through the tall yellow grass across the field.

When they reached the group of Hyksos, Achilles spoke to them. "They were surprised to see me alive. My father is in the village and he is mourning my death. He will be happy to see me.

"Diomedes was taking the men out to hunt bison when they heard us in the woods. They thought we might be downriver Hyksos coming to attack the village."

The small group of Hyksos moved into a circle around them as they led Khons and the other two Mayans down a gradual slope through the forest.

When they reached the bottom of the slope, Khons could smell something cooking. Then the smell vanished.

At the entrance to the village, Diomedes signaled to someone up in a tree.

Then Khons could see something move high up in the foliage. It occurred to him that this person must be some kind of sentry, guarding the village.

They moved into a clearing and Diomedes turned around and held up his hand.

The group stopped.

Khons noticed that all three of them were surrounded by a ring of Hyksos warriors.

A small man charged out of a hut across the opening. He ran up to the horse and grabbed onto Achilles' right leg and hugged it.

Khons was so struck by the emotion of the man that tears rose into his eyes. "That must be Achilles' father," he whispered to Narmer.

Private Kamose turned. "Yes, it's Zeus, his father."

Achilles started to climb down from the horse.

Narmer moved forward.

Two warriors stepped up behind him.

"Here, let me help you down, Achilles." He turned to Kamose. "Private, help me, will you?"

"I am a great hunter. I can get down by myself."

His father interceded.

Kamose smiled at the man and handed him a translator.

The father clipped it onto his right ear.

"I am a doctor. He'll pull out his stitches," said Narmer. "He needs help getting down, no matter what he says." Narmer pointed to the patch of gauze on Achilles' back.

"Don't be a blockhead, My Son. Listen to the medicine man."

Narmer, Kamose and Zeus helped the teenager down off his horse.

"How did you get hurt?"

Achilles slipped an arrow out of the quiver hanging off the side of his horse. "This is from a downriver Hyksos. They shot me in the back when I wasn't looking."

"What were you doing at the village of the Mayan people from the sky?"

Achilles skin flushed pink.

His father turned to Khons. "You are grinning. You must know. I am Zeus his father and I must know why he was doing this stupid thing."

"I think it was the girls, Sir."

Zeus nodded and smiled. He turned to Achilles. "You were watching the girls. We have plenty of girls here and they are prettier anyway."

Achilles was staring down at the ground. He didn't respond.

Zeus faced Narmer and Khons. "We welcome you to our village. You have saved my son. That has made me very happy."

Khons noticed that a rather tall, pretty girl had walked up to Diomedes and was talking to him. He noticed her because she had nodded toward him.

Her father scowled and shook his head.

The girl turned away and walked back to a fire pit in the middle of the village.

Khons moved with the group toward some logs lying in a loose circle around the fire pit.

Zeus turned to them. "Sit down. We will give you some food and some drink to thank you. And I will send back a freshly killed bison to your village to thank your people for saving my son."

Khons sat down on one of the logs and Private Kamose sat to his left.

Councilman Narmer was standing next to Diomedes. Finally, he clipped a translator onto the man's ear and they began to talk.

The next thing Khons knew, a pair of feet in moccasins below slender legs appeared before him.

He looked up.

In front of him was the young woman who had been talking to Diomedes. She was smiling and holding a bowl of what looked like stew and a wooden spoon.

"I think she wants to give you that food, Khons."

He looked at Sile Kamose. "Yeah, I guess." Khons rose up off the log. He took a translator out of his shirt pocket and held it out.

The girl's blue eyes were riveted on his and she was smiling.

Khons reached around to her small left ear and slipped on the translator. He held his left hand in front of his mouth. "I'm Khons. Are you giving me that stew?"

The girl seemed startled. Then she reached around with her free hand and touched the translator.

"That's a translator. I'm holding my hand in front of my mouth so you're not confused by my lip motions. I'm speaking my own language, Mayan, and you're hearing it as your language, Hyksos."

She pulled the translator off her ear and uttered something in her native tongue.

Khons pointed to her ear.

She handed the translator to him and her blue eyes focused on his.

"She wants you to put it on."

Khons glanced at Sile. "Really?"

"I think she has a thing for you."

Khons smiled at the girl. "She's very pretty."

"I guess."

He turned to Sile again. "Hey, she is."

"I don't like my women with orange hair."

Khons faced the girl again. He reached out with the translator.

She took his hand and guided it to her ear. All the time she was doing this, her blue eyes were riveted on his.

Khons felt a stirring down low. With his hand shaking, he slipped the translator onto her ear.

"I like it when you do it."

Khons could feel his skin heat up.

"You are blushing."

Khons shrugged. "Yeah, I guess."

"Would you like some bison stew?"

"Yes, sure."

She handed him the bowl and the spoon.

"Thank you."

"I have not eaten breakfast. I will eat with you." She walked back to the fire and picked up a wooden bowl and spoon from a small table next to the fire. She scooped stew out of the pot into the bowl with a large wooden ladle that had been hanging from the spit outside of the supporting triangular stand on the right side of the fire.

When she finished, she returned the ladle to its place on the spit and pivoted around. Then she walked back toward Khons.

It was then that he noticed the man with the shield, Diomedes, was watching. Khons wondered if this father approved of his daughter befriending a stranger.

The girl sat down to his right. She turned. "I'm Athena. I am Diomedes' only daughter. I know he's staring at us because he's not sure about you Mayans."

Khons held out his hand. "Hello, Athena, I'm Khons Imhotep."

She looked at his hand. "What should I do with your hand?"

"Clasp onto it with your right hand and I'll show you."

Her blue eyes looked into his. "This won't be something that will make my father angry, will it?"

"I don't think so."

Athena held out her right hand.

Khons clasped it and shook it once. "How do you do, Athena. Nice to meet you. You're very pretty."

Athena blushed and grinned. "Father says I'm too tall and that is why I'm not married yet."

"I don't think you're too tall. I think you're just right."

"But you are taller than Hyksos men."

"Not really."

"Oh, yes. The men in our tribe are all shorter than you. Many of them are shorter than me."

Khons glanced around. "I guess you're right."

"You don't think I'm too tall, do you?"

Khons shook his head. "Absolutely not."

She touched the translator. "This translator thing is wonderful magic. Zeus told us that you Mayans had many magic things and that you came from some place far up in the western sky. Are you going to stay here very long or are you just stopping for a while."

"Oh, we're definitely staying for good."

Athena's face brightened. "That's wonderful. My father thinks that you will steal all our bison and all the women in the tribe because they are prettier than your women, and then you will fly away in your big thunder stick."

Khons tasted the stew. "Boy, this is really good."

"I made it. Father says that a woman should know how to cook for her man." Athena blushed.

"We Mayans came here to find a place to live. Our own planet became unfit to live on. It took us forty-nine years to get here."

"I don't understand years."

"You'll have to translate it into Love Moons, Khons."

He turned to Sile Kamose. "How much time is that?"

"A month, approximately. It's when the two moons seem to connect. It occurs approximately every thirty days." Sile thought a minute. "We traveled across the universe for about six hundred love moons."

"Oh my!" Athena's eyes became very large. She turned to Khons. "Then you are very old."

He shook his head. "No. I'm about two hundred fifty-two Love Moons old."

"That's good because I'm two hundred and four Love Moons."

"Seventeen."

Khons turned to Private Kamose. "Really? She doesn't seem that young."

Kamose shrugged. "Does it matter?"

"I am old to get married."

Khons turned. "You are?"

"Most Hyksos women are married much earlier when we are full-grown women. We are taught all the wisdom of our mothers when we become full-grown women. My father said he would not be able to marry me off because I am too tall."

"I don't think you're too tall."

The blue eyes focused on Khons. "Not for you."

"No, not for me."

Athena blushed and turned away. She spooned some stew into her mouth and chewed. Then she turned to Khons again. "Eat your stew. It's getting cold."

"Yes, Ma'am."

Athena's blue eyes stared at Khons.

He smiled. "Just kidding."

"What is kidding?"

"Making jokes."

"You're cute."

Private Sile Kamose was grinning. "You'd better be careful, Khons."

"He doesn't have to be careful about me. I would be good to him."

CHAPTER TWENTY
"Alert"

Starship Hope
Compartment 76
Level 4
Pod 1
3M, Day 28, 96 A.D.
8:42 a.m.

Ramses rested his left arm on the countertop at the end of the kitchen. Naqada was sitting to his right. He had the phone in his wrist control module set on speaker.

"We've been working hard every day," said a female voice coming from the phone.

"What kind of work, Intef?"

"Oh. . . digging and things like that. Khons Imhotep was working with us yesterday. He found this young Hyksos in the woods with an arrow in his back. We took him back to the hospital tent and they operated on him to remove the arrow.

"To me, he looked pretty young to be a warrior. One of the girls said she didn't think he was. She said that she'd spotted him at the edge of the woods before, staring at her. He looked like a little kid, but they're all small people."

"How small?"

"Oh, I'd say the men are like. . . maybe five feet seven or eight. And they all have this kinky orange hair. It's kind of weird actually."

Naqada glanced at Ramses. "We've been hearing that the military's going to confiscate all the batteries for their communication devices. That's what your dad told me, anyway."

"That's why I called. I heard that they're going to take all of them today. I wanted to call you before I went out to work just in case I couldn't later on."

"Won't you be able to call us at all?"

"I don't think so, Mother," said the voice on the phone.

"I was hoping you'd meet some guy down there, Intef." Naqada looked into Ramses' eyes.

This had been one of his hopes too. Unlike her mother, Intef didn't seem to be very aggressive when it came to men. Here she was at forty-four years old and she was single. Based upon what Ramses had observed, it wasn't for lack of interest in male people. She just hadn't found the right one, apparently.

"There are a lot of guys down here. Most of them are quite young – in the military and everything."

Ramses looked over at his wife. He had noticed something in his daughter's voice that was different. She was holding something back. "Sometimes those military guys are very good people, Intef."

"Hi, Dad."

"Hi, Honey."

"Well. . . actually there is this one guy. He's really good-looking and I don't know. . ."

Maybe it was time to press this issue. Ramses always felt his daughter opened up to him more than anyone else. "What's his name?"

"Sile Kamose."

"And he's in the military?"

"Yes. He's only a private, but he's really nice. I've talked to him a few times. . . well, actually twice."

Naqada leaned closer to the phone. "How old is he?"

There was silence on the other end for several seconds. Then Intef said, "I have no idea."

Ramses knew the real answer. This Sile Kamose was younger than his daughter. Ramses was tempted to say something about age not mattering, but he decided to just keep his mouth shut.

"He's not around this morning, as far as I can tell. He must be out on patrol or something."

"Do they send out many patrols, Honey?"

"I really don't know, Daddy. It seems like there are a few. I suppose it's for special reasons because Colonel Ra likes to keep most of them right here to defend this place."

"I just hope they set up some kind of call center for everyone down there, Honey, so that you can call us again."

"Colonel Ra has been talking about it. That mouthy councilman, Narmer, has been bugging him. I think he's obnoxious but he does get things done."

Ramses grinned. "Narmer will be a big pain until the colonel does something, I'm sure. I've dealt with Narmer before. Once he gets onto a pet project, he's hard to get rid of. I have confidence he'll do something so you guys down there can call up here."

"Well, Mom and Dad, my friend, Omina, is here. I've got to go out and work in the garden."

"Honey, over the next few days – maybe a week or so – we're going to be real busy up here."

"Why is that?"

"There's a meteor shower coming toward us. We'll be on high alert all during that time. I'll be up on the bridge almost constantly. If you do call us, I'd wait about ten days or so. Okay?"

"Sure, Dad."

"And say hi to that Kamose guy for me."

"I don't really know him that well."

"Introduce yourself to him, Honey. He might be a great guy. You never know about those things."

Naqada leaned close to the phone. "Say hi to Khons for us. His grandma and grandpa miss him a lot."

"I will, Mom. Bye now."

"Good-bye, Honey."

Ramses tapped the face of his wrist control.

Naqada looked over at him. "I think she has a thing for this Sile Kamose guy."

"Sounds like it. I just hope he knows."

"Is it true what you said about being on high alert?"

Ramses nodded. "Yes, but we're trying not to panic everyone. Just the military, my officers on the bridge and the Emergency Repair Crew are informed of the alert. Unfortunately that ERC guy named Hapmen is down on the planet. He's really sharp. I wish he were up here for this. I'd feel a lot more comfortable about this meteor shower."

Naqada reached out and touched her fingers to the side of Ramses' face. "Everything will be fine, Dear. I have this good feeling about it. You'll handle all of it just right and everything will be fine."

His wife always tried to be encouraging. That was one reason why she was a good wife. In fact, Ramses really appreciated her attitude. This time, however, she just might be dead wrong. According to Doctor Buhen, this shower could be huge and it was definitely headed their way.

CHAPTER TWENTY-ONE
"The Plan"

Hyksos
The Colony
3M, Day 29, 96 A.D.
8:01 a.m.

"**I** Want to know, Colonel, why this young man is being punished."

"Councilman Narmer, I understand your concern, but I have to maintain discipline here in my military unit."

"Look, this young man was worried, as was I, about the way this Hyksos boy, Achilles, would be treated by your men, one man in particular."

Colonel Djoser Ra knew exactly which man Narmer was referring to, but he had to defend his military unit against this mouthy protester. If his unit lost credibility over this, there might just be a moment when he would need their trust and he wouldn't have it. "I will check into that, Councilman. I promise you. In the meantime, however, I have a mission to carry out."

"What about the community phone, Colonel?"

"We're working on that, Councilman."

"These people need to keep in touch with their relatives up on that starship, Colonel. They must maintain that channel of communication. I can't tell you enough times how important that is to these people. A single community phone would do that, and it would mean the use of only one battery."

"Look, Councilman Narmer, if this mission works out, we'll have our generator back and this whole issue of dying batteries will be ancient history."

Colonel Ra turned to Private Kamose and Sergeant Smendes. "Sergeant, I'd throw Kamose into the brig but we can't spare the manpower. What I want you to do is give him the toughest jobs you can find, and then throw him into the brig at night."

Smendes saluted. "Yes, Sir."

"Colonel, may I say something, Sir?"

Colonel Ra turned to Kamose. "I don't know why I should let you say anything, Private."

"Colonel, Private Kamose was instrumental in getting us to the Hyksos village safely and now we have established a good relationship with those people."

"I wouldn't trust them for a minute."

Kamose turned to Sergeant Smendes. "Sir, they're peaceful people - the upriver tribe is. The downriver Hyksos are the ones who have been attacking us."

"I don't trust any of them."

"You don't think that bison carcass was given in good faith, Sergeant?"

Sergeant Smendes looked at Councilman Narmer. "It might just be a trick."

"You have a very limited view of other people, Sergeant. I think you're letting your prejudices cloud your judgment. While it's true that the Hyksos are not a particularly attractive people, they are intelligent and peace-loving."

"Colonel, Sir. . ."

Colonel Ra turned to Kamose. "What is it, Private?"

"Colonel, I wouldn't use this downriver Hyksos man as your guide. I'd get Zeus or Diomedes to guide you to that downriver Hyksos village. This guy might lead you into a trap."

"We've spared his life. He won't turn on us, Private."

"Not if what Achilles told us is correct, Sir."

"We can take care of ourselves, Private." Colonel Ra moved by Private Kamose out through the tent flaps.

Waiting outside was a contingent of five soldiers with assault rifles slung over their shoulders and one Hyksos with his wrists tied together behind him in a plastic zip strip. Next to him was Unas, a newly promoted sergeant.

"Are we all set, Sergeant Unas?"

The handsome soldier near the end of the line stepped forward and saluted. "Yes, Sir."

The colonel turned back toward the men in front of the tent opening. "You handle things while I'm gone, Sergeant Smendes. We should be back some time this afternoon. We won't be contacting you unless we need reinforcements."

"Colonel, Sir, I really wouldn't use this guy as your guide, Sir."

Colonel Ra made eye contact with Private Kamose. For just a split second, he wondered if perhaps this kid's warning might be important. Then he thought of the technological advantage his little squad had over these primitive people. After all, they had five assault rifles and the Hyksos had spears and crossbows. It was no contest.

Though it was true the men only had four clips of ammunition apiece, these weapons could deal with anything these primitive people could dish out.

He turned to Unas. "Form the men up, Sergeant."

"Yes, Sir." Unas turned. "Okay, you guys, form a line behind this primitive here." He pointed at the Hyksos.

Colonel Ra turned to Sergeant Smendes. "You're in charge now, Sergeant." He started to walk away. Then he stopped and turned around. "By the way, Sergeant, when I get back, we can discuss a promotion for you."

Sergeant Smendes saluted. "Yes, Sir, Colonel, Sir." There was a sly grin barely hidden in his lower face.

Colonel Ra led the line of soldiers to the edge of the colony. Then he moved back next to the Hyksos. He clipped a translator onto his own right ear, then onto the other man's left ear. "I understand your name is Menelaus. Am I correct?"

"Yes, you are right."

"We want you to lead us to your village, Menelaus. We do not mean to cause your people any harm. We only want our generator back."

"What is this generator?"

"It was the machine below the windmill I showed you."

The small orange-haired man nodded. "Yes, I remember. My chief, Hector, wanted it because of all the bright metal. He said it would make pretty jewelry."

"Jewelry?"

"My chief has good taste in jewelry. He likes metals."

Colonel Ra made eye contact with the little man. These people were not to be believed. They were so damned primitive. Of course, if one wanted to stay on their good side, maybe he shouldn't get into that. After all, they didn't even know what a generator was, so why wouldn't they think the parts would make pretty jewelry?

Colonel Djoser Ra had been in the military for over thirty years and he had never experienced anything like this. There had been no preparation for this in their training exercises all those months as they entered the CM Draconis solar system. Certainly there had not been anything to prepare him for dealing with people so primitive.

The manual did say, however, that they were supposed to be prepared to think on their feet, trust their instincts and go with their gut feelings. However, nothing this extreme had been described in the manual.

His mind popped back to Private Kamose. Had that young man really been afraid of what Smendes would do to that Hyksos boy? Smendes was kind of a crude individual. He drank to excess at night, but never when he was on duty.

Colonel Ra had often wondered what kind of upbringing Smendes had experienced. It certainly wasn't what his family was like. Colonel Ra's grandfather had been the original commander of the starship and his father had served five terms on the council.

Yes, compared with Smendes, Colonel Ra was convinced that his upbringing had been a high quality one. Of course some of his best soldiers came from disadvantaged situations. Apparently Smendes was one of those.

Colonel Ra walked slightly behind the left shoulder of the Hyksos warrior, Menelaus, as they moved into the deep forest. He noticed that the small man would look up into the trees every so often. The colonel wondered if that was significant or whether it was just a habit the little man had. They were in an open area now so Menelaus had stopped looking up.

An idea occurred to Colonel Ra. He stopped and turned around. "Sergeant Unas, send a man ahead of us several hundred yards as a scout. I would suggest that he carefully check high up in the trees for any activity."

"Have you seen something, Sir?"

"No, but our friend, here, has been glancing up into the trees."

The Hyksos warrior's head turned.

"Private Mastaba, front and center." Sergeant Unas stepped out of the line.

A lanky man with very dark skin moved up the line. "Yes, Sir?"

"Mastaba, move up into the woods and scout about two hundred yards ahead of this column. If you see something, get on your radio right away. Check up in the trees for any movement."

"Yes, Sir." The lanky man jogged up along the side of the column and into the path ahead of Menelaus, the captured Hyksos warrior. He continued to jog until, eventually, he disappeared from sight.

"Radio check," said an artificially high voice.

"We read you loud and clear, Mastaba." Sergeant Unas leaned close to his left wrist. "Keep your eyes open, Private."

"Yes, Sir," said the voice. "Standing by, Sir."

"Out, Mastaba." Sergeant Unas tapped his wrist control.

They were trudging out of the tall grass into the forest. Colonel Ra moved up next to the Hyksos warrior, Menelaus.

The little man glanced at him, then focused on the trail ahead. "You Mayan people would not make good hunters."

"Why is that, Menelaus?"

"You do not see what is right in front of you."

"I'm sure we miss a lot. We're not used to living out in nature like this. We've been on a starship for many years. Before that, we lived in plastic domes. We haven't lived out in the natural world for several generations. I'm sure we are a bit rusty in that regard."

When Colonel Ra heard the first man drop, he had no idea what it was, but then the man behind him collapsed into his right shoulder, almost knocking Ra to the ground.

Colonel Ra scrambled to his feet with his assault rifle aimed in front of him.

What happened next was a complete surprise. He heard a hollow "puff" like a large horn.

Something sharp slammed into the left side of his neck. Then darkness.

CHAPTER TWENTY-TWO
"One Little Moment"

Starship Hope
The Bridge
3M, Day 29, 96 A.D.
5:06 p.m.

R amses sat behind the two pilots, drinking a cardboard cup of tea. It wasn't as good as the tea Naqada made, but it was okay.

Outside the starship windshield he could see the green and blue surface of the planet below. At this moment the margin of night was slowly moving toward the colony. He had seen it many times before, but it always seemed to be a very dramatic event. He truly enjoyed watching it.

Today he was more relaxed than he had been for a long time. Most of the meteor shower had passed. The starship wasn't completely out of danger, but the greater part of the shower had swept by the planet far out in space, hundreds of thousands of miles away from Hyksos, and that was very good. Ramses supposed that calculating where meteor showers would go had to be an inexact science because this one had missed them completely.

Even though they had this astrophysicist genius, Doctor Ahmose Buhen, aboard the starship, apparently it was next to impossible to calculate these things with any degree of accuracy. Ramses was just relieved that they had dodged the bullet.

He studied the well defined margin of night and day crossing the green and blue of the planet from the white of the northern polar region all the way to the South Pole. In an hour or so there would be small pinpoints of light in the darkness, marking the location of the colony.

On cloudy nights you couldn't see anything of course. Tonight would be clear. Even though his shift would be over soon, Ramses liked to stay for a while to see the lights appear down on the planet.

This made him feel closer to his daughter, Intef. It was also a sort of affirmation that everything down there was all right. Those small lights were like tiny beacons of assurance in the dark night.

Yes, life would continue up here in the starship as long as they could repair the systems that sustained them. The real future, however, was down on that planet.

He and Naqada had not heard from Intef lately. All phones in the colony had been confiscated by the military for the batteries. The ship had received a text message yesterday saying that Colonel Ra was going to try to negotiate with the Hyksos people to get the generator back. If that worked, then everything would be good.

Ramses wondered if his daughter had followed up with that army guy she had her eye on. What was his name – Kamose? Probably not. Intef was a wonderful young woman but she had never possessed confidence around men and she was not willing to assert herself.

He wasn't trying to be an interfering father. Ramses just wanted the best for his daughter, as any father would. What always amused him was how different Intef was from her mother. Naqada had never had a problem getting what she wanted. She would always find a way.

With your kids, you never knew. He just hoped Intef was happy. She seemed to be, so Ramses guessed that everything was really fine and his daughter would have a good life down there.

He stared out the starship windshield. These days the lights they saw at night down in the colony were watch fires set by the military. It was a way of providing light for their sentries. Again, Colonel Ra was trying to save all forms of battery power. There was no electricity, unless they got that generator back, so it had to be bonfires.

Ramses checked the time on his wrist control. Commander Menes would be here in about an hour. He came on duty to replace Ramses at six o'clock. Usually he arrived five minutes early.

Then Ramses could go down to Pod One to his compartment and spend a nice quiet evening with his wife, Naqada. It was funny about their marriage after all these years. Just spending time with his wife was somehow healing. It felt good.

There was a violent lurch.

Hot tea slopped all over Ramses' hand. For just a second, he realized that this was different. All the tea in his cardboard cup had spilled - every last drop. That was odd.

A siren sounded.

The pilot turned to him. "Sir, it's Pod One! Something's wrong, Sir!"

Ramses thrust himself up to a standing position. "Turn on the cameras."

An image of Pod One appeared on his screen.

What Ramses saw was bizarre.

A large hole was blown clean through the pod. There was debris floating out in space. Then he saw two bodies, one a woman with long hair. "My God!" he whispered.

"Sir, we're losing air fast! I'll have to shut down the portal to Pod One or we'll lose all our air in Pod Two!"

Ramses hesitated. "Naqada," he whispered.

"Sir, shall I shut down the portal?"

Ramses could feel tears coming. He had to focus. "Yes."

"Portal closed!"

Ramses reeled and fell against the console. Then he bounced onto the deck.

The ship shook violently.

He clawed his way to a standing position and dropped into his seat. Then he belted himself in.

The starship was shaking.

"Mastaba - What's happening?"

"Sir, we're oscillating! If we continue like this we could compromise our orbit and head down!"

"If we do head down, Mastaba, can we recover?"

"No, Sir!"

"What's causing us to oscillate?"

"Pod One seems to be loosened from its mounting, Sir!"

Ramses stared at the oscillating view of the planet Hyksos.

"Commander we have to eject Pod One or we won't survive!"

Ramses could feel tears running down his cheeks.

Mastaba was staring at him.

"Do we have time to evacuate, Captain?"

The younger man's eyes blinked. Then he shook his head. "No, Sir!"

Ramses swallowed hard. "Eject Pod One, Captain."

"Ejecting Pod One!" The pilot pushed a button on the console in front of him. "Pod One ejected, Sir!"

There was a violent lurch.

"We have to pull free of this orbit, Sir! Move out into space! We'll need all the power we can muster! I'm going to override the controls on the shuttle and use it for more thrust! Do I have your permission, Sir?" Captain Mastaba turned.

Ramses stared at the other man through a blur of tears. "Yes."

"Overriding the shuttle controls, Sir!"

Ramses wiped the tears off his face with his shirtsleeve. Then he flicked a switch on his console. "This is Commander Ramses Tutan! Prepare for launch! All people aboard, if you haven't already belted yourself into your launch seats, do so now!"

He waited. "I repeat! Belt yourselves into your launch seats immediately! Any of you in the general meeting areas of the ship away from launch seats, lie on the floor and grab onto anything! Prepare to launch!"

Ramses flicked off the switch. "Fire when ready, Captain."

"Ready, Sir!"

Ramses hoped it had happened so fast that Naqada didn't have time to be afraid. "Captain Mastaba, engage all rocket engines. . . in five, four, three, two, one – fire!"

The starship shuddered.

Ramses' body slammed against his seat. The skin on his face pressed back.

In the periphery of his vision Ramses could see the two bodies floating by the windshield of the starship like giant rag dolls lost among the myriad white stars in the black of space.

He wished so much that he had been granted just one little moment to say good-bye to Naqada, just one little moment.

CHAPTER TWENTY-THREE
"Little Pet"

Hyksos
The Forest
3M, Day 29, 96 A.D.
6:02 p.m.

They had left the colony an hour ago, heading south. Up ahead of the column of soldiers, the forest was getting dark.

Avaris Khufu wasn't all that fond of the forest in the dark. At least now the unit was out in a grassy field and they could still see the blue sky, but the forest was right up ahead. He wasn't looking forward to that.

Avaris twisted his head around, as if to check the men behind him. Actually he was looking at the first lieutenant bar to the right of his shoulder. That was pretty cool. Smendes had made him a lieutenant.

There wasn't any ceremony. Earlier today, Smendes had just walked up to Avaris and said, "Look, Khufu, I know I can trust you, so I'm making you my lieutenant – okay?"

"Sure."

Then Smendes had handed him the lieutenant bars and said, "Put these on."

"But, Sarge, I don't understand."

Smendes had pulled him off to the side behind the tents next to the bulwarks bordering the colony. "Look, Khufu, I'm the general of this fuckin' outfit now, and you're my lieutenant. Got it?"

"What about Colonel Ra?"

"He's a gonner. We heard some weird radio transmissions. His unit was attacked. They haven't come back and it's been almost twelve hours. He's definitely a gonner and maybe the whole patrol too."

Smendes had decided they should go out looking for Colonel Ra. The general had figured that since they had night vision goggles, they had an edge at night, so they should do it after dark.

"Get down!" whispered a voice behind him.

Avaris dropped to his right knee. He pointed his assault rifle in front of him. His eyes automatically scanned the trees at the edge of the forest.

He didn't like being out in the open like this because you were an easy target, but he also didn't like being in the forest because these little Hyksos runts could climb trees like monkeys.

"Lieutenant," whispered someone behind him. "Lieutenant . . . I think General Smendes wants you. He's up ahead, waving." That sounded like Gurab. The guy was always a busybody, always acting like he should be in charge.

Now Avaris could see the general standing in the darkness just inside the line of trees.

The lieutenant rose to his feet and trudged forward through the tall yellow grass. His legs swished against the long dry strands of grass.

Smendes was holding an assault rifle in his right hand with the barrel pointed skyward.

Avaris stopped next to him just inside the line of trees. "Yes, Sir, Serg. . . General? What's up, Sir?"

Smendes beckoned with the assault rifle. "Follow me."

Avaris walked behind the other man into the dim forest.

The sun had gone down behind the line of trees to the west so that the forest was almost completely dark.

Avaris didn't like looking up when it was close to night like this because once you did that, your eyes got used to the bright blue sky and you couldn't see a goddamn thing down close to the ground, especially in the forest.

In a matter of seconds, he knew why the column had stopped. The pathway in the woods was littered with bodies. They were scattered in a strange uneven pattern next to the trail.

None of them had run very far. That meant they had been surprised and killed almost instantly.

There was the low uneven buzz of flies in the stillness.

Avaris had seen bodies like this before. In a matter of minutes they would be covered with black flies. Sometimes the flies were so thick on the eyes and mouth of the dead man that you couldn't clearly see his face.

Smendes waved the barrel of his assault rifle around in a sweeping gesture. "They were surprised. Never had a chance. It was that fuckin' Hyksos guide the colonel used. Led him right into a fuckin' trap."

Smendes rubbed his eye lids with the index finger and thumb of his left hand. Then he turned around to face Khufu. "Lieutenant, tell Corporal Sobek to pick up all the ammo they can find on the bodies. Tell him to take two other soldiers for the detail."

"Yes, Sir." Avaris saluted.

"Don't salute me, Khufu. If one of these Hyksos assholes is up in a tree and sees you doin' that, he'll shoot my ass with a crossbow."

"Yes, Sir." Avaris moved away.

"Khufu!"

The lieutenant turned. "Yes, Sir?"

"Tell the men in your unit to put on their night vision goggles. These woods could be crawlin' with those little red-haired assholes."

"Yes, Sir." Avaris started to raise his hand for a salute, but he stopped it at his waist. He turned away and moved through the trees out into the open field.

Now he was beginning to wonder if he should leave his lieutenant bars on his shoulders. They sure gave away your rank. Of course Smendes had those gold general's stars on his shoulders and he didn't seem all that concerned about it.

The lieutenant moved down the line of crouched soldiers until he saw one man who was larger than the rest. He stopped and dropped down to his right knee. "Sobek, take two men and go into the woods and pick up the cartridge belts off the bodies."

"What bodies?"

The men near the lieutenant turned.

Khufu glanced around. "Look, assholes, Colonel Ra's patrol was ambushed because the colonel used that fuckin' Hyksos guide. It was a trap – okay? Don't get all bent out of shape about it."

He faced Sobek again. "Just get the ammo belts. And take any pistol clips you find. We need the fuckin' ammo." He looked into the small brown eyes in the flat expressionless face. "Any questions?"

"Got it, Lieutenant."

Avaris stood up. "Good. Now get going."

"Yes, Sir." Sobek saluted.

"And don't salute."

Sobek stared at the lieutenant.

"I don't want to be a fuckin' target for some Hyksos."

"Oh, yeah." The large soldier made a halfhearted smile and moved away. "Hey, Hetep and Abu, come with me."

Two other smaller soldiers stepped out of the line and fell in behind Sobek.

Lieutenant Avaris Khufu paced up and down the line of soldiers. "Okay, you guys, listen up. When we enter the woods, you should have your night vision goggles on. Keep checkin' up in the trees. These Hyksos are like fuckin' monkeys."

Avaris reached down to his own belt and ripped up the Velcro cover on his night vision goggles. He moved up toward the front of the line at the edge of the woods.

General Smendes walked out of the woods with another man.

Avaris recognized who it was - that weird guy, Manetho. Smendes had made that guy a colonel.

He felt creepy when he was around Manetho. There was just something about him. Maybe it was those grey eyes. Sometimes they looked like the eyes of a dead man.

Up ahead, Smendes swept his arm in a beckoning gesture.

Avaris stuffed his night vision goggles back into the pouch on his belt and pressed the Velcro strip. Then he moved through the tall grass up to the general. "Yes, Sir?"

"Where are the guys with the crossbows? We need them up in front when we go into these woods."

"I'll get them, General." Avaris walked back down the row of men.

The crossbows were their new unit. They had taken three of these weapons off the dead Hyksos after the attack on the colony. Then Smendes had this idea to develop a special unit.

Lieutenant Khufu saw a crossbow. "Private Hem, move up in front of the line." He touched another arm. "You too, Teti." At the end of the line, was Gurab. "Move up, Gurab. The general wants you crossbow guys up in front."

"Why?"

The lieutenant's head jerked around. "What did you just say?"

"I asked why, Sergeant."

"I'm a lieutenant."

"You aren't any more of a lieutenant than Smendes is a general."

Avaris put his hands on his hips. "Tell you what, Gurab, I'll turn you over to that guy, Manetho. How'd you like that?"

The tall private stared into Khufu's eyes. "You wouldn't do that, Sarge, would you?"

"I'm a lieutenant – and, yes, I would. So get your fuckin' ass up there."

"I don't like bein' up in front, 'specially in the woods."

"I don't either, Gurab, but I'm gonna be right behind you, so get up there."

The tall private shrugged. "Guess I might as well. All of us are gonna get our asses kicked anyways."

Khufu grabbed the taller soldier by the arm. "Look, Gurab, you keep talkin' that way and you'll end up dead." He pushed the other man away. "Now get your ass up there and put on your night vision goggles."

The tall soldier shuffled through the tall yellow grass toward the front of the line.

Up ahead at the edge of the woods the two other crossbow specialists were standing next to General Smendes.

Avaris looked around at the soldiers near him. "Keep your fuckin' eyes peeled. Those little assholes hide in the trees."

The lieutenant walked up the line to the front.

Wearing night vision goggles, the three men with crossbows crouched low and moved into the dark forest.

Smendes and Manetho followed them.

Avaris ripped open his night vision goggle bag on the left side of his belt and tugged out the strange goggles. Then he lifted off his soft camouflage hat and slid his night vision goggle harness down over his face. He pulled on his hat again.

Looking through the green ambience of the night vision goggle lenses, Avaris checked the column of men behind him. All of them were wearing their goggles.

The lieutenant swept his arm. "Come on. Let's move." Khufu stepped into the dark forest.

Behind them, the light in the sky was dimming.

In these woods, it would be dark very soon. Out in the open it would still be light for maybe an hour or more.

The lieutenant scanned the trees up in front of the column, moving his head slowly back and forth. He could hear the buzzing sound of the flies near the bodies.

He stepped around a body without a head. His stomach jerked, as if he were going to wretch. He controlled himself.

"Zip!" An arrow stuck into the ground next to his right foot.

Avaris dropped to his left knee and swung his assault rifle down off his shoulder. He aimed it upward toward the trees.

"Zip!"

There was the crashing, crackling sound of someone falling through the limbs of a tree.

"Got him," said Gurab's voice up ahead.

General Smendes moved back down the line carrying a crossbow and a quiver of arrows. He handed the crossbow and quiver to a soldier several feet behind Lieutenant Khufu.

"I don't know how to use it, Sir."

"Use it anyway. Get up there."

The soldier slung his assault rifle over his right shoulder and grabbed onto the bow and quiver.

Smendes moved by Avaris toward the front of the line. The soldier, a man named Unas, followed the general.

Avaris thought this was a stupid idea, arming this kid with a crossbow when he didn't really know how to use it. But then, he wondered what he would do in this situation - maybe the same thing.

The crossbows were important. They were stealthy. They wouldn't give away your position.

Avaris wondered who had been shot with the Hyksos crossbow. Obviously it wasn't Gurab.

Seconds later, the column moved forward. They had decided earlier to move in a column so that they would know where everyone was. Smendes had told them back at the colony that once they found the downriver Hyksos village, then they would spread out.

Avaris's foot bumped into something. He stopped and looked down. The green imaging of his night vision goggles revealed the body of Private Teti. There was an arrow through his neck and his mouth was wide open, almost as if he had been trying to shout a warning.

He stepped around the body. Through the green haze of his night vision goggles his eyes scanned the trees as he moved forward in the dark forest.

The sound of the flies had lessened now. He supposed it was because the temperature was dropping.

But he couldn't think about those bodies and the flies. He had to watch the trees for another Hyksos with a crossbow.

They moved like this in the darkness for what seemed a long period of time. Avaris had no idea how long. He wasn't about to press the face of wrist control because it would light up his face and make him an easy target.

It occurred to him that maybe the Hyksos didn't know they were coming. However, another voice deep in his mind whispered that these people were hunters and they had lived in this forest for a very long time. They were not easily surprised.

Much later in the darkness, Lieutenant Khufu could smell something different. He didn't know how much time had gone by. They had walked through the woods at a slow pace for what seemed to him to be at least an hour, maybe more.

He could tell they were near the river because he could hear it off in the distance to the right. Sometimes you could even smell the mustiness of the wet ground and the water. He had noticed that he had begun to recognize smells better now that he had been down here on the planet for awhile.

Now he realized what he was smelling. It was food, yes, but it was mixed with other smells like body odor, or sewage smells maybe.

The column stopped.

Smendes crept back down the line. He leaned close to Avaris's left ear. "We're near the village. We're gonna send the crossbows up ahead. Spread the men out."

The general's head moved away.

"Which way is the village?" Avaris whispered.

The general leaned closed to his ear again and he pointed toward the southeast. "Over there, best as we can figure." He looked at Avaris. "Spread the men out along here." He swept his arm back and forth. "And wait until I come back for you."

"Yes, Sir."

The general crouched and moved away.

Hunched over, Lieutenant Avaris Khufu walked back down the line of soldiers. "Let's spread out and be quiet," he whispered. "We're close to the village so don't step on any twigs or anythin'." When he reached the last group of soldiers, he repeated the message. "No noises. . . spread out."

The line of soldiers moved to the right and left off the trail.

A twig snapped.

Avaris's head jerked around. He wondered who the hell that was.

He crouched down and moved to the left off the trail. He knelt behind a tree and peered around the trunk.

In the green haze of his night vision goggles he could see three figures moving through the tall trees toward the southeast.

He would hate to be in that crossbow unit, especially with that one kid who had no idea what the hell he was doing. Of course, waiting back here and not knowing what was going on was no fun either.

You just had to stay in one position and watch and listen. Sometimes Avaris would hear things and he would wonder what they were. What he really hated were sounds behind him. That gave him the creeps, almost as much as that Manetho guy gave him the creeps.

He forced himself to stop thinking about Manetho. He had to focus.

He scanned the trees up ahead. Nothing was moving as far as he could tell.

"Zip!"

Something crashed down through the trees and landed with a "thump."

Two figures moved back into the small clearing behind the trees. One of the figures waved his arm in a beckoning motion.

Avaris lurched to a standing position and moved forward across the space between them.

When he neared the figure, he recognized General Smendes. Manetho was standing next to him. For the first time, Avaris realized that Manetho was not carrying an assault rifle. He had only a pistol. He held it in his left hand.

Smendes leaned close to Avaris's right ear. "Once we get to where we can see the village, open fire. Spray the whole place. Kill all the little ass-holes. Got it?"

"Yes, Sir, General."

Smendes moved away. "Let's go." He swept his assault rifle forward in a beckoning motion.

To Avaris's right and left, a line of soldiers moved through the trees. They were crouched down with their assault rifles held ready to fire.

Up ahead, Avaris could hear voices. He thought at first they were his own men talking, but then he realized that it was the Hyksos.

General Smendes dropped to one knee and raised his assault rifle to his right shoulder.

A burst of flame shot out of the barrel. Stuttering echoed in the trees.

Down the line soldiers fired toward the sounds ahead.

There were screams and yelling.

Avaris stepped to Manetho's right and fired his assault rifle in a sweeping motion.

Arrows zipped through the trees.

Khufu shot in that direction and swept the rifle back and forth. He held the trigger until the weapon stopped stuttering.

There was silence.

He pressed the ejection lever.

A clip dropped to the ground.

He dug out a new clip from a square case on his belt and slammed it into the slot under the weapon. Then he yanked back the latch.

It made a "snap."

Smendes stood up. "Let's move!"

When they pushed through the brush up ahead, Avaris saw a cluster of an old man, two young women and some children. They were standing huddled together. They looked like a family.

The area around them was littered with the bloody white bodies.

A Hyksos warrior lunged out of the forest with a spear.

Smendes' assault rifle stuttered.

The echo faded in the silence and the man fell face first next to the fire pit. The spear dropped next to him.

Smendes swung his assault rifle around and fired into the cluster of people.

The women rushed to their children. Bodies jerked.

The old man tried to run and bullets ripped through the left side of his body. He spun around and fell on top of a dead woman.

The stuttering echoed in the woods. Then silence.

Avaris could hear crying.

A little girl wearing fur shorts stepped out of a hut off to the right.

Manetho climbed over the bodies and knelt down next to her. "Well, aren't you the most beautiful little thing."

Avaris's body tensed. His right hand reached down to his holster and pulled back the Velcro cover.

As if this hand were somehow separated from the rest of his body, it slid down into the cloth holster and tugged out the pistol.

With complete detachment, Avaris raised the pistol up in front of his right eye. He closed his left eye and aimed.

He cocked back the hammer, and then placed the sight on the tiny girl's chest.

He squeezed.

A deafening sound filled his ears.

The small body jerked and flopped to the ground. The little mouth was wide open and the blue eyes were large.

Manetho swung around. "Why did you shoot her? I wanted to make her my little pet."

Avaris held the pistol aimed at the space where the little girl had stood. Deep down somewhere inside, in some secret place, he wanted to move the pistol over just a little to the left and pull the trigger.

His hand shook. Suddenly he felt ill. He lowered his right arm and stuffed the pistol down into his holster. He pressed the Velcro strip across the top.

Then he turned around and stumbled into the woods.

He stopped next to a tree. He thought he was going to fall. His knees felt so weak.

Avaris Khufu reached out his right hand and leaned against the rough bark of the tree trunk. Maybe if he waited just a little while, the nausea would pass.

The stutter of assault rifle fire broke the silence.

Avaris swung around and dropped to his left knee. He raised his assault rifle to his shoulder.

"Zip!"

An arrow stuck in the ground next to him.

He scurried around behind the tree.

Large numbers of men came crashing through the underbrush toward him.

"Zip! Zip! Zip!" Arrows were flying all around them.

The men scurried behind the trees.

General Smendes and Colonel Manetho lunged out of the brush and ducked behind a tree a few feet to Avaris's right.

"General, what's going on?"

"They're counter-attacking! Let's see if we can get this mob organized and set up a defensive line!"

A large soldier staggered out of the brush and fell forward to his knees. An arrow was sticking out of his back.

Avaris recognized him. "General, help me with Gurab!" The lieutenant dropped his assault rifle and rushed forward. He grabbed Gurab by his right arm. "Get up!"

The large man staggered to his feet.

Avaris and General Smendes led him back behind a tree.

Smendes leaned around the tree. "Medic!"

CHAPTER TWENTY-FOUR
"Falling Star"

Hyksos
The Colony
3M, Day 29, 96 A.D.
8:13 p.m.

Intef was exhausted. She was smelly and dirty. It was twilight so it was hard to see close to the ground in the garden and they didn't have flashlights now that Colonel Ra had confiscated all the batteries.

All the girls who worked in the garden were headed back to the village. The main group was in front of her.

The one thing she hoped at this moment was that the army guy she had a thing for - that Private Sile Kamose - wouldn't see her like this. This would definitely not make a good impression. Of course, Sergeant Smendes had taken out a patrol looking for Colonel Ra so maybe Kamose was with him.

She was walking next to Councilman Narmer. Every so often she would stop and drink water from her bottle. Thank goodness the work was over for the day. She would sneak down to the river tonight, take off all her clothes and bathe. She was such a mess. Of course, now they put the drawbridge up at night, so maybe they wouldn't let her out.

Intef had bathed in the river many times before. She always made it quick because she didn't want any of these soldiers to catch her naked. Most of them seemed to be pretty good guys but you never knew for sure.

If anything happened, she wouldn't be a virgin anymore. Being a virgin was something she was actually kind of embarrassed about. After all, she was forty-four years old. Most women that age had given birth to at least one child.

Of course with the strict rules aboard the starship concerning numbers of children, there had to be some women that age who had never birthed a child. On the other hand, most of those women weren't virgins either.

"I hope Colonel Ra was successful in getting the generator back from the Hyksos people."

Intef looked up at Narmer. "Have they returned? I thought Smendes took some men out to look for him. That's what one of the girls said. Some soldiers left right around dinner time."

The tall man shrugged. "I have no idea what the army is doing. I've been busy out in our garden. We finally got some seeds into the ground and have marked the rows. That should pay off in just a few months based upon the weather we've been having."

Intef liked being part of something like this. It made what you did seem worthwhile. She would have helped to dig the ditches but she didn't know much about that kind of thing. Besides, there was a large group of men who had been doing that.

They had finished all the ditches all the way around the colony. Now, when people went back into the colony, they had to cross a drawbridge that was guarded. The sharp log bulwarks behind the ditch weren't finished yet. That seemed to take more time and she had heard that the army guys were running low on fuel for the chainsaws.

Up ahead, the first of the girls reached the bridge. It was still down. Maybe they were waiting for the soldiers to come back.

A guard appeared in front of them. "Who goes there?"

Councilman Narmer stopped. "For God's sake, Corporal, you know who we are."

"Sorry, Sir. I'm supposed to say that." The soldier stepped aside.

Intef followed Narmer and the young girls across the plank bridge to the grass on the other side.

Councilman Narmer stopped. "Is that a man on that thing?"

Intef looked off to her right.

In the shadowy twilight was a large wooden T. On it was a man whose arms were tied to the top bar.

Narmer shook his head. "This is Sergeant Smendes' doing. The colonel wouldn't stand for this kind of thing." He turned to the group of young girls. "You get on home, ladies, and thank you for your hard work today. We'll see you at eight o'clock sharp tomorrow morning."

The girls walked away. There was murmuring sound among them.

Narmer glanced around. "Let's give him a hand." He began walking toward the figure on the wooden T.

Intef fell in next to him.

Not until she was within a few feet of the T did Intef recognize who it was. "Private Kamose." She hurried ahead of Narmer.

When she reached him, Kamose's eyes opened. "Water," he whispered.

Intef unscrewed the cap from her water bottle and held it to his lips. Kamose tipped back his head and drank.

Councilman Narmer came up to them. "Sergeant Smendes did this to you, didn't he?"

Kamose gasped for breath. "He had this guy named Manetho beat me up. Then they tied me here before they went out on patrol."

"I'll speak to him. I'll get to the bottom of this, Private. Colonel Ra will see to it that Smendes is punished."

"Ra's not coming back."

Narmer moved closer. "What happened?" he asked in a lower voice.

"We got this strange radio transmission, like somebody's radio was turned on accidentally and we could hear these weird yells and screams. Then it stopped."

"We'll cut you down from here, Private. Then I'll confront Smendes."

"He's gone."

Intef stared at Kamose. "We've got to get you down."

"Don't tell the army guys. I have to get out of here – have to go to the Hyksos village. When he gets back, Smendes will kill me. He'll do it tonight when everybody's asleep."

"He wouldn't dare."

"He'll do it, believe me, Councilman."

Intef touched Narmer's arm. "You cut him down. I'm going to get my backpack. He needs somebody to help him."

There was a hollow puffing sound.

Private Kamose's head snapped to the right. "That's a Hyksos blow gun."

Intef swung around.

A small figure appeared on the near end of the drawbridge.

"That's Achilles." Kamose looked at Intef. "Get your backpack. Bring some food."

Intef jogged across the open area at the end of the rows of tents. She rushed down the first row and stopped by the third small tent on the left. She ducked down and crawled inside.

Her roommate, Omina, looked up from her clothing bag. "Who was that guy tied to the wooden thing?"

"Private Kamose." Intef grabbed some of her clothing out of her bag and stuffed it into a backpack. "Do you have any granola bars?"

"Sure."

"Can I have everything you've got?"

"Everything?"

Intef turned. "Yes, everything."

"I don't understand."

"Look, Omina. I'm just going to say this because I don't want you to know too much. I'm leaving. That's all I'm going to tell you."

"Where are you going?"

"I don't know."

"You're weird, Intef."

"If I tell you, Sergeant Smendes will beat the hell out of you to find out. The less you know the better."

The teenager stared at Intef. "You're serious."

"Yes."

The girl dug into another bag near her sleeping bag and brought out a fistful of granola bars in wrappers. She held them out to Intef.

"Do you have any water?"

"I've already drunk from it."

"I don't care."

Omina handed her a water bottle.

Intef stuffed the granola bars and the water bottle into the outer compartment of her backpack. "I'll be back."

"Sure, okay."

Intef crouched low and crossed to the tent flap. She pushed her head out and checked both ways. Then she stepped out, swung the backpack around to her shoulders and buckled it.

She had lied to Omina about coming back. If Colonel Ra was really dead, then Sergeant Smendes would be running the army unit. Coming back would no longer be an option.

She ran down the row of tents toward the drawbridge. When she got to the wooden cross, nobody was there. She stopped and gazed around.

Across the ditch along the edge of the woods in the dim twilight she saw a small white male figure waving his arms.

Intef charged toward the bridge and ran across the wooden surface. She passed the body of the bridge guard lying on the ground, and then jogged across the field. When she reached the edge of the woods, she stopped.

"In here!" a male voice whispered.

She stepped into the darkness among the trees.

Councilman Narmer appeared in front of her. He handed her a translator. "Put this on. Achilles and I got Private Kamose up onto Achilles' horse." He patted her on the shoulder. "Good luck, Young Lady."

"Thank you, Sir." Intef slipped the translator onto her right ear.

Narmer turned to Achilles. "Get going before I return to the colony. If I'm seen coming out of the woods, the army men might know where to find you, and send out a search party.

"I heard some shouting and laughter when I was cutting Private Kamose down. The army guys must be having a party. That may give you more time to get away." Narmer pulled his translator off his right ear and stuffed it into his pocket.

He smiled down at Intef. "Take care, Young Lady. I probably won't see you again so I wish you luck."

"Thanks, Sir." Intef moved up to the right side of the horse.

Achilles led the horse by the reigns. Out in front of him there was another Hyksos youth.

Intef saw the translator on Achilles ear. "What's your name?"

"Achilles, son of Zeus." He nodded toward the other Hyksos. "That is Alexander, son of Diomedes. You are safe with us."

Alexander drifted back toward them.

Achilles motioned with his head. "Go to the edge of the woods and check for the army men. Most of them are drunk but someone may have discovered the one we shot with the dart."

Alexander muttered something in their language and drifted off to the left toward the colony.

Intef looked up at Kamose who was sitting astride the horse. She wanted to take care of him, wanted to treat his cuts and bruises and make him well.

She touched his leg.

He turned and looked down at her.

"Are you all right?" she whispered.

"I've been better. We aren't going to be able to stay with the Hyksos very long. Smendes will figure it out and come after us. Besides, I don't want to bring trouble to the village. They're good people."

Intef smiled at him.

"Why did you do this?"

Intef didn't answer. She wanted to tell him she'd been watching him since they had come down here to this planet, but when she thought about saying that, it sounded kind of juvenile.

Besides, he was younger than she was, probably in his early thirties. He might think she was a silly older woman.

Intef was very tired, but there was something about this journey that was absolutely right. She was convinced that she would have been willing to do it even if she had worked in the garden two days without sleep.

There was just something different here. Intef didn't believe in fate or any of that kind of thing, yet this course of action seemed right, almost as if she was supposed to do it.

Were their lives laid out for them ahead of time? She doubted that. However, she did know there were choices one made, and there were turning points in one's life. This felt like a turning point. She didn't know where this event would lead, but it felt right.

It was possible that once she was out here in the forest, wherever they were going, that she would never speak to her parents again. That was kind of sad when she thought about it.

A bright light streaked across the black night sky. "A meteor," she whispered.

Kamose looked up. "If that's a meteor, it's a big one."

"They say that seeing a falling star is good luck." Intef smiled. Maybe that old superstition was right. She sure hoped it was.

CHAPTER TWENTY-FIVE
"Large Matters"

Starship Hope
Conference Room 2
Level 1
Pod 2
3M, Day 30, 96 A.D.
7:58 a.m.

Naomi Imhotep stepped over the curved threshold into the conference room.

The door sucked shut behind her.

She turned to check the door. After the tragedy with Pod One, sealed compartments suddenly made a lot of sense.

The guard held out his hand. "Your identification, Ma'am."

Naomi handed him her I.D. card.

"Doctor Naomi Imhotep?"

Naomi smiled. "Yes."

The guard handed the card back and stepped aside. "You may sit down, Ma'am."

"Thank you, Private." Naomi crossed the short distance to the conference table. There was one remaining seat open by the starship commander, Ramses Tutan. She knew why it was open. People didn't like to sit next to somebody who had recently been bereaved. It made them uncomfortable.

Naomi didn't feel comfortable doing this either, but Ramses was a good guy who could probably use a friendly gesture this morning. He had just lost his wife when the meteor hit Pod One. In fact, she had heard from her husband, Amun, that Ramses had given the order to eject Pod One. That would be terrible.

She moved around the end of the table and sat in the last seat next to the commander. "Hello, Ramses. How are you doing this morning?"

He seemed startled. "Oh, hi, Naomi." He shrugged. "I'm all right."

"If you want, you can stop by our compartment any time."

His blue eyes met hers. "Maybe I will. We may need to work together anyway."

"Yes, I thought that might be happening."

Dr. Ahmose Buhen, the astronomer, rose from his chair at the opposite end of the table. "Good morning Gentlemen. . . and Lady." He smiled at Naomi.

She returned the smile.

Dr. Buhen's face became serious. He turned to the guard. "Young Man, perhaps it would be best if you stepped outside."

"Yes, Sir." The guard moved to the door and pressed his hand against the pad to the right.

The door rattled open.

The guard stepped out into the corridor.

Buhen faced the table again. He nodded toward the environmental expert. "Dr. Pithom and I have called this meeting this morning to explain some things and to lay out a plan."

He looked around the table. "As all of you know, we have suffered a serious loss of friends and loved ones because of the meteor strike yesterday. I won't go into those details. Suffice it to say, Pod One slipped into the atmosphere of Hyksos early last evening. It caught fire upon entry and disintegrated."

He stared down at the tabletop and cleared his throat. Then he looked up again. "We just pray that all of those aboard at that time had already died from lack of oxygen.

"I feel responsible in so many ways for that event. I am the resident astronomer. However, unfortunately meteor showers are totally unpredictable. Believe me when I say that if I could have done something to prevent that, I certainly would have. May all of those poor souls rest in peace."

Doctor Buhen sat down and covered his eyes with his hands.

Doctor Pithom, the environmental expert, patted the other man's shoulder and rose to his feet. "Doctor Buhen and I have been going over all the data very carefully. This is our situation. The oxygen regeneration system aboard this starship has been damaged beyond repair."

He looked down the table at Ramses. "Commander Ramses Tutan urged the Emergency Repair Crew to work on that system around the clock. They have done just that. Early this morning they reported back to Commander Tutan and myself that the system could not be repaired."

The pudgy man glanced around the group of people. "This means that we have only a few weeks left before our oxygen supply becomes so compromised that we won't be able to survive."

He turned to the astronomer sitting next to him. "Ahmose, do you want to tell them or shall I?"

The other man looked up. "You do it."

Doctor Pithom looked around the table. "Ahmose lost his wife. You'll have to forgive him." Pithom cleared his throat again. "This is what Ahmose has suggested. He has proposed that we move this starship out into this solar system between Planet Three, which is Hyksos, and Planet Four. Further, he suggests that we establish an orbit around CM Draconis, this solar system's sun.

"What Ahmose told me was that if we do this, then there is a good chance that this starship will stay intact and that our people down on Hyksos will someday in the future be able to find it out here in its orbit."

Doctor Ahmose Buhen rose from his seat. "I'm okay, Sethos. I'll take it from here."

The other man sat down.

The astronomer gazed at the faces around the table. "I think it's pretty obvious that it will be at least a hundred years' time before our people on the planet Hyksos will be able to get back up here to this starship on their own. In fact, it's likely to be more than one hundred years. They will have to develop the science, the engineering and the manufacturing capacity to build a shuttle to get off the surface of Hyksos."

Doctor Buhen gazed around the table again. "The only way this starship will survive that long is if we place it in orbit around this solar system's sun. I have gone over and over the numbers and that's the only possibility.

"If we return to an orbit around Hyksos, it will be only a matter of time before that orbit deteriorates and the starship heads down into the atmosphere. That would destroy it.

"If we establish an orbit around the sun, CM Draconis, there is a remote chance that what's left of this starship will suffer some future meteor damage. However, if we make a point of storing everything, including our engineering data, information about where we came from and our cultural history, in a secure place aboard this ship in sealed containers, then I think there is a great chance it will survive for several centuries."

He nodded toward Naomi. "Doctor Imhotep, how is your history project coming?"

Naomi rose from her seat. "We could use some help, Gentlemen."

"Then we'll get you the help you need."

"That would be great. I will be glad to give out my phone number and my email address so you may contact me either way. Considering what has been said here this morning about our current situation, I think this project of saving our history is of the utmost importance. The project group can use any help you are willing to give us. Just contact me." Naomi sat down.

Doctor Buhen looked around the table. "This is not something I enjoy saying to you, but I will say it anyway. The truth of the matter is that we are all going to die within a few weeks.

"Therefore, we should make a real effort to insure that everything we know is stored for future generations. Our people down on that planet will, at some point in the future, find this starship. We must preserve the history of our people."

He focused on Ramses. "Commander, when can you be ready to move this starship out toward Planet Four to establish an orbit around the sun?"

Ramses stared down at the tabletop for several seconds. He looked up. "I should guess that it can be done in a matter of hours. We'll have to announce it to all those aboard because we are still held to some extent in the gravitational field of Hyksos. Everyone will have to buckle into their launch seats."

"Please let all of us know when this will happen."

"I will, Doctor Buhen. I'll contact all of you at least thirty minutes prior to making the announcement on the public address system."

Naomi was watching Chancellor Apis Dahshur who was sitting along the left side of the table next to Doctor Pithom. The chancellor had lost much of his handsome luster that was a hallmark of his image. It occurred to Naomi that maybe he had also lost a loved one when the meteor struck.

The normally engaging man was acting a little like a chastised child, one who had been caught with his fingers in the candy dish. Dahshur's normal thing would have been to at least give her a flirtatious glance, but his glowing confidence seemed to have dimmed - maybe even vanished.

In fact, Naomi was beginning to feel sorry for him, and that was nearly an impossibility considering how she had always mistrusted him. But then, these were extraordinary times and, therefore, extraordinary things happened.

The chancellor's feelings were small stuff. Naomi had an important mission to accomplish and she didn't have much time to do it. The Mayan people must know their own history and she would make sure they did.

Doctor Buhen glanced around the table. "Do any of you have questions for either me or Doctor Pithom?" He waited several seconds. "This meeting is adjourned."

CHAPTER TWENTY-SIX
"The Discovery"

Hyksos
Inland
4M, Day 1, 96 A.D.
Early Night

Intef felt a little safer bathing out here on the trail. That seemed strange but there were only three men and two of them were Hyksos - Diomedes and Alexander. The third was Private Sile Kamose and she wasn't sure about how she'd feel if he saw her naked.

She didn't have any soap but just sitting here in the river was so cooling and soothing. She had wet her hair and she knew it was a mess, but at least she had rinsed it.

Up above, the fast moving Man Moon was far across the sky. It was never up there more than a few hours. She figured it would set before she went to bed. Of course, these days it was hard to tell what time it really was. She wasn't wearing a wrist control anymore. Colonel Ra's men had confiscated all of them because of the battery problem.

In a way, it was kind of liberating because you weren't held to a particular time, but then it was also disorienting because you had no idea what time of day it was. Oh, you could guess by checking the position of the sun, but it was definitely just guessing.

Sile Kamose had shown her an ancient way of telling time by putting a stick in the sand and figuring where the stick's shadow was. He had done that when they took a break late this afternoon, after they had crossed through the mountains. But then Alexander had gotten angry and rubbed the figures out of the sand. "Leave no signs," he had said.

He had been really serious about this. It seemed like they had traveled so far that Intef had the impression they were safe already. Apparently Alexander thought differently.

They were headed east through some mountains. Sile had been trying to guess how many miles they had traveled during this second day. Intef didn't want to know. She just knew she was tired and, until this bath, she had been filthy.

"Hey." It was Sile's voice.

Intef slid farther into the river until her shoulders were underwater. "I'm here in the water. . . naked."

"Are you. . .under the water?"

"Yes." She could see his shadowy silhouette on the riverbank in the moonlight.

"Then you're covered - right?"

"Yes."

"I need a bath."

Intef couldn't see clearly in the white moonlight, but she could tell he was stripping off his clothes. Then she saw him advancing into the water. She tried not to stare, although it was very interesting. But she couldn't see much anyway.

When he was several feet away, he dropped down into the water. There was a subtle splash. "Oh, man, this feels great. I'm so dirty."

"Same here."

He was a few feet away from her. He slid down farther into the water until he was up to his neck and moved closer. "This is great. I'm going to soak here for awhile, and then I'll dress and go back to the camp and sleep."

His head turned to her above the slow-moving water. "I don't have a change of clothes or I'd wash the ones up there on shore."

"I don't either." Actually that was a lie. She had four changes of underwear. She didn't know why she had packed just four. Of course there wasn't a whole lot of room in her backpack anyway.

Things were silent for a moment. Intef listened to the distant gurgle of the water and the frog sounds from farther down the riverbank. Then she looked up at the Man Moon, which now was nearing the western horizon. It would set very soon and the sky would be black, except for the millions of stars.

Sile's voice broke the silence. "Why did you help me? I mean – I do appreciate it a lot, but why? You took a big risk."

Intef could feel her body tingle.

The croaking sound of frogs filled the night air.

Finally, her bare shoulders shrugged. "I don't know," she said in a low voice.

His head turned so that he was facing her. "I noticed you around the colony. I never said much to you. I'm not real good around females."

Intef smiled. "That makes two of us."

"Around females?"

"I meant around males."

Sile chuckled. "Would you believe it?"

"Believe what?"

"It took the two of us to be way the hell out here to finally really talk to each other."

"And in the dark. . . naked."

Sile laughed again. "Yeah. Isn't that the hell of it? Life sure is weird." He wrapped his arms around his submerged knees. "Look, Intef. . ."

She waited.

The river gurgled in the distance.

"Well. . . what I'm trying to say is that you'll have to be patient with me." He turned to her. "Okay?"

"This is strange."

"What's strange?"

"I was just going to say the same thing to you."

"No kidding?"

Intef nodded. "Yes - exactly the same."

He was facing her now. Intef could see his handsome face in the shadowy moonlight.

Sile smiled. "You know - my mom and dad would never believe this."

"Are they back at the colony?"

"They're up in the starship – Pod One, Level Five. They never got a winning ticket."

"My parents were too old." Intef wasn't going to take that part of the conversation any further. "Do you know where they're taking us?"

"You mean Diomedes and Alexander?"

"Yes."

"All I know is east to 'the big water.' That's what they call it. Maybe it's some kind of huge lake or something. I don't know any more than you do."

"We'll never see Mayans again, will we?"

Sile looked over at her. "Probably not. Well. . . there might be others who want to get away from Smendes. I mean – that's possible."

Something occurred to Intef. "Would you do something for me?"

"What?"

"Will you wash my back? I can't reach it."

"Sure." Sile started to stand up. "Oh, sorry." Instead he rose to his knees and crawled around behind her.

When she glanced back, Intef could see that he was kneeling behind her. She saw a firm flat stomach and then some dark hair leading downward.

"I'd better sit down."

She could feel his legs slide by her hips.

He brushed water up and down her back in the white moonlight. The strokes were cool and gentle. Her back tingled and she closed her eyes and enjoyed the feeling of his hands on her bare skin.

"Your skin's real soft."

Intef opened her eyes. "Is that a compliment?"

"Sure. . . I guess."

"I wish I could talk to my mother and father."

Sile didn't respond right away. Finally he said, "I don't think we'll be able to do that, ever again."

Intef looked back over her left shoulder. "I'm glad you're here with me."

"Yeah – I feel the same way." The water sloshed behind her and Sile came around to her right and then settled down next to her. "Want to learn about the stars?"

"You know about them?"

"It's one of my many brilliant talents."

Intef grinned. "I like you."

"Same here."

CHAPTER TWENTY-SEVEN
"Underneath"

Hyksos
The Colony
4M, Day 2, 96 A.D.
Late Afternoon

Khons Imhotep walked next to his father and Narmer across the grassy area toward the drawbridge. He had been thinking about Athena a lot lately. He just couldn't seem to get her out of his mind.

The whole thing was crazy. She was a Hyksos and she had that bushy red hair. In spite of all that, he did want to see her again. However, he just couldn't go walking off into the forest alone. He would need somebody with him. Maybe his father would agree to go.

"I've been telling this Smendes that we can't operate without some public input, but he won't hear of it. I have half a mind to form a council and create a citizen's movement of some kind." Councilman Narmer turned to Khons and his father. "Would you two like to be part of this?"

Khons said nothing.

Aten nodded. "It sounds reasonable to me, Tanis. We do need some public input. Now that we have this ditch dug and the bulwarks in place and the drawbridge, there's enough security. I think we're ready for some civilian input." He turned to his son. "What about it, Khons?"

"I don't want to get involved, Dad."

"Oh, yes. You're interested in that Hyksos woman. What's she like anyway?"

Khons shrugged. "I don't know. She's just nice."

Aten turned to the councilman. "What do you think about that, Tanis? My son, here, has taken up with this young Hyksos woman."

"She's really quite attractive, Aten. I met her when we took Achilles back to his people." He turned to Khons. "I have to say, Young Man, that I wouldn't mention this around Sergeant Smendes. He has real prejudices about these people. And the man is crude and backward. I really think he's capable of all kinds of unsavory things."

A loud siren pierced the silence. It rose up higher and higher to a crescendo and then it died down in a sweeping humming sound until it groaned down to low basso rumble, then dissipated into nothing.

"Thirty minutes until the gate closes." Narmer turned to the group of girls moving along next to them. "Is everybody accounted for, ladies?"

"We can't find Omina."

Another girl spoke up. "She went into the woods with that little Hyksos guy."

Khons turned. "Achilles?"

"I think so. He's been hanging around a lot. Finally he talked to her - made some strange noises. Then they got some translators."

"Yes, that's right. She borrowed my translators." Narmer turned and looked toward the woods. "Well, she heard the siren so I'm sure she'll come in."

They reached the drawbridge.

The guard counted them as they walked by and checked an electronic device hanging from his neck. "One girl is missing."

"She went into the woods, Corporal Gerzean."

Khons had an idea. "I'll go find her as soon as I get rid of my tools."

His father looked at him. "The drawbridge is going up in less than thirty minutes."

"Do you want to leave her out in the forest all night, Dad?"

Once inside and away from the guard, Khons turned to his father. "I have to go see Athena, Dad," he said in a low voice. "There are some things I have to discuss with her."

"So, you're not really interested in saving this Omina after all. You really want to see this Hyksos woman."

Khons shrugged. "Well, actually, yes. But then Achilles and I can also take Omina to the village. She wants to stay there all night."

"If you're going to the Hyksos village, I'll go with you. You shouldn't travel alone in that forest."

"I won't be alone. I'll go with Achilles."

"To be honest, Son, my real motive is that I want to meet this young Hyksos woman you're so interested in."

An army sergeant walked up to Tanis Narmer. "Councilman Narmer, General Smendes wants to see you."

Narmer turned. A sarcastic smile formed on his mouth. "So, the sergeant has had a promotion. And he skipped several ranks, including lieutenant, captain, major and colonel."

"He wants to see you, Councilman Narmer – right away."

"Can't he wait until I've cleaned up and had some dinner?"

"No – right away."

Narmer looked at Aten. Then he glanced back at the officer. "Just a minute. I have to give something to my friends, here." He pulled his small pistol out of his pocket. "Here, take this, Khons."

Khons stared at it. "I don't want that, Councilman."

Aten grabbed onto it. "I'll bring it back tomorrow, Tanis."

"No hurry." The councilman turned away. "Lead on, Young Man." He gestured toward the pathway between the first two rows of tents.

Khons watched as the young soldier led Narmer away. "I wonder what that's about."

Aten turned to his son. "I have no idea, but if you're going to travel to the Hyksos village, we have to get going before they pull up the draw-bridge."

"Let me get my backpack." Khons handed a hoe to his father. Then he ran away toward the second row of tents. He jogged down the row to a large one, four tents down. He flipped up the cover over the entrance, bent down and stepped inside.

His mother was buttoning a shirt.

"Sorry, Mom."

"No problem."

Khons moved over to his sleeping bag. He opened the clothing bag next to it, dug inside and removed several items. Then he stuffed them inside his backpack and picked it up.

He turned around to his mother. "Do you have any granola bars? I also need water."

"We have only two left." His mother opened a trunk and pulled out a bottle of water and two wrapped bars.

"I'm going to the Hyksos village to see Athena. I'll be back tomorrow, Mom. Okay?"

"Sure." She handed him the two granola bars.

He kissed her cheek. "I think Dad's coming with me."

"You'd better hurry. They'll be raising the drawbridge."

Khons hustled across the tent. Then he stopped. For some reason he could not explain, he thought of the sealed book his father had.

He turned around and rushed back to the metal chest in the back of the tent.

"You have to hurry, Khons. What are you doing now?"

"Just getting something." He dug into the chest and pulled out the cloth bag with the plastic container inside.

"Why do you want that thing?"

Khons stared at the cloth bag. Then he looked at his mother. "Ever have a feeling you can't explain?"

She shrugged. "Sure."

"I'm having one."

She leaned forward and kissed his cheek. "You be careful. When will you be back?"

"Probably tomorrow."

"Be careful, Honey."

"I will."

"You'll have to introduce me to that girl you've met."

Khons grinned. His mother was always so cool. "Sure."

"Hurry, Honey."

"I'm gone." Khons rushed across the tent, pushed up the flap and stepped outside. He turned and dropped the flap in place. Then he jogged down the row of tents toward the clearing next to the drawbridge.

He could see his father standing with the guard in front of the bridge. Next to them was the hand-crank siren.

Khons broke into a run across the muddy grass to the bridge. When he reached his father, he was out of breath.

His father turned to him. "The corporal, here, says we only have about eight or nine minutes before they crank the siren again and pull up the drawbridge."

"Why do you have a backpack? And you brought that history book."

"I just thought it would be smart to have some supplies in case we have to stay outside overnight."

The corporal stared at Khons. "General Smendes wouldn't like it if you stayed outside."

Khons immediately felt on the defensive. "What harm can we do outside?"

"He just wants everyone inside. He doesn't trust the Hyksos." Corporal Gerzean hesitated. Then he added. "I didn't tell you this." The young soldier glanced around, and then leaned closed to Aten. "Smendes is planning a raid against that village upriver."

"Why would he do that?"

The corporal glanced around. He leaned closer. "I didn't say that – okay?" he said in a low voice. "But I just thought I should tell you. I was there when we attacked the downriver Hyksos. He told us to kill everybody. . . even children. But you never heard that from me."

Khons looked into the corporal's eyes. "Okay, I understand." He started to cross the bridge and turned. "Thanks for the tip."

"Hey, you didn't hear it from me."

Khons grabbed his father's arm. "Come on, Dad, we're wasting time." He glanced at Corporal Gerzean. "We'll try our best to get back. I'm just worried about that girl."

They moved across the drawbridge.

"Why did you bring that thing?" Aten nodded toward the cloth bag his son was holding.

Khons shrugged. "I don't know. I'll tell you just what I told mom. I had this hunch it would be a good idea."

"It's crazy bringing it out here."

"Bear with me, Dad. Okay?"

Aten shrugged. "Hey, fine. But you carry it. I'm not going to."

Khons began jogging. "Come on, Dad, hurry."

Aten followed him at a slower pace.

Khons wanted to get into the woods and find the path before the sun started down. Once he was on that path, he could probably find the way to the Hyksos village.

At the edge of the woods, he stepped inside. He stood in a clear area and waited. He could hear voices a short distance away.

Khons watched as his father made his way toward the edge of the woods.

He wished his dad would speed it up. Of course, he didn't really understand, himself, why he had hurried. There was just this uneasy feeling he had about Smendes. The guy was out of control. If Smendes was planning a raid, he had to warn the upriver Hyksos people.

"Why are you out here?" said a girl's voice.

Khons swung around. "Omina, you scared the hell out of me."

Achilles said something in Hyksos.

Khons slipped his hand into his side pocket and pulled out his translator. He clamped it onto his right ear. "You guys scared me."

Achilles smiled. "I am good, huh? I can stalk animals and they don't even know I am there. Why did you come? I was going to take this pretty girl back." He nodded toward Omina.

"Let's wait for my father. I wouldn't take her back if I were you."

"Why not? I am no danger to these Mayan people."

"Sergeant Smendes is planning a raid on your village. You're the enemy."

Achilles seemed puzzled. "We have done nothing to him."

"You helped Private Kamose escape."

"So, now he will attack our village?"

"Look, Achilles, I don't understand it either. I was just told this by the army guy at the drawbridge. The soldier at the bridge said Smendes ordered them to kill all the downriver Hyksos when they raided the village, even the children."

"That is evil."

"I agree. I wouldn't take Omina back near the colony if I were you. Smendes might just put you in custody."

"I will run away."

"Then he might shoot you."

"He is a crazy man."

Khons nodded. "Yes, I think you're right." He turned to Omina. "I'm not even sure if it's safe for you to go back."

"But my clothes are back there."

"I wouldn't go back, Omina. I wouldn't chance it if I were you." A thought about his mother popped into Khons' mind.

The siren broke through the silence.

Khons jumped out of the forest into the clearing. "Dad, come on!"

"What's the hurry?"

"The siren's early. Something's wrong!"

The "crack" of a rifle broke through the siren sound.

A bullet whizzed by Khons. "Get down!"

His father bent over and charged into the trees.

The stutter of automatic weapon fire cut through the siren sound now descending toward a low growl.

Bullets whizzed into the trees.

Achilles crouched low and ran with Omina deeper into the woods.

"Hurry, Dad!" Khons charged after Achilles.

Once they were several yards into the woods they caught up to Achilles.

Every so often Khons would look back over his shoulder. He had this uncomfortable feeling that they might be followed. He suddenly remembered the gun his father had. But it was just a small thing – not very much protection. "They're going to come after us."

Achilles turned. "Why do you say this?"

Khons shrugged. "I just feel that it's going to happen."

"You would make a good hunter. If what you say is true, we must move quickly. We must warn my village the ugly sergeant is coming."

Khons wasn't sure what he was so worried about. All of it was like this strange premonition. He didn't really believe in such things, but he was certainly feeling something right now.

What was strange was that in the midst of all of this feeling of impending doom, when he thought about Athena, he felt better. For some reason she gave him hope.

The journey through that night was a strange one. The Man Moon moved overhead above the high forest trees casting shadows on the forest floor.

Achilles moved at a fast pace. At one point when they were near the village he moved back behind them and dropped to the ground and placed one ear against the surface of the forest floor. Then he stood up. "I hear people coming. They are not far behind us. We must move quickly."

When they were within sight of the village, Achilles put his hands around his mouth and made a ululating sound up toward the treetops.

A ululation came back, echoing through the silent forest.

Achilles turned to Khons. "You lead them back into the village. I will stay out here."

Khons did as he was told. When he neared the edge of the village, he noticed that there was no fire and there were no torches. There was absolutely no light, except for the white moon.

When they walked down the slope into the village, someone grabbed Khons and Omina.

Khons was pulled inside a hut and taken to Athena who smiled at him in the dark.

There was the "stutter" of automatic weapon fire.

Khons grabbed onto Athena and pulled her down. He lay on top of her.

He could feel her breathing against his neck.

He heard a man yell, then another. Then there was silence.

Minutes later, Achilles appeared at the front of the hut. "They are gone."

Someone lit a torch.

Khons rose up off Athena.

She smiled and reached up to touch his face.

He grinned at her and dug in his shirt pocket for his translator. He clipped it onto her small left ear.

"Is this Athena?"

Khons turned. "Oh, Dad – there you are. Yes, this is Athena."

She stood up and reached out her right hand.

Aten clipped a translator onto his right ear. Then he reached out and took her hand.

She shook it once. "Good to meet."

Aten was grinning. "You're very pretty, Young Lady."

"Thank you, Khons' father."

"You may call me Aten."

"Aten is easy to remember."

Khons put his arm around Athena's shoulders. "Where is your father, Athena? I'd like to have him meet my father."

"Diomedes is far to the east. He is taking your Private Kamose and his woman friend to the fish people on the big water."

"When will he be back?"

"It will be two days – maybe more. If it rains, they will be longer."

Khons turned to his father. "Maybe you can meet him later, Dad."

His father shrugged. "Sure." He stared down at Athena. "For a Hyksos, you're quite tall, Young Lady."

"Khons says I am just right."

Aten looked at his son. "Is that so?"

Khons shrugged. "Hey, she's real nice."

Aten turned to the girl. "Is this serious?"

"Hyksos women do not love a man for fun. I want Khons to live with me and give me many children. I will feed him well and take good care of him. I am the best cook of any of the young women of this tribe."

"She is a good cook, Dad. You ought to taste her bison stew."

Aten nodded and smiled. "You sound like a good match for my son. However, there is one thing. You're a Hyksos and he's a Mayan."

"We are not so different, Aten." Athena touched her own arm. "My skin is white." She touched Khons' arm. "His is brown."

She pulled on her kinky hair. "My hair is orange." She looked up at Khons. "His is black."

She stabbed at her arm with her index finger. "But let me tell you something. Underneath our skins we are the same. If you cut my arm, I will bleed red blood just like you.

"When I saw your son, I knew I loved him right away and I could see in his eyes that he loved me.

"Love is something that does not make any sense. It happens because our souls connect." She touched Khons' chest and then her chest. "We are connected inside with love."

Aten leaned forward, wrapped his arms around the Hyksos girl and hugged her. Then he held her shoulders at arms' length and looked down at her. "You have my approval, Young Lady. Actually – you're quite the catch."

Khons was overcome with emotion. He could feel tears rising into his eyes.

Athena grabbed onto his right hand with both of hers and squeezed.

CHAPTER TWENTY-EIGHT
"The Only Way"

Hyksos
The Colony
4M, Day 3, 96 A.D.
8:13 p.m.

"So, Sergeant Coptos, what do you have to report about last night's patrol?"

The man stared down at the matted grass in front of the general's desk. "We were ambushed."

"Ambushed? What kind of fuckin' excuse is that? Did you kill them?"

The man looked up. "No, Sir."

"You were lookin' for Aten and Khons Imhotep and some girl. Is that right?"

"Yes, Sir."

"Where are they?"

"I don't know, Sir."

General Smendes thumped the knuckles of his right hand on the desk. Then he turned toward Badari Gerzean. "Corporal, take Narmer down to the drawbridge. Colonel Manetho is in charge. He will know what to do with him."

Earlier, Corporal Bedari Gerzean had left Councilman Narmer outside the tent. He had taken him down from the wooden T that was also used for Kamose. Councilman Narmer was barely able to stand. Colonel Manetho had beaten him for several hours last night and had tied him to the wooden T. They had left him there all night and all day today.

Luckily Gerzean hadn't seen the beatings. He had been on guard duty.

Tonight, with the help of Akhenaten and Nefera, Corporal Gerzean had brought Narmer here to the General's tent, as he was ordered.

"And Saite. . ." General Smendes turned to the man standing back in the shadows. ". . . bring back that Imhotep woman. She's in tent number four in the second row. Maybe she knows where her husband is." The general shrugged. "If she doesn't know, we'll kill her."

He glanced at Corporal Gerzean, then turned to Manetho. "Bring her back before you do anything, Saite, and make sure Gerzean, here, is with you."

Manetho smiled. "Certainly, General."

The general turned to Corporal Gerzean. "Carry on, Corporal."

"Yes, Sir." Badari Gerzean saluted, pivoted around and marched out of the tent into the night air. He had a bad feeling about all this. It was as if he was waiting for something to happen. Nothing had happened all day, but it was coming. He knew that for sure.

He had been at the drawbridge last night when the Imhoteps had left. General Smendes hadn't addressed that matter yet. Of course, he had also warned the Imhoteps that Smendes was planning a raid on the upriver Hyksos village. Smendes couldn't know about that. He hoped to hell Smendes didn't know that.

Right after Corporal Gerzean stepped out of the tent, Saite Manetho appeared from under the low entrance.

The blond-haired colonel was carrying a length of heavy rope. He studied the cluster of men sitting on the ground next to Councilman Narmer who was on his back in the mud. "So this is the unit that was ambushed."

A large man with an assault rifle slung across his shoulder nodded. "Yes, Sir."

"And how did that happen, Private Nefera?"

"The Hyksos were hiding up in the trees, Colonel."

"You look like you're big enough to deal with almost anyone."

Manetho pointed at another large man. "What's your name, soldier?"

"Private first class, Menes Akhenaten."

The colonel studied a bloody man lying in the mud with his hands tied behind his back. "Would you gentlemen please pick up Councilman Narmer, here."

Private Nefera rose to his feet. "Yes, Sir."

Akhenaten slipped his assault rifle off his shoulder and leaned down to help. They raised the councilman to his feet.

Councilman Narmer's right eye opened. "You can't get away with this, Smendes."

"Shut up, Narmer." Saite Manetho walked over to the battered councilman. "Narmer, we're going to hang you by the neck until you're dead."

A cynical smile slipped onto his lips. "However, we have a special treat for you. I'm not going to drop you off a horse or a cart or whatever. That would break your neck and you would die almost instantly. There's no fun in that.

"Instead, Councilman Narmer, we're going to raise you slowly so you choke to death. I find that much more entertaining. And entertainment is terribly important, don't you think?" Colonel Manetho smiled. "You always were entertaining, Councilman. This will be your big moment and I, for one, just can't wait."

He beckoned with his right hand. "Bring him."

Nefera took hold of Councilman Narmer's left arm.

The colonel turned to Gerzean. "Walk with me, Corporal. We have something to discuss."

"Yes, Sir." Gerzean moved up next to the colonel. He felt a little uneasy about this strange blond man with the grey eyes.

Ahead of them was a muddy lane between the first two rows of tents. At the end of the lane was a torch in a metal stand jammed into the ground.

Farther ahead was the wooden T next to the bulwarks and, beyond that, was the drawbridge pointing straight upward with support posts on either side. The light there was brighter because there were two torches, one on a stand on either side of the bridge supports.

Earlier Gerzean had been the guard on duty at the bridge, but he had been called to take Narmer down from the T and bring him back to the general's tent. The man was in such bad shape that Gerzean had ordered Nefera and Akhenaten to carry him.

Colonel Manetho had tortured Councilman Narmer. That made Corporal Gerzean wonder about picking up this Mrs. Imhotep. He didn't want to be involved in torturing anybody, especially a woman.

Gerzean had thought several times about just taking off into the woods some night when he was on guard duty. He always had an assault rifle when on guard. That would give him a lot of protection.

Unfortunately, he had left his weapon back at the general's tent. Probably it was this whole thing of worrying about what Smendes would do. He could get the assault rifle later.

Of course, the ammo would be gone. The other army guys were stealing ammo all the time now. Everybody was running short. They were all kind of nervous about it. Oh, there was plenty of pistol ammunition, as far as he could tell. It was the assault rifle ammo that was short.

He and the colonel reached the clearing at the end of the row of tents.

Colonel Manetho stopped and turned to face him. "Corporal, what I understand is that you were the guard at the drawbridge when the Imhoteps left the colony yesterday." The empty grey eyes scrutinized his face. "Is that right, Gerzean?"

"Yes, Sir."

The colonel nodded. "Yes, that's what I was told. Why did you let them out of the colony?"

Corporal Gerzean could feel his throat tighten. "There was a girl out in the woods, Sir. She was on my check list, but she hadn't come back from working in the garden.

"I couldn't go into the woods to look for her because I had guard duty at the drawbridge. The Imhoteps said they'd get her. I figured they'd be right back."

"Didn't you know that General Smendes was going to pick up the Imhoteps for questioning after Narmer?"

"No, Sir." The corporal noticed that Colonel Manetho was smiling and staring at him.

"Corporal, you fucked up. Don't you know that?"

"I don't see how, Sir. I didn't. . ."

"Don't interrupt!"

Gerzean swallowed. "Yes, Sir."

"What punishment should we give you, Corporal?"

Gerzean looked over toward the two soldiers standing next Narmer. Private Nefera's lower face slipped into a sly smile.

A chill darted up Gerzean's spine. He wanted to run, but there was no place to go. The drawbridge was up.

Gerzean had dreaded this moment since the group of soldiers had rushed by him across the bridge and fired into the forest yesterday. It was just after Mister Imhotep and his son had left. Right then, he knew something was terribly wrong. He knew he had made a serious miscalculation.

Colonel Manetho had been there at the bridge too.

"You haven't answered me, Corporal."

Gerzean figured he had nothing to lose. "I don't think I deserve any punishment, Sir. I followed protocol."

"Don't insult my intelligence, Corporal!" The colonel stabbed Gerzean's chest with his right index finger. "You will drag Mrs. Imhotep out of her tent. I want her to see Narmer die. Maybe that will improve her attitude."

It was something like cold water running down Gerzean's back. At this moment all of it became brutally clear. He saw how it was going to be.

They would hang Narmer. Then they would beat up Mrs. Imhotep and maybe do worse things. Then maybe hours later they would kill her, maybe even hang her too.

But who would kill Mrs. Imhotep?

Now the answer to this question became all too clear. Of course, he would be ordered to do it. Then, obviously, they would kill him. Probably Manetho would do that.

Gerzean couldn't see himself killing this woman. He had noticed her around the colony. She was in her forties and somewhat attractive, if you thought a woman in her forties was attractive. She was a mother and a wife, much like his mother.

However, his mother was up there on the starship, Pod One, Level One, Compartment eighty-six. His father had died several years back of a sudden brain hemorrhage. They said it had to do with the reduced gravity aboard the starship and some genetic defect.

"The Imhotep tent is right over there, Corporal Gerzean."
Colonel Manetho pointed. "Go get her."

"Yes, Sir." The answer had been automatic. However, now Corporal Gerzean's mind was working. When he realized that he was going to die, his thinking gained a new precision.

He stopped in front of the tent. He glanced over his left shoulder toward the blond-haired colonel.

"Get her, Gerzean."

The young corporal unstuck the Velcro flap of his holster and pulled out his pistol. He held it up in his right hand and snapped back the slide. There was a loud "click" in the silence.

"Who is it?" said a female voice from inside the tent.

Gerzean pulled back the flap and leaned down. "Good evening, Mrs. Imhotep." He crouched low and stepped inside. Then he stood upright.

In the dim light of the one lantern, Isis Imhotep placed a paper plate with a half-eaten sandwich down on a folding table. "Have you heard anything from my husband?"

"No we haven't, Ma'am." Gerzean moved closer. He glanced over his left shoulder toward the loose tent flap. "Ma'am, Colonel Manetho wants to see you for questioning."

"Why would he want to question me?"

"You're about the same age as my mother."

Isis Imhotep smiled. "From the sound of your voice, I'd say that you haven't seen your mother for awhile."

"No, I haven't, Ma'am. She's aboard the starship." Gerzean cleared his throat. "You seem like a nice lady, Ma'am, so let me be completely honest with you." Gerzean hesitated. For her sake, he had to get this just right. "The colonel will try to beat information out of you."

The woman's warm smile eclipsed. "I don't understand."

"They want to know where your husband is."

"He's. . ."

The corporal raised his left hand. "Don't."

"I was just about to tell you."

The young corporal nodded. "They'll kill you anyway, Ma'am," he whispered. "They'll kill you no matter what."

"But why?"

Gerzean shrugged. "Maybe they're crazy," he whispered.

Gerzean took in a deep breath. "I'm going to do you a big favor, Ma'am." He raised the pistol.

Isis Imhotep stared at him. "Is that what they ordered you to do?"

Corporal Gerzean put his finger to his lips. "Shhh! Listen." He stepped forward and leaned close to her left ear. "I'm going to walk you outside in front of me with my gun drawn. When I say the word, 'Down,' you drop to the ground. Got it?"

He stepped back and looked into the soft brown eyes.

"What are you going to do?"

Gerzean put his finger to his lips. "Shhh."

The tent flap opened and Colonel Manetho's head appeared. "Corporal, bring out Mrs. Imhotep."

Gerzean turned. "Yes, Sir."

The tent flap dropped.

Gerzean waved the pistol. "Get in front of me, Ma'am."

"Are you sure you want to do this?" she whispered. "Can't we reason with them? I don't know anything."

Gerzean shook his head. "It won't work, Ma'am. This is the only way."

Her eyes searched his. Then she said, "I trust you."

"When I say 'Down,' you drop." Gerzean made eye contact. "Got it?"

"Yes."

"Ready?"

The woman's eyes looked into his. "Yes."

"When you get outside, stop. Don't move. I need you to cover my pistol."

She turned and walked across to the tent flap. She bent over and stepped through the opening.

Gerzean was close behind her.

Once outside, he spotted the colonel off to his left.

Manetho smiled. "Good evening, Mrs. Imhotep. So good to see you. We thought we'd provide a little entertainment for you." He nodded toward Councilman Narmer. "We're going to hang the councilman. I thought you'd like to watch."

"Down!"

Mrs. Imhotep dropped.

Gerzean aimed and fired at the colonel's chest.

"Pop!"

He fell backward.

Gerzean swung around and crouched. He fired. "Pop!"

Nefera fell against a tent.

Private Akhenaten swung his assault rifle.

Gerzean aimed and fired.

"Pop!"

Akhenaten dropped backwards.

Gerzean grabbed Mrs. Imhotep's arm. "Come on!"

She scrambled to her feet.

Gerzean moved over to Narmer, grabbed his bayonet out of his own belt and cut the ties on Narmer's wrists. "Come on, Councilman, we have to get out of here."

The battered man shook his head. "No. I can't make it. Give me one of those assault rifles."

Gerzean rushed across to Akhenaten and slipped the rifle out of his hands. He ran back and handed it to Mrs. Imhotep. "Come on. Let's get going."

Gerzean helped the councilman to his feet and led him out into the open in front of the drawbridge.

When they were part way across the opening, Narmer dropped to one knee. "I can't go any farther. Give me that rifle."

Gerzean lowered him to the ground and handed him the assault rifle.

Narmer looked up at him out of his right eye. "You get that drawbridge down. Use a knife to cut those ropes."

Gerzean stood upright. He glanced around. Among some shovels, rakes and chainsaws lying along the side of the trench he spotted an ax.

He charged over to the tools and grabbed the ax.

Mrs. Imhotep was standing next to the drawbridge.

Gerzean ran over to the drawbridge crank. He raised the ax above his right shoulder and swung the flat end against the wooden chock in the gear wheels.

The chock flipped into the air.

The gear wheels whirred and the bridge landed with a loud "thump." Dust billowed upward.

Gerzean heard the "stutter" of automatic weapon fire.

Bullets whizzed around him.

Gerzean dropped the ax. "Come on!" He grabbed the torch out of the stand and ran.

There was the "stutter" of an automatic weapon. Narmer was firing at an advancing trio of men.

Gerzean charged across the bridge. When he reached the grass, he stepped off to the side and crouched behind the bulwarks.

Isis Imhotep ran off the end of the bridge.

A man appeared in the opening and raised his assault rifle.

Gerzean aimed his pistol. "Pop!"

The man jerked backward as if stunned. He raised his weapon again.

Gerzean fired twice. "Pop! Pop!"

The man dropped.

Gerzean threw the torch onto the bridge. Flames shot upward.

Mrs. Imhotep was next to him now.

"Come on!" He swung around and ran as fast as his legs would move.

There was a "stutter" of automatic weapon fire.

Something smashed into Gerzean's left shoulder. He stumbled and fell.

Isis Imhotep crouched next to him. "Get up!"

He scrambled to his feet. There was a terrible burning ache in Gerzean's left shoulder.

He could see the forest just a few feet ahead. If they could only make it into the cover of the trees.

CHAPTER TWENTY-NINE
"The History"

Starship Hope
Pod 2
Level 3
Compartment 775
4M, Day 4, 96 A.D.
9:23 a.m.

Naomi Imhotep poured coffee into Ramses's mug. She marveled at the fact that she automatically poured it half way up. They had lived in this sixty percent gravity for almost fifty years. Now, all of this was a habit.

The time had raced by. Back on Mars, she had been that struggling student, working on her studies at home in a locked bedroom at night. She could never have imagined all these events in her life. Back then, her whole focus had been making it through her classes at University Five – just surviving the process.

She had become more contemplative of late. She often wondered what had happened to her brother, Sile. He had died, certainly. The whole planet of Mars had died after this starship left.

She remembered Sile fondly. He had been her hero – a wonderful brother who had protected her.

Her mother and father had been another matter – both alcoholics. Now, all these years later, she could forgive them some of the time. At other moments, she wondered why she should. She certainly wouldn't forgive them if they were just anybody she happened to know. Then she would consider them losers.

That whole business with her father had tainted her for the rest of her life. Luckily she had married this very sweet, gentle person, Amun Imhotep, and she loved him today as much as she ever had. Now that she was in her seventies, Naomi was convinced that love had more depth – was somehow richer than it had been years ago.

She and Amun had been allowed only one child aboard the starship and they had named him Aten, after his grandfather, the man who had designed these compartments.

"You're awfully quiet, Dear."

Naomi turned to her husband. Then she shrugged. "Just thinking back to when all of this started."

Farther down the counter, Ramses Tutan put his coffee mug down and swallowed. "A whole lifetime ago. If Amun's father hadn't adopted me, I wouldn't have gotten here."

Amun smiled. "Naqada wouldn't have let that happen."

Naomi put her hand on Amun's arm.

"What wrong? We can talk about it, can't we?"

She looked farther down the counter. "Is it all right with you, Ramses?"

He shrugged. "Sure."

"So, how are you doing, anyway?"

"I'm all right. It's strange. . . we all have this built-in desire to survive, but lately I've sort of wanted to get this over with. I don't mean to be morbid or anything. I just miss Naqada. I guess I believe underneath it all that I'll see her again, once this is over."

Amun leaned back and folded his arms. "I don't believe in that kind of thing – the afterlife. We just die."

Naomi patted his arm. "Please, Honey, let's not talk about it. Okay?"

Amun looked at his wife and smiled. "I'm sorry."

"How is that history project coming, Naomi?"

She put her fork down and turned to Ramses. "We've stored almost all of our Mayan history, including the journey across the galaxy. Now we're working on things that have happened since we've arrived here in this solar system."

Ramses leaned forward on the counter. "Do you think you'll finish?"

Naomi nodded. "I think so. Of course, one of the problems is that we've lost much of our communication with the planet Hyksos and our people down there. The past few days there haven't been any calls at all."

"I'm not getting any new updates from Colonel Ra. I wonder why."

Amun shrugged. "Maybe he's just very busy. They were having trouble with those native people, weren't they?"

"They were attacked that one time. The last I heard from the colonel he was going out with a patrol to retrieve his generator."

"If they don't get that back, things are going to become very tough, I would think."

Ramses looked at Amun. "Yes, very tough – no electricity. Those batteries in their communicators will only last so long. If they could use those solar batteries on the translators in their other devices, then they might be all right."

Amun shook his head. "I don't think so. If I remember correctly, those are two separate systems."

"True. I haven't heard from Intef either, by the way. Have you heard from Aten and his wife?"

"No, we haven't. I'm assuming it's because of the battery situation. Once they get that generator up and running again, we should be hearing from them."

Naomi thought it was time for something more pleasant. "I've made some blueberry shortcake for desert. Do you want some, Ramses?"

"Heck, yes. Where did you get the blueberries?"

"I know the manager of the hydroponic farm."

Ramses grinned. "It's still who you know, isn't it?"

Naomi rose out of her seat and picked up her plate, then her husband's. "In this instance, it definitely is."

She started to move, but then stopped and dropped the plastic plates to the countertop.

"Are you all right, Honey?"

Naomi opened her eyes. "It's this thinner air."

Ramses pushed his plate across the counter toward her. "They've cut the oxygen by seven percent. Trying to make it last."

"Do you want whipped cream on your shortcake, Ramses?"

He smiled. "Absolutely."

"How about you, Dear?"

"Sure."

Naomi picked up the plates and carried them toward the sink. Here she was being very domestic for a change. It was kind of nice, actually. It was almost like those meals back at the Imhoteps' condo on Mars fifty years ago. Too bad Naqada couldn't be here.

CHAPTER THIRTY
"The Journal"

Hyksos
The Colony
4M, Day 4, 96 A.D.
10:03 p.m.

General Abydos Smendes swung around in front of three rows of men. "Attention!"

The troops snapped their heels together and stood with straight backs, the butts of their assault rifles rested on the ground next to their right boots and the barrel ends held with the tips of their fingers next to their right legs. Off to the left stood a small group of men holding crossbows.

"Some of you guys fucked up real bad the other night! You let Gerzean and that Imhotep woman get away! So we're gonna use this here problem to our advantage. We're gonna solve this here Hyksos problem once and for all!" He turned and strode down the row of men, eyeing each face.

At the eastern end of the row was the wooden T next to the bulwarks a few feet north of the drawbridge. Tied to the T was a man's body. It looked strange in the shadowy flickering light of the torch jammed into the ground next to it.

The general turned. He stopped and studied the scarecrow-like figure tied to the wooden T with its arms drooping and the bloodied head hanging down.

Smendes' face broke into a smile. Narmer was out of his hair for good. The mouthy, old asshole was dead and now he, General Abydos Smendes, could carry on and do things like they ought to be done. He wouldn't have to listen to that fucking old windbag anymore.

The general pivoted around and faced the line of men again. "We're gonna solve our problem by wipin' out that upriver Hyksos village tonight. We'll capture Gerzean and that Imhotep woman. Then we're gonna kill every one of them little orange-haired runts and then. . . we're gonna burn that village to the ground!

"When I get through with those little shits, there won't be a single one alive! We did it to that other Hyksos village downriver and now we're gonna do it to this one!"

Smendes pointed off to his left. "We have our new crossbow unit with us tonight. They'll be movin' out ahead of us and they'll take out those little bastards hidin' up in the trees before they know what happened!"

"I figure the guys in our unit who fucked up the other night ought to get out there and kill themselves some of those little orange-haired assholes! Fact is, for each Hyksos any of you kill, cut off a left ear so you have proof and I'll give you a six-pack of beer for each one."

Smendes scanned the faces up and down the first row. "The men who fucked up know who they are. So get out there and make up for the mess you made! And all of you bring me back some of them ears!"

He turned to the man at the near end of the row. "Captain Khufu, move them out."

Captain Avaris Khufu hustled out in front of the troops. "Crossbow unit, move out double-time, Assholes."

The small unit carrying the antiquated weapons trotted double-time in front of the rest of the troops and crossed the muddy field to the drawbridge. Their boots thumped in a sporadic rhythm as they tromped across the wooden bridge.

As Smendes watched them, he took pride in this unit he had created. He could just imagine Colonel Ra, the wimp, creating a unit like that. He'd probably create a negotiating unit that would sit around and fucking talk all night. What a pussy that guy was.

Well, good old Colonel Ra had led the small squad toward the Hyksos village downriver, and guess what? He got ambushed. No surprise there. The man was a fucking wimp.

General Smendes was sure the smart thing to do was to wipe this bunch of little orange-haired runts upriver off the face of the planet. That way he wouldn't have to worry about those little assholes attacking the colony anymore. What's more, people who fucked up here wouldn't have a place to run and hide either.

"General. . ."

Smendes turned. "Yes, Khufu, what is it?"

"Sir, what do you want me to do?"

"Hang close to me, Captain. I may have some special work for you to do. When we find that Gerzean, we're gonna make him pay for turnin' traitor. Traitors are the lowest animal on the face of this planet, Khufu."

Captain Avaris Khufu nodded. "I agree, Sir. What about that Imhotep woman and the rest of the Mayans?"

Smendes smiled. "We'll have somethin' special for them, too." He turned around and checked the group of men crossing the bridge. "Tell the men to keep it quiet. No radio unless necessary." He turned to the young officer. "Got that, Khufu?"

"Got it, Sir."

"Then let's get out there and do this." Smendes stepped onto the bridge. He had a good feeling about this raid tonight. After all, his men had night-vision goggles and those guys up front with the crossbows should be able to take out any sentries posted in the trees around the village.

As they moved across the muddy field, the general stopped and pivoted around. Sometimes he liked to look at the colony from the outside.

He had made that place what it should be. Someday, far into the future, people would appreciate what he had done. Maybe they would write it down in the Mayan history books.

With a thing like that you couldn't just wait for it to happen or take your chances that somebody would write it down. What he would have to do tomorrow or maybe the next day is find himself someone in the unit or one of the civilians in the colony who could write pretty well. Then he would have that person begin writing a journal.

Hell, he could keep a journal himself. You couldn't leave these things to chance. He was going to have to write some of this stuff down. After all, this should be recorded so people in the future would know how much good he had done for the Mayan people.

You'd never know about great men unless you could read it, so the thing you had to do was to get it written down. Then someday he might be talked about in Mayan history classes. That would be the absolute coolest thing of all.

CHAPTER THIRTY-ONE
"The Escape"

Hyksos
Forest
4M, Day 4, 96 A.D.
Night

Isis Imhotep didn't know how long she could continue to help Corporal Gerzean walk. He had been leaning on her for what seemed like hours. She didn't know how long it had been. These days she had no way of telling time – no wrist controls anymore.

In some situations, like this one for instance, maybe it was better not to know how much time had elapsed. The only thing that gave her a sense of the passage of time in this dark forest was the Man Moon.

It had risen in the east a while ago. At least with the rising moon she had a better sense of direction. She knew the river was off to her left. She couldn't see it. The trees hid it from sight, but she could hear it.

Isis was aware that the river traveled in a north to south direction, approximately. She knew generally where she was going.

She was getting really tired carrying Corporal Gerzean's arm around her shoulders and supporting his weight. "I'm going to have to put you down for awhile, Corporal."

"Understood," he whispered in a breathy voice.

When she lowered him to a fallen tree trunk, he made a grunting sound.

"Sorry," she whispered.

"It's okay." He held out his pistol. "Here, take this. I'm afraid I'm gonna pass out and drop it." He pressed a lever next to the handle and the clip dropped out.

He stuffed the empty clip into a small container on his cartridge belt. Then he pulled out a new clip and slipped it into the black gun's handle. He snapped back the slide, and then lowered the hammer.

Gerzean held the gun out to Isis. "Here, keep this. You may need it."

Isis clasped onto the heavy pistol with her right hand.

Gerzean pointed. "You cock back the hammer and it's ready to fire. Okay?"

Isis shrugged. "I guess."

"Mrs. Imhotep, I can't go on anymore. You're gonna have to go to the Hyksos village and get help."

The cool breeze swept the choral croaking of frogs up through the tall trees from the river valley to their left.

Isis wondered how she had gotten herself into this situation. Here she was with a wounded man, fleeing toward a village with people who didn't even speak her language. "Well, maybe I'd better get going. I don't know if the army people are following us or not."

Corporal Gerzean winced and moved slightly. "Lots of pain in that shoulder. As far as Smendes goes, I don't know. My gut tells me he'd come tomorrow, but maybe I'm wrong."

"Are you okay?"

Gerzean slid off the log to the ground and leaned back. He winced. "God that hurts."

"Maybe I shouldn't leave you."

"No, you have to go. Get some help. Tell them to bring a horse or something."

Holding the heavy pistol in her right hand, Isis moved off into the dark toward what she thought was the north. The moon was off her right shoulder. She would have to work to keep it there because when you moved through these woods you had to take detours around all kinds of obstacles.

She wondered what kind of reception she would have in the village. Of course, her son, Khons, apparently had his eye on a girl in that same village, so it seemed that they accepted him.

Isis didn't know how she felt about that girl. One side of her said that these people were primitive. They were at least hundreds, more likely thousands, of years behind the Mayans. The Hyksos girl was hard to accept, especially when it came to her own son.

On the other side of the equation was the reality of their situation. They were living in rather primitive conditions themselves and it looked like those conditions might even become more primitive as time went on. They had no electricity and no running water. Perhaps she should adjust her thinking to accommodate these new realities.

When the Hyksos warrior came upon her she was completely surprised.

The Hyksos grabbed her arm and put his finger to his lips, as if to tell
her to be quiet. He was wearing a translator on his left ear. He tapped it
twice.

She shook her head. "I don't have one," she whispered.

He checked both her ears and nodded. Then he led her north
through the forest.

What struck Isis as almost miraculous was how fast this little man
moved among the trees. She had difficulty keeping up with him.

When they neared the village, the Hyksos cupped both of his hands
around his mouth and sounded a ululation into the night.

Another ululation echoed back through the trees. He motioned to
Isis.

She followed him down a long sloping hill toward a village. When
she stepped into the clearing several warriors appeared.

"Mom!"

She turned. It was Khons and her husband Aten. "Corporal Gerzean
is out in the forest wounded."

Khons was wearing a translator. He spoke to the man who had
brought his mother into the village. "Zeus, there is a wounded man out
there in the woods. We have to bring him in."

Zeus said something in his own language.

"Mother, were there any men following you?"

Isis shrugged. "I don't know."

Khons turned to the Hyksos. "She doesn't know."

Zeus walked away and spoke to one of the other warriors.

A pretty, red-haired Hyksos female moved up next to Khons and
slipped her hand into his.

He smiled at her. Then he turned to his mother and handed her his
translator.

Isis slipped it onto her ear.

"Mom, this is Athena."

The girl smiled at her and made a finger wave. "Good to meet you,
Khons' mother."

Isis noticed that three men were leaving the village with a horse. They
were headed south. She assumed they were going after Gerzean.

Athena pointed at one of the warriors. "He is my father. He is Diomedes, the best hunter in the tribe."

Isis looked toward the man's back as the three men left the village.

"Mom, they are going after Gerzean." Khons nodded toward the black pistol in her hand. "By the way, why are you carrying a gun?"

"Corporal Gerzean gave it to me."

"Put the thing away, Mother."

Isis slipped the pistol into the waistband of her jeans. "There. Is that better?"

"Much better. I need my translator." He reached out his hand.

His mother slipped it off her ear and handed it to him.

Her husband moved up closer. "What happened back at the colony, Isis?"

"Smendes tortured Narmer. He was going to take me into custody, but that Corporal Gerzean saved me. We escaped, thanks to him."

"Did Smendes' men follow you?"

Isis shrugged. "I don't know. I don't think so."

Aten frowned. "Smendes has to be stopped." He looked at his son. "We should go back there tomorrow, Khons, and confront him. He can't go on doing these things."

"That won't stop him, My Dear."

Aten turned to his wife. "This is preposterous. He has no right to do things like this."

Isis nodded. "I know, but he's doing them anyway. Apparently he doesn't care what anyone thinks."

"Well, we'll see about that."

Zeus suddenly appeared at the edge of the village.

Khons pointed. "Something's wrong."

The small man rushed across the open area next to the fire. He said something to Khons.

Khons turned to his father. "Dad, Smendes and his army are coming. Get that book. Zeus is going to lead us into the forest."

"Do you think I really should take the book?"

"Absolutely."

Aten hurried away.

Khons motioned to his mother. "Come on, Mom, we'll grab some food."

Zeus shook his head and said something in his own language. Then he led them across the village to the east end. He crouched down and looked back.

There was a ululation high in the trees.

Something crashed down through the branches and landed with a "thump" in the brush at the edge of the village.

Aten hurried across the open area toward the small group.

Zeus led them into the dark forest.

Khons and Athena were directly behind Zeus as he moved swiftly through the darkness.

For a while, Isis held onto her husband's hand. Soon, however, it became obvious that it would be easier to travel in single file.

Aten fell back behind her.

CHAPTER THIRTY-TWO
"The Small Flashlight"

Hyksos
The Forest
4M, Day 4, 96 A.D.
Night

Khons was glad his mother had finally met Athena. Sure his new girlfriend wasn't exactly what she had planned for him, but he was hoping his mother would see how cool Athena really was.

Unfortunately, out here in the woods at night with Smendes looking for them was not a good way to get to know someone.

Athena stopped suddenly. She pointed to her right.

Khons started to open his mouth.

She put her finger to her lips.

Now he knew what she was telling him. There were people over to their right in the woods. Khons had not heard a thing, but of course, he had not learned how to notice these sounds.

He was always amazed by what the Hyksos could do. They could climb trees like nothing he had ever seen and they could hear the smallest noises long before any Mayan could.

The distant stutter of automatic weapon fire echoed throughout the forest.

Khons' instinct was to drop to the ground, but that assault weapon was back at the village. He did not want to think about what Smendes might be doing to those poor people. There were women and children.

He wished he could help them, but what could he do? He was out here in the forest and he was unarmed.

Zeus crouched suddenly.

Athena motioned for Khons to get down. He dropped to one knee and turned to his parents.

His mother started to speak. Khons shook his head and put his finger to his lips. Then he pointed off to the right.

Athena quietly moved around to the rear of the group.

Khons followed her.

When she stopped, she indicated with her hands that she wanted to be at the back of the line with him in front of her.

Then Khons understood. She was indicating that there should be a Hyksos on both ends of their small group. He supposed it was a way of protecting them better.

After several seconds of waiting, Zeus rose to his feet and moved forward. He had his crossbow in his left hand with an arrow already in the slot.

Khons assumed that Zeus sensed that they were close to Smendes' people.

What happened next startled Khons. He heard a subtle "zip."

Zeus fell.

Athena grabbed Khons and pulled him into a bush.

There was another "zip."

"Oh!" Aten dropped.

Khons looked around for Athena. She had disappeared.

He lunged out of the bush to help his father.

His mother was standing with the pistol held up, aimed toward the treetops. She was moving around slowly in a circle.

There was another subtle "zip."

Something heavy crashed down through a tree off to the left.

Athena appeared out of the woods on the left. She was carrying a crossbow and a quiver of arrows was slung by a loose leather strap across her left shoulder. "Take your father down toward the river. There are caves," she whispered.

The arrow in his father's back didn't look very deep. Khons reached for the arrow and pulled hard.

"Ugh!"

The arrow didn't move.

"Sorry, Dad," he whispered. Khons lifted his father to a sitting position with his mother's help. Then he crouched down onto his knees. "Put him on my back," he whispered.

Athena and his mother struggled with the limp body and they moved his father upward so that he was lying on his stomach across Khons' back.

Khons grabbed onto one of his father's arms and one leg. Then he struggled to his feet.

Athena leaned close to his ear. "I will stay behind and look for more of the enemy. You be careful, My Man."

Khons looked into the pretty eyes under his father's limp body. "You be careful, too."

"I will be fine. I killed the man who shot your father. I will hide up in the trees and look for more of these men who kill Hyksos." Athena moved off into the shadows. Then she disappeared into some brush.

Khons struggled forward with the huge weight on his back.

His mother walked ahead of him with the pistol in her hand.

Khons was sure she didn't know how to use it, but the noise might be a deterrent. Luckily she hadn't shot it when his father was hit with the arrow. Smendes' men would know where they were.

The journey to the river bank seemed to take forever. The ground was uneven and several times Khons lurched and almost dropped his father. He was sure that if he did drop him, he and his mother could never get his father up again.

At the river bank they found a formation of rocks that rose up into the dense trees.

Still holding onto his father, Khons motioned for his mother to come near. "You find a cave," he whispered. "I'll wait here."

His mother nodded her assent. She handed the pistol to Khons and moved away.

He held it up in the shadowy moonlight. She hadn't even cocked the hammer back. At least he knew enough to do that, but he was not about to cock it now. If he heard something, then he might.

Khons' original idea was to wait with his father across his back until his mother returned. However, after several minutes of holding the weight, he could stand it no longer.

He dropped down to his knees and eased his father off face down into the bed of leaves.

The night was filled with the noises of insects and frogs and the gurgle of the river.

In the white of the moonlight, his father looked like a little boy sleeping on his stomach.

For Khons, his father had always been there, no matter what. He did wonder, however, if this time things might be different. It felt like his entire life had turned upside down.

Most of all, Khons was worried. If his father stayed out here in this forest without medical attention, what would happen?

"Up here," his mother whispered.

"Help me."

His mother moved closer.

He handed her the pistol. "Take this," he whispered. "By the way, for it to work, you have to cock back the hammer."

"I knew that."

Khons bent down. "Okay. Help me drag him. I can't pick him up again."

Khons grabbed onto his father's left arm and his mother the right. They dragged him on his stomach up a sloping leaf-strewn path of black rock next to a rock wall with juts and crevasses.

When they were half way up, his mother stopped. "This is hard work," she whispered. "Not much farther." Isis Imhotep rose to full height and rubbed her back. "Your young woman friend is very pretty, Khons," she whispered.

"She's a good person, too, Mom. I know she's not what you had in mind for me, but things have changed a whole lot."

"True, she's not what I had in mind, but you're right – things have changed."

"I was thinking of a career as a history teacher. Obviously that's not going to happen."

"Maybe you can keep our history alive. Maybe you can write some of it down – write your own journal."

Khons nodded and looked up at the Man Moon, now almost two-thirds of the distance across the star-filled night sky.

"Let's get at it," said his mother. "I want to hide him where he'll be safe."

As Khons leaned to grab onto his father's left arm, he wondered about his mother's statement. How could his father be safe out here? The big thing was to get him some medical help, and, obviously, it couldn't be Smendes' people.

It would have to be the Hyksos tribal medicine man. From what Athena had told him, these medicine men knew a lot of cures.

Minutes later, his mother stopped. "We're here," she whispered.

Khons looked around. "Where?"

His mother pushed a bush aside. "Back here."

In the moonlight, Khons could see a small opening in the side of the rock.

"I've been inside already. There's nothing in there. It looks like some-one used it some time in the past, but not recently."

His mother flicked on a flashlight.

"No!" Khons whispered.

The light went out.

He motioned toward the bush. "Move that out of the way."

His mother stood off to the side and wrapped her arms around the tangle of bush. She pulled back.

Khons grabbed both of his father's arms, crouched low and moved backward step-by-step into the cave.

A flashlight glared in his face.

Now he could see where he was going. Actually this cave was quite large. Three or four people could sleep in here.

He pulled his father back toward the wider area deeper in the cave.

When Khons felt his father was far enough inside, he released the arms and sat down to rest.

His mother moved inside with her small flashlight. "I kept this with batteries. I suppose I should have given them to the army like everyone else did, but sometimes I'd wake up in the night and it would be so dark it would scare me."

Her soft brown eyes looked over toward the cave entrance. "I used to get out one of my old paper books and read with this flashlight."

She turned to Khons. "It was a form of comfort for me in this strange world we came to. I'm not a nature lover. I don't like snakes and frogs or bears and wolves. I'd rather be back on the starship."

She smiled at Khons. "I came down here for you and your father. He said that maybe someday I could go back up to the starship if I wanted – when we got very old. He said that he would go up to visit me now and then."

She stared down at her husband's body lying in the dirt on the floor of the cave. "I don't think that's ever going to happen." She smiled. "Your father gets these ideas in his head and he holds onto them – like that his-tory of the Mayan people. He has it tucked inside his shirt."

"Dad needs help, Mom. I'll find Athena again. She knows the tribe's medicine man. He can get that arrow out of his back."

"I don't want some primitive medicine man working on my husband."

"Mom, we can't take him to Smendes. He'll kill all of us."

His mother nodded several times. "Yes." She looked at Khons. "You'd better find her. She might be in some danger."

"Don't worry, Mom, she's just fine." Khons stood up and bent over below the cave's low ceiling. "Do you have some water?"

His mother pulled a half-empty water bottle out of her jacket. "Yes, I have a little. I can always go down to the river if I have to."

Khons smiled at his mother. The next thing he did without thinking. Months after this, he would wonder if he had experienced some kind of premonition at this moment.

He leaned and kissed his mother's cheek. "I love you."

Tears appeared in her eyes. "I'm worried about your father."

Khons nodded. "I am too. I'll be back." He moved to the mouth of the cave, and then turned around. "Don't waste the battery." He nodded toward the flashlight.

The light went out.

Suddenly it was very dark. Khons had this overwhelming urge to find Athena. He didn't want her to be captured by Smendes' men.

CHAPTER THIRTY-THREE
"Very Soon"

Hyksos
The Forest
Fourth Man Moon
Night

Athena leaned back against the tree trunk. She had succeeded in wedging her shoulders between two limbs. This way if she dropped off to sleep, she would not fall out of the tree.

Her father had taught her these things. She supposed he did that for her because she was still around the hut. She should have been married about thirty-six Love Moons ago right after she became a full woman, but it had never happened.

Now she had her man. He was very handsome. She touched the translator on her left ear. She liked to wear it even when Khons wasn't near because it reminded her of him.

He didn't know anything about hunting, but he knew other things. Besides, she could teach him about hunting or maybe her father could. That would be even better because then her father would see how smart Khons was.

Her father had yelled at her a lot about Khons. Finally she had just told him that now she had found a man so what was he so upset about?

So what if his skin was brown and his eyes were brown and he was so tall. Did that matter so much? He was handsome so her children would be pretty and he was smart so her children would be smart. He was kind, so he would be good to her. What else did her father want?

Sometimes Athena had wondered if her father might be jealous because Khons' people knew all these magical things her father knew nothing about – like those little fire sticks they could shoot bison with and the big bird that flew them out of the sky and those talk things they used to wear on their wrists. They stopped wearing those because of problems with those things they called batteries.

Besides Khons was cute. In fact, every time she saw him she wanted to rub that little thing where she peed. It would get all tingly down there.

Her mother had told her not to touch that in front of people. She said it was impolite to do that. She said that a woman should let her man touch that little thing and then everything else would happen and there would be sex between them and it would be wonderful and there would be children.

Khons had not touched her that way. She wanted him to, but she wanted to make sure he was truly her man before that happened. Athena knew of this girl in the tribe who had let three different boys touch her and then there had been fights. Athena didn't want that.

Of course, because she was so tall, there hadn't been any boys interested in her all that much. For awhile, Achilles had seemed to show interest, but then he had tried to kiss her once and he had to stand up on his tiptoes. That part he didn't like, or at least Athena guessed that's what happened, because Achilles never came back after that time.

She wanted Khons with her now. This could be the first time they would sleep together – well, not in that way.

Athena grinned in the dim moonlight. She turned her head and looked toward the west. The Man Moon was near the horizon. It would be dawn in awhile. She should get some sleep before then.

In a way she wished she could get out of here. She knew by the sounds she had heard in the woods tonight that Smendes' army men were all over the place.

What had made her want to kill those men was when she saw the huts of the village on fire after Khons had gone. The flames didn't last long. The straw roofs had gone up in a blaze. That meant this Smendes had killed the Hyksos people. He would not make slaves of them. He would be stupid and kill everyone.

Athena had some friends among them, but she hoped they had escaped. Those friends were married and had small children. It made her sad to think that some of the children might have died when this Smendes man attacked the village. Killing children was against all that was good. It was a very bad thing.

A twig snapped in the darkness.

Athena's eyes popped open. Her first natural impulse was to move, but her father had taught her to look first. He had taught her to see what was around you before you moved.

Athena studied the wide expanse of forest beneath the tree. Then to the west, she saw a figure moving toward her. The figure passed through a beam of moonlight. He was a Mayan. She could tell by the dark, straight hair.

She carefully moved forward out of the crotch of the two limbs bracing her shoulders. Then she pulled an arrow out of the quiver on her left shoulder and slipped it into the slot of the crossbow.

At this point something occurred to Athena. Her man was a Mayan. Up here so high, she couldn't tell for sure who was down there.

She would be better off climbing down to the ground and following this intruder to see who he was. She didn't want to shoot Khons. She hadn't even made love with him yet. Besides, why would you shoot a man so handsome and so kind?

She shoved the arrow back into the quiver and slipped the crossbow up her arm to her right shoulder. Then she lay forward so that she could wrap her arms around the tree limb on which she sat.

Once she had a good grip, she swung down to the next tree limb. Before she moved down again, she studied the forest toward the west.

The intruder was getting closer. She would have to move down fast so that she wouldn't be spotted until she was sure who it was.

She leaned and hugged the limb, then swung down to the one below. The next few were close together. She moved around the tree trunk to the opposite side so the intruder wouldn't spot her. Then she stepped down on the closely aligned limbs one after the other.

When Athena reached the last wide limb some eight feet above the ground, she stopped. Then she carefully moved around the tree trunk on the north side, away from this person who was coming.

Once the intruder was close to the tree, she recognized him. "Khons," she whispered.

He stopped and looked around.

"Up here, above you."

He looked up.

She motioned to him. "Come up here with me," she whispered. She pointed to a low-hanging limb. "Use this."

Khons grabbed onto the limb and swung his boots upward.

They landed on the limb.

He pulled himself upward until he was sitting. Then he clambered to his feet.

Athena stepped around the tree trunk to a limb next to him. She leaned close to his ear. "We have to go up and hide very high so we're not seen," she whispered.

When he turned, she kissed his lips and darted her tongue into his mouth.

This was the first time she had done that with her tongue and she liked it very much.

He leaned close to her ear. "My father's wounded. We need to find your medicine man."

"We must wait until dawn to see where Smendes' men are." She motioned with her hand. "Come, follow me." She reached above her head for a limb and pulled herself upward.

For Athena, this was good. Her man was safe and he was with her. Maybe they could sit high up in the tree and hold hands and fall asleep together. There wouldn't be any touching tonight. Maybe some other time very soon.

CHAPTER THIRTY-FOUR

"Buried History"
Hyksos
The Forest
4M, Day 5, 96 A.D.
Early Morning

Aten Imhotep heard his wife's voice before he was aware of anything else.

"Sweetheart, would you like some water?"

Aten opened his eyes. There was dirt against his face and everything was cool and shadowy.

He was aware of bright light some distance to his left. He moved his head. "Yes, water." He rolled over toward his right shoulder.

A sharp pain pierced his back.

Now he remembered - the arrow. He had been shot by an arrow in the dark.

He could now see the oval opening to the cave. There was light outside. He could hear water gurgling. They must be near the river.

"Here."

Aten turned his head farther to the left.

Isis was kneeling next to him. She had a bottle of water. "Here, Sweetie, drink this."

He turned his head farther.

Lukewarm water trickled into his mouth. He had never tasted anything better. The water was so good.

"Can you sit up?"

Aten tried to move.

Pain shot through his back.

He closed his eyes. "God, that hurts!" he whispered.

"I have to leave you, Honey. I have to find a doctor."

Aten opened his eyes. "Where's Khons?"

"He left last night to find that girl, Athena. He said she knew a medicine man who would take out that arrow. He hasn't come back."

"Be careful. Smendes' men."

Isis nodded. "Yes, I know." She turned toward the mouth of the cave. Then she looked at him again. "I'll leave you the water right here, where you can reach it." She placed the plastic bottle next to his left hand.

Her eyes studied his face.

Aten noticed that her eyes were eyes full of concern. He supposed she was worried about him. He would be all right if someone could just get this arrow out of his back.

Then Aten noticed something. He couldn't feel his legs. He wondered about that. Well, maybe it was because he had lain here so long. Maybe it was because of the pain from the arrow.

He tried to move his legs, but he couldn't tell if they moved or not. "Did my legs just move?"

Isis looked down. "I didn't notice anything."

Aten tried again. "Now?"

She shook her head. "No." Then Isis's soft brown eyes focused on him. They were concerned eyes again. Finally, she smiled and the eyes brightened. "I'll get you a doctor."

Aten was going to assure her he would be all right, but he didn't feel like expending the energy to do so. He seemed to have used an awful lot of energy to try to move his legs and now he felt tired again.

He didn't realize that he had closed his eyes until he heard Isis.

"I'll be right back. It shouldn't take me more than fifteen or twenty minutes."

His eyes popped open.

His wife leaned and kissed his cheek.

Aten could smell the faint fragrance of a familiar perfume. Then he watched as his wife moved toward the mouth of the cave, obscuring the bright light.

At the last minute she turned and made a finger wave.

Aten tried to smile. He wasn't sure how much of a smile he had made with his face against the dirt like this.

Now the light at the mouth of the cave was bright again. The sound of rushing water swept in with a faint breeze that moved the limbs of the bush at the opening.

Aten felt at peace. His wife would be back. That's what he held in the front of his mind. But then he considered how weak he was, just laying here like this, and he began to wonder how long his wife would take.

Some other thing drifted into his hazy consciousness just then. It was the possibility that he would stay here and he would drop off into his final sleep right here and there would be peace.

That had a certain appeal. He didn't know why. Perhaps it had to do with nature telling his brain that he was going to expire, bite the dust, leave this life, and pass on. There were so many ways of saying it. "Bite the dust" had a certain relevance. After all, his face was in the dirt.

Then he remembered the plastic enclosed book of Mayan history. It was tucked inside his shirt. He had put it there yesterday for safekeeping.

Now that he thought about it, he could feel the hard plastic rectangle pressed against his abdomen. What if something happened to him? What if Isis never came back? He wouldn't want Smendes' men to take possession of this book. Those animals would probably throw it into a fire or something.

Aten considered the matter. If he buried it, the book would be safe. And if Isis did come back, he could always tell her he had buried it. On the other hand, if she didn't, he wouldn't want all that precious information lost. Smendes would probably burn it in a fire. He was such a beast.

Aten moved up onto his right shoulder.

Pain shot through his back.

He closed his eyes and waited for the pain to ease.

Finally, it receded to a tolerable level.

He unbuttoned his shirt with his left hand, all the way to his waist.

Then he closed his eyes and waited.

Finally, summoning all his strength, he pulled on the soft bag containing the plastic enclosed book.

For several seconds he was sure it wasn't going to move.

Then it jerked free.

Pain shot through his back.

Aten closed his eyes and waited for it to subside. While he lay there with his eyes closed, he had an image of the joy of someone finding this book someday. It would be a great revelation. It would tell the story of where the Mayans had come from and what they had done.

It would tell of the great journey across the galaxy. It would tell of finding this new planet. It would tell everything.

But how was he going to dig a hole to bury it?

Aten's eyes popped open. He scanned the area near his head.

Just above his head, there was a little stick. Maybe that would work to dig a hole.

Aten raised his left hand toward the stick.

Pain shot through his back.

He stopped his hand.

The pain subsided.

He moved his hand again. This time he was braced for whatever came and he was determined to push through it no matter what.

His back came alive with searing pain.

He pushed his hand upward until he clasped the stick. Then, holding it tightly, he lowered his hand.

He had expected the pain to go away.

It didn't. It lingered like a burning, searing thing, as if someone had pushed a hot poker into his back.

"Dig," he whispered. "Forget the pain and dig."

Using the end of the stick, he began scraping the loose sandy dirt away from under his chest. For some reason which he did not completely understand, Aten felt that he must hurry.

Finally, when he stopped to rest, he understood the reason for his haste. He smiled ironically. "Not going to make it, are you, Aten?" he whispered.

Now he was more determined than ever. His left hand scraped and scraped the dirt away from underneath him. He dug and dug and dug.

Then he looked down and gauged the size of the hole and the size of the book. No, he had not dug enough. It did not have to be very deep, but he had to be able to cover it with dirt.

When he had reached a point where he thought he might have dug the hole wide and deep enough, he heard a single gunshot echo in the woods outside. "Pop!"

Then he heard the stutter of automatic weapon fire.

That would be one of Smendes' men shooting someone. An image of Isis passed through his mind, but he waved it off. No, that would have been a single shot, not one of those assault rifles.

He placed the stick where he could easily reach it and slid the book out of his shirt into the hole.

It wasn't perfect but it was a pretty good fit. Now he had to swipe the dirt back over the book to cover it.

He reached out with his left hand cupped and swept dirt back over the book. He swept and swept and swept and swept and swept, until he estimated that it was covered with about two inches.

Now when there was a breeze outside the cave, warm air wafted in through the bush.

Yes, it was getting warmer – probably late morning.

Aten felt tired. Maybe he should just lie down on the buried book and close his eyes. When Isis came, she would wake him.

Even as his eyes closed, he knew there was a distinct possibility that Isis would never return. There was also the possibility that if she did, she might be too late.

What was strange, however, was that Aten wasn't really all that concerned about either scenario. He was just very tired. The arrow in his back didn't hurt anymore, so that was good. Maybe now he could get some rest.

Isis would wake him when she came back.

CHAPTER THIRTY-FIVE
"Fire Stick"

Hyksos
The Forest
4M, Day 5, 96 A.D.
Morning

Khons was dreaming about flying above the forest. He was concerned because it seemed to him that this bird he was riding always wanted to dive like some kind of hawk. The giant bird would swoop down in deep dives barely missing tree limbs.

Now Athena was with him, sitting behind him. He was surprised because he didn't remember her being with him during the other dives.

Unfortunately, this time the bird swooped too low and they were going to crash into a tree. He yelled.

A hand clamped over his mouth.

Khons' eyes popped open.

Athena's face was inches from his. "Shhh. You're making noises," she whispered.

Her hand slipped away from his mouth.

Khons glanced around. He was high in a treetop wedged between two branches waist high and was sitting on a larger branch. He tried to remember how he got here.

"Army men are in the forest," Athena whispered. She pointed downward toward the southeast.

A large man wearing camouflage clothing and carrying an assault rifle made his way through the underbrush in an easterly direction.

The man crouched down and studied something on the ground. Then he rose to a standing position.

Athena moved away from Khons. She pulled her crossbow off her left shoulder, slipped an arrow into the slot and cocked the bow. She held it up in front of her face and aimed.

The man checked the forest, moving his head in a precise arc back and forth. Then he scanned the treetops to the northeast of his position.

Athena followed his movements with the bow.

The man raised his left wrist up near his mouth. With the index finger of his right hand he tapped the surface of his wrist control. "All clear to the east of the village, General."

There was a buzz of static, then a muffled voice.

"Yes, Sir." The soldier tapped the surface of the control with his right index finger.

He then turned as if to go back the way he came and as he turned, his head tipped upward. Then his right arm swung back toward his assault rifle.

"Zip!"

The arrow struck him in the chest.

He fell backward with a crash into the yellow grass.

As soon as the soldier landed, there was another "Zip!"

An arrow struck his neck.

His large body thrashed and rustled in the tall grass and leaves. Then, it stopped.

Athena turned to Khons. "We have to go. They will find his body and know where we are."

"Why did you shoot him?"

"He saw us."

"How could you tell?"

"His right arm moved to raise his fire stick."

"Assault rifle."

"Okay, assault rifle. We have to go."

"What about my parents?"

Athena's blue eyes studied Khons' face. "We will have to come back for them later when the soldiers are gone. We are on the eastern edge of where the soldiers are. We must move farther east into the mountains."

"My dad needs medical attention, Athena. If he doesn't get it, he'll die."

Athena nodded. "Yes, but if we stay here, then all of us will die. There are too many soldiers."

Khons' emotions pulled on him to stay, but he knew Athena was right. Besides, what good would it do his father if all of them were dead? "When can we come back?"

Athena shrugged. "I don't know. Maybe tomorrow. Maybe not tomorrow."

Athena slid her crossbow over her right shoulder and swung down to a limb below. She looked upward. "Come, we must hurry," she whispered.

Khons wiggled forward on the limb until he could free his upper body from the short limbs holding his chest. Then he leaned down onto the limb, wrapped his arms around it and swung his boots down to the next limb.

He glanced below.

Athena was almost down to the last limb above the ground.

Khons dropped onto his butt, then leaned and wrapped his arms around the wide limb. He swung his boots down again.

When he finally reached the lower limbs, he saw Athena. She was holding an assault rifle and an ammunition belt. He wondered why she had taken those off the soldier.

At the last limb, Khons swung down and dropped to the ground.

Athena moved nearer the tree. "Here, take these," she whispered. She held out the assault rifle and the ammunition belt.

"I don't know how to use them."

She grinned. "My sweet, gentle boyfriend. We are at war with these army people. We need everything we can get."

Khons had to admit – this made sense. He reached out and took the belt. When he tried to buckle it around his waist, it was much too large.

Athena rested the rifle against the tree trunk. She grabbed the belt and slung it over Khons' left shoulder, then buckled it down by his waist on the right side. She grinned. "My gentle boyfriend looks like a warrior." She bent down and picked up the assault rifle. "Here."

Khons reached out and grabbed onto the heavy rifle.

Athena pointed at a small lever in front of the trigger guard. "Safety is on." Then she turned around and moved quickly through the tall grass.

When Khons passed the dead soldier, he noticed that the arrow in the man's neck was gone. There was blood all over his neck and shirt front. The flies were buzzing around his open mouth and his neck.

The man's brown eyes were wide open and empty.

Khons turned away. He didn't want to see people who were dead. It made him think of his father and he would rather not think about that. He had to focus on Athena and getting away.

He felt protective about Athena and that was one reason he was willing to move eastward into the mountains. When he considered his sense of protectiveness, it seemed kind of silly. She was very capable of taking care of herself – and even taking care of him, in fact.

Athena moved at a fast walking pace. Every so often she would look over her left or right shoulder. It was as if she expected that somebody was following them.

Khons tried to listen for sounds but he couldn't hear anything above the whir of the tall pines and the sound of his own feet. Every so often, he would stop and listen. He found, however, that this tactic didn't work because Athena would get too far ahead.

Suddenly Khons heard water gurgling. Then he almost stumbled into Athena. She was crouched in a copse of bushes.

He opened his mouth to say something.

Athena had her index finger at her mouth. She motioned for him to crouch down. Then she touched her ear. It was the one with the translator.

Khons was going to reach up and check his translator. Maybe it was loose.

He heard men's voices. He turned his ear toward the sound and listened. They were speaking Mayan - soldiers.

Athena moved over close to him and twisted off the safety on the side of the assault rifle. She then leaned close to his ear. "There may be too many for this crossbow," she whispered. "You will have to shoot your fire-stick."

Khons' skin felt clammy. This was one thing he had never wanted to do – kill people. He looked at the pretty face in front of him. He would have to do this for her, for Athena.

That idea gave him strength. It was strange how these things worked. At this moment, he was sure he was really in love with her.

"Okay," he whispered.

Athena motioned for him to move forward. She pointed at the ground.

She had done that before. Khons recognized it as a warning to avoid stepping on something that would make a noise, like a dried stick.

He moved slowly forward. Then he began to see where the soldiers might be. There was brighter sunshine ahead. That would be the riverbed.

The soldiers might be taking a break. Khons hoped that meant they had put down their assault rifles.

When he reached a point where he could begin to see naked chests and faces, Athena moved away off to his right. A short time later she climbed a tree.

Khons crouched down and waited to see what she would do.

Athena placed herself two branches high in a position where she could see him. She pulled her bow off her shoulder and loaded an arrow into the slot. Then she cocked it back.

She motioned with her arm for Khons to move forward.

He rose to crouching position and stepped carefully through the brush and tall yellow grass. He could feel his knees and legs shaking. His insides were rubbery.

When he reached a row of bushes, he stopped and crouched low. He could clearly see the soldiers now. There were six of them.

He scanned the area to the north, then to the south. There was no one else around as far as he could tell.

Then he looked over at Athena.

She held up her bow and then pointed at him.

Khons raised the rifle butt to his shoulder. He closed his left eye. He had seen soldiers do that in the videos on the starship.

Then he focused his right eye on the short telescope sight. He put the crosshairs on the back of a large soldier.

"Zip."

The sound was so subtle that it surprised Khons.

He squeezed the trigger.

The rifle stuttered and hammered his shoulder. The barrel climbed upward.

The sound echoed in the forest.

He pulled the rifle down, squeezed the trigger and moved the barrel back and forth.

The stuttering echoed again.

He could smell something dusty and metallic.

The stuttering stopped.

Khons snapped the trigger again and again. Nothing.

He lowered the rifle.

He heard moaning.

Now he could see Athena moving through the underbrush toward the bodies lying on the rocks.

"Zip."

The moaning stopped.

Athena stood between him and the bodies. She was beckoning for him to come forward.

Khons rose up to his feet and stumbled through the tall grass. His knees were still shaky and his insides felt like loose putty.

When he reached her, she grabbed the assault rifle and popped out the clip. Then she pulled a clip out of her pocket and shoved it into the slot.

She held the rifle out to him. "We are good together, you and me. We won. They are all dead."

Khons saw a motion out of the corner of his eye.

He grabbed the rifle and swung it to his shoulder. He squeezed the trigger.

Bullets sprayed the trees.

The stuttering of automatic fire echoed throughout the forest.

The man dropped into the clearing.

Khons released the trigger and lowered the assault rifle. He stared at the bare-chested body lying face down in the tall grass.

Then he swung around, first to the left, then to the right. "There may be more."

"Let's go." Athena motioned with her hand.

Khons followed her. He held the assault rifle ready with the safety off.

When he passed the man he had just shot he saw the bare back and the blood and the pistol in the man's hand. The flies were buzzing around the bloody spots on the back.

When he and Athena crossed through the deep, slow-moving river, Khons raised the assault rifle high above his head.

He caught a glimpse of the slaughter off to his left. There were bodies lying across the rocks and there was blood in the creek water. He turned away.

Athena smiled. "My gentle Khons."

Earlier he had been thirsty, but now he would never drink that water. The thought of the blood in the water made him feel sick.

Besides, they had to keep moving. The sound of the assault rifle had probably attracted someone's attention. Of course, in these woods it might be hard to trace its source.

They moved into the foothills. Now the walking became more diffi-cult because they were trekking up the side of a hill.

Khons twisted the safety and swung the strap of the assault rifle onto his right shoulder. It had become obvious to him, because of the encounter with the soldiers at the river, that going back for his father and mother right now would be dangerous, maybe fatal.

What Khons tried to keep in the front of his mind was that his mother was quite resourceful. She would probably find a way to get med-ical attention for his father.

By the time the sun was up in the middle of the sky, they had reached the top of the first mountain.

Khons could see when they were in clearings that the mountains ahead were much higher. He supposed they would have to cross those as well.

From what his grandfather had told him about Olympus Mons back on the planet Mars, these mountains were not nearly as high. He was glad about that. However, they still looked pretty high.

Athena turned to him. "You stay here and I will see if the soldiers are following us." She reached up for a low limb on a pine tree and climbed upward.

Khons had become much more sensitized to the necessity for cau-tion. So while Athena was climbing the tree, he moved into some bushes, knelt down and twisted off the assault rifle safety.

He stayed crouched there, facing west, and he listened. All he could hear was the wind in the pines and the occasional rattling of the leaves on the deciduous trees. There was also the sound of his own breathing.

When Athena came down from the tree she motioned for him to move forward.

He twisted on the safety, slung the assault rifle over his shoulder and walked over to her.

She was waiting for him under the large pine tree. She held out her hand.

Khons looked at her palm. "Nuts?"

"Yes. They are good food. We cannot stop and cook. We must keep going."

"Were there any soldiers following us?"

Athena shook her head. "I didn't see any, but the forest is very thick at the bottom of the mountain. When we go up the next mountain, I will look again."

Khons crunched one of the nuts in his teeth. Then he smiled at her.

"Why are you smiling?"

He shrugged. "You're something else."

"What does that mean?"

Khons narrowed his eyes and thought a moment. "That was a compliment. It means I'm quite impressed with my new girlfriend."

Athena grabbed his shoulders and kissed his mouth. When she pulled away from the kiss, she said, "We will sleep together tonight. But they say it is not good luck to do anything sexual until you are married."

Khons could feel his face heat up.

Athena grinned. "My gentle Khons. I have embarrassed you."

He shrugged. "Yeah, I guess."

"You're cute."

CHAPTER THIRTY-SIX
"Little Blue Planet"

Starship Hope
Bridge
4M, Day 5, 96 A.D.
2:37 p.m.

Ramses stared out the windshield of the starship. He could see this tiny blue-white planet far away in the blackness of space. That was Hyksos.

It made him feel good to look at Hyksos. He knew his daughter Intef was down there somewhere. He missed her. He wondered if she ever did anything about that army guy. As Ramses remembered, his last name was Kamose. Intef seemed so awkward around males. Well, maybe it would work out for her. Ramses didn't care as long as Intef was happy.

He missed her mother too, but if there really was an afterlife, he would see Naqada soon enough.

He had tried to believe in those things for years. He had always found it difficult. It seemed to him that this afterlife idea was the way humans had enabled themselves to deal with their own mortality. Humans feared death, so why not create a myth about something afterward, something better than life?

Ramses didn't know if he believed any of it. Right now, he hoped it was true because he missed Naqada. She had been taken from him so abruptly. What was worse, he had probably been instrumental in her death.

The chance that Naqada had been killed when the meteor struck, before he ejected the pod, was very small. There was no doubt. He had killed his own wife. No matter how many times he had told himself that he had done what any starship commander would have done, he still doubted that decision.

He had gone over and over the possibilities of saving Pod One. When he thought the whole thing through each time, however, he came to the same conclusion. He had been given no other viable choice.

That didn't make it any easier. In fact, believing that even Naqada would have approved of his decision didn't help much either.

Ramses opened his left hand.

Inside was a tiny brown envelope. Everyone had been issued one of these envelopes. In the envelope was a pill. All you had to do was pop it into your mouth and drink some water.

He felt relatively confident that everything was in order. All of it had been organized carefully and all those history records had been stored in that one compartment aboard the starship.

The idea was that the Mayans down on Hyksos would someday find this starship. They would find the records and they would know everything.

Ramses wondered about the importance of these things. Of course, for the Mayan people it was probably important.

Perhaps these future Mayans would find a way to go back to their home planet or even to the planet Earth. Doctor Buhen, the astrophysicist, and Doctor Pithom, the environmentalist, had both affirmed that one day the planet Earth might be habitable.

All of that was in the records. Probably after a hundred or two hundred years have passed, the Mayans down on Hyksos would come back up here and they would find these records. Then they would perhaps make plans to return to their home solar system.

That thought and the possibility that he would see Naqada again were the things that Ramses tried to think about right now. They made him feel better about this thing he had to do.

He slipped the small brown envelope into his left jacket pocket and pulled himself to his feet. Once standing, he waited for his head to clear. The air in this ship was very thin and it smelled foul.

If he didn't take this pill today, he would probably die in his sleep tonight. Suffocating in your sleep didn't sound too good. The pill was a much better idea.

Ramses picked up a half empty water bottle and shoved it into his right side jacket pocket. He would need that in a few minutes.

Holding onto the console in front of him, he shuffled around the end of it. Still holding onto the console, he moved toward the pilot's seat directly in front of the windshield.

Before he reached the low seat, he stopped to let his head clear. Then after several seconds, he shuffled forward.

He dropped down into the pilot's seat and closed his eyes.

What struck him as kind of amusing was that his fear of death was virtually gone. Lately with this thin air, it had been difficult to live on the starship anyway.

Then, of course, he missed Naqada. He was living in a single's compartment. It was a residence which, right from the beginning, had possessed a very temporary feeling.

Of course it had a temporary feeling because it was temporary. Anybody would know that.

Ramses smiled. He was being such an idiot about this. One should try to be noble when one died – do it with some dignity. But honestly, what was dignified about dying?

Of course you should try to do your best at it, if you had the opportunity to make any choices. The choices part would be critical.

With this situation, you had only two choices. You could die naturally, which would be extremely uncomfortable, or you could just pop this pill and take a drink of water. In a few seconds you might feel a little nausea and it would be all over.

Honestly, that wasn't any choice at all.

He opened his eyes.

Outside in the black of space, with the myriad stars, he spied Hyksos again, the bluish planet with a subtle film of white. From their orbit it appeared to be the size of a marble, a blue marble at that.

Beyond Hyksos was a cluster of stars. If he remembered correctly, that was the approximate location of their own solar system, farther out in the next ribbon of the galaxy.

My, they had certainly come a long way, hadn't they? It had taken them slightly over forty-nine years.

As he stared at the small blue marble out in the black of space, he had a good feeling about the future of the Mayan people. They would do great things. After all, they had made a good beginning here. Now it was a matter of holding it all together and moving forward.

He reached into the left side pocket of his jacket and clasped the tiny brown envelope with his index finger and thumb. He slipped out the envelope and placed it on the console directly in front of him.

Then he tugged his bottle of water out of the pocket on the right side of his jacket and twisted off the cap.

The clear liquid sloshed upward. It looked almost as if it were going to leave the bottle neck. The sixty percent gravitation did that kind of thing.

Ramses raised the bottle to his lips and took a small drink. He swallowed carefully. It was so much harder to do these simple things here in the starship when there wasn't enough oxygen.

He carefully placed the water bottle on the console. Then he picked up the envelope and using the thumb and index fingers of both hands, he ripped it open at one corner.

With his right hand he shook out a small white pill into the palm of his left. His face broke into a smile.

It would be good to see Naqada again. In fact, it would be okay with him if he just spent all of eternity dreaming about her.

Ramses raised his left hand and dropped the little white pill into his mouth. Then he lifted the water bottle, tipped it and drank.

The water and pill slipped down his throat.

He placed the water bottle on the console and screwed the cap back onto it.

Then he stared out the starship's windshield at the little blue planet suspended in the black of space.

CHAPTER THIRTY-SEVEN
"Domestication"

Hyksos
The Forest
4M, Day 5, 96 A.D.
Late Evening

Athena chose the place for their camp. It was at the top of a hill with a panoramic view.

Khons assumed it was part of her plan to have a view of the valley behind them. "We will sleep in trees," she told him. "Safer there."

Tree sleeping wasn't one of his big things, but Khons had seen some of the large cats that roamed the wilderness and the wild boar and also some of the constrictor type snakes. In light of all that, sleeping in a tree didn't seem like a bad idea.

He was sure the most important reason for sleeping in the trees was the fear that they were being followed by Smendes' men. To Khons, the reasoning just didn't make sense. Why would those army guys waste time pursuing two people in the forest? Of course, they might assume there were more than just two.

What made Khons even more nervous about this, however, was Smendes, the man. A long time ago, Khons had concluded that this guy was at least neurotic and he was sure neurotic people were not necessarily very logical. In other words, a neurotic might pursue two people for miles into the forest, even when it was totally unreasonable to do so.

That's what worried Khons. It wasn't something he thought about all the time. It was more like this gnawing fear, lurking in the corner of his mind.

Athena held a sharpened stick in her hand. "Let me show you how to dig for roots."

Khons stared at her.

Athena grinned. "We have to eat and we can't have a fire. It would be seen for miles, even the smoke in the daylight." She pushed a bush aside and jammed the stick into the ground. She churned it around and tipped up the side of the bush.

Then she pulled out her knife and cut off the roots. She then tucked them into the pocket of her loose animal skin pants.

She repeated the same process with an adjacent bush. Then she motioned for him to follow her.

Athena led him to a cold mountain stream where she kicked off her moccasins, then strode into the water. She pulled the roots out of her pockets and washed them in the water. Then she walked to the shore and handed them to Khons.

She rinsed off the stick she had used and commenced to sharpen it with her knife. When she had honed it to a sharp point, she slipped the knife into her belt.

"Have you ever eaten raw trout?"

Khons made a face. "No."

"It is really good. But most important, it is good for you. It is good food."

"What are you going to do with that stick?"

"I'm not going to stab you, sweet Khons." She grinned.

"You're pretty."

"Yes I am and you're handsome. We will have beautiful children. Some of them will be white like me and some of them will be brown like you, but they will all be beautiful."

"We aren't married."

"We will be."

Khons was somewhat amused by her confidence. "How do you know that?"

"Because I know you love me and I love you."

"And how do you know that?"

"I see the way you look at me." She turned around and moved into the deeper water near an overhanging sweep of branches. "Besides, we are a good team."

She stopped and became motionless in the knee deep water. "I have to focus on fishing, now. Please do not talk."

Khons laid the assault rifle on the ground and sat down on a rock.

"You should go to the top of that little rise and watch for Smendes' men."

"Sure." Khons rose from the rock and picked up the assault rifle. "If I see something, what should I do?"

"Make a bird sound."

"How would I do that?"

"Whistle."

Khons shrugged. "Sure – okay." He turned around and walked upward to the top of the low rise. When he reached that position, he realized that he couldn't see much.

He checked the sun just above the horizon to the west. It wasn't going to be up very long. Maybe he should walk slightly westward to the edge of that ridge and check the forest down below to the west.

Khons moved across the level ground under huge pine trees. He didn't know why he was going to all this trouble, but something inside urged him on.

Oh, he knew what it was. It was his tendency to worry, to nitpick and fuss over things - always the details. However, the details were really important sometimes.

When he reached the edge of the ridge, he stopped and looked down on the thick forest below. The foliage was so heavy that he was sure he wouldn't be able to see anything, even if there was somebody down there. Besides, it had to be nighttime down that low.

Then he saw something that startled him - a flash of light. He slipped his assault rifle off his shoulder and twisted off the safety.

He tried to think what would cause light down there. It had been just a momentary flash. Was there a mountain stream with an opening to the sky that would cause a reflection?

Khons thought about the country they had walked through today. His head turned toward the south. Yes, the stream was over there, not down here at the base of this hill.

He saw the flash of light again.

Khons raised his assault rifle to his shoulder and put his right eye up against the short telescope sight. He aimed at the area he had seen the light in.

Then after thinking about it, he moved the rifle barrel slightly downward, closer to the base of the hill.

The light flashed in front of his telescope sight and he saw something moving.

He tipped his assault rifle downward. Two figures popped into the opening in the darkness. One was holding a flashlight.

Khons lowered the assault rifle. He had to think about this. They had to be a half a mile away.

He looked up into the trees. There was only a slight breeze, but still it would be a difficult shot. No, he had to tell Athena. She would know what to do.

He ran across the flat area among the pines. He scrambled over the uneven ground and around the huge tree trunks.

When he reached the top of the low hill, Athena was coming out of the stream with a large fish wiggling on the end of her wooden spear.

Khons waved his hands.

Athena jabbed the handle of the spear into the sand. Then she ran up the low hill toward him.

When she was in front of him, Khons said, "There are two men down at the base of the mountain. I spotted their flashlight. They're coming this way."

"Smendes?"

"Yes. I'm sure they're his men."

Athena moved in the direction he had pointed.

Khons stepped in next to her.

"Why didn't you whistle?"

"I was afraid they would hear me."

She smiled. "Good thinking. You're learning."

At the top of the steep hill Khons stopped short of the slope downward. He motioned with his hand. "They're going to be closer."

Athena dropped to her knees and crawled forward. Khons did the same.

When Athena reached a point a few feet from the edge, she dropped to her stomach and crawled.

Khons followed her example. When he reached the edge, he saw nothing. He had learned from Athena, however, to wait and watch.

Then he saw them – two men struggling their way up the hill among the trees. Now they were in more sunlight so the flashlight was out.

One man looked upward.

Khons' first reaction was to duck, but he didn't. Athena had taught him that motion is detected more easily than anything else.

He waited for the soldier to focus on the hill in front of him again, then Khons ducked down.

Athena pulled back and moved over close to him. "It will be dark soon," she whispered. "They will climb to this rise. If they don't know we're here, they will use their flashlight and they will be easy targets."

Khons and Athena crawled several feet away from the edge of the steep hill.

Then Athena rose to her feet and walked back to a stand of trees that was thick. "This will be good cover for us." She pointed at Khons' assault rifle. "Have you checked your clip? I don't think you have much ammunition left."

Khons pressed the lever on the side of the assault rifle.

The clip popped down into his hand. There was one round in it.

Athena slipped the round out and stuffed it into the right front pocket of Khons' jeans. She then handed him the empty clip. "Put this in your belt." She nodded toward the cartridge belt slung across his left shoulder.

Khons pressed each one of the four compartments for clips. The third one was empty. He ripped up the Velcro strip, then slid the empty clip into that compartment and pressed the Velcro strip.

He then ripped open another compartment and pulled out a clip. He snapped it into the slot in front of the plastic stock. Then, just for safety's sake, he ripped open the remaining two compartments. He had two more full clips inside, one in each.

Athena had chosen a tree. She jumped up and grabbed the lowest limb. Then she swung her body upward to a near branch and pushed herself to a sitting position.

"Where do you want me?"

She pointed to a tree some fifty feet away. "There. Find a good branch where you can sleep so you don't have to move."

Khons crossed the space toward the other pine tree. This tree was slightly behind where Athena was located and to the north of her position.

When Khons rose to his feet on the first limb, the upper rim of the sun was just above the western horizon. He noticed that because he knew it would become dark very soon and he wanted to be in a good position in the tree by that time.

Khons pulled himself up to the next grouping of limbs on the huge pine tree. He made sure he was facing west every time he moved. Then he looked for Athena. It took him several seconds, but finally he spied her high in the other tree.

He climbed upward.

At one point a small branch snapped.

Khons stopped and stared toward the clearing at the top of the hill.

He climbed again, going up several levels, each time checking toward the west. He was rather amused because he was sure he would never get this tree climbing thing down, not to the point that Athena had.

Three move levels upward, he stopped and turned once more toward the west.

What he saw startled him.

A light beam flashed back and forth across the ground.

Khons turned around completely. He wanted to sit down, but that wasn't going to be possible.

He knew what Athena was doing. She was holding her crossbow up and taking aim, but she would wait until they were closer.

Khons thought about the safety on the assault rifle. Had he twisted it off? He was trying to remember. He turned the assault rifle slightly so that he could see the safety, but his eyes had been dazzled by the flashlight and he couldn't see it.

After several seconds of wondering about this, he knew he had twisted it off. The assault rifle was ready to fire.

And he must get ready. He raised the assault rifle so that his left arm was resting against the side of a heavy branch. Then he peered through the telescope sight.

It was easy to see the man with the flashlight, but he would have to make sure he got both of them.

He pulled his face away from the sight and checked his arm and his position in the tree. He didn't want the recoil of this thing to make him fall.

He had learned to press the butt of the rifle tightly against his shoulder. The first time he had used it, he had made his shoulder black and blue from the hammering of the stock.

After Khons had checked carefully, he pressed his right eye against the rubber flange around the short telescope sight. He aimed the crosshairs on the man to the right of the man carrying the flashlight. He figured the flashlight guy would be easy to find.

He held the assault rifle like this for what seemed to be an eternity and followed the two men approaching from the west.

He was waiting for Athena, but she was so slow to react this time, that he was wondering if she was waiting for him.

When the two men were less than forty feet from his tree, Khons heard a "Zip!"

A man shouted.

Khons squeezed the trigger.

The assault rifle stuttered and the butt hammered against his shoulder.

Khons swung the rifle back and forth, emptying the clip.

When the stuttering stopped, the echo pulsed throughout the dark forest.

He swung the telescope sight back and forth, trying to see what had happened.

The flashlight lay on the ground casting bizarre shadows across the two bodies in the tall grass.

Khons heard a whistle.

He ducked under the heavy tree limb to his left and aimed the telescope sight in that direction.

In the shadows he caught a spit-second glimpse of Athena moving through the tall grass.

He pressed the lever on the side of the assault rifle.

The metal clip clattered downward out of the tree.

Khons ripped one of the Velcro strips off a clip container. He pulled the clip out, felt for the pointed bullet ends. Then he flipped it around and shoved it up into the slot on the rifle.

He aimed the assault rifle at the two bodies lying on the ground.

Athena was there now.

He could see her through the telescope sight.

She pressed her foot on one of the men's chests and yanked an arrow out. Then she motioned for him to come down.

Khons started to move. He stopped and felt the right side of the assault rifle. He twisted the safety. He didn't want to shoot himself or Athena while climbing out of this tree.

He slung the rifle strap up onto his right shoulder, and then sat down on the limb he was standing on. He lay on the limb and swung his boots down the next level.

He did this all the way down the tree. At the last limb he hung down and dropped the few feet to the ground.

Athena was waiting for him. She was carrying several items in both hands. She handed him a flashlight. "Don't use now. There might be other soldiers."

He stuffed the small flashlight into his left front pocket.

Then Athena handed him four clips of ammunition. She tapped on one of them. "This is not full."

Khons reached into his right jeans' pocket and pulled out the cartridge.

Athena grabbed it, slipped it into the clip and pressed down.

The cartridge popped under the catch on the side of the clip.

She handed the clip to him. "We need all we can get in case there will be more soldiers."

She began to move into the tall grass.

"Aren't we staying here?"

Athena turned. "No."

"Aren't you tired?"

"Yes, but I'm alive. Alive is good."

Khons smiled. "You're right, of course."

Athena began walking toward the east and Khons fell in at her left slightly behind her.

He really admired this girl. She was not only good-looking; she knew how to survive. Besides that, she was a leader. That amused Khons. After all, here was this seventeen year old leading him around like he was a child.

However, she was not only seventeen; she was smart. In fact, when he thought about it, he realized that she was also loyal. Heck, she could have left him out here and, frankly, her chances of surviving alone would be greater than with him tagging along.

Khons was convinced that without him, Athena would be a lot farther in this journey toward the east. He wondered where this place was. All he had ever heard was it was "the place of the big water."

Athena stopped. She clamped her hands onto his cheeks and kissed his lips. Then she said, "We are a good team. Do you want some roots to chew on?"

"What kind of roots?"

She shrugged. "Just roots."

Khons realized that he really should trust this girl. After all, she had taken good care of him so far. "Sure."

CHAPTER THIRTY-EIGHT
"At His Side"

Starship Hope
Compartment 775
Level 3
Pod 2
4M, Day 6, 96 A.D.
8:21 a.m.

Naomi had been awakened by her difficulty with breathing. She didn't know why she hadn't taken the pill before this.

It was probably that old thing about being in control, that attitude of hers about somehow coping with whatever came along. After all, she was the college student who had posed as a college teacher. Obviously she had the temperament to survive.

She had even survived her father and her mother, who were drunks. Young Naomi Nefera had done this. That was her name back then – Naomi Nefera. She had become Thoth Strabo to get aboard this starship. To her amazement, it had worked. Knowing Mister Aten Imhotep had helped. He had been quite influential.

She remembered so well her first impression of her husband's family, the Imhoteps. Here were these people with money and position and, here she was, this kid from a totally dysfunctional home. The Imhoteps could have cared less. They liked her; they welcomed her.

Mister Imhotep had admired what she had done, posing as somebody else to get aboard the starship, even though it was illegal. He had told Amun that very thing.

Naomi heard a noise. She turned on the bar stool. "Is that you, Am. . .?" She ran out of breath before she finished the sentence.

Amun stepped though the doorway. He was wearing a tee shirt, jeans and slippers. He stopped to catch his breath.

Naomi noticed that his skin seemed a lot whiter lately and he looked much older. No doubt she did too. Well, both of them were seventy-one. It was hard to believe. All that time had gone by, all forty-nine years of it aboard this starship.

They had been married forty-six years. Their anniversary would come up in two months.

Naomi had always wondered if she could deal with marriage, after what had happened with her father. It was easy with Amun, however. He was gentle and sweet and he had been so patient with her.

Many times she had stopped him when he touched her, even after they were married. Eventually, she had learned to trust him. That had been the magic ingredient. Then the physical side of their marriage began to work.

Amun smiled. "Hi, there, Beautiful."

"I look awful."

"You're beautiful."

Naomi doubted that. She was still in her bathrobe and pajamas. With this thin air it just took so much energy to do anything.

Amun moved over to the coffee pot on the counter. He slid the pot out from under the drip top and poured some of the black liquid into the mug sitting on the counter. He then shook sugar into the mug from the dispenser next to the pot. He picked up a spoon and stirred.

Finally, he slid the mug across the breakfast bar and sat down with one stool between them. "I keep thinking. . ." He caught his breath. ". . . I can't call Ramses. He did it yesterday." Amun stared down at his coffee mug.

"He's okay."

Amun nodded. "Better than before."

"He missed Naqada."

"Not now." Amun raised his coffee mug and sipped from the black liquid. He lowered it to the counter and looked at her. Then he smiled. "I love you."

Naomi smiled back and she could feel tears rising into her eyes.

"I've been waiting."

She nodded. "I know."

"You always win, but. . ." He stopped to catch his breath.

Naomi knew what he was going to say. This time she couldn't win. This time, no matter how smart and determined she was, nothing was going to work. "I realize that."

He looked at her and grinned. "You're so cool."

"You're blind."

"Not at all." He drank from his coffee and returned the mug to the counter. "I wonder about Aten . . ." He stopped.

"And our grandson."

He nodded. "Yes, Khons."

"They're fine."

"I hope so." He raised the white coffee mug and sipped. Then he lowered it to the counter. "Hope they don't know."

"About us?"

"Yes."

"How can they?"

He shrugged. "I just hope."

"They don't."

Amun raised his coffee mug again, but stopped. He placed it on the counter closer to her. He slowly moved over one bar stool, so that he was directly next to her.

He sat for several seconds with his eyes closed. Then he opened them again and turned to her. "I have the pills."

Naomi wondered about that. She had wondered about a lot of things lately. She had wondered who would find this starship someday. Whoever it was would find all of them right here where their lives had stopped.

Some of the men had moved Ramses body to a couch at the back of the Bridge Command Center. With this thin air it was much too difficult to move a body any farther.

Ramses should be left in the Bridge Command Center. That was where he had worked. That was where he had sacrificed his own wife for the good of the starship.

Pod One had slid downward into the Hyksos atmosphere and it had burned up like some huge meteor. Nobody would ever know one way or the other what had happened to the people inside. Obviously they had died. Knowing that was enough.

"You've been great."

Naomi turned to her husband. She smiled. "You too."

Amun dug into the right front pocket of his jeans and pulled out two small brown envelopes. "How. . .?"

"Together."

Amun smiled.

It was then that Naomi noticed that his eyes were wet. He was crying. "I couldn't have without. . ." She couldn't go on. Her head began to swim and she thought she might pass out.

"without you."

"Same here." Amun slid his hand across the grey surface of the breakfast bar until his fingers reached the back of her left hand. "I love you."

Naomi smiled and tears ran down her cheeks. This was the man she just had to have. This was the only one she would ever have trusted. Many times over the last forty-six years she had thanked God or whoever was out there that she had found Amun Imhotep.

"Ready?"

Naomi wiped off her eyes with the back of her right hand. She nodded. "Yes."

He moved his hand off hers and ripped open an envelope. He shook the pill out in front of her. Then he ripped open the second small brown envelope and shook out a pill next to his coffee mug.

He picked up his pill.

Naomi picked up hers.

"I love you," said Amun.

"I love you."

Amun pushed the pill into his mouth with his right index finger and gulped some coffee.

Naomi pushed the pill into her mouth and then raised her coffee mug and drank.

The coffee was cold, but that was unimportant. She was with the best man she had ever known and she had been fortunate enough to marry him and have his child.

It had all worked out much better than she had ever thought it would. Now they would die together. As usual, he was right there with her. He had been right there for forty-six years.

Naomi didn't expect there would be an afterlife. She couldn't be that lucky, but if there was, she would be with him. Wherever he was, she wanted to be there. He was the only man she could ever have loved, the only one she ever did love. Now, she was right where she wanted to be – at his side.

CHAPTER THIRTY-NINE
"Limited Amount of Time"

Hyksos
Big Water Village
4M, Day 8, 96 A.D.
Late Afternoon

Sile Kamose sat along the windward rail of the sailboat. He was one of a crew of seven men. The hull of the boat was full of fish. He still hadn't gotten used to walking through the piles of slimy fish in his bare feet. The Hyksos took it in stride.

What always stuck in his mind was how willing these people were to accept Intef and him into their village. He really wasn't sure that Mayans would have accepted Hyksos people into their colony like this.

Sile's upper body was bare. At first, he had tried to practice precaution in the sun, fishing like this each day, but a shirt, even a thin one, was hot. Besides, he had only the clothes he had worn on his back when he came here and he had to save them. Then he would have to figure out how to make the Hyksos animal skin clothes.

He had told Intef that they would have to adjust to this new life. Actually, to his surprise, she seemed quite happy with it. He hadn't expected this from her. Sile was very much aware that she was well educated and from a more affluent background than he was.

He could live with that. She was so nice it didn't seem to matter. Besides, they were happy here.

He was glad to be away from General Smendes. The one thing he feared was that Smendes would find this village. If he did, he would probably try to destroy it.

"Coming about!" shouted Cronos, the man at the helm.

Sile automatically slipped down into the piles of fish in the hull. He ducked under the wooden boom that was swinging across the body of the boat.

He climbed up onto the other side. He had begun to learn the Hyksos language. It wasn't all that complicated. Now that they didn't have translators, both he and Intef were learning the language fast. They had to.

Cronos pointed. "A flag!"

Sile turned to look.

Sure enough, a man on shore was waving a giant animal skin flag. The man holding it moved his body in accentuated swings back and forth. There were some people standing with the flag waver. He wondered who they were.

"Hey, Sile, Monster Mayan Man, they are telling us to come in, but we are coming in! It could only be some dumbass Mayan waving that flag!" Cronos laughed.

Sile hoped there wasn't a problem of some kind like the village was under attack or something. He wouldn't wish that on these people. Cronos didn't seem to be very worried about it. He was making jokes like he always did.

Sile shaded his eyes against the sun. As he studied the uneven string of people on the sandy shore, he could swear that he spotted one Mayan.

The open boat swept forward on the crests of the whitecaps toward the beach.

As they came closer Sile was sure now that the one man was a Mayan. He was definitely darker skinned than the Hyksos people around him, and he was taller. The man had an assault rifle slung over his shoulder. That wasn't good.

"Get ready to beach!" Cronos shouted.

Crouched down, Sile and the other crewmen moved forward along the rails on each side of the boat.

The sail was now pointing directly out over the starboard rail, making a right angle with the hull.

"Bring up the centerboard!"

Hephaestus, the second mate, cranked the wooden winch at the back of the open slot in the middle of the boat.

The giant wooden board pushed up through the hull just behind the mast and dead fish flipped back into the piles on either side.

"Haul down the sail!"

Hephaestus whipped the large halyard loose, then, hand over hand, wrestled the billowing animal skin sail down onto the boom. Immediately, he wrapped ropes around the sail and the boom and tied them.

As soon as Sile clearly saw the pebbles on the bottom, he grabbed the rail and vaulted over the side into the water.

The rest of the crew followed. They ran along next to the boat, gripping the gunnels and pushing the hull forward.

Finally there was a "crunch" as the pointed bow cut into the sandy beach.

Sile had learned to love being out on the water. There was something about the smell of the salty air and feel of the sun and the almost constant breeze in your face. When you came in at the end of the day, you hauled the fish out to be gutted and salted. Then you bathed in the ocean to clean off the sweat and the fish slime.

At night you slept so soundly. He had never slept better in his whole life. Sometimes he would dream about being out on the ocean with Intef. She would be naked and she would open her arms to him. At times like those he would often wake up and reach over and touch her and they would make love in the darkness of their hut.

To his great surprise Intef had been a virgin. He knew she was somewhat older and that's why he was surprised.

The age difference didn't seem to matter out here. The Hyksos accepted her as Sile's woman and he was Intef's man. These people didn't care about age or social distinctions. Sile had figured out why. They were all about survival, the good of everyone and the good of the village. Beyond those three things, nothing mattered.

That had often made him wonder if more primitive people didn't have a better grasp on the important things of life. Maybe civilization, at least as the Mayans knew it, had a lot of downsides.

Once the boat was secure on the beach, Sile walked up to the Mayan man standing next to a tall Hyksos woman. He held out his hand. "Hello. I'm Sile Kamose."

The Mayan gripped his hand and shook it. "I'm Khons Imhotep." He turned. "And this is my girlfriend, Athena."

Sile recognized her from his stay in the other Hyksos village inland to the west. He smiled and held out his hand. "How do you do?"

Athena shook his hand. "I am fine. We have escaped Smendes' army people and we have come here."

Sile's head canted to the left. "How far did they follow you?"

Athena shrugged. "Maybe two days into the forest."

"It's a four day trip. In other words they came half way."

Athena nodded. "Yes."

Sile looked at Khons. "Were you in the army?"

"No. We took this assault rifle off a soldier she shot with her crossbow."

"Have you had any food?"

"Very little."

"We'll get you some food."

"I have a question."

Sile turned to Khons. "What's your question?"

"Is Intef Tutan here?"

"Why do you ask?"

"She's my cousin."

"No kidding?"

"Actually, her father was adopted by my great grandfather, but we still call ourselves cousins. Her father is the senior commander of the starship."

Sile stared at Khons. "Ramses Tutan?"

"Yes."

Sile suddenly felt uneasy. She had never told him about that. Ramses Tutan was older. Was she really his daughter?

"Is everything okay?"

Sile nodded. "I was just surprised. Intef never told me about any of this."

"You sound like you know her pretty well."

"She and Councilman Narmer and Achilles saved my life." Sile hesitated. "We've been living together."

"Really?"

Sile didn't know how to take Khons' reaction. The guy seemed somewhat surprised. "She's in the village." He nodded toward the grouping of grass-roofed huts near the edge of the forest. "I have to help the men with these fish. We'll talk later. I want to catch up with what's going on."

Khons moved away with the tall Hyksos woman.

Sile turned and walked back to the boat. The men were already hauling out the fish to the cutting boards lying on the beach. They were handing the fish to a group of women who were kneeling at the boards and slicing them open with knives.

Every so often one of the women would walk with a handful of fish guts over to a large wooden box attached to a travois strapped onto a horse.

Sile had learned that they used the fish guts as fertilizer in their gardens. They would mix it with the horse manure in a compost pile at the northeast end of the gardens. They placed it there because that was a point farthest from the village and the winds usually came from the west so the smell of the compost would blow out to sea north of the village.

This year's fish guts became next year's fertilizer. Sile thought that was very efficient. These people wasted nothing.

Hauling the fish out of the boat hull took, perhaps, half an hour. Sile was never sure about those things anymore. He had lost his sense of time. He would always check the position of the sun.

Once he was finished with the fish, he walked into the sea water and washed off his hands. A month ago he would have used a towel. Now he wiped them off on the sides of his shorts.

They were his old military camouflage pants that he had shortened, simply by cutting them off with a knife. He had found that they were too warm full length, especially when he was out fishing.

When he stepped back up onto the beach, he was curious. He picked up a stick and drew a circle. He looked up at the sun. It was far down into its decline in the sky.

He stuck the stick into the middle of the circle. The shadow fell into a position at about five o'clock. He wondered if it really was five o'clock.

But you had to wonder. Was it that important? He was living in a primitive Hyksos village. To these villagers it certainly wasn't important.

He wondered sometimes what would happen if Intef became pregnant. How would his children grow up? Would they know anything about where their parents had come from?

Thinking of Intef made him wonder about all this information she had withheld from him. One side of him was hurt by this revelation, yet Intef had saved his life.

What was even more important was the fact that he had never known a woman who connected with him like Intef did. Maybe that's why this hurt so.

He scuffed the primitive sundial in the sand and yanked out the stick and threw it. He had better get back to the village and Intef. They would have to have a talk about this.

Barefoot, he walked across the warm sand toward the north.

Cronos, the fishing boat captain, fell in next to him. "I see that you have a Mayan friend here."

Sile turned. "He's not my friend, Cronos. I was just talking with him about how far General Smendes' men had followed him. I was worried about the safety of this village."

"I have heard about this Smendes. He sounds like an evil man."

Sile nodded. "Yes. He beat me pretty badly. If Intef and Achilles hadn't saved me, he would have killed me."

"Why would he do that?"

"Because I didn't follow his orders."

Cronos tapped his right temple. "He has the devil in his head. His head is sick."

Sile stopped. His eyes scanned around the perimeter of the village.

Cronos came to a halt a few feet away and walked back to Sile. "What is it, Monster Mayan Man?"

"Maybe we'd better make up a battle plan or something. I have a bad feeling about this."

"You mean this Smendes with the sick head?"

Sile nodded. "Yes. I think we should post sentries and get ready to defend ourselves."

"But this Smendes, he is one of your people."

Sile looked into the short man's blue eyes. "Not anymore, Cronos. Now the Hyksos are my people. You've been good to Intef and me. I will fight for the Hyksos people now and I'm sure this Mayan man, Khons, will too."

Cronos grinned. "That is good." He slapped Sile on the back. "You are learning how to fish and crew a boat. You are not very good at it yet, but you will be. Maybe someday when I am very old and don't have any teeth, you will be captain of the sailboat."

Sile had an idea. "You know, Cronos, that sailboat may come in handy if we have to fight Smendes' people."

"How so? It is only a sailboat."

Sile nodded. "Yes, but I know how the Mayans fight and I know what their weaknesses are. I have an idea about how to use the sailboat if they attack us."

Cronos studied Sile's face. Then he smiled. "It is good to have a friend who has been on the other side. He knows the ways of the other people."

"Exactly. Let me ask you something, Cronos. Would it be possible to anchor the boat out from shore some distance? I mean - we would anchor it in water shallow enough so that we could walk out and climb aboard."

"Yes. That is possible, except when there's a storm. Then it is good to have the boat on the beach so we can tie it down."

"What I'm thinking is that the boat might be safer off shore if we're attacked."

Cronos nodded. "Ah, yes. That is a good idea. I will do that."

"Can we do it tonight?"

Cronos shrugged. "Yes, I suppose."

"And I'd make sure we have some sentries posted up in the trees."

Cronos smiled. "I am glad you are with us, Sile. You are a good warrior."

Sile patted the other man's shoulder. "When you want to move the boat, let me know. I have to go speak to this Khons Imhotep and his girl-friend, Athena. They will be with Intef."

Sile walked away from Cronos at an angle. He had built his hut closer to the ocean. It was the only space available. The first few nights he and Intef had slept in another family's hut. What had shocked him was that the woman in the house had asked him why he and Intef didn't have sex at night.

For the woman, it was apparently an innocent enough question. Sile had tried to explain to her that Intef was very modest and easily embarrassed. That wasn't really the reason. It was that Intef and he hardly knew each other, but that explanation seemed to satisfy the woman.

The whole village had helped them build their hut. They used natural materials. The Hyksos had shown them which branches worked better for the sides of the hut and which ones worked better for framing the roof.

It took most of three days to build and to his surprise it was really quite comfortable. It was certainly better than a tent. At night it stayed reasonably warm and during the day the straw roof worked like a layer of insulation and kept them cool.

When he came upon Intef and Khons, they were talking. Sile noticed that Intef seemed somewhat watchful, even self-conscious. He wasn't sure why.

"Hi, how was the fishing?"

"Very good." Sile looked at Khons. "You and your girlfriend can stay in our hut tonight if you want."

"No, that's not necessary, but thank you. We're staying with Achilles. Athena has gone to speak to him about his father."

"Zeus?"

"Yes. He was killed during a skirmish. Smendes burned down the whole village. I don't know what he did with the women and children." Khons Imhotep looked down for a second. Then his brown eyes focused on Sile. "Maybe I don't want to know. I will have to go back to find my father very soon."

"Was he captured or something?"

"He was wounded."

Sile nodded. "I wouldn't recommend going back. I have a feeling, in fact, that Smendes is coming here."

"Why would he do that?"

Sile shrugged. "I don't know. The guy's crazy. He has to control everything. I really wouldn't go back. I think you'll run right into his army."

"If they're coming here, these people have to prepare."

"Yes. I'm going to get together with the boat captain, Cronos, and the village elders to plan something."

Khons nodded. "I'll help you, Sile. Smendes killed all those villagers who were so kind to us."

"Achilles told us about that battle, but he said he thought the Hyksos won. Of course, he left just as the thing started. He didn't want to take a chance that Smendes would get his hands on Omina, his Mayan girlfriend. He brought her across the mountains to our village. Did Smendes kill all of them?"

"We're not really sure. We had to get away ourselves. Athena said our lives were in danger."

"Are you two an item, Cousin?"

Khons turned to Intef. "Yes, definitely. She's really a neat person."

Intef smiled. "I see you've been smitten."

Khons glanced around. "Where's Achilles hut?"

Sile pointed. "Over there at the south end of the village."

"I feel I should be with Athena. I've wondered if her father made it out alive. She hasn't said anything."

Sile pointed to Khons right ear. "If you lose that translator, you can learn this language pretty fast, Khons."

"You're probably right. For now, I'm going to wear it, especially if we're going to be attacked. I want to be able to communicate. I'll just have to stay close to Athena. As far as I know, she's the only Hyksos wearing one." Khons moved away. "See you two in a little while," he said over his shoulder.

Intef watched him walk away. "It's nice to have family here."

"You didn't tell me that your father's the starship commander."

Intef turned to Sile. "I didn't think it was important."

He shrugged. "I guess it isn't."

"You seem angry or something."

Sile focused on the soft brown eyes. "Look, Intef, you mean more to me than any other woman I've ever known. And even though I haven't known many, that's important. I've told you everything about me. I figured it was what you're supposed to do when you love someone. But you didn't tell me about you."

Intef looked off toward the blue water of the ocean. "I was afraid you wouldn't want me. I was afraid you'd think I was this nasty old maid."

"Why would I think that?"

"Because I'm older than you." She turned to Sile. "I'm forty-four."

Sile was surprised.

There were tears running down Intef's cheeks. "I've never been good around men. It's always been difficult for me, but then I met you and it felt different. The only problem was you were younger. I didn't want to tell you who my father was so you'd figure out my age."

"I'll have to admit I'm surprised." Sile shrugged. "But what difference does age make if you love someone?"

He moved closer to Intef and put his hands on the sides of her shoulders. "Hey, there are real advantages to this."

Intef's head tilted. "Advantages?"

"Yes. You see – this is the problem. You have only a limited amount of time left to have children, so we'd better get screwing – like every night."

Intef grinned. "I'm okay with that." Her face became serious. "I really do love you more than anything, Sile."

"And I love you."

Intef looked off toward the ocean again. "It's been wonderful living here with you."

"It's sure different."

She turned to him. "There's something so simple and wonderful about it. I've never been happier."

"Me either."

CHAPTER FORTY
"Bent on Revenge"

Hyksos
Ocean Village
4M, Day 11, 96 A.D.
Before Dawn

S ile Kamose's eyes opened when he heard the ululation.

He heard it again and this time it sounded like it came from the forest to the west. That meant one thing - Smendes.

He rose up from his sleeping mat, pulled on his shorts and grabbed the black pistol and the two clips of ammunition.

"Where are you going?"

"He's here."

"Who?"

"Smendes."

"How do you know?"

"There was a signal. Get dressed. You're coming with me."

Itef rose out of bed in her underwear. She pulled on jeans and a blouse.

Sile handed her the pistol and clips. "You know how to use this. I want you to stay close to me. This whole thing with Smendes could get brutal. Understand?"

"Yes."

"You're going out on the sailboat with me."

"Like we talked about?"

"Yes." Sile took the crossbow off a hook on the wall of the hut and the quiver of arrows behind it. Then he slung the quiver over his left shoulder.

Seconds later, he pushed his head out of the hut. He had heard nothing specific yet, but he just knew it was Smendes.

Intef stepped out after him.

He grabbed her hand. "Hurry. We have to get down to the boat."

The whole community of huts was alive.

Men were carrying their crossbows and quivers of arrows. Some had several small spears - some blowguns. Others had brought in their horses from the stockade.

Older women were bringing children together in a group.

Over the last two days, Sile had talked strategy with them. The one thing that slowed them down was the village elders. They weren't convinced that if they just gave up Sile, Intef and Khons to Smendes everything wouldn't be all right.

Finally they seemed to understand that even if they gave up these Mayans, Smendes would still destroy the village. Achilles was the one who had convinced them. It was simply because he, too, was a Hyksos. He told them what had happened to his own village and he warned them that it would happen to theirs.

Down at the ocean shore Sile led Intef into the water. They waded out to the sailboat. Cronos was waiting for them with the crew and many more men. There were about twenty-five of them armed with crossbows.

"Come, you slow Mayan Monster Man." Cronos grinned. "You said this would work but we have to get out from shore first."

Sile helped Intef into the boat.

"You have brought your woman, Sile?"

"She's special, Cronos. She knows how to shoot that fire stick."

"And you have the crossbow?"

"I know who's boss."

Cronos grinned. Then he turned to the crew. "Okay, you lazy-ass fishermen, let's get this old rag boat out of here."

The crew leaned into the oars and the boat moved away from the land.

What Sile had counted on was that the sailboat would go unnoticed by the Mayans. He had told Achilles and Khons to keep the Mayan army busy over toward the north side of the village. If they did that, they would have Smendes' men backed up against the river.

Sile's plan was to come around their right flank and attack Smendes' army from the rear. He had also considered starting a fire in the forest to block their escape.

The problem, of course, was he didn't know what the prevailing wind would be this morning. It usually came out of the west, southwest. But some mornings were different, and it came from the northeast.

Achilles was going to use his spearmen on horses to charge the army after he had softened them up with showers of arrows. At Sile's direction, they had also created some primitive catapults from springy young trees. They had used a pair of horses to cock them back. They had tried this already with some success.

They would shoot flaming bundles of straw. With any luck that would catch some of the pine trees on fire. Catapulting up high into the pines would be the best. That could cause some real havoc in the Mayan army ranks.

From the boat, Sile could hear the stutter of the automatic weapons. One thing he did notice right away was there seemed to be fewer of these weapons. Maybe three or four. Then he remembered the problem with ammunition. If that were the case, this battle would start out on a more equal basis because when it came to crossbows, the Hyksos had far superior skills.

He carefully studied the edge of the thick forest as the boat moved along parallel to shore heading south. Finally he could see the motion of the camouflaged soldiers of Smendes' army charging into the opening next to the village.

Out of the south, almost right in front of the boat, a string of horses with riders charged on the Mayan's right flank.

Now Sile could clearly see where most of Smendes' men were. "Go farther down, Cronos. We'll land there." He pointed toward a sandy beach far down the shore.

"After we're on the beach, you and Hephaestus take the boat back out on the ocean where it will be safe."

"Good idea, Monster Mayan Man. Are you going to send your woman out with us?"

To Sile, this sounded like a good idea. "Yes." He turned to Intef. "You'll be safer out here. Why don't you give me the pistol and the clips?"

Intef handed him the pistol with her right hand. The clips were in her other hand. "I don't want you to get hurt."

Sile smiled and slid the pistol into his right pants pocket. He dropped the clips into his left pocket. "I won't get hurt, Intef."

"I'll be very mad at you if you get hurt."

Cronos was chuckling and shaking his head. "You'd better not get killed, Monster Mayan Man, or she'll kill you all over again."

Some of the crew members near Sile grinned.

"Either way, Mayan Monster Man, your ass is cooked." Cronos broke out in a belly laugh and some of the crew members laughed with him.

Others seemed unaffected and their faces remained very sober as if they were afraid of the coming conflict.

Sile found that he was grinning. "Thank you, Cronos, for all the good information. You're so full of shit your breath stinks."

The crew broke out laughing and Cronos laughed too. "If you didn't try to kiss me, Mayan Monster Man, you wouldn't know how my breath stinks."

The crew laughed again. Some of the warriors in the bow looked back over their shoulders and grinned.

Suddenly Cronos's face sobered and he pushed the tiller over and let out the mainsheet.

The boat turned around toward shore and the sail swung out off the side. The small wooden craft rode the waves toward the sandy beach.

Cronos looked around at his crew. "You crewmen will have to hold us off shore while everyone gets out. Then you will turn us. Hephaestus and I will stay aboard this time. Any questions?"

Sile didn't know if this flanking idea would work but they had to try something. These village people had their backs to the water. There was no place for them to run.

One thing he was counting on was Achilles hate for Smendes. Ever since Achilles had heard about his father's death, he had been fuming with hate. He was bent on revenge.

This Khons Imhotep was a nice guy but Sile didn't see him as necessarily a strong fighter. However, his girlfriend, Athena, was very capable. Both of them were with Achilles.

As Sile thought about it, he became more confident in that side of the defense force. Now, to make this flanking maneuver work.

When the boat reached shallow water, Hephaestus winched up the centerboard and Cronos dropped the sail and wrapped it around the boom.

The crew members jumped over the gunwales, Sile with them. When he grabbed onto the edge of the gunwale, Intef was sitting above him.

She leaned down. "I love you," she whispered. She leaned lower and kissed his lips. "You come back," she uttered in a low voice.

"Of course. We have to make babies, every night."

Intef grinned. "I love you."

"Same here," he said.

Once the warriors had climbed out of the boat, the crew turned it seaward.

Cronos raised the sail and swung the boom out over the side.

The sail caught the soft offshore breeze and the boat moved away with only the gentle gurgle of the water off the stern.

Intef waved at Sile.

He waved back. Then he turned to the warriors who were waiting in the knee-deep water. "We are going to go around behind Smendes' army. I think we should close in on them before we shoot the arrows. The best time to attack them is when Achilles' group is launching an attack.

"We will use whistles and ululation like we planned. Are there any questions?"

One man raised his hand. "Monster Mayan Man, suppose this doesn't work and they attack us?"

Sile made eye contact with the man. "Well, let me put it this way. If this fails, your village is doomed. Everyone you know and love will die. Your children who are hiding with the old women out in the woods will be found by Smendes' army and they will be killed. No – they will not just be killed. Some of them might even be tortured."

He stared at the man. "Do you understand, Hector?"

The small man nodded. "Yes, I understand, Monster Mayan Man."

Sile smiled at him. "You know, Hector, it would be much easier just to call me Sile."

The other man's white face broke into a grin. "I know, but I like to make fun of you."

The men chuckled.

"I love you too, Hector."

The men laughed.

"Okay, Men, let's get moving. Remember, keep it quiet."

Sile walked out in front of the men through the shallow water up the slow slope onto the beach. Then he led them into the forest. As they moved into the dewy undergrowth, Hector cupped both hands around his mouth, tipped his head up and made a ululation.

The birdlike sound of a ululation came back from the far left in the forest.

They had decided on this as a way to keep track of where their forces were. They couldn't see very far in this thick undergrowth.

Sile had estimated that they were about two hundred yards behind Smendes' men, but he knew from experience that things were often vague and uncertain during a battle. He wished he had binoculars with him but that was a luxury right now. The best he could count on was his own eyesight and the keen perceptions of the Hyksos warriors.

When they had trudged through a swampy area, suddenly there was a frantic ululation up ahead to the left.

Hector moved over close to Sile. "They have spotted Smendes' men."

"Let them know we heard them, Hector."

The small orange-haired man cupped his hands around his mouth and tilted his head back. The sound that projected from his mouth this time was slightly different.

Sile had never asked about this, but he was convinced there were certain sounds that signaled certain things.

"Hector, do you think all of the men know we have spotted Smendes' army?"

"Yes, they will know, Monster Mayan Man."

Sile grinned and slapped the little orange-haired man on the back. "I'm happy to be fighting next to you, Hector."

"We will get rid of this Smendes forever."

"Let's hope." Sile slipped his crossbow off his shoulder and loaded an arrow into the slot. Then he cocked it back. He noticed that Hector moved away and remained slightly behind him. The man was still carrying his bow over his shoulder.

Sile spotted something. He motioned to Hector to get down.

The small man crouched, slid his bow off his shoulder, loaded it and cocked it.

Sile aimed at the area in front of him. He waited and watched. Then he saw a camouflaged back move. He pointed with his right hand and looked over at Hector.

Hector nodded.

Before Sile could aim he heard a "Zip!"

An arrow struck the man in the back of his neck.

He fell into the brush.

Suddenly another man appeared.

Sile aimed and squeezed the trigger.

"Zip!"

The arrow struck the man in the stomach.

He grunted and fell onto it.

There was thrashing in the underbrush.

Sile followed Hector's lead.

Hector waited, and then with his bow cocked he moved forward with slow careful steps.

Sile moved with him.

"Zip!"

An arrow narrowly missed Hector.

Sile caught the motion in the tree. He dropped to one knee and aimed. He couldn't see anything.

Then he saw an arm and he knew where the man was. He squeezed.

"Zip!"

There was the clatter of a body falling through a tree, and then the resounding "thump!" as it hit the ground.

Hector rushed through the tall yellow grass toward the fallen sniper.

Sile followed.

Apparently the man was still alive.

Hector grabbed the left arm and slashed the soldier's throat.

Sile knelt next to the dead soldier. He leaned close to Hector. "Was he on his radio?" he whispered.

Hector pointed toward the wrist control. "He was talking to this."

Kamose put his finger to his lips. Then he ripped the Velcro strap loose from the wrist control and wrapped it around his own wrist. He remembered one officer in particular, a guy named Nubia.

"Nubia, come in, Nubia."

"Reading you loud and clear. Is that you, General?"

"Is everything okay in your sector?"

"Yes, Sir, everything's good, Sir."

"Glad to hear it. Keep me posted. How is it going over on the north sector, Captain?"

"We're losing some ground there, Sir, but we'll get it back. I'll give you a call when I know more, General."

"Do that, Nubia."

"Yes, Sir, General. Over and out."

Sile Kamose tapped the face of the control.

"What this man say?" Hector pointed at the control.

Sile converted his mind to Hyksos. "He said they were having trouble over there in the north sector." Sile pointed.

"That is good, right?"

"Yes. Now's the time for us to launch a major attack."

Sile ripped up the Velcro on the dead soldier's holster and pulled out the pistol. Then he checked the ammunition belt for clips. He found three.

He decided it was a better idea to take the ammunition belt itself. With Hector's help, he pulled the belt out from under the body. Then he clipped it onto his own waist and stuffed his two pistol clips into the ammunition compartments on the belt. He put the new pistol back into the holster, first checking it to make sure it was loaded.

He snapped back the slide to put a cartridge into the chamber. Then he lowered the hammer. The other pistol he stuffed into the left side of the cartridge belt.

Hector smiled. "Now you are ready to be a warrior."

"Let's get at it, Hector."

"I'm with you, Monster Mayan Man." The small orange-haired man grinned.

CHAPTER FORTY-ONE
"Safer"

Hyksos
Ocean Village
4M, Day 11, 96 A.D.
Morning

Khons Imhotep couldn't believe that Smendes would actually attack in the morning. It was stupid. The Mayans were facing east; the sun would be in their eyes.

It turned out to be an advantage for the Hyksos, not a big one, but it was an advantage all the same. Besides, it was so much easier for the villagers to see the Mayan army this way. They were advancing in bright morning sunlight.

Khons felt strange fighting against these people that he knew. He had been out here beyond the forest for several days now, living among the ocean Hyksos. While they were kind and accommodating, they weren't his own people.

Of course, once he married Athena that might be a whole different thing. If they had children, some of them might have that kinky orange hair and white skin. Then he would be part of the Hyksos community for sure.

He had wondered when this battle with Smendes was over if he might try to go back and live among the Mayans. Of course Smendes would have to be out of the picture. Would the Mayans accept Athena?

What was strange about all this was that he knew very well he would be accepted better among the Hyksos than Athena would be among the Mayans. It was an unpleasant truth, but there it was.

Right now, there seemed to be a slight lull in the fighting. Athena and he were crouched in some bushes waiting. She had warned him about standing up and exposing himself to snipers. They had discovered that Smendes' men had killed the Hyksos sentries up in the trees and replaced them with Mayan snipers with crossbows.

Athena touched his arm. "You stay close so you don't get hurt. Achilles is reckless because he is hot for revenge, but that is dangerous. Don't you get reckless like him."

Two horses were brought up in back of some trees off to their right behind their own lines. The horses' harnesses were tied with a rope to a young tree that had been stripped of foliage. A wad of straw was tied to the end of the tree.

Almost directly behind them, Achilles rose up onto his horse. He yelled something in Hyksos.

"Duck," said Athena.

Khons lay down in the brush and turned over on his side so he could see.

Behind him one of the Hyksos was lighting the wad of straw.

Achilles yelled.

A young warrior cut the rope between the tree and the horses.

The tree swung skyward and the wad of straw sailed in an arc high above the forest. It dropped into some pines.

There was a scream, then the crashing sound of someone falling through the brush.

"One of Smendes' snipers fell out of a tree." Athena raised her head to look.

Behind them Achilles yelled. Then he rode by their position wielding a handful of small spears.

Five other horsemen rode in from the cover of trees at different angles and followed Achilles toward the Mayan lines.

Arrows zipped through the air.

One horseman tumbled off his horse and rolled in the tall grass.

The rest of them charged on.

Khons rose to a kneeling position and raised his assault rifle.

A cluster of Smendes' men appeared out of the brush with their cross-bows aimed.

Khons squeezed the trigger.

The "stutter" of the assault rifle echoed in the trees.

He swept the barrel of the rifle across the staggered men in camouflage uniforms.

Several of them collapsed. One turned his way.

Khons pulled the trigger again.

The man dropped.

Something slammed into Khons' shoulder. He dropped backward.

The assault rifle was yanked out of his hands.

He was looking up at the blue morning sky but it all became vague now. The blue began to dim and look more distant. He could hear the "stutter" of an assault rifle near him. The sound continued. Then it stopped.

He could feel Athena fumbling for a clip in his cartridge belt.

The stutter of the assault rifle echoed among the trees. These were short bursts.

Khons blacked out.

He dreamed he was rising in the air and a beautiful woman with kinky orange hair was hovering over him. His journey through the air was full of jostles and bounces.

He could smell gunpowder. If he was dead, it was strange that he would smell gunpowder.

Then he could hear humming and shortly after, there was pain, terrible pain in his shoulder. Now he could hear voices. One of them sounded like Athena but he couldn't understand what she was saying. "I need my translator."

He understood that he had lost it or it had been taken off his ear.

Now he dreamed about tree catapults where people would be launched upward through the air and they would yell and laugh and fly away into the sky above the jungle.

His eyes opened.

It was dark.

He blinked and moved his head to try to determine where he was.

Pain shot through his shoulder. "Ugh!"

Athena's face appeared above him. "Is my Khons all right?"

"What happened?"

"You were shot with an arrow during the battle. You are in Delphi's hut. He is the medicine man for the ocean Hyksos here in this village. He took out the arrow and put healing ointments on you."

Khons turned his head. His shoulder hurt again. He stared at the small, bare white shoulders next to him. "You're naked."

"Of course. I'm in bed. When I go to bed I sleep naked."

"But you're on this mat with me."

"I'm protecting you."

"Is there still fighting?"

"No. We beat them. We killed most of them. The rest ran into the forest and went back toward the west."

"What about Smendes?"

"He's still alive. Achilles is tracking him."

"Revenge for his father's death."

"He loved his father very much." Athena rose up so that the animal skin slid down off her breasts.

In the near darkness Khons stared at the small white breasts. Then he looked into Athena's eyes. "You're beautiful."

She grinned. "I know, and I'm your girl. We can get married by the tribal elders. Then we can do sexual things together. You want to do that, don't you?"

"Which part?"

"All of it."

Khons stared into the pretty eyes in the dim light of the hut. "You know what's strange?"

"What is that?"

"When I was up there in that huge starship I never would have guessed that I would find a woman like you down here on this planet."

"It was meant to be. You were meant to find me and I was meant to find you."

"A few weeks ago I would have said things don't happen that way."

"Have you changed your mind?"

Khons thought a minute. "Yes."

Athena leaned and kissed his cheek. "My gentle Khons, we should sleep now."

"Yes, we should."

Athena moved up closer to him under the animal skin and pressed her naked body against his. She closed her eyes.

It wasn't until Khons felt the patch of bristly hair against his hip that he realized he was naked too.

He found this amusing, but then there was also something sweet and innocent about it.

His eyelids flickered. Then they closed. Khons drifted off into a peaceful sleep. He dreamed about embracing a beautiful, naked woman with white skin and orange, kinky hair.

Throughout this dream he realized that he had never felt more completely whole and more content. He had never felt safer at any time before in his entire existence.

CHAPTER FORTY-TWO
"Eye for an Eye"

Hyksos
The Forest
4M, Day 11, 96 A.D.
7:26 p.m.

Captain Avaris Khufu didn't like being out here in the forest alone. Otherwise he would have left Smendes a long time ago.

The two of them had been walking west for hours. This forest was so damned big and they had a long ways to go – four days on foot.

Besides that, there was only the sun and the compass on your wrist control to guide you, and the battery was getting real flakey.

The control would work for a few minutes and then it wouldn't. That had happened to a lot of the guys lately. Avaris supposed eventually their wrist controls would die and they would have to learn to do things without them.

"We'll keep movin' right through the night, Captain."

Khufu turned to Smendes. "All night, General?"

"Yup. There's somebody followin' us. I can feel it."

Avaris Khufu checked over his right shoulder. Then he looked back over his left shoulder. He saw nothing. In fact, he heard nothing either.

He turned to the man on his left. "General, this walking is exhausting. We need to stop sometime."

Smendes didn't look at him. "We'll keep movin'."

Avaris shrugged. He didn't know what the hell to say. He felt this was stupid, but he had learned from being around the general that the man was not always rational.

More important, Smendes didn't like to be crossed and he had a terrible temper. That's why they had gone over the mountains to attack the ocean Hyksos. Smendes was pissed off at all the Hyksos, no matter where they were, and he couldn't be talked out of this stupid campaign. They had lost a lot of soldiers, and for what?

Avaris could see the reason for the attack on the downriver Hyksos. That village had stolen their generator.

After that battle they found pieces of it all around the village. Some of it had been made into jewelry and was on the bodies of the men and women they had killed.

They had brought all of the pieces back, hoping to rebuild the generator. Moses Hapmen, the repair guy, had said that some of the parts of the electrical contacts had been filed down. He told Smendes that he would try, but he was doubtful he could reassemble all of it into a working generator again.

So they had killed every last Hyksos in that downriver village and they still didn't have a generator. The event that stuck in Avaris Khufu's mind was the little red-haired girl. He dreamed about her every night.

Sometimes he would dream that she was begging him not to let that awful man, Manetho, take her away. Avaris would wake up in a sweat and he would feel bad about shooting her, but what if Manetho had taken her? Avaris didn't want to think about that.

As far as Avaris was concerned, there was only one good thing that had come out of all of this shit lately. Manetho was dead. Corporal Gerzean had shot him when he went AWOL.

But this whole thing of going to the Ocean Hyksos village was crazy. They had marched out here into the forest and crossed through this mountainous country over a period of four days. Then they had attacked the village.

They lost the battle and lost a whole mess of their men too. Avaris had no idea how many men were left.

Now, out in these woods, General Smendes thought somebody was following them. Avaris was sure the general was imagining this shit. Why would anybody follow them? The Hyksos had beat them real bad.

Sure, there was a need for security around the colony, and all that, but Smendes did things to the extreme. He was crazy sometimes. That often made Avaris wonder if he really wanted to stay in this army.

Eight years ago he had taken the tests and joined the army because he thought a military career was going to be his life's work, but he hadn't signed up for anything like this. He didn't like working for this crazy man.

Avaris had cleverly avoided the nastiest details. He had never been involved in any of those tortures. When he saw something like that coming, he would volunteer for some unpopular duty, like going on patrol in the forest.

What he figured was that he would take his chances out there with the Hyksos tribesmen before he would be part of torturing anyone. Because he had volunteered for these duties so often, Smendes considered him one of his most loyal officers.

Everything changed when he shot that little red-haired girl. It was so hard to shoot her, but he couldn't let Manetho take her.

He had told himself over and over again that shooting her was the only answer. It was the logical answer, but logic didn't always work. His emotional side kept reminding him that he had done an unforgiveable thing, and if there were gods somewhere, he would be punished in the afterlife.

He could not think about the little girl now. He had to focus on staying alive, on getting over these mountains and back to the Mayan colony.

Avaris gazed up through the tall pine trees toward the west.

The sun was low in the sky. It would be getting dark soon down in the lower areas of the forest next to the riverbeds. Once they reached the high mountains, the sun would be down completely.

Avaris certainly hoped Smendes' wrist control was working better than his. At night they would definitely need a compass unless there was a moon to guide them west. He wasn't sure if there was going to be a moon early tonight.

The Man Moon came up every night but it came up at different times. Sometimes it rose real late.

"Zip!"

Avaris Khufu swung around.

Off to his left, Smendes clutched his stomach and fell forward onto the arrow shaft.

It pushed through his back.

"General!" Avaris glanced around, and then charged across the open area under the trees.

At some point farther into the forest he heard the noise of a horse's hooves. He jumped behind a tree.

After he had caught his breath, he carefully leaned around the rough bark of the massive trunk. He studied the forest.

A Hyksos on horseback appeared in a clearing. He was holding a length of rope. It was tied around something lying on the ground.

Then Avaris realized what was on the ground – Smendes.

The Hyksos warrior kicked the sides of his horse.

The horse charged forward.

The body at the end of the rope dragged through the tall yellow grass.

The horse galloped around in a wide circle in the clearing with the body bouncing across the rough ground. This went on for several minutes.

Finally the horse stopped. The warrior swung the end of the rope around and around above his head and flung it up over the low thick limb of a pine tree. He moved the horse under the tree until he was able to grab the end of the rope on the other side of the limb.

He kicked the sides of the horse.

The horse moved away at a right angle to the limb. When the animal had moved several feet, it balked.

The rider kicked the sides again.

The horse lunged forward.

Smendes' body rose up off the ground. It was tied by the ankles.

The Hyksos rode the horse to a nearby tree and wrapped the rope around a thick tree limb and tied it.

Then he moved the horse over in front of the body. It was hanging upside down with arms dangling.

The Hyksos thrust a knife into the stomach and pushed downward, ripping the abdomen.

There was a deep grunt.

Avaris Khufu jumped behind the tree. He squeezed his eyes shut and bit his lower lip.

CHAPTER FORTY-THREE
"Discoveries"

Hyksos
The Forest
5M, Day 3, 96 A.D.
(3 weeks later)
Mid Afternoon

Through the trees, Khons studied the drawbridge to the Mayan colony. It was still daylight, but the bridge was up. What was going on? They always had it down during the day.

He looked toward his left where the garden was located, just to the south of the colony. There were various plants growing in rows, but there were also weeds, hoards of them.

He recognized bean plants, tomatoes and small corn stalks. It seemed to him that there had not been a whole lot of work done in the garden for several weeks.

Khons stared at the wall of wood on the other side of the wide ditch. He had belongings inside the colony, but there was no use worrying about that. Probably Smendes' men had confiscated them a long time ago.

His right shoulder was still sore and stiff. He had been exercising it to try to work out the stiffness. Apparently that was helping because the shoulder was much better now than it had been even a week ago.

Khons studied the bulwarks around the colony. This might be the last time he would see this place.

Obviously he wasn't wanted here. He couldn't imagine what they would think of his new wife. "This doesn't look good, Athena. Let's check out your old village," he whispered.

"We have to be careful. We don't want to be caught by these people."

"You're right. There might be patrols." Khons felt strange about this. After all, they were talking about Mayans – his people. At least, they had been his people at one time.

Athena peered through the brush at the bulwarks. Then she faced Khons. "I don't mean to insult you, but your people are very strange. Some of them do strange things."

"I agree." Khons smiled. "You know, even with that translator on your ear, you're beautiful."

Athena's head tipped coyly. "Are you trying to have your way with me, Khons Imhotep?"

"Maybe later." He looked toward the bulwarks. "Let's get out of here," he whispered.

They moved through the underbrush side-by-side toward the north.

Khons knew which way they were going. It only seemed natural that they should check the Hyksos village where Athena had been brought up. "Are you sure you want to go back?" he whispered.

The pretty face turned to him. Now the blue eyes were sad. "Yes. It is not a happy thing, but I should do it out of respect for my parents."

"I understand." Khons looked down at the worn path in front of him. Finally, his head came up. "I don't think my parents are still alive."

Athena stopped. "They were not alive when we left here, Khons."

"How do you know that?"

Athena touched her chest. "I felt it in here."

"Intuition."

"I felt it in my heart."

"Same thing."

Athena smiled at him. "We are good together, you and I."

"I think so." Khons had considered this before but now maybe was the time to tell her. "I want to learn the Hyksos language."

Athena's face beamed. "You do?"

Khons began walking again. "Sure. These translators won't last for-ever. Besides, I want to be able to speak to my children. I might teach them Mayan and teach them about the great history of the Mayan peo-ple."

"About their giant firebirds flying down out of the sky?"

"Of course." Khons remembered something. "My father's history book - I wonder where it is."

"When we find your father, we will find that also."

Once they reached the perimeter of the Hyksos village, they began to discover skeletons.

The remains were Hyksos. Khons could tell by the size. He stayed close to Athena and watched her. If he were in her shoes, he would find it very difficult.

Along the edge of the village compound, which was now piles and piles of charred wood and thatch, Athena stopped near a tree.

There was a crossbow and a small skeleton.

She dropped to her knees and picked up a bracelet made of a thin bronze wire strung with various colored, polished stones. She held the bracelet against her chest and tears came to her eyes.

Khons knelt beside her. "Are you all right?"

She turned to him. "My daddy." She held out the bracelet. "I made this for him when I was a little girl."

Khons put his arm across her shoulders and pulled her against him. He kissed her forehead. "I'm so sorry, Athena."

After several minutes Athena rose to her feet. She slipped the stone bracelet onto her left wrist.

Khons stood up. "Do you want to bury him? I'll help you."

"No. He loved the forest. Let's just leave him here where he'll be happy."

Khons walked through a small grove of trees and stepped into the edge of the charred remains of the village. He stopped.

Several feet in front of him he saw a larger skeleton and two tiny ones. The larger skeleton was on top of the smaller ones. Perhaps the mother had been trying to shield her children.

He turned away. "I can't do this. I don't want to see anymore."

Athena touched his arm. "My gentle husband." The blue eyes focused on Khons. "Do you want to go back to the ocean Hyksos?"

"Yes. But first I have to find my mother and father." He looked into the soft blue eyes. "I've been dreading this for a long time, Athena. I know it's been hard for you, too."

"I try to think of their spirits flying up into the sky. I try to think of them smiling down on us. Then I can feel them here." She touched her chest.

Khons smiled. "You're so full of beautiful wisdom."

In silence, they moved farther to the north, and then swung around the edge of the village toward the river. Khons had the sense that this was approximately where they had been with his parents that night.

At one point he turned to Athena. "You have a better sense of direction out here in the woods. Is this about where we were with my mother and father?"

"Yes."

Several minutes later they came upon a skeleton with an arrow through the rib cage.

Athena crouched down and studied the clothing. "He has no cross-bow or quiver. I took them off his body that night. This is Zeus."

She turned and studied the trees to the west. "This is the way you took your father." She motioned with her hand. "Come."

She moved westward through the thick undergrowth. Suddenly, she stopped. Then she looked back at Khons.

"What's the matter?"

Athena pointed. "Your mother," she said in a soft voice.

Khons moved forward. When he saw the blouse, he stopped. Just beyond the finger bones of the right hand there was a black pistol lying in the underbrush.

For a split second he had this idea about picking it up, but he couldn't make himself move any closer.

He pivoted around and leaned with his right hand against a tree. He thought he was going to vomit.

"She's up in the sky above us, Khons. She's fine now."

His eyes filled with tears. "She was a good person. I'm so sorry she had to die like this."

"She's happy now, Khons."

"Yeah," he whispered. Khons didn't know whether he believed in the afterlife or not, but it was a beautiful idea.

"We should look for your father and that book."

Khons shook his head. "I don't think I can stand this anymore." He sniffed and wiped his eyes. "Let's go back east to the Ocean Hyksos village." He turned to Athena. "Is that okay with you?"

"Yes." She smiled sweetly and took his hand. "Come, my gentle husband, let's go home."

They walked hand-in-hand eastward into the forest.

Khons had learned from Athena what to listen for in the woods. He was still learning to detect unusual sounds, but he had nowhere near the acuity of hearing of a typical Hyksos.

A few minutes later there was a small sound that caught his attention. Athena let go of his hand. "I have to run off and pee."

Athena vanished into a bush. There was a slight rustling. He expected to hear the typical sound of her relieving herself. She was quite innocent and not terribly bashful about such things. Very often she would just step off the side of the path, drop her animal skin pants and squat.

"Put your hands up high!"

Khons' skin crawled.

"Up!"

He raised his hands.

Someone behind him slipped his crossbow off his right shoulder and his quiver off his left.

"Where's the Hyksos woman?"

Khons shrugged. "I don't know."

"She was just here."

"What do you want with me?"

Something hard slammed into his back and Khons stumbled forward.

Now the man was facing him. A second Mayan came out of the woods. "Can't find her, Sergeant."

"Where's the Hyksos woman?"

"I don't know."

The second man walked around behind Khons' back. He grabbed his arms, pulled them back and handcuffed him.

Pain shot across Khons' right shoulder. It was the wound.

"What's your name?"

"Khons Imhotep."

The man grabbed the translator off Khons' right ear and put it on his own left ear. He cupped his hands around his mouth. "Listen, Hyksos Woman. If you want your man back, give us Sile Kamose! We want Sile Kamose!" he shouted.

The Mayan soldier waited.

An arrow struck the shorter soldier in the back and he fell.

The man with the translator jumped behind Khons. "Shoot at me and you kill him!"

Khons' eyes studied the trees to the east. He could see nothing.

The man with the translator grabbed Khons' cuffed hands and led him backwards through the brush.

For a split second Khons saw white skin and orange hair high in a tree to the east.

As he was being led through the woods toward the colony, he had this bad feeling about what was going to happen. His one bit of hope was based upon the fact that these were Mayans, his own race, his own people. Beyond that, he didn't see much of a chance to survive.

The army sergeant led him backwards to the ditch next to the colony. There he shouted orders for the drawbridge to be lowered.

Once he was inside the colony, Khons felt truly alone.

At the headquarters tent a small, wiry man stepped outside. He stared at Khons. "You're an Imhotep. Yes, I remember your family. Welcome home, Mister Imhotep. I'm General Khufu." He turned to the sergeant. "Put him in the brig."

* * *

Athena had followed the soldier leading Khons back toward the colony, but she could never seem to get a clear shot. If he had only been a little taller than Khons it would have been possible.

Once she had seen the soldier take Khons inside the bulwark walls, she realized her only option was to get back to the Ocean Hyksos village. There she could get some help.

Her emotional reaction was to run as fast as she could, but that was dangerous. There might be other Mayan patrols out here in the forest.

She had gotten careless. People who are in love sometimes did that. She would not make this mistake again. Because of her carelessness, her wonderful husband had been captured by these ruthless people.

Staying in the shadows of the brush and thicker stands of trees, Athena worked her way eastward. She could not take a chance of being seen out in the open.

When she reached an open area of yellow grass, she moved quickly and headed for cover as soon as possible.

Once she had gotten far enough east so that she could rest and drink some water, she began to feel lonely. He was such a sweet lover-man, her husband. She would do anything to get him out of that colony.

They wanted this Sile Kamose. Why did they want this man? What had he done?

Athena had seen him around the Ocean Hyksos village. He had learned the Hyksos language and was working with Cronos on the fishing boat. This Sile Kamose seemed nice enough.

Maybe that woman, Intef, he was living with belonged to some other man. That might be the problem.

Athena moved eastward through the forest. Every so often she would climb up high into a tree to check the trail behind her. She did this three times before she reached the mountains.

She planned to travel through the night. Time was important. Besides, without her sweet Khons by her side, she didn't know if she could sleep.

If she could travel two nights in a row, then she might be able to get to the ocean village in less than two days. For now, that was her plan.

She didn't understand most of these Mayan people. They were crazy. Why would they kill their own? What was so important about this Sile Kamose anyway? Didn't they have elders to solve their problems like the Hyksos did?

Khons was smart. He could help them solve their problems. Athena was sure that wasn't going to happen because there were bad people running the Mayan colony. They needed people like Khons to make things better, but Athena had the feeling this was not going to happen.

Once she was far beyond the location of the Mayan colony, Athena moved eastward through the forest at a slow jog. She might be able to keep up this pace until the Man Moon was half way across the night sky.

Sooner or later, however, she would have to eat roots or something. She did not have time to stop to make a fire and she was sure a fire was a bad idea anyway.

After all the teasing and all the time she had spent as a young Hyksos woman who was too tall to find a man, she was not going to lose her lover man. Besides, Khons was so sweet and good and he was handsome. He was a good lover too, although she would teach him more about that.

No, there was nothing that would stop her from getting back her man – nothing.

CHAPTER FORTY-FOUR

"Gift from the Gods"
Hyksos
Ocean Village
5th Month, 5th Man Moon
Early Morning

Sile Kamose felt extra chipper today as he walked down the beach toward the fishing boat. He was chewing the last bite of a sweet cake Intef had made for him this morning over the fire. The sweet cakes were made from ground corn meal and honey and they were browned in a fry pan over the fire – real tasty.

He used to miss coffee in the morning. The Hyksos didn't know what coffee was. He didn't really miss it anymore.

This morning he felt just super. Intef was pregnant. What made it better is that she was all excited about this. Sure – she was a little nervous about bearing a child with a midwife.

She had described the way the midwives looked. They were all old, wrinkled women. Of course, who would know more about bearing children than old women who had suffered through birth themselves lots of times and later helped many other women do the same thing?

Intef was so excited. The joy of being pregnant far outweighed everything else. She told him frankly that she had never thought at her age she could get pregnant. She was a little worried about a deformity or a child born with some kind of mental problems.

Sile had told her not to worry. She was healthy, happy and he was going to make sure she was fed good foods and had all the love and care she needed.

That was his mission – to make sure his lovely wife had a successful pregnancy and that she had a healthy child. He would give her back rubs, or absolutely anything she wanted.

She had actually taken on a glow and Sile was convinced that she was prettier now than she ever had been. He knew it was the joy of being pregnant.

As for him, he had wondered lots of times about having children, but he had never seen himself as a father. Once Intef had told him last night, however, Sile had begun to think about it and he became convinced that this really did fit into his life.

In fact, he had stayed awake for a long time, staring up at the grass ceiling of his hut, feeling the wonder of it. He was actually going to be a father.

He thought about how immature he had been for most of his life. Now, he had the biggest responsibility of all, raising a child.

Up ahead, in the dim predawn, Sile could see the fishermen waiting by the sailboat. He had been a little late getting out of his hut this morning. He was so excited about this pregnancy.

When he neared the sailboat, Cronos waved. "Hey, Monster Mayan Man, where the hell have you been? I've been getting older just waiting for you to get your lazy ass out here!"

Sile waded into the shallow water and stopped by the side of the boat.

"So, I see you're smiling like a jackass even though you're late. What would make you smile like a jackass when you have to get into a boat with a mouthy old guy like me?"

"I was having a hard time making myself come down here because I knew I would see your ugly face, Cronos."

The little man threw back his head and laughed. "A man as ugly as you calls me ugly? Now there's something!"

"Intef is pregnant. That's why I'm late."

Cronos slapped Sile on the back. "Congratulations, Monster Mayan Man."

"Thank you, Cronos."

The bearded little red-haired man turned to the other fishermen. "So, can you imagine? Now there will be another ugly Mayan around the village!"

The men smiled. One in the back spoke out. "No other Mayan can be as ugly as this one!"

Cronos laughed and bent over. "Now, that's the truth." He looked at Sile. "Well, I hope it's a boy because you sure are ugly and I can't imagine a girl as ugly as you."

Sile grinned. "Thank you - I guess."

Cronos slapped him on the back. "Come on, Monster Mayan Man, let's get this old boat out onto the ocean so we can catch some fish."

Sile grabbed the starboard gunwale and helped to push the bow around.

There were two Hyksos men next to him pushing as well.

When they had turned the boat, Cronos climbed over the stern and sat down at the tiller.

The crew continued to push the boat farther out until they were in waist deep water. Then they climbed up over the gunwales and grabbed oars.

They dropped them into the square slots cut into the gunwales. Then they began to row the boat outward. Sile sat in the stern just in front of Cronos, looking toward the sun rising above the brim of the ocean to the east.

"Hey, Monster Mayan Man, it is a great gift from the Gods to have a child. You should be a happy man."

"I am."

Cronos nodded. "I can see that." He looked at Sile. "If it's a boy and he is handsome, then you can name him after me." Cronos broke out into uproarious laughter.

Some of the crewmen at the oars looked back. One shook his head and rolled his eyes.

Sile had wondered over the last few months about living out his life here with these people. Things had changed so much.

Not more than a year ago, he had been living aboard an interstellar starship that had crossed the galaxy forty-seven light years distance. Now he was in a small fishing village on an ocean he knew nothing about, with people who were far back in history. He had no idea how far back they were, but these people definitely lived a primitive life.

However, Sile was never going to return to the colony and live with the Mayans. Even though Smendes was dead, the Mayan army might still behave just like they had before. He wanted nothing to do with that.

These Hyksos people were primitive in many ways. One thing, however, was very common in this village. They seemed to have a respect for life and a respect for people who respected them. That was actually quite civilized.

Sile liked living in this Ocean Hyksos village. Once in awhile he would feel lonely and he would think back to what he had come from. Then he would walk across the village and stop by Khons Imhotep's hut.

He hoped Khons and Athena were okay. A couple of days ago they had gone back to the Mayan colony to find Khons' mother and father.

Now that Sile was living with the Hyksos, everything was different. He was never going to be able to send this unborn child of his to college. He didn't go to college himself, but he always figured that if he did have kids someday, he would definitely send them.

There was no need for college in this life here among the Hyksos. You had to learn how to work for the whole village and you had to learn how to hunt and fish.

When you got old, you took care of the children while the women worked in the garden or made clothes, and the men hunted or fished. Then when you were very old, you were taken care of.

He had heard that the oldest people who were very sick were given a drink made from herbs taken out of the forest. Then they would drift off into a long sleep and never wake up.

Of course, that kind of thing was a long time away. Right now, he had to help catch fish so that they could smoke them and store them.

Sile turned to the little red-haired man at the helm. "The only time I would name my boy after you, Cronos, would be if he was both ugly and stupid."

The small crew of the sailboat broke out into laughter and Cronos slapped Sile on the back and laughed. "That was a good one, Monster Mayan Man."

Sile grinned. Actually, he liked Cronos very much. The man was a tough captain, but he had never lost a crew on this ocean. He kidded around with his men and that made the long days out here on the blue water in the hot sun tolerable.

Sile moved forward to the man at the oar in the left rear position. This guy looked older than the others. "Do you want me to take over for you for awhile, Aeneas?"

The man turned and looked up. "Yes, that would be good, Monster Mayan Man. My old back is sore." The small man moved around Sile toward the stern.

Sile sat down on the heavy plank astride the boat. He leaned forward, pushing against the oar.

"Now we will go as fast as the wind. The Monster Mayan Man is rowing this old boat!"

Sile looked back over his right shoulder and grinned. "Why don't you yell off the stern, Cronos! Maybe your big wind will make the boat go faster!"

The crew burst out laughing.

CHAPTER FORTY-FIVE
"Proposal"

Hyksos
Ocean Village
5th Month, 5th Man Moon
Early Evening

Intef had never been a person who especially enjoyed hard work. She had learned, however, to pace herself so that she could do the weeding and hoeing for hours. At the end of the day, she could feel the sting on her skin of sunburn. Inevitably, her back would ache.

With this pregnancy, however, she was avoiding the hardest labor. When she explained to the other women about the pregnancy, they didn't seem to understand. Finally one woman named Aphrodite told her that Hyksos women worked anyway, pregnant or not.

She said that everyone was happy for you when your child was born, but they expected you to be back out in the fields within three days. You might do lighter work and you might have your baby in a sling in front of you breastfeeding, but you were expected to work.

Today she had been weeding and hoeing. Weeks ago they had to replant a lot of the garden because it had been destroyed during the raid by the Mayan army. Some of the crops would be coming in late. Hopefully those plants would be mature before the dry season.

Intef noticed the motion at the edge of the forest before she actually knew what it was. Late in the day like this, she had sometimes seen nocturnal animals coming out early. Most of them looked harmless enough.

She expected this would be some such animal. Then she saw the orange hair and she realized it was a Hyksos.

She rose upright. It was a woman, moving at a very slow pace, halting sometimes.

Intef dropped her hoe and picked up a ceramic jug from the grass next to the garden. This late in the day, the jug was light. Most of the water was gone.

She hurried across the large open area toward the figure. Now she recognized her. It was Athena.

Intef broke into a slow jog and brushed through the tall yellow grass. As she approached, she noticed that Athena was staring straight ahead and didn't seem to notice her at all.

When Intef finally stopped in front of the orange-haired woman, she spoke. "Water."

Intef pulled the cork stopper out of the jug and held it out to Athena. "Here, drink."

Athena took the jug, and then dropped to her knees into the tall grass. She raised the jug to her lips and drank several gulps. Then she lowered it. "They have Khons."

"My cousin?"

"Yes."

"Who has him?"

"The Mayans."

"Why?"

Athena hesitated, and then she looked into Intef's eyes. "They want your Sile."

Intef scowled. "Why do they want Sile? I don't understand."

Athena drank from the jug again. Then she set it down on the ground and slammed the cork stopper in with the palm of her right hand. She rose to her feet. "I intend no disrespect, Intef, but your Mayan people are very strange."

Intef looked off toward the ocean shore. The sailboat bow was jammed into the sandy beach. Sile would probably be helping with unloading the fish.

She turned to Athena. "Come on, we should talk to Sile." She grabbed the water jug.

Athena moved in next to her and the two women trod through the tall yellow grass toward the cluster of huts.

Intef turned to Athena. "You look exhausted."

"I've traveled two days without sleep."

"You should have some sleep, then."

"First, I must tell Sile. He will know what to do. He will talk to the village elders and the warriors and they will make a plan."

Minutes later, when they arrived in the village, the men were crossing the beach away from the fishing boat. Cronos was walking next to Sile.

He stopped in front of Intef. "Hey, woman, you're with child. Sile was telling me. That is wonderful."

Intef smiled. "Thank you, Cronos."

"By the way, the best midwife is Hera. She has only four teeth left, but she's the best midwife by far. It is said that she has never lost a baby."

"I'll remember that, Cronos."

The little man turned to Sile. "I must get home to my woman. If I am late for my dinner she will chew on my ears for the rest of the night and she still has all of her teeth." Cronos threw back his head and laughed.

Sile grinned. "See you in the morning, my friend."

Cronos waved as he walked away. Then he turned suddenly. "Oh, Sile's woman, I forgot to say may the gods bless your child. Now I have said it." He laughed and moved northward among the huts.

Sile turned to Intef. Then he noticed Athena, standing in the shadows. "Athena, you look awful. What's wrong?"

"The Mayans have captured Khons. They want you to come back. Then they will let him go. I've been traveling for two nights and one and a half days without rest or much food. I must sleep now. But we must go back and get Khons. I will fight with you."

Sile put his hand on the side of her shoulder. "We'll get him back, Athena. We'll figure out something."

Athena nodded. "I must sleep now. I will see you in the morning. Then we must go to the Mayan colony and save Khons." She shuffled down the pathway toward the village.

Sile watched her, and then he turned to Intef. "We can't let them hold Khons for something I've done."

"You're not going back there, Sile."

"I have to."

"They'll kill you."

"If I don't go back, they'll kill Khons."

"Talk to Cronos."

Sile nodded. "Good idea."

"Here, I'll go with you." Intef took his hand and they walked together across the compound toward the north. "You realize that we should get married before this child is born."

Sile's head turned. "Are you proposing?"

She shrugged. "I guess I am. A marriage will make our child legitimate."

"These people don't care about that, Intef."

"I do."

"If it's that important to you, we can get married. I don't know how we'll do it. Do you want to do a Mayan ceremony?"

"I'm not sure."

"We may have to do it Hyksos style. That's the only thing these people know."

"I guess I'd be okay with that."

Sile put his arm around her. "We'll get married, but first we have to take care of this."

They stopped in front of a hut with a camouflage Mayan army shirt spread across the roof just above the animal skin over the front opening.

"Hey, Cronos, can you come out? I have to talk to you."

The brown animal skin moved aside and Cronos stepped out of the low doorway. "Ah, it is the Monster Mayan Man."

"Cronos, we have talked to Athena. She has just returned from the Mayan colony to the west. The Mayans have captured Khons and they want me or they won't give him up."

"Why do they want my friend, the Monster Mayan Man?"

"I disobeyed an order."

"Was that an order from the horrible Smendes?"

"Yes."

"Then you don't have to worry. Achilles killed Smendes. Now it doesn't matter."

"That's not the way Mayans do things."

Cronos placed his hand on Sile's shoulder. "Sile, I like you, even if you are a Mayan, but I have to say that your people are crazy."

"That may be true, Cronos, but they do have Khons."

"What has he done to them?"

Sile shrugged. "Defended this village."

"You Mayans are strange people, Sile."

"Cronos, I have this idea."

The small man laughed. "Now, that is a surprise, Monster Mayan Man. Usually you have sweet cakes and a smile. At least that's what you have in the morning."

"No, really, Cronos, I have this idea that we can use to defeat them once and for all."

CHAPTER FORTY-SIX
"The Plan"

Hyksos
The Colony
5th Month, 8th Man Moon
Late Afternoon

S ile stood close to the travois leaning against the tree. Cronos had brought him out here tied onto the travois behind a horse, pretending that they had hauled him across the mountains.

Now Sile's hands were still tied together and the other end of the rope was tied to a tree.

They had come up with this idea three nights ago at the ocean village. Sile didn't really want to be the bait but he figured that this was probably the only way they could get Khons out of the Mayan colony.

Cronos stood on the other side of the travois with his arms folded across his chest. He was wearing Athena's translator. "These Mayan people are dumber than you are, Monster Mayan Man. All they have to do is bring this Khons to the gate and walk him out," he said in a low voice.

"They probably suspect it's a trap, Cronos."

"Do you think they killed this Khons?"

Sile had wondered about that. Even if Smendes was dead, did this mean there would be no more torture and killing?

Frankly, he didn't know. That's why he wanted this travois and the horse left nearby. He wasn't sure that the Mayans wouldn't try to kill him right here.

Cronos cupped his hands around his mouth and tilted his head back. "Mayans. . . we are waiting!"

"I wouldn't push them, Cronos."

Sile heard the drawbridge "creak" before he saw any motion. Then a string of army men appeared along the top of the bulwarks.

"Do you see the men at the top of the bulwarks, Cronos?"

"Yes, I see them, Monster Mayan Man."

The bridge rumbled downward and made a loud "thump" on the ground. Dust billowed upward.

Sile began to sweat. Yes, they had planned this out carefully, but these Mayan army people might just shoot him.

The whole trip here through the woods had reminded him of his escape with Intef months ago. Frankly, he had never wanted to come back here.

Intef had come with him. She had insisted. She had told him over and over that she would kill anyone who even threatened him. It was funny, but she had become very protective since her pregnancy.

"Here they come, Monster Mayan Man, and I have only a dagger in my belt."

A party of three men appeared on the bridge. The one in front was apparently Khons. His face was wrapped in a black cloth blindfold. Behind him were two army men holding pistols.

"They have pistols, Cronos. They can shoot both of us."

"But that would be foolish because they would die too, Monster Mayan Man."

"Stay close to the travois. I don't trust them." Sile watched as the three advanced to the end of the bridge. They stopped. One of them raised his wrist control toward his face. He seemed to be talking to somebody in command.

A man appeared at the top of the bulwarks. "Bring Sile Kamose to the drawbridge!" he shouted.

Cronos cupped his hands around his mouth. "You bring Khons to us!"

The man on top of the wall raised his left wrist. Apparently he was in contact with someone else in charge.

Sile studied the blindfolded figure. It really did look like Khons Imhotep, although he couldn't be absolutely sure. It might be a ringer who could also be armed.

In fact, he could have an assault rifle strapped to his back. Then at some point he would drop to his stomach and one of the other two would shoot the assault rifle.

Sile turned to Cronos. "Our people aren't going to come out of the woods, are they?"

Cronos was studying the bulwarks. "No, Monster Mayan Man. Why do you ask?"

"It's possible that the blindfolded man has an assault rifle strapped to his back."

"I had not thought of that, Monster Mayan Man. Now I will watch to see if I can spot such a trick."

"What are you looking at Cronos?"

"I am looking for your assault rifles. I do not see any on the bulwarks. Maybe they are out of bullets."

"That's possible, but it would only take about two clips of ammunition to wipe out all the Hyksos in the woods."

"We would kill him first, Monster Mayan Man." Cronos continued to scan the bulwarks back and forth, from north to south, then north again.

The officer on the bulwarks tapped his wrist control. Then he put his hands on his hips and stood with his feet apart. "If you do not bring Sile Kamose to the drawbridge, this exchange is over!"

Cronos continued to scan the bulwarks. "I will wait to give them an answer, but we cannot take you to the bridge. They would kill all of us."

"I think you're right, Cronos."

The small man cupped his hands around his mouth. "Then this is over!" he shouted.

Sile moved closer to the travois. "Watch for any motion at all, Cronos."

"I was doing that before you were born, Monster Mayan Man."

The guard on the drawbridge to the right of Khons raised his wrist control and spoke into it. Then he tapped the surface with the index finger on his other hand.

Both guards grabbed onto Khons' arms and moved backward across the drawbridge.

Sile watched the soldiers at the top of the bulwarks. He was waiting for one to raise his crossbow.

"Crack!"

A bullet nicked the side of the travois just above Sile's head.

The horse whinnied.

Sile ducked behind the travois next to the horse and dropped to his knees.

Cronos jumped behind the travois.

A shower of arrows zipped across the open space and one soldier on the bulwarks fell forward landing on a spiked log. His body thrashed and thrashed, then it jerked and stopped.

Sile looked over at Cronos in the darkness behind the travois. "We have to do something."

"Tonight we will attack when they are asleep, Monster Mayan Man."

"Khons may be dead by that time."

"We must attack anyway, Sile, or they will attack our village again."

"Maybe I should just give myself up."

"You have a child, Monster Mayan Man. He will need his father."

Sile stared into the blue eyes. He felt a link with this little orange-haired man like he never had before. "Cronos, we can't let Khons die."

"Then we must go back into the forest and think of another plan."

CHAPTER FORTY-SEVEN

"An Old Trick"
Hyksos
The Colony
5th Month, 8th Man Moon
After Dark

Achilles had agreed to do this trick only because he still felt anger toward the Mayans for killing his father.

The inside of this gutted bison was dark and slimy. Achilles was lying on his right side with the translator on his left ear so that it wouldn't be knocked off. Holding onto the loop in the leather strap was not easy when the horse moved and the travois bounced on the ground, but Achilles was focused and determined.

Agenor, one of the hunters, had come up with this idea of tying the bison to the travois and then slipping a leather strap through the neck to the interior of the bison's gutted body. The bottom end of the strap was tied into a loop. This was what Achilles gripped with his right hand. The top end of the strap was tied to the travois frame.

"This is a little present for you Mayans!" shouted Cronos. "It is fresh bison meat! We were hoping we could talk you into making the exchange of Sile Kamose for Khons Imhotep."

"They're up on the bulwarks," whispered Cronos. "They're looking at us. Don't move."

"Get out of here!" shouted a man from on top of the bulwarks.

"Fresh bison! If you don't want it, we will come here again later tonight and take it back to our campfires and cook it for ourselves."

Through an opening in the bottom of the carcass, Achilles could see Cronos' feet move away.

The feet stopped. "We will leave it here for awhile," Cronos shouted. "We thought some fresh meat might make you easier to deal with."

The horse snorted and the travois jiggled.

It occurred to Achilles that Cronos might just irritate these Mayan soldiers. Then maybe they would shoot at the bison carcass with their assault rifles. But Sile Kamose had said that they didn't have many bullets left, so maybe they wouldn't do that after all.

For someone who liked to move about quickly, lying inside this slippery, bloody bison was not the way Achilles usually did things. Yet, here he was.

He lay on his right side, hanging onto the leather strap and listening to bits of conversation from inside the colony. It was too far away to hear clearly. He hoped it was at the drawbridge and the Mayans would come out and get the bison carcass so he could leave this smelly, slippery place.

Was he afraid? Yes, of course. But fear sometimes made you a better fighter. He had learned that a long time ago from his father.

Achilles had planned what he would do when he got inside the Mayan colony. Yet he was smart enough to know that these things didn't always go as planned. Suppose somebody decided to look inside this bison carcass. Then, he would have to be lightning fast.

He decided it was better not to think about all of this. He would just stay here and wait.

Achilles reached out his left hand and with his index finger slowly pushed up the flap of the outer hide at the neck. With his left eye he could see two Mayan soldiers up on the bulwarks. They were standing with their crossbows loaded, peering toward the forest from their high lookout positions.

They would see nothing. Unlike Hyksos people, these Mayans could not see things that were right in front of them.

What Achilles heard next made the nearer of the two soldiers on the bulwarks turn to look. There was a loud "creak."

It was the drawbridge.

There was a rumbling sound and a loud "thump."

Achilles tensed.

Somebody walked by the flap he was holding up.

The horse made a low guttural sound.

Achilles lowered the flap very slowly. Then he waited.

The travois began to move. The jarring loosened his grip on the strap.

Achilles grabbed it with his left hand.

The flap rose, exposing the side of a Mayan soldier's head. The flap dropped.

Achilles held on with both hands.

The travois jostled across the boards of the bridge.

What if the strap broke? He would fall and he would have to stab one of these Mayans with his knife and take the crossbow. Then he would have a real weapon.

The jostling stopped.

The horse snorted.

Achilles waited, listening. His knife was in the left side of his waistband, right below his left elbow. Once his right hand was free, it would be easy to grab.

He could hear voices. Then he heard the creaking of the bridge being raised.

He moved his left hand ever so slightly, and with his left index finger, he slowly raised the flap of the outer hide.

In front of him was the left side of a Mayan soldier's face. The soldier was talking to another soldier a few feet away.

Achilles' natural response was to drop the flap, but he knew if he did, the soldier's left eye might catch the motion.

He held the flap still.

The other soldier moved out of sight.

The soldier directly in front of him turned away and walked toward the bridge.

Achilles raised the flap higher.

Now he could see another soldier winding the crank for the drawbridge. The wooden bridge finally reached the top of the wooden frame.

The second soldier wedged a chunk of wood into the wooden gears of the drawbridge crank.

Achilles moved his left hand down the edge of the flap of hide. He stopped at about the chest cavity.

These two men were the only ones here at the drawbridge. There were two more up on the mound of dirt behind the bulwarks toward the south. Those were the guards he had seen when he was outside.

He moved his hand farther to his left. There were two more guards on the mound of dirt behind the bulwarks north of the drawbridge. He supposed there were more guards at other places on the bulwarks around the colony.

Where was the other soldier who had left? Was he sent away to notify a general about the bison? If that was true, very soon there would be many more soldiers here.

Achilles heard voices.

He slowly moved his index finger farther up toward the neck of the bison.

Both of the soldiers who had been at the bridge were standing next to the bison carcass.

Achilles yanked his knife out of his belt and rolled out of the carcass. He swung his arm around the first soldier's neck and slashed underneath.

There was a cough and the man fell forward.

Achilles swung around and stabbed the second soldier straight into his neck.

The man's brown eyes bulged and he dropped to his knees.

Achilles yanked out the knife.

The soldier spat blood and then fell forward onto his face.

Achilles grabbed the crossbow from the second soldier's right shoulder and cut the quiver of arrows off the left. Then he scurried around behind the bison carcass.

He loaded and cocked the bow. He aimed at the back of the nearest soldier to the south. He squeezed the trigger.

"Zip!"

The arrow struck the soldier's back and he fell forward out of sight.

The first soldier to the left of the drawbridge turned.

Achilles loaded and fired.

"Zip!"

He fell face-first into the compound.

There was shouting.

Achilles aimed and fired at the second soldier on the left.

"Zip!"

This soldier fell down the bank tumbling in the dirt.

The second one far to the right was running along the top of the hill.

Achilles knelt and fired.

"Zip!"

The arrow missed.

The soldier stopped and loaded his bow.

Achilles shot again.

"Zip!"

The arrow pierced the soldier's stomach. He flopped forward and then rolled down the dirt mound.

Achilles charged across the open space to the wheel at the bridge. With the heel of his right hand, he slammed the wooden chock.

It didn't move.

He yanked the knife out of his belt and sawed the rope on the right side of the drawbridge.

It snapped loose.

The bridge crunched and the right side slung down, away from the wooden frame.

He charged across to the rope on the left side of the bridge.

An arrow whizzed by him.

He jumped down into the shallow area of the ditch next to the bridge and began sawing on the rope.

Strands of rope popped and the bridge sagged. The last strand snapped.

The bridge rumbled down. It landed with a loud "thump."
Dust billowed upward.

"Zip!" An arrow ripped his right ear.

Achilles jerked around and ran over to the bison carcass.
He dropped to one knee and peered beneath the horse's belly.

Cronos and Sile Kamose charged across the drawbridge with a group of Hyksos men behind them.

Sile stopped next to the horse. He was wearing a translator. "You're bleeding!"

Achilles rose to his feet and touched his right ear. "I'm okay."

"Let's get Khons Imhotep."

*　*　*

Sile was relieved that they had been able to finally get inside the Mayan colony. Their plan with the bison carcass and Achilles had worked.

The question now was whether Khons Imhotep was still alive.
Because Sile was the one the Mayans actually wanted, he felt a huge sense of responsibility for Khons. It had weighed heavily on his mind during the three-day journey over to the colony.

He had wanted to be happy about Intef's pregnancy but this thing about Khons Imhotep had been preying on his mind night and day.

Sile moved between the first two rows of tents.

Achilles walked next to him.

Unarmed people were peering out of their tents. Some were just standing, watching.

He motioned to them. "Stay down and out of sight or you might get hurt!"

In front of a large tent at the end of the row, a short Mayan soldier with gold stars on his shoulders stood with his arms folded across his chest. "I'm General Khufu. I'm in charge of this colony. How dare you break into my compound and attack my people!"

Sile grabbed the man by the shirt collar. "Unless you want this Hyksos to gut you, tell us where Khons Imhotep is!"

Achilles yanked his bloody knife out of his waistband.

The general's eyes grew large. "The brig."

Sile released the man's collar. "Show us!"

The general led them to the right, down a narrow path between two rows of small tents to a huge tent at the back of the colony next to the bulwarks.

When he pulled the flap away, a soldier stepped out with his hands held high. "I surrender!"

"Release Khons Imhotep, Private."

The soldier moved back inside the tent.

The general followed.

Sile entered the huge tent behind the general.

Inside were large cages, most of them occupied by a single man in each. Some were empty. The whole area was lit by a single gas lantern hanging from the center pole.

Sile glanced around. "What are these men in here for?"

The general shrugged. "Various things."

"Order them released, General, or I'll give you to this Hyksos and I'll release them myself."

General Khufu nodded at the young private. "Release them."

The soldier unlocked the first cage.

The tent flap opened behind them.

Achilles spun around and crouched, holding out his knife.

A grey-haired Mayan man stepped inside. "Who's in charge of the Hyksos warriors?"

Sile stepped forward. "I am."

The man held out his hand. "I'm Moses Hapman."

Sile shook his hand. "Sile Kamose."

"Mister Kamose, I've been actin' as leader of the civilians in this colony. We had nothin' to do with the massacre of that village. We have no quarrel with the Hyksos people."

"I'm afraid the Hyksos are going to have a hard time believing that."

Moses Hapmen studied Sile's face. "You were the soldier tied on the wooden T."

"Yes I was."

"Sile Kamose?"

He pivoted around.

Khons Imhotep walked up to him.

"Khons. . . how are you?"

"Where's Athena?"

Sile motioned with his head toward the front of the tent. "Out there somewhere."

Khons crossed to the tent flap, flipped it back and disappeared outside.

Sile turned to Moses Hapmen. "If what you say is true, we should have a meeting of your people and the Hyksos. Maybe we can stop this senseless killing."

CHAPTER FORTY-EIGHT
"Good Reason"

Hyksos
Ocean Village
6th Month, Love Moon
Early Night

Cronos raised a wooden cup above his right shoulder. "I make this toast to Sile Kamose, the Monster Mayan Man. May he and his new bride be happy, even though Sile doesn't know his ass from a hole in the ground!"

The whole crowd burst out laughing.

Sile grinned and put his arm around Cronos' shoulder. "If I didn't know you loved me, I'd punch you in the nose, Cronos."

"I'm not worried. You have been drinking so much joy juice I don't think you could even find my nose!"

The crowd laughed again.

Khons moved with Athena over to where Intef was standing. "Congratulations, Cousin. I know you'll be happy married to Sile. He's a good guy. When are you expecting?"

"I think about seven and a half months. I'm not really sure."

"I'll be an uncle . . . or a cousin . . . or something."

Athena stepped in next to Khons. "I want to congratulate you too. I know you'll be happy." She looked up at Khons. "I hope I can get pregnant soon."

Khons felt his skin heat up.

Intef grinned. "You're blushing."

He shrugged. "I do that sometimes."

"My gentle Khons." Athena tugged on his arm. "Let's go for a walk."

Khons made a finger wave to Intef. "Again, congratulations on the marriage, Cousin."

Intef smiled.

Athena led Khons away from the crowd around the fire down the row of huts toward the south.

Once they had cleared the edge of the village and the torches, there was only the shower of white moonlight.

The large Woman Moon was high in the sky and heading down her gradual slope toward the western horizon. In the east, the smaller Man Moon was racing across the black sky.

Khons turned to his wife. "I have a question for you. When the Woman Moon is up in the sky like this and the Man Moon comes up higher and nears her, what does that mean to your people?"

"They're your people now, Khons."

"That's true. But what does it mean?"

"It means that the Man Moon is chasing the Woman Moon and he catches her – well, almost catches her."

Khons stopped. "Why did you say, 'Almost'?"

Athena took his hand and squeezed it. "It's a female thing, my gentle husband."

"What female thing? I don't understand."

Athena's face was streaked with moonlight shadows. "Men don't understand it. That's why it's a female thing."

Khons stared into the pretty eyes. "You're playing with me."

Athena's head canted to the left. "What makes you say that?"

"You didn't answer my question."

"Yes, I did."

"No, you didn't. You said I didn't understand because I was male. You never explained it."

Athena grinned. "Females like to have secrets. It's part of our nature. It's what makes men want us. They think they will find out our secrets if they make love to us."

"But they won't?"

"I didn't say that."

"I think we're having our first argument."

Athena took his hand and led him down the beach bathed in moonlight.

The waves swept in with a soft, drumming rhythm and the water left wet arcs on the sand that glistened in the white moonlight.

After they had walked awhile, Athena stopped. "Let's sit and watch the Man Moon chase the Woman Moon." She dropped to the sand. She leaned forward and wrapped her arms around her knees.

Khons dropped down into the warm sand next to her. "What I said back there doesn't matter. What matters is that I love you and you love me. I had to travel far across the galaxy to find you and I'm glad I did."

Athena turned to him. "I'm glad you did, too."

"It's strange how those things work out, isn't it?"

"It's supposed to be that way, Khons. The fates make it happen that way. We just did what we were supposed to do. I knew the first time I saw you that we were meant for each other." She touched her chest. "I felt it in here. . . in my heart."

"I just thought you were beautiful, and your bison stew was very good."

Athena looked out at the water.

The white pathways of two moons splayed two white pathways across the wavy black surface.

"It was a long trip across the galaxy to get here." Khons wrapped his arms around his knees. "I was born in the starship. That Moses Hapmen was too. He was born the first year, while the starship was still in the old solar system."

He turned to his wife. "Wasn't his story about his father saving the starship interesting? It shows that only one person can make a big difference."

Athena looked at him. "Whenever you talk like that I think of my father." She touched the stone bracelet on her left wrist. "He was such a good man and I still love him, even though he's gone far up into the sky. But when I think of him, I become sad."

"Don't be sad." Khons put his arm across his wife's shoulders. He looked up into the night sky.

At that moment he wondered about the starship. He used to be able to see it at night, every now and then. It was like a fast moving star. He hadn't seen it for a long time. He wondered why.

Well, someday, they would make contact again. It would take awhile, but they would do it. Then he could introduce Athena to his grandparents over the phone and tell them about what had happened to his parents. He wondered if his grandparents would accept Athena.

He turned to her. "I miss my parents. I'm sure my father's dead. I'll have to go back and look for him someday, and that history book. The people up on the starship wouldn't want us to lose that."

Athena wiggled over closer to him and leaned her head against his shoulder. "Let's make love tonight. Let's do it so we are defying these sad things like this talk of death. Let's do it so we are saying that we are alive and that we will have many children and we will be in love and be happy together forever."

Khons squeezed Athena's shoulders and leaned forward to kiss her forehead. Then he looked upward toward the approaching Man Moon.

It was strange how these things worked out in life. It was almost as if they were planned.

THE END

Dear Reader,

CONSTELLATION DRACO is Book II in a series of eight novels entitled BIRTH OF THE GODS.

You might consider going back to the first novel, THE END OF DAYS. That story begins on Mars 11,500 years ago. It's about a planet that's running out of breathable air.

By lottery, the government is choosing the few people who will leave Mars to make a forty-seven light year journey across the galaxy. As you know from reading CONSTELLATION DRACO, this journey ends at the planet Hyksos.

You might also want to read the other novels in this series:

Book III - DARKNESS VISIBLE

Book IV – THE TALES OF AGENOR

Book V – ORION FOUR

Book VI – SPACEPORT ATLANTIS

Book VII – EMMANUEL

Book VIII – FOREVER

Thank you for reading CONSTELLATION DRACO. I do hope you enjoyed it.

Yours sincerely,

J. R. Bacon

johnbaconauthor@gmail.com
http://www.johnbaconauthor.com